I0772365

# LAKE OF SAPPHIRE

## ALLIUM SERIES BOOK ONE

MALLORY BENJAMIN

Editors: Nancy Kohutka and Glasswing Editing
Proof Editor: Mary Benjamin
Cover and Interior Design: Mallory Benjamin
Cover Art: Trey Benjamin / Shutterstock

ISBN 979-8-9868674-1-0 (paperback)
ISBN 979-8-9868674-0-3 (hardcover)
ISBN 979-8-9868674-2-7 (ebook)

# LAKE OF SAPPHIRE

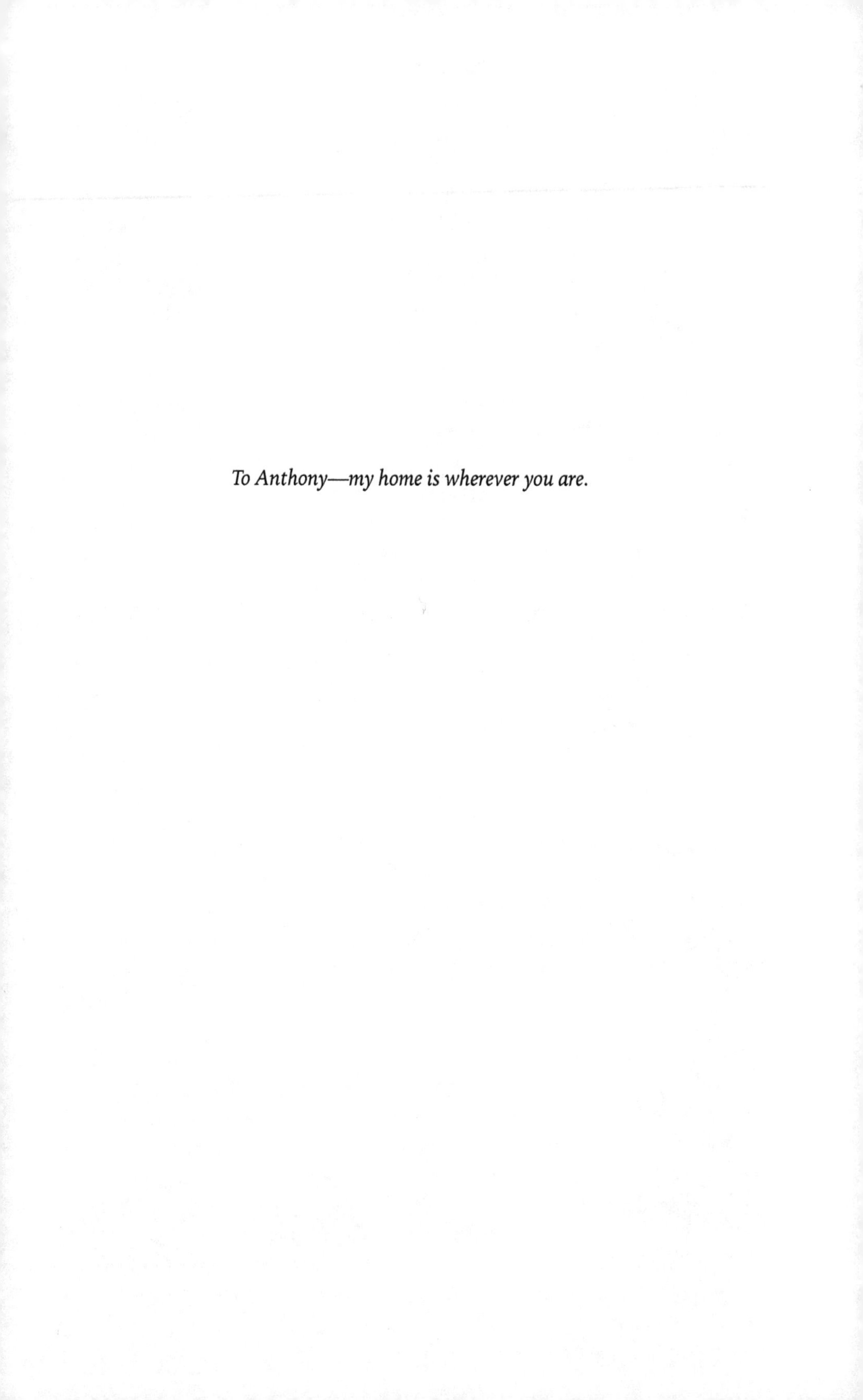

*To Anthony—my home is wherever you are.*

NARWAY
KITLARN
THE DARK KINGDOM OF TENNEBRIS

BACKERLY
PALM
ADDLER
LAKEWOOD

# PROLOGUE

"What if I don't have any powers?" my daughter asked.

"You do," I assured her. "You have the Luxian markings. If you didn't have any abilities, the designs wouldn't appear on your skin when you get wet." For emphasis, I ran my fingers over the spot where her black markings emerged every time she bathed or swam in the ocean.

Possessing the markings were vital. It meant you had abilities. It was simple: markings meant power. To have blank skin like the humans represented weakness, and I knew my daughter was anything but. I performed the ancient Luxian ceremony when she was born and submerged her in the ceremonial basin I kept hidden. It used to be widely exercised back on Allium to note which infants would grow into elemental powers. But it was banned since coming to this planet. For the first time, our kind started to have no powers. The Luxian markings didn't materialize on our skin when submerged—we looked too similar to the humans. I shuddered, thinking of how mothers killed their babies by accident, keeping them under the water for too long, praying and pleading for their newborn's skin to change.

My daughter watched me closely, seeming to think over what I said before asking, "But what if the other kids make fun of me because I don't know what my powers are yet?"

"It's completely normal that they haven't manifested. It can take some Advenian children a while to figure out what they're capable of. That's why you're going to school—to practice. You'll have plenty of years to train before you have to take your Trials."

I silently prayed to our Goddesses that her powers were ordinary because Luxian civilians seemed to disappear when they emerged with rare or special abilities. My stomach tightened, and I felt my anxiety giving way in the shape of knots. I couldn't discern what her markings meant. I didn't want any attention drawn to her. I just wanted her to be average, to get through this long life unnoticed. I was thankful each day that her powers hadn't manifested. But I knew whenever the day came, there would be no hiding them.

I was envious of the Tennebrisian markings and sometimes found myself wishing we'd been born to that kingdom instead of Lux. The Dark Kingdom of Tennebris could easily hide what powers they possessed. Their golden markings only awoke on their skin when their abilities were being used, and even then it was usually just pretty patterns and spirals. But the Luxian markings were a tell-tale sign of what you could do. Flame markings meant you possessed fire, waves were water, wings were air. Trees, flowers, or branches were signifiers for ground manipulators. Even the more rare abilities like healers or Alluse users had specific symbols.

"I hope I have water powers like you!" my daughter exclaimed as she stared at me. I followed her gaze and saw my own markings, now appearing on my forearms due to the sweat coating my skin. Black wave-like designs ran over the tanned length of my arms. There would be no doubt to any Advenian that I could manipulate the water element. I smiled briefly, momentarily forgetting about my anxieties concerning my daughter, thinking of when she used to ask to color on my arms, spending what seemed like hours adding blue to the canvas on my skin.

I prayed that we would have more times like that—coloring together and swimming in the ocean under the blazing sun. But the sweat enveloping me had nothing to do with the scorching heat this island succumbed to. I was nervous. I didn't want her to attend school. Six years old seemed too young to start her gruesome training this golden city mandated, all leading toward the Trials upon graduation. She would only have twelve years before she'd have to take the most important test of her life.

The school was supposed to be a balance, focusing on our history while training the children in the specific abilities they possessed. They would learn about our long and complicated past regarding the Ability War that caused the destruction of our planet, Allium, forcing both Advenian Kingdoms to discover Earth and remain hidden from the humans. No Advenian was fond of their new home on Earth, but both kingdoms had agreed to the newfound peace out of necessity.

Lux, the Kingdom of the Light, home to elemental powers, was marooned to an island in the Atlantic Ocean. Tennebris, the Kingdom of the Dark, possessing psychic abilities, was stranded on the snow-laden coast of Antarctica. Our new homes—ones we could never leave.

I hugged my daughter tightly, knowing that starting school would be so much more than just learning about our history. She was about to enter the most grueling part of her life, and I couldn't shake the feeling that her ability would be her damnation. Because in this King-dom, the powerful were just as cursed as the weak.

# ONE
## SCOTLIND

"WHAT DO WE DO WITH THE OTHERS?" A DEEP VOICE grunted, waking me from my sleep.

"Eliminate them."

I flung off the bed sheets, aware that my body was drenched in sweat. My room was abnormally hot, too hot even for a scorching summer day in Lux. Every inch of my white nightgown was soaked, plastered to me like a second layer of skin.

"Mama—" I choked on the words. They were barely audible, catching in my throat as I gasped for air. My windpipe was now scratchy and raw. I closed my mouth as I squinted around my room, my eyes adjusting to the dark as my hazy bedroom came into view, tinged with smoke.

"Mama" was on the tip of my tongue again, begging me to scream for her. *She would know what to do,* I thought, but I swallowed back the plea for help, too scared to draw the attention of whoever was here.

A distant, muffled scream reverberated through the house, heaving me into action. I jerked upright in my bed.

Large beads of sweat began to drip down the back of my neck, collecting at the base of my spine. I didn't think it was possible to sweat any more than I already had. My heart was pounding so fast and loud that I thought it would crack a rib. Whoever was here was getting closer. I could hear heavy footsteps growing louder with each step. Fumbling off my bed, I scurried underneath it, just as my bedroom door forcefully swung open.

My eyes blinked, rapidly adjusting to the bright light shining through the now open door. Two black-tipped boots stepped inside the doorframe, blocking my only exit. Smoke engulfed the room as it propelled in with such a violent force that it was an effort to keep from coughing. I could only make out his legs from where I was hidden under the bed. His boots paused in front of me before he sauntered around it.

He started scavenging the room, throwing the blankets off my bed, pulling the drawers from my dresser, and rummaging through my closet. I flinched, wanting to sink into the floor and disappear beneath it as a drawer flew across the room and collided with my vanity mirror. I pulled my hands over my head in reflex as shattered glass scattered across the tile.

I tried to steady my breathing in an attempt to stifle my panic, but it didn't work. With each breath I took, a cough threatened to escape as the thick smoke scratched my windpipe. I clamped a sweaty, shaky palm over my lips as two more figures entered the room.

"Stop making a ruckus and breaking things. We're supposed to be discreet. It's not going to seem like an accidental fire if you keep this up," one of them barked.

Another voice growled, deeper and more menacing than the first, "What's taking so long? Find the girl, and let's get out of here."

Nausea crept into my stomach and formed a thick lump in the back of my throat. *They were here for me, but why?* I willed my eyes to shut in an effort to relax and calm the bile threatening to spew from my mouth.

Black-tipped boots paused in his search. "What about the others?"

"They've been taken care of. You're the only one who's taking forever with your task."

"I'm looking for her! She's not in here."

The scarier of the three growled, "She's a child, there are only so many places she could hide. She's here, keep looking."

Smoke still poured in through the open doorway, and I could now make out erratic and angry flames stretching through the hall. What did he mean *they were taken care of*? And took care of who? Panic raced in my head as I realized the muffled screaming from earlier had stopped.

My breath was wheezing unevenly through my hands. Whether from the smoke or the panic, I couldn't tell. But my effort to quell it was futile. Tears swelled in my eyes and poured down my cheeks as my mind raced with worry for my family. Where were they? I needed my mother's hug so desperately. I wanted to curl into her arms and have her tell me that everything was going to be okay.

Silently, I sent prayers to the Goddesses of Allium as the intruders continued to tear apart my room. I sent an extra plea to the Highest Goddess, Pylemo, to keep my family safe and alive. I prayed they weren't the ones the males were talking about. Then I prayed for myself, in the off chance they wouldn't find me and I could escape.

I couldn't make out what they were mumbling and grunting to one another over my pounding heart. I was surprised they didn't hear the beating. It was all but deafening to my ears.

My eyes were still clamped shut when I felt a rough, calloused hand grab hold of my ankle. A shriek escaped my lips as I was yanked backward across the tile. My knees burned as they dipped into the crevices of each indent. The small shards of glass embedding into my skin, drawing blood as I was pulled across the floor. I reached for my bedpost in a desperate attempt to stop myself, but it was no use. The intruder holding my ankle overpowered my frame. I swore I saw the male with boots playing with fire, tossing a tightly wound ball between his hands, as he gawked at my struggle. Like he knew only one of them was needed to keep me in place. The scarier of the three was just standing there, accessing everything while the third held me down.

Without second guessing myself, I pushed back. I couldn't give up. I had to get to my family. I had to make sure they were safe. I kicked with my other leg, ramming it against something hard. I knew I'd made impact when I heard a grunt followed by a curse.

I tried to wiggle free, but the hand holding my ankle advanced further up my leg, tightening its grip as it went. It didn't stop until it reached my hip before flipping me onto my back. My head slammed against the tile. I tried to focus my vision on their faces, to see if I could recognize them, but they were all wearing masks hidden beneath black hoods, making them look more like demons.

With my free hand, I reached for my head, checking where it had slammed into the tile. Warm liquid immediately seeped into my fingers. Before I could react, the male grabbed both of my hands in his. I continued to struggle against him, kicking and screeching for my parents, calling for my mama.

"Gag the brat already," the scary one deadpanned. "I'm sick of hearing her scream."

The booted one, who was playing with fire, grew impatient. He stormed toward me. The fire in his hands vanished as he ripped the sock off my foot before shoving it into my mouth and clamping it shut. I heard a rip, then felt as he wrapped tape over my lips, continuing until it made a full circle around my head.

"Much better," he sneered.

Tears were overflowing from my eyes, obstructing my view. They continued down my freckled cheeks like two running rivers. I wasn't sure if the crying was attributed to the smoke burning my irises, or the realization that my life was likely about to end.

"Is this even the right girl?" the one holding me down asked the other two.

"Only one way to find out." My head was lifted off the tile as I was dragged into a seated position. The back of my nightgown was pulled down, exposing the upper portion of my back. "I need your water abilities. The girl we're looking for only has markings on her back."

Through my blurry vision, I saw the scary one step to the side as he moved to position himself in front of my back. Water spewed from his outstretched hands. A moment later, a cold rush of fluid hit my flesh, mixing with the sweat as it poured down my body.

"That's her alright. Let's go."

I was jerked to my feet, my head whipping back as one of the males dragged me from my bedroom and toward the flames. I tugged at his grip and planted my foot on the floor, trying to catch him off guard. It worked. Except instead of running for freedom, I fell backwards.

I landed in a lump of something burning. A searing pain coursed through my body as my right leg became engulfed in flames. An agonizing throb took over my calf, and the smell of charred flesh filled my nostrils. The male who possessed the water abilities threw his hands in my direction, dousing the flames before they consumed more.

I tried to push up onto my feet to run away, but my legs gave out. I crawled all of two steps before one of them threw me over their shoulder. Now seeing the world upside down, I was carried out of my house as the fuzziness further took over. The entire place went up in flames just before everything went dark.

When I opened my eyes again I didn't know how much time had passed. I was freezing, my body was shaking uncontrollably. It was a cold I'd never experienced before, even on the chilliest day in Lux. I tore at the tape around my head, not caring how much hair I pulled off with it as I ripped the makeshift gag from my mouth, gasping uncontrollably.

A coughing spell took over me as I attempted to inhale the crisp air. Mercifully, there was no smoke, but the air felt cold and wrong. My chest was rising and falling rapidly as I heard the familiar sound of waves crashing onto the shore. Slowly, I turned my aching head to take in my surroundings. I had been dropped on a beach, left to rot in the sand, but I didn't see the clear blue water that always surrounded the Luxian island.

The ocean was dark, almost black, with mounds of white mountains stretching in the distance. The peaks were almost too bright to look at. The sun reflecting off the white, icy material was blinding. How long had I been passed out? It was night in Lux, but now it looked more like midday. I shielded my eyes as I scanned the beach, noticing a fine layer of snow covering the black sand beneath. *Black sand.* Goddess above, where was I?

I picked up a pile of the white fluff, letting it escape through my fingers. I'd never seen snow before, but there was no mistaking the cold substance. It left traces of water droplets in its path as my fingers turned numb.

Dread crept up in me as I realized I wasn't home anymore. I wasn't even on my island. This was not the beaches of Lux with its beautiful golden sand, almost always too hot to touch. There were no aqua-blue waters that felt refreshing against the constant heat and basking sun. I found myself wishing for the warmth of it as shivering overtook my body.

I scanned the rest of the beach, searching for any indication of where I was, but there was nothing. Everything was vacant and unmoving, except for the dark ocean at my back. Strong winds were whipping all around me, making the waves seem more vicious like it'd swallow me whole if I got too close. Miles of the snowy black sand separated me from a dense forest at the other end of the beach. But even the trees were dead. There were no vibrant green leaves or colorful flowers like there were in Lux. I couldn't even hear a bird chirp or an animal stir, as if the climate was too harsh for them.

I tried to pry myself up to stand, but my legs were wobbly. They felt heavy and numb, and I couldn't bear any weight on them. A burning pain seared through the right side of my leg as I pressed my knees together.

I braved a look and wished I hadn't. Angry, red blisters had formed over my entire right calf where my skin used to be. A particular section was singed down to the muscle with thick, white blisters scattered over the ruined flesh. The site was repulsive. Bile instantly rose in my throat and poured onto the ground in front of me.

I had to get off this frozen beach. My parents told me enough about the cold to realize I wouldn't last long. My numb fingers seemed to scream at me in agreement. The process had already begun.

My teeth chattered so rapidly that they produced a constant rattling sound, overpowering the crash of waves behind me. I scanned the rest of the beach. I was alone as far as I could tell. Slowly, I began to crawl away from the ocean, away from my pile of vomit.

It was painful. I didn't know where I was crawling to, or what I was crawling from, but I told myself it didn't matter as long as I kept moving, kept breathing. *Just one more push. Don't lie down yet*, I kept repeating to myself.

I could have been crawling through the snow-laden, black sand for seconds, minutes or hours. Time seemed to still, and I lost focus of my surroundings. I could only concentrate on the next inch of land in front of me. One awkward, painful crawl at a time, inch by inch, as I slowly made my way across the unfamiliar beach.

I didn't see someone approach me until it was too late. I recognized the same pair of black-tip boots as my stomach twisted in knots. I glanced up at the male who wore them. Two lavender eyes burned down at me from above. He no longer wore a mask. A faint, demeaning laugh escaped his mouth as he towered over me with his arms across his chest. Laughing at me, laughing at my poor attempt to escape. His laugh was the last thing I heard ringing in my ears before everything went black again.

———

THE RAYS from the sun streamed through my dorm window as I peeled myself out of bed. Careful not to wake my roommate, I quietly slipped out of my sticky nightgown and tugged my training outfit over my sweat-slicked legs. I didn't bother bathing, I was only going to get more sweaty.

Once I accepted that I could do nothing about being in Tennebris, that this was my new reality, I started training. Every morning I woke before classes and ran to the training grounds to practice. It helped me shake off the lingering terror that occurred every night.

I had long since mastered masking the after effects of my nightmare. I forced slow breaths out to control my heavy panting as I got ready, but it wasn't always like that. Every night was the same. The same nightmare from the day I was kidnapped, the same night sweats, the same jolted wake up call that brought me back to consciousness in a panic right as the male on the cold beach reached me. But at least the screaming had stopped.

The nightmare never changed, and somehow, it slipped into my dreams every night as an ugly reminder that I didn't belong here. It was the only memory I had before I was taken from my home in Lux and brought into the Dark Kingdom of Tennebris.

Eleven years had passed, and I still couldn't remember anything about my life from Lux. I couldn't remember my family, what they looked like, if they loved me, or if I had any siblings. I knew that I had a family, but every time I searched my mind for any trace of my parents, I was left with nothing. My only childhood memory was a horrible fragmented one of being ripped away from my home, my island, and the place I belonged. My only memory was that night.

I had long stopped wondering if my parents were alive, if anyone from my island even knew I was missing, or if they believed I had died in that fire. I used to hate myself for dwelling on it. It would send my mind to dark places, making me wonder why I was brought here in the first place, and if those males were coming back for me.

Now, I welcomed it each night, along with the scarred, burned flesh on my right calf and the Luxian markings on my back. They were the only remnants of my previous life. Those three things—my nightmare, my scar, and my markings—were my only reminders that I once belonged to Lux, that I was not crazy, and that I didn't make up what had happened to me.

When I first realized I was left in Tennebris, I tried to explain myself. After blacking out on the frozen beach, I awoke in a confined room and was only allowed to see one person—my *counselor*—until I was deemed ready to rejoin society. I pleaded with my counselor to take me back to Lux, that I didn't belong here. I told her my story in the hopes that she would listen, but she never believed me. She claimed I was a confused, that I was deflecting from my traumatic past. It didn't help my case that I developed a fear of fire ever since. It took me years to be able to go near an open fireplace or hold a small candle. I chose to sit in complete darkness rather than brave a flame.

It made winters my living nightmare. I soon found out that Tennebris didn't have a normal *night means darkness and day means sunlight*. They had six months of constant light, where the sun never set and six months where everything was cast in shadows. Every building that didn't have electricity required fire to light the space. It was another reminder to me of how different things were between the two kingdoms. Another reason I so desperately pleaded with my counselor and wanted to go home.

She'd tell me what I was claiming was impossible as she shoved a folder in my face concerning my parents from *Tennebris*. It stated that we lived in one of Tennebris' six villages called LakeWood, and that my parents both died in a horrible fire, making me an orphan. A tragic accident. But I knew better.

*I had my scar, I had my Luxian markings, and I had my nightmare.*

I often wondered if the pictures in the folder were my real parents, or if they were just random photographs of people who somewhat resembled me. They shared the same brown hair, lean frame, and high cheekbones, but my eyes were different from anyone in Tennebris —sapphire.

An unnatural shade of blue, so bright and deep there was no hope of blending in amongst the varying shades of black, brown, hazel, and green eyes of Tennebris. Unique eye coloring was a Luxian trait, and unlike my back, my eyes were something I couldn't hide. Blue eyes weren't completely unheard of in Tennebris, but rare amongst the sea of earth tones.

My counselor claimed I was making stuff up for attention. That was the story she fed me. She brushed it off by saying I was a child who made up lies to cope with my past. Fighting back only landed me with the label of being traumatized and countless more hours of being detained.

I didn't care. My first couple of months here, I pleaded with her. I begged for a new counselor, for someone who might believe me, but it was only ever her. I was kept locked in her office for months while I was *coping*.

It wasn't until my counselor threatened me with treason that I learned to keep my mouth shut. She said it was forbidden to live on the wrong soil. Tennebrisians and Luxians didn't mix. Unless you had a work visa, which I clearly didn't due to my age, I would either be killed immediately or sent to prison. She also informed me that I would beg for death if I was given the latter judgment.

I had to endure years of her "therapy." So much that I actually started believing some of the things she told me. It became difficult to separate reality from the fabrications I was spun. I wasn't able to attend Tennebris' schools or speak with any other Advenian until I was compliant.

The time in isolation landed me the reputation of being the freak orphan girl. Growing up in LakeWood, the furthest south of the six villages, made it difficult to make any friends. So I kept to myself and I trained.

The crisp air hit my face as I walked outside. I inhaled sharply and exhaled a sense of relief. I'd now gotten used to the cold, rough weather of Tennebris, not that I liked it. We were taught in school that when Luxian air users created the shield around the Kingdom of Tennebris, they kept out most of the bitter weather. It never felt like that to me. Every day, I yearned for the warm breeze and blinding sun of Lux. But I would never again see the tropical island that I used to live on. I was stuck pretending to be a Tennebrisian.

Mornings were my favorite part of the day. Peaceful, free, calm. It was the only time I could be myself. It was the only time I felt relaxed. I didn't have to worry about who was watching me. I didn't have to be careful to cover the black markings on my back, even though I always kept them hidden out of habit. This early in the morning, the entire school was still sleeping, leaving me utterly alone.

I was greeted by intermittent gusts of wind, breaking through the shield, as I headed toward the school's gym and training grounds. I embraced my runs every morning. The feeling of my legs moving one after the other, the air filling my lungs, making me believe I could escape the world behind me if I could only outrun it. It cleared my mind. I didn't think about anything as I sprinted toward the NorthEnd of the school's campus that housed the athletic arena. I didn't think about how I was from Lux, and that if I was now discovered, I would be killed for it. I didn't think at all. I just ran.

LakeWood's campus was one of the few schools that was named after the town it resided in. It was divided into five different sections. The center of campus, known as the Hub, was where the students' social life lived. It was home to the dormitories, the library, the Great Hall, auditorium, cafeteria, and a few small tea and book shops. The EastEnd of the campus held the teachers' quarters. The SouthEnd, the classrooms, and the WestEnd consisted of a pathway to one of the residential areas of the village that typically housed the upper class.

Past WestEnd, was the town of LakeWood, situated a few miles from the campus. The pathway there had an Advenian-made garden with picnic tables scattered every so often. On a warmer day during summer, I usually found an empty table to sit and read. Only a few flower patches and bushes were spread out along the path at West-End, but I still found myself gravitating toward it.

I never understood why the town or the school I attended was named LakeWood. There were no bodies of water and no woods. In school, we learned that when Tennebris first made roots in this glacier climate, the Luxian ground users changed the layout within the shield. They added unnatural forests and vegetation throughout the six villages. Apparently, just not in LakeWood. Besides the small path of WestEnd, all this dreadful town had were vast, rocky, snow-capped mountains.

The campus wasn't much better. The grounds were old and boring. The same brown brick framed every single building, making them identical, except for the small, rustic looking sign outside of each one.

The gardens were the only unique part of LakeWood, but they were still nothing compared to the pictures of Lux that were depicted in our textbooks. Since the Light Kingdom housed the elemental ground users, Lux was known to be flourishing with beautiful botanicals as they bent the soil to their will, creating a vastness of color and beauty. It was only because of the Treaty that Lux agreed to create anything at all in Tennebris. If it wasn't for the ground users, there would be no mountains or trees, just frozen ground covered in snow.

The large mountains engulfed the surrounding area, giving it a false alluring presence of seclusion. To me, it was just a reminder that I was trapped in this valley I couldn't escape from. The mountains were mostly bare of wildlife and nature. Dirt, rocks, and rubble laid below each white crest.

The only opening through the mountainous perimeter was one road, Laten, which led to the other Tennebrisian villages. Since I was still a student, the only time I would be able to leave on it was in a week, after graduation.

I finished my run to NorthEnd and entered the familiar, musky gym. The summer sun remained high in the sky, shining through the floor-to-ceiling windows, lighting the space with golden rays. I began my usual workout routine of punching and kicking drills before moving on to weapon training. In class, we had to familiarize ourselves with each weapon of the kingdom. Even though most of our fighting focused on abilities, our instructor always enforced that we couldn't rely on our powers, that if we only trained with them, it would become a crutch. I had no dark abilities I could use, so I made myself skilled with weapons.

We practiced with swords, knives, staffs, bow and arrows, and axes. Whenever I had a choice, I always chose the large staff. I liked the feeling of letting everything out, of not having to hold anything back or keep anything in. With a dagger or sword, I had to draw back my throws to not injure my classmates. One wrong cut could be fatal without a Luxian healer stationed at the school. But with a staff, as long as I avoided headshots, I let whoever I was sparring against feel my wrath.

The palms of my hands felt raw by the time I finished my weapon training. Thankfully, I developed thick calluses long ago, so my hands no longer were left with open blisters.

Most days, I opted to walk after my training. Being out in nature calmed me. I would walk until the last possible second before I had to head back to my dormitory to wash and prepare for class, knowing I would repeat everything again tomorrow.

I usually ended up on the trails near the mountains, wondering if the cold, snowy beach from my nightmare was on the other side. Scanning the perimeter out of habit, I would search for an opening other than the guarded road of Laten. But I knew the only way out was up and over the mountains. Despite my failed attempts every day, I walked, picking a new area to stroll and discover.

Today was different though. I only had a week left of classes before our Trials this weekend. I always thought that if I found the black-sanded beach, the memories of my previous life would come rushing back to me, and I would know why I was brought here.

It was wishful thinking. I knew some of the Advenians of Tennebris possessed mind-controlling abilities. I didn't doubt that the male with the lavender eyes had my memories from Lux wiped by a Tennebrisian. Only it didn't all take. The memory of my capture was left, either on purpose or by accident, but I always wished I could remember everything. It bothered me not knowing the names of my real parents. Not being able to recall their faces or remember if they loved me.

I'd spent countless nights not sleeping, trying to figure out who kidnapped me. Lavender eyes were a Luxian trait and I swore the kidnappers possessed elemental abilities. Even though my memories were tampered with, I didn't doubt that recollection. I re-lived it every night. But what purpose would someone from Lux have for leaving me in Tennebris?

Impulsively, I decided to try to hike up one of the nearby peaks. Grabbing my worn leather gloves from my front pocket, I quickly threw them on and shoved my workout pack over my shoulders.

It was harder than I thought. My legs grew sore and stiff from hiking up the cutting terrain, but I pushed myself to go further. The air became thinner, causing my breath to become more ragged. The temperature dropped the higher I climbed. I could feel the frigid air seeping through my clothes. It was so cold that it felt like it was burning my skin the closer I got to the top of the shield. I slipped on an icy patch, but managed to catch myself before tumbling all the way down.

The next time I slipped, I didn't see the large rock behind me as I stumbled. My pants tore at the knee, opening up to a raw cut. Blood covered my kneecap and dripped down my leg. My bare skin felt chilled against the wind. I knew from the throbbing that it would leave a nasty scar in its wake. I clutched my knee to my chest as I surveyed the distance I had climbed. Disappointment coursed through me as the realization sank in that I still had miles to go, and the slope would only get steeper and icier the higher I climbed.

I decided to rest on the rock as I slowed my breathing. The change in altitude wasn't helping. I took my water out of my pack, took a sip, and frowned as it was nearly half gone from my workout. Classes would be starting soon. I momentarily thought about skipping them to continue hiking, but decided against it. One mark on my record could tarnish my chances of passing the Trials.

Part of me knew that even if I made it over this mountain, it wouldn't end there. It wasn't like the beach was going to be waiting for me on the other side. The villages of Tennebris were spread out, and all I had was a scant amount of water and an apple. I didn't even bring my coat for warmth. Frustrated, I sighed as I started the slow descent back down the mountain.

By the time I reached my dorm, my roommate, Vallie, was sitting at her desk with her arms crossed, tapping one foot hard against the floor. Her red hair was tied up in a messy bun that somehow still looked perfect as her amber eyes glared at me.

"Where have you been? We're going to be late for class," she blurted the moment she spotted me. She stood, pushing the chair aside so she was looming over me.

"I know. I'm sorry. I got caught up with my training. I'll be super fast." I promised her as I threw my pack down, kicked off my boots, and rushed into the bathing room.

I could hear Vallie call after me as I locked the door and jumped into the cold bath she must have filled for me, "You better! This is not the time to be late with Trials coming up this weekend."

"I won't make us late," I shouted through the locked door as I vigorously scrubbed the grime and dried blood from my body. The dorms in Tennebris were only lit by windows or candlelight. The Dark

Kingdom hated electricity and seldom used it as it reminded them of Lux. But even though the bathing room was dark, I didn't bother lighting a candle. I still avoided them whenever I could and I loved the select rooms that did have electric lights.

She huffed. "You better not, Scotlind Mae Rumor. I don't care how strong you are from all your training, I'll beat you myself if you make us late."

"Vallie, I would pay to see you try to fight anything," I teased as I hopped out of the tub in record time. In all the years I'd known her, she didn't do anything that could get her even remotely dirty. *That'll ruin my makeup,* she would say anytime I tried to get her to join me.

"You're lucky we're friends, Scottie," she shouted. I could imagine her large smile even though she was on the other side of the door. "I've never known another Advenian who doesn't care about dating and literally doesn't do anything fun."

"Just because I don't like to go out partying with you and Miles, doesn't mean I don't like fun things."

"Running outside and reading does not count as fun."

I laughed. I was lucky Vallie was friends with me. She was my only friend. Well, her and her twin brother, Miles. Everyone else at Lake-Wood looked at me with disgust. I was the strange child who survived a fire that killed her entire family. A child with no abilities as far as they knew. I was a loner at LakeWood. The only female trying out for the King's Guard at the Trials. Everyone looked at me as if I was foreign, but little did they know, I was.

# TWO
# SCOTLIND

Vallie and I were both panting by the time we arrived at our first class of the day. Breathless, I leaned over one of the wooden desks that filled the classroom. We had just made it—our teacher wasn't here yet. We smiled at each other triumphantly, realizing we barely got out of getting detention as we claimed the only two empty seats left.

I grinned at Vallie. "See, I told you I wouldn't make us late."

She rolled her eyes at me, but I saw a hint of a smirk appear just as Professor Gibs wobbled in on her cane. She was the oldest professor at LakeWood and had been teaching Mortal-Allium History for as long as anyone could remember. Other than her slight limp and silver hair, she looked young. Everyone of our kind did. An Advenian could be a thousand years old, but still pass for a thirty-year-old mortal.

"Students, as you are all aware, your Trials are approaching. I was instructed to remind you of its significance and how the weekend will go. The first portion will be an examination. The exam will be an accumulation of everything you have learned over your years at Lake-Wood," Professor Gibs said. "It will make up one-third of your overall Trial. I suggest you all take it seriously. The test will determine your knowledge and rank you amongst your peers. The last two-thirds of your Trial will take place the following day. You will have your rank evaluations to classify what Dark powers you possess as well as your physical Trial for the career you've selected."

She paused as she scanned the room, staring down at us. "All three sections—the exam, the rank evaluations, and the physical Trial—will be used to determine your worth to our society. As you're probably already aware, members of the High Council of Tennebris will be at the ranking and Trials to evaluate your performances. They will ultimately be the ones who determine your future. You have the freedom to try out for any career, but not everyone gets the job they've selected, so you must do well in all three parts. This is your one chance to carve the pathway for your future. Whatever worth and job the High Council grants you, will be yours for the rest of your life."

The entire class fell eerily silent. Everyone knew the Trials were this weekend. We'd been preparing for them ever since we were little, but the fact that they were only a few days away was starting to sink in. By the end of the week, my life would be changed forever. For good or bad, I would finally be leaving LakeWood.

"The majority of your examination will consist of Tennebrisian history and abilities. However, do not pass over your study material on Lux. Although we live separate lives, knowledge of Lux is just as important. You will be tested on everything." Professor Gibs tapped her cane on the ground. "Now, let's review. Who can tell me the differences between Luxian and Tennebrisian abilities and markings?"

She peered around the room, glancing over all of us from the top of her pointed nose. No one raised their hand. We knew by now it didn't matter, Professor Gibs would call on whoever she wanted anyway.

"Yuri John," she called.

All eyes immediately went to Yuri. She smiled broadly, aware of the attention focused on her as she flicked her hair over her sharp shoulders. I rolled my eyes as a blonde curl bounced behind her back.

Yuri gently cleared her throat. "Of course, Professor Gibs. Our kingdom, Tennebris, is the Dark Kingdom. Our powers consist mostly of the inner mind. When we use our abilities, if we are lucky enough to have any—" Yuri paused deliberately and twisted in her chair to face me. A few snickers echoed throughout the room at what she implied. Her hazel eyes met mine before she continued, "—our bodies will produce golden markings unique to each individual. As soon as we are done using our abilities, the markings will fade from our skin, allowing us to blend in with the human race if we ever had to. The Advenians from Lux, the Light Kingdom, tend to have abilities that are more prone to the elements. Their markings are black and appear on their body whenever their marked skin comes in contact with fluid. It doesn't matter if they are using their powers or not."

I hated being reminded of my different markings. Luckily, my black markings of Lux were confined to my back, so I'd been able to hide them from everyone in Tennebris. If mine were in a more visible area like my hands or face, I would have been discovered years ago. Now, I just had to keep my back covered at all times.

"Very good," Professor Gibs said with a half smile. Leave it to Yuri to be the one who could turn our Professor's frown into a grin. "Can anyone tell me how the abilities are ranked and how the two kingdoms determine strength?"

Professor Gibs pointed toward a student near the back of the class. The boy's voice was shaky as he answered, "Our abilities are tested throughout our schooling and our final ranking will go on our official record during our rank evaluations at our Trials. They vary from rank zero, which is having no powers, to rank five, which means you have the strongest and rarest powers. Everyone will be evaluated by how many abilities they possess and how powerful and rare they are. A rank five for Tennebris is extremely rare. Mediocre abilities score a rank of one or two. And those who have no abilities are tainted with human blood. They are *nixes* and are given a rank zero."

Someone coughed my name, and a few laughs echoed throughout the classroom. Professor Gibs either didn't hear it or chose not to. I knew without turning my head that the entire class was now glancing my way.

I had no Tennebrisian abilities, my skin would never turn golden, no matter how badly I wished it could. No one from the Dark Kingdom knew I wasn't one of them, except for the man with the lavender eyes who captured me all those years ago. But even he had belonged to Lux with the way he manipulated the fire and left me to the mercy of my old counselor. To everyone here, I was a worthless nix of Tennebris, the scum of society, and I was happy to keep it that way. At least it would keep me alive.

I remembered the day I realized this. I was eight, a year after being in Tennebris, and we just had a lecture about the differences between the two kingdoms in our Magical Theories class. After spending the entire year being manipulated into thinking I made everything up, I had started to believe it.

Having no memories of my childhood, except for the night of my capture, I questioned if I really was crazy. Was I really just an Advenian of Tennebris, an orphan, and a nix? Was everything in my head?

I remembered sprinting back to my dorm immediately after the lecture about our markings. I lit all the candles in the bathing room and jumped in the bath, scanning my body in a rushed state to search for any markings. I normally opted for darkness when I bathed over the flame of a candle so I never really paid attention to what my skin looked like in water before. I was so disappointed when I found no black designs dotting my skin that I sobbed as I hopped out of the tub. I was using my towel to wipe off a section of the mirror and almost didn't notice as I turned around.

My entire back was covered in the dark, black markings of Lux, glistening and glowing from the water droplets running down my spine. I kept craning my neck to get a better look. I couldn't make sense of all the symbols and designs.

The golden markings of Tennebris were mostly patterns, circles, lines, dots, and spirals, but mine took shapes. A large tree with thick bark around the trunk ran up my spinal column. Beautiful feathered wings covered in flowers were spread across my shoulder blades with water and fire entwining around either side. Other symbols were scattered across my skin, symbols I didn't recognize. Symbols that covered every inch of the flesh on my back.

I searched my body one last time to make sure I didn't have markings anywhere else, anywhere that I might have missed, but I found none. Blank—the rest of my body was utterly blank. I stared at my back, watching the black markings disappear with each drying drop of water.

I was exuberant for a brief moment as revelations flashed through my mind. *I was not a nix. I had abilities.* I had no idea what they were, but I had powers. The markings indicated I wasn't truly a rank zero. That meant something to know I wasn't crazy. I didn't make everything up. I was Luxian. I had a life before this, a life I was uprooted from. I had a family in Lux. A family I needed to find, or at least, figure out what happened to them.

Then the dread and realization of what that actually meant sunk in. My entire back was covered in black markings, and if anyone saw them, they would know I was from the Light Kingdom. I would be killed. I couldn't comprehend why I was brought here. Why did those men start the fire just to abandon me in Tennebris? What was the purpose of me growing up here? No matter how hard I thought about it, I never got closer to figuring it out.

I sobbed for days after realizing I would never have a normal life here. I would have to hide my identity forever. It would have been easier if I really was just a nix.

Since it was illegal to intermix between the two kingdoms, I could never take a husband in Tennebris. My markings would appear whenever any fluid made contact with my bare skin. I wouldn't be able to keep them hidden from a spouse. I would be exposed and branded a traitor or spy. There would be no logical reason I could give as to why I was living here. Nothing I could explain, or at least, that anyone would believe. I had already learned that the hard way.

That was why I chose to try out for the King's Guard. After that bath when I was eight, I realized it was my safest option and the only possible career path for me. A guard was the only career that didn't encourage marriage. I would never have to worry about someone discovering who I was. I vowed that day to never marry anyone from Tennebris, to never even let myself date.

I also vowed to never leave myself defenseless. Never again would I be uprooted and forced into a situation where I couldn't defend myself. So I started training...

Every. Single. Day.

I would wake up before classes to do physical training. I attended all the guard classes in our curriculum, and read about the different fighting techniques and styles during my spare time.

And although I hated thinking about it, I knew my nightmare would serve as a reminder. I would become strong. I would be able to defend myself. Never again would anyone overpower me. Never again could anyone take me from my home. Never again would I be helpless and not able to protect the ones I loved. *I would not be weak.*

I tried to not let it bother me that this only gave my classmates more reasons to loathe me. On top of being the orphan nix who survived a tragedy, and the deranged child who made up stories and told lies, I was trying out for the guard. The only female to do so at LakeWood. The only rank zero to do so. Both were unheard of.

The males in my guard classes made sure I didn't forget where I belonged. They never held back when sparring with me. In the beginning, I would come back from practice covered in bruises, barely able to walk. Every day was like that until I learned to use my frame to my advantage. I focused on technique since I couldn't fight with abilities. I became faster, more agile. I learned to predict my classmates' movements, zipping out of the way before they could overpower me in brute strength. I learned to fight back.

"I will not tolerate the use of harsh language in my classroom," Professor Gibs warned, forcing me out of my thoughts. "You're all aware that the use of the term 'nix' is forbidden at our school. Even though rank zeroes have no power, there is no connection between them and mortals. They are still Advenian. They still possess our long lifespan and, as such, will be treated fairly in our society."

Calling someone a nix was the worst kind of insult, except perhaps to be called a mortal.

"Then how do you explain why rank zeroes only existed after our kind came to this planet?" someone mumbled under their breath.

"It's because our ancestors were disgusting and actually fornicated with the mortals. They tainted and weakened our blood."

Someone else responded, "Rank zeroes shouldn't exist."

"Do not speak out of turn," Professor Gibs yelled as she jabbed her cane against the brick wall.

Vallie leaned in to whisper softly, "Don't listen to them."

Once Professor Gibs wasn't looking, I turned to smile toward her. "Thanks," I mouthed.

It didn't really bother me, not anymore. At least, I didn't take it personally, but I felt for all the naturally born rank zeroes. It wasn't right to treat someone poorly just because they didn't have an ability. Their life shouldn't be viewed as worthless because they couldn't teleport or manipulate dreams. Unfortunately, I was one of the few Advenians who thought that way. Tennebris thrived off the ranking system, and from what I learned through our studies, it seemed like the Luxians were even worse. I liked to believe that even if I grew up in Lux and wasn't considered a nix, I would feel the same about rank zeroes. That I would still hate the ranking system even though I wouldn't know firsthand what it felt like to live at the bottom of it.

Most rank zeroes were selected as servants after their Trials, even if they chose a different career path to test in. It was another reason why I trained so hard. If I was going to spend my life serving the Dark, it would be on my own terms. Not mopping floors and cleaning up after the high ranks. I wanted to prove that the ranking system was flawed and that a number didn't define your worth to society. I wanted to prove that a zero could still fight.

A boy with slick hair and chestnut eyes raised his hand. "Yes, Bradley. What is it?" Professor Gibs grumbled as she pinched the bridge of her nose.

"Why don't we just work with Lux and overthrow the human population? Mortals are weak, and we're so much stronger, and Lux is far more advanced. Why can't we overtake Earth instead of being confined to our hidden kingdoms?"

Professor Gibs flashed him a stern look. "Perhaps I should assign the class to read the Treaty? It's apparent you do not understand why our ancestors signed the document that ended the Cold Time and the Ability War."

The whole class groaned as she continued. "It would violate the Treaty if we attacked the human race and made ourselves known to them. We must learn from our ancestors' mistakes. Yes, we have abilities far greater than the creatures inhabiting this planet. However, they outnumber us twenty-fold with their bountiful reproduction systems. When our kind first came here, it had been decided that it would be too devastating to completely invade the planet. Too many lives had already been lost—our planet had been lost. We couldn't risk that again.

"Another war could cause the destruction of this planet, just like it had on Allium. We do not want to risk a repeat of our time stranded in space. It took our ancestors many centuries to find Earth. And that was centuries of not being able to use their powers due to the confined walls of a space-craft. It's a blessing to be able to breathe in air, to be able to wield the powers that were gifted to you at birth by Pylemo. Furthermore, this is not our planet. As you are aware, becoming an astronomer after the Trials, if that is what one desires, is a highly praised career path. Second only to the High Council and the king himself. Tennebris has the best space program and has been working diligently on searching for a habitable planet for our kind. One that is barren of inhabitants, so we may claim it as our own. We must be patient. Once on a new planet, it will be wise to keep the peace between our two kingdoms. We do not want to start another magical war."

A girl in the back raised her hand. Professor Gibs sighed. "Yes, Krancy. What is it?"

"If our intention here is only to hide to bid time until our kind finds another planet, why have we adapted one of the many mortal languages?"

Professor Gibs was speechless for a long moment as if she wasn't sure of the answer herself. The language of Allium was still taught and mandated for all to take, but the fluency of it had been lost. No one spoke it anymore. Only ancient documents like our Treaty were written in Allium, which was probably the only reason we were still required to learn it. Vallie was an expert at it, but I could never grasp the written language and was thankful that the humans found a simpler way of communicating.

"That is a question perhaps that might be better suited for your Mortal Relations teacher. I'm sure Professor Madick can shed some more light on the subject," Professor Gibs finally stated. "It's unclear why our ancestors switched our language all those years ago, but we have been speaking one of the mortal tongues for almost seven centuries. We have now adapted it and claim it as our own."

Professor Gibs rambled on for another twenty minutes before she assigned our homework and study materials for our examination.

The rest of the day dragged on. Class after class after class. I hated the days I didn't have guard practice. It made me antsy to be forced to sit through boring lectures all afternoon, and today, my training had been canceled because of the King's Tournament. But I was so excited that they were going to broadcast the competition for the first time that I almost didn't care.

Almost.

# THREE
## SCOTLIND

I jumped in my chair from the commotion around me as the final chime rang out, signaling the end of our school day. The entire class started buzzing around me, giddy because the tournament for the new king was tonight.

Vallie skipped over to me right away. "I'm so excited. Do you think the Hall will be crowded? Of course it will, Sie's fighting," she rambled, answering her own question. "Let's hurry so we can get good seats."

I groaned. "I'm not looking forward to that."

Vallie halted her skip in her step as she turned to look at me. Her arched eyebrows rose even higher. "I thought you were excited to watch the tournament. It's the first time they're airing it live, so you don't have to read about it like you normally do."

"I am excited to watch the fighting. I want to see who will be crowned the new king. I just meant I'm not excited for all the squealing girls and how packed it's going to be."

"Scotlind Rumor, I will be among those squealing girls, so I demand you take that statement back right now!"

I purposely kept walking to get a rise out of her. Vallie gasped loudly when I refused to respond, slapping her hand across her chest like I'd offended her. She untangled her other arm out of mine and pinched my hip hard until I finally gave in.

"Okay, okay," I laughed. "Yours is the only squealing that doesn't bother me."

"Damn straight it is." She smiled as she yet again took my arm, my elbow lifting up to match her height. "Also, it's a known fact that Sie is going to be the next king."

"That's not true, Vallie. No one knows for sure what the outcome of the tournament will be."

"Scottie, Sie is Tennebris' only rank five. He's going to win the free-for-all fight and get to move on to challenge the current king. There is absolutely no way he loses. He's the strongest Advenian alive."

Vallie didn't need to add the strongest *Tennebris* Advenian alive. Lux was known for breeding rank fives. The curriculum in Tennebris even hints at Lux being the stronger kingdom, though they don't outright say it. Lux and Tennebris are supposed to be described as a delicate balance. A yin and yang on a scale that wouldn't tip. Lux symbolizes the golden sun, while Tennebris represents Allium's twin pink moons. Night and day. Darkness and light. But the balance had been skewed for a while. The only reason Tennebris still has a standing is because they possess compulsion and illusion.

"Just because he's a rank five, doesn't mean that he will automatically win," I countered. "It takes more to win the tournament than just being a high rank."

Half the females were only watching the fight tonight because it was the first King's Tournament that Sie was competing in. Now that Sie had turned twenty, he was eligible to fight. It was a law that an Advenian had to have already graduated from school in order for their Trials to be reviewed. You needed to have a rank in order to apply. And Sie graduated two years ago with a rank five. He only had to wait for the king's ruling decade to finish for another tournament to happen. Everyone in Tennebris knew his name. Ever since his powers manifested at such a young age, Advenians had been waiting for him to come of age to claim the crown.

I loved the idea behind the King's Tournament—that every decade someone could rise up and be better than the current king. The ruler of Tennebris could never hold on to his title without being deemed worthy. The king's rule could last for centuries, but every ten years, he had to prove he was still the best choice to govern the kingdom. It didn't matter what family you were born into, but merely what abilities you possessed could make or break your life.

I just hated the fact that only males with a rank of three or higher could apply to compete. I also hated that everyone spoke about Sie as if he was already the king.

"They say he graduated top of his class in combat skills and scored perfectly on the examination for his Trials. He's going to win," Vallie continued as we headed toward the Hub of campus. "I can't wait to see him fight."

I couldn't help but roll my eyes. "Vallie, don't pretend you actually want to see him fight. You're only watching the tournament because you want to see what he looks like."

"Well, duh... I think that's the reason every girl is going to be watching tonight, except you. Everyone says that he's super tall and ridiculously hot, but I need to see for myself," she squealed as she squeezed my arm. "Can you imagine marrying him and being queen? You would literally go down in history as the girl who married a rank five."

"Just because he isn't married doesn't mean he doesn't have someone in mind. I'm sure he's betrothed but just keeps his personal life to himself," I said. Sie was the youngest to ever be accepted to fight in the tournament. Usually, the males competing were already married, automatically making their wife the queen. But if you entered the competition without a wife or a betrothed, you must agree to an arranged marriage, as the Tennebrisian law states a king must have a queen before his coronation.

I found the whole thing ridiculous. Why must a king be married in order to lead, and why couldn't a queen rule?

"If he had someone in mind, he would be betrothed or married by now. I'm sure he doesn't," Vallie insisted.

"Vallie," I questioned, "how did you jump to him getting married when we don't even know if he's going to win?"

"You're living under a giant rock. Just wait until you see him on the screen. Then you'll be drooling over him too."

"Yeah, right," I remarked.

"I'll take that as a challenge," she said as she pulled me in through the door of the Hall.

Long rectangular tables stretched out the length of the room. Wooden benches that were normally tucked underneath were filled with students. The Hall was packed since it was the only place that received broadcasts from the other villages. It was the only monitor LakeWood had in the school and anytime a mandatory announcement was made from the king or Council, the students filed into the cramped room. Most of the students were turned to face the lone monitor mounted on the wall. Even though night was approaching, the sun was still shining through the windows, settling in as rays of orange mixed with hues of blue shown through the stained glass.

Golden swirls that represented the Tennebrisian markings were scattered in between each piece of glass. The window was a map, illustrating how the six Dark villages were spread throughout this glacial slab of ice. A thin purple line banded around the entire thing where the shield was strategically placed. My eyes followed the purple curve of the shield, indicating the parts of our kingdom that remained hidden from the mortals. I often wondered if the black-sanded beach was within the shield or outside of it in the mortal territory.

"It seems like everyone wants to see him fight," I mused as we scanned the crowd for open seats amongst the flock of females. I figured it would be crowded, but I'd never seen the Hall this full before.

I groaned as I realized Yuri was at the only open table left, positioned directly in front of the large monitor. Not because no one wanted to sit with her, but more likely because everyone was too afraid to approach her.

"Ugh, Vallie, please no," I pleaded once I realized my friend's eyes were narrowed in on the empty chairs. "I would rather stand than sit next to her." I emphasized *her* in order to get my point across. It wasn't a secret that we didn't get along.

"Scottie, I know you don't like her, but I want a good view of the screen. Plus, the tournament is long. I don't want to stand all night, I'm wearing four-inch heels."

I crossed my arms across my chest as I glared up at her. We were forced to wear our school uniform for all our classes, but it didn't apply to our shoes and Vallie almost never left our dorm without heels. "I'll switch shoes with you," I begged. I wanted to watch the tournament in peace, and I was losing my patience with putting up with Yuri's snide remarks.

Vallie huffed a laugh. "As much as I would love to see you in heels, you know my feet can't fit into your boots."

Vallie turned, her red hair whipping me across the face, as she placed two hands over my shoulders. "Please, Scottie-cat. We graduate right after our Trials, and I won't be able to see you again. I know she isn't always the nicest toward you, but we can ignore her. You are my best friend and I want to sit with you before I won't have the chance anymore." She pouted, dragging out the word, "Please."

"Ugh, fine," I groaned. I could never say no to Vallie when she guilted me about our limited time together. In truth, I didn't want to think about the fact that this time next week, I wouldn't be able to hang out with my friend. I wouldn't be able to hear her infectious laugh or see her glowing smile.

"Yay!" Vallie clapped her hands together as she jumped up and down. "Come on, if I miss Sie's interview, I will kill you." I was grateful Vallie took the spot closest to Yuri and her friends as I slumped onto the bench to Vallie's left. I always felt slightly guilty seeing the two of them together. She and Yuri used to be friends before I ruined it when Vallie ultimately defended me. They're still civil toward one another, but Yuri hasn't invited Vallie over to her place since the night she brought me.

"Hi, Vallie," Yuri's high-pitched voice rang through my ears as she smiled at her. I did my best to zone them out as they started talking about Sie's abs and what it would be like to be his queen. I focused on the monitor screen. It didn't look like we missed the fighting portion of the tournament. Still, with the buzz and gossip flying across the room, it was hard to hear anything coming from the screen.

I felt a tap on my shoulder and turned to see my only other friend at school. "Hi, Miles," I smiled as he pushed Vallie out of the way to squeeze down in between us.

"Hey, Scottie. Hey, sis." Miles grinned at his twin and me. There was no denying that Vallie and Miles were related when they smiled. They both shared the same wide grin with teeth that were too large for their mouths. They were both on the tall side, but while Miles was lankier, Vallie had a more feminine figure. She had curves in all the right places, something I wished I had. Miles' hair was a shade lighter than his sister's. More of a strawberry-blonde while Vallie's was a flaming red. She stuck out in any crowd. Especially in the sun when the light hit her hair just right and hues of orange and gold shined through, complementing her amber eyes.

Vallie was gorgeous, and her personality matched her looks. She was light-hearted, open, and sweet. She made friends wherever she went. Miles was more of a loner like me. In fact, he probably didn't have any other friends either. He always had his head in a book, studying for the AASP, the Allium Advenian Space Program. Whenever we would hang out without Vallie, we didn't talk much, and usually just read our own books in silence.

Vallie stuck her tongue out at her twin. "Nice of you to join us, Miles."

Miles gave her a nod before turning his attention to me. "How is training going?" I bit my lip as his russet eyes met mine. He sometimes made me feel uneasy with the intensity of his gaze. I would catch him looking at me, and he wouldn't look away. I wasn't used to the undivided attention he gave me, no matter how much time I spent with the two of them. Most Advenians avoided me altogether. He was attractive, and I was aware there were many females interested in him, but I just never thought of him in that way, and I was thankful that, because of Vallie, he never made a move on me.

"It's good," I managed to choke out.

Vallie slapped my arm, saving me from whatever Miles was about to say next. "Ah, Scottie, that's him! Oh. My. Gosh. He is so… hot."

I looked up at the monitor, and I had to agree with her. A reporter was currently interviewing Sie as he appeared front and center on the screen. The man staring back at me had a dark, masculine persona. He was tall, really tall, about a head above everyone else.

Some of the other males standing in the background were bulkier than him, but he looked more athletic. Powerful in a different kind of way, every inch of him corded in lean muscle. His facial contours captured my attention as his dark, black messy hair fell into soft waves over his forehead.

As he shook his head to brush the few strands away, I caught a glimpse of his eyes. They were the most striking feature about him. His dark gaze was piercing. He didn't smile and kept his mouth set beneath his straight nose, exposing his angular jawline. Every feature somehow fit him perfectly, making him appear like a weapon, like someone you wouldn't want to face in battle. He didn't even look like someone you would want to hold a simple conversation with. He looked dangerous in a cold, menacing kind of way.

The screen zoomed in on Sie's left wrist which had the number five burned into it. After the Trials, once you received your official ranking, everyone had to get their number branded onto them. It was meant to symbolize your strength.

I found it cruel. Most people had the one or two rank burned onto them, a common number. Fewer had a three or a four, but no one in Tennebris had a five. Not until Sie. At least not anyone who was still alive. I found that rankings were just a way for Advenians to brag, giving them an excuse to feel superior over others. All the competing males had their gazes transfixed on Sie. They looked nervous, intimidated by his number.

Vallie leaned over her twin and pretended to wipe something off my chin. "Drool," she smirked with a gleam in her eyes.

I swatted her hand away. "Did we miss the beginning?" I asked the group of girls we were sitting with, wholly ignoring Vallie's comment. Miles seemed to notice too.

One of the girls responded, "Yeah, the written portion of the tournament just finished. It took about an hour for everyone to be done. Sie finished first, of course."

"Oh," I responded, slightly disappointed. I knew that it was generally the boring part, but I wanted to watch the entire thing. The tournament had three stages: two fighting stages and a written exam in the beginning. Thousands of males apply for the tournament every decade, but only the top fifteen are accepted to take the written exam.

"I never understood why they have to take a written exam. It's a waste of time if you ask me," Yuri huffed.

Miles looked at her in disbelief. "You're kidding me, right?" When she didn't respond, he added, "You're telling me that you don't want to make sure the future ruler of Tennebris is intelligent? The fact that he has to be able to make logical and just decisions for our kingdom and is responsible for meeting with Lux every year to negotiate the Peace Treaty, doesn't concern you at all?"

"Isn't that the purpose of the High Council?" she asked as she inspected the ends of her blonde hair.

"The king gets the final say. He has more sway than anyone. If the king—"

"No one cares, Miles," Yuri cut him off as she turned her focus back to the screen. Miles continued to stare at her in disbelief.

"Did the results come back yet for the written exam?" I asked, hoping to break the tension. I wanted to know how many passed and would proceed to the fighting portion.

"Yeah, the results are back. Ten people failed it," another girl answered. "Sie and four others passed. I honestly forget their names. They just started the interviews, so they should come up on the screen soon."

As an interviewer asked Sie a question, the whole room grew silent. "As you know, during the first round of the tournament, you and your opponents will be fighting all at once. Are you aware of the rumors circulating that the other opponents may try to team up against you? Since the first round is combat only, you won't be able to rely on your powers at all. Does this concern you?"

Sie looked at her unamused by the question as if he expected it. Everyone was gossiping that the only way to beat him was for all the contestants to work together from the start, take him out first and then fight amongst themselves. It was a good strategy, and probably the only feasible one, if what they said about his fighting skills were true. I just didn't think it was fair.

"No," he remarked. His voice was flat as he added nothing else.

"He sounds cocky and arrogant," I blurted as I sat back on the bench. Everyone around me, including Vallie and Yuri, hushed me so they could hear what else Sie was saying. Miles chuckled.

The interviewer continued to ask question after question, trying to get a juicy remark out of him, but he didn't indulge her. I wondered if he was even capable of speaking more than one-worded answers. He maintained a serious and composed face the entire interview, showing no signs of emotion.

She finally asked him, "I have one final question for you. The Tennebrisian law states that the winner must take a wife prior to the coronation if they are not yet married. If the tournament ends in your favor and you're victorious today, do you have someone in mind? All the other competitors today are already married. Are you, perhaps, engaged and keeping it to yourself?"

Everyone in the Hall fell silent. All the females leaned forward in their seats, simultaneously holding their breaths. After all, this was why half of them were watching. They wanted to know if there was a chance to be chosen, to be his wife.

Sie was silent for so long that I didn't think he would answer. Then he said, "No, I'm not engaged, and I don't have anyone in mind."

A few girls squealed. Yuri and Vallie both visibly sat up a little taller. Yuri, with a massive smile plastered to her face, Vallie with her hands covering her mouth.

"So if you don't have anyone in mind, you're aware that the High Council then chooses a wife for you in an arranged marriage?" Sie gave a subtle nod. The interviewer grinned excitedly, believing she was finally getting into the juicy questions. "Does this concern you? Tennebrisians pride themselves in marrying for love. If you win today, you will be giving up that right. You will be forced to be with whoever the Council selects for you for your entire life, not just your rule."

This was yet another reason Tennebris varied from Lux. The Dark Kingdom encouraged marriage. Everyone had to marry, except the King's Guard. I remembered when I was younger, my professor explained the reason why Guards don't have significant others—because an Advenian would always choose to save their loved ones over whom they are supposed to protect. The nice thing about the Dark Kingdom was that you had the choice. You could select anyone you wanted. You could marry for love. That's why there had been so much talk about the only rank five not yet choosing his bride. He could have anyone he wanted. He could choose, yet he didn't.

"Duty is more important to me than a wife. It hasn't been my priority to take one. If I am to be the king after this, I have no issues with the High Council choosing her for me."

Vallie frowned a little bit as Yuri said, "I'm sure he just hasn't met the *right* girl yet. Once he sees me, he will change his mind." All of Yuri's friends nodded in agreement. I rolled my eyes. How thick and self-centered could she be to assume that she would marry him?

"Dream on," Vallie chimed in. "He's mine."

"To me, it sounds like he only cares about being king and having power. I wouldn't get your hopes up on love. I'm pretty sure a marriage to him would be platonic at best," I remarked, quieting their giggles.

One of Yuri's friends added softly, "That's probably true. I heard he has lots of Advenian females throwing themselves at him. I wouldn't be surprised if he has a ton of mistresses and affairs. He doesn't really seem like the type to love someone. He's too cold and closed off."

Yuri ignored her friend's comment and glared at me. "No one asked your opinion, nix. Just because no one will ever choose you, doesn't mean there isn't a chance for the rest of us. Who would want to marry a nix anyway?"

Vallie gave me a weak smile, reaching across her brother to squeeze my hand before she frowned at Yuri. "Be nice."

Yuri ignored her, but once her gaze settled on Miles who looked like he was about to punch her in the throat, she turned her attention back to the screen.

"Don't listen to her," Miles leaned in to whisper to me. "Any guy would be lucky to have you." I gave him a small smile before I turned my attention to the screen as well. The only perk of being a known rank zero was that no one was interested in me. Yuri wasn't wrong, but I didn't feel like hashing it out with her. I had to be on my best behavior with the Trials just days away. I couldn't risk having another fight on my record. The Goddess knows I had too many already.

After Sie's interview, they interviewed each of the four remaining contestants individually. One of the males seemed promising. His name was Robert Bashington. He stood about a foot shorter than Sie in height but made up for it by being ridiculously broad. I was surprised he could fit through a door frame. His hair was shaved so short that I could only determine his true hair color by his dark bushy eyebrows. He was a rank four and competed ten years ago in the last tournament, but didn't make it past the second round. At least he would have the advantage of knowing what to expect, and had probably dedicated the past ten years to training harder.

The rest of the interview process took about an hour. Most of them talked about Sie and how they planned to beat him. It was crazy to me how this whole tournament seemed to revolve around him.

The second portion finally started, and we watched the screen as all the men were ushered around the base of a small enclosed arena. Steep bleachers were erected high off the ground in a circle, completely surrounding the competitors. The stands were filled with members of the high rank society who were watching the tournament in person. Maybe one day, if I became a guard, I could watch the King's Tournament from the stands too.

The screen panned the crowd, then landed on the current king. He looked apprehensive, slouched shoulders, sweat beading down his forehead and building in his thick mustache. I wondered how he felt about all the gossip regarding Sie.

If Sie did win today, it would make King Lunder's rule short. With only three King's Tournaments won, he would only have ruled for thirty years. It would also make Sie the youngest king ever elected for Tennebris and the first Dark King in a long time to be a rank five.

King Lunder made a short speech reciting the same lines every king made at the beginning of the tournaments according to the books I'd read. I found myself zoning out his words and staring at Sie. I couldn't take my eyes off him. He didn't seem nervous about what was about to happen. He had an air of confidence, even though the other four males held murderous gazes all directed at him.

After King Lunder's speech, an announcer who introduced himself as Effin came on. "Thank you, King Lunder, for those words of encouragement. What an honor it is to be hosting another King's Tournament by your gracious side. We will now begin the second round of the tournament. Five men passed the written portion and will be fighting against one another. Now remember, abilities are prohibited during this round. You will fight until your opponent is either unconscious or surrenders. There will be no deaths. I will announce the competitors one at a time as they enter the arena, along with their official ranking and their passing scores for round one."

Effin paused dramatically. "Robert Bashington, rank four, scored ninety-one percent. Adam Ontinio, rank three, scored ninety-three percent. Sie Noren, rank five, scored ninety-six percent." The crowd burst into cheers that Effin was desperately trying to quiet before he continued. Sie stalked out toward the center of the arena, his shoulders wide, head held high as his dark eyes narrowed, taking everything in. He nodded toward the other two opponents as he joined them at the center.

"Please welcome Savern Abre, rank four, scored eighty-nine percent. And last, but certainly not least, Nathan McRee, rank four, scored ninety-two percent." Effin didn't stop the cheering this time as all five men gathered at the center. A loud bell chimed through the speakers, lingering a few seconds before the announcer exclaimed, "Begin."

# FOUR
## SIE

I zoned out the deafening roar of the crowd as soon as the announcer bellowed to begin. I turned toward my opponents, sizing them up. I quickly realized that all the males stood together, facing me.

"So this is how it's going to go," I mumbled under my breath as they launched toward me in unison. I knew I had to take one of them out immediately—a knockout. I wouldn't make it long in the fight if it remained four on one. I had to scare them all from the start, making them hesitant to come at me.

The announcer said Adam Ontinio was a rank three. I scanned them, searching for the three brand across their wrists. He stood about a foot shorter than me, with lanky limbs and a scrawny body. Good enough.

I used my footwork to position myself in front of him, letting him come to me. Giving him false hope, he threw wide.

I leaned back on my heels, balancing my body weight as I dodged his fist. I didn't hesitate as I landed a front kick to his face in a matter of seconds. My leg snapped up and I heard a sharp crunch of bones, breaking something. He stumbled backward, trying to steady himself.

His scream echoed throughout the arena as he clutched his nose, attempting to stop the gush of blood pouring out.

The other three males hesitated. Good. That was precisely what I was counting on.

I sprang toward Adam again. I needed to get him out of the fight. I kicked, extending myself as my foot slammed into his thigh. Then before lowering my leg, I leaned back, giving myself more power before landing another kick to his jaw.

Adam's eyes rolled back in his head. One moment, he was standing before me. The next, he was falling flat on his back. The other males stopped short, gawking at Adam's leg. He was lying in a pool of his own blood.

My own eyes racked his body, just for a moment. Bone was protruding out of his thigh. Shit. I didn't think I'd hit him that hard. It would heal. He might not walk the same, but it would heal.

I tore my gaze from the bloody mess on the ground to stare at the three remaining opponents. I couldn't afford to get distracted. I had to finish this fight as quickly as possible so I didn't deplete my stamina. I smiled, letting a vicious curve take over one side of my mouth. I knew I looked malicious, but it would do the job. Horror briefly flashed across their faces as they took in Adam, then my coy grin standing above him. They were hesitant. They were scared. They were exactly where I needed them to be.

I barely heard the announcer shout, "That's unbelievable! Sie Noren took out an opponent in ten seconds! I think that's a new record for the fastest fight we have seen during the tournament."

The most tenacious male out of the bunch—I think his name was Robert—pulled his gaze away from Adam to stare at me. He resumed his pacing around the arena, looking for a weak spot, a way in. The other two followed closely behind him.

Robert met me first and heaved a strong arm in my direction. I dodged his punch, only to be greeted with a hard kick in the ribs from the one named Savern. He flashed me a wicked grin as I grunted from the pain searing in my side.

Clutching my ribs, I staggered away from them, trying to catch my breath.

I collected myself, staying light on my toes. If I got caught in the middle of those two, I'd be done for. I clung to the outside of the ring, making sure to keep them in front of me at all times.

Now joined by Nathan, the three of them worked together, not letting me catch my breath. They lunged at me one after another. All I could do was swerve, hoping to counteract with a kick or punch of my own. They were trying to tire me, but I'd practiced my whole life for this. I had stamina. I could push through the ragged breathing, the bruised rib, the tiredness of my muscles. Thanks to the forced training my father had put me through, I knew what exhaustion felt like. I knew I could handle whatever pain they shot at me.

Savern and Nathan were smaller. It didn't take long for them to fatigue, feeling the effects of each blow I made toward them. Robert, though, was clearly ready for a good fight. He landed a solid jab to my face just above my eyebrow. I staggered back as blood began to seep into my vision. In one swift motion, I wiped the blood off with the back of my hand.

Robert, thinking he had me, let his guard down. I lunged. He was stronger than me, but I was faster. I landed three blows and then side-stepped before he could counter.

I glanced at the red clock flashing by the announcer's booth. The fight had only been going on for nine minutes when I finally pinned Nathan and Savern to the ground, leaving just Robert. It felt longer. Those nine minutes felt like a lifetime from the toll it took on me. I already had too many open wounds and was covered in black and blue from various bruises starting to develop.

Robert threw a powerful kick to the already tender spot on my ribs. His next punch landed straight to my sternum, knocking the wind out of me. I gasped as I stumbled backward.

He grumbled something under his breath. The smirk and mocking demeanor of his face told me it was vulgar and vile. I couldn't make out his words through the coughing spell that followed his punch, the ringing in my ears, and the constant cheers from the crowds, but I knew he was taunting me.

It was enough to set me off, reminding me of my father. I didn't know if it was the mere act of fighting, the tone of his voice, or the fact that he had the same dark brown eyes. It didn't matter. I saw red right before I charged at him, losing myself to the fight.

When I came back to myself, my own chest was rising and falling in time to my heavy panting as I stood towering over Robert, his face flat on the ground. I was straddling him. One foot planted on the rubble as my other leg rested on a wobbly knee. My fists were clenched around his shirt, lifting him just slightly off the ground.

He let out a groan, which gave me a moment of relief until I noticed the pool of blood that sprayed out around him. I glanced down at my own knuckles. They were bloody, scabbed, and raw. Shit. How hard had I hit him? How long was he in this state before I stopped?

I peered toward the crowd, who seemed transfixed in our direction. In awe or shock, I couldn't tell. The arena grew deathly quiet until the announcer came on the loudspeaker, "And our winner is Sie Axel Noren!"

Only then did the crowd erupt in exhilarated cheers. I stumbled off of Robert. I couldn't make out what the announcer was saying, the ringing in my ears was meeting its crescendo—the tournament was far from over.

# FIVE
## SCOTLIND

"HOLY SHIT," MILES BREATHED. "HE'S AN ANIMAL."

He was the first person to break the silence after Sie's fight. The Hall, which was usually loud and chaotic, felt ominous in the minutes after Effin announced Sie as the winner. With only the distant clicking of someone tapping their finger against the table, the silence was penetrating.

I'd heard rumors of Sie being an amazing fighter. Everyone thought he would be good, but I didn't realize he would be *that* good. Ever since he was little, when his abilities first manifested, everyone talked about him. Sie probably grew up knowing he would someday be the future King of Tennebris. I just never truly comprehended how powerful he was until today.

The only rank five alive in Tennebris. A weapon even without his abilities. He moved like lightning, striking the ground before the thunder roared. His movements were nimble and deft—and deadly.

"Yeah, and that was just him fighting with his combat skills. He didn't even use his abilities," Vallie replied, her eyes still glued to the screen. Her gaze was transfixed on Sie as he walked out of the arena. "They got what they deserved. All teaming up on him like that wasn't right."

Images of Adam's bone protruding through his skin flashed in my mind. Sie did that in a matter of seconds. *Seconds.* I forcibly shook my head to clear my thoughts, to erase the mangled, bloody limb from my brain. And then the way he attacked Robert... it was like something in him had snapped.

"I can't believe Sie only has fifteen minutes to recover before the next fight," Yuri yelped. "That's so unfair. He was so beaten up, and now has to fight the king right away."

I snorted. "Haven't you read about the previous King's Tournaments before? It's always like this. The competitor has a disadvantage since the king is starting out fresh. Someone has to be truly powerful to win. It's one of the reasons a king's rule can be so long."

"Don't worry, Yuri. Sie gets to use his abilities in this round, so there isn't as much physical fighting. It's not as bloody," one of Yuri's friends responded, trying to cheer her up.

It seemed to work. Yuri perked up. "That's right. He will surely beat King Lunder. What are his powers, anyway?"

Goddess above. She was so desperate for Sie to be king, yet she clearly knew nothing about the tournament or his background. I shook my head at Miles in a silent communication to mock Yuri. It was one of the things we bonded over; we both despised Vallie's old friend.

During the break, Sie was taken out of the arena through a tunnel appearing under the raised stands while they interviewed King Lunder. They asked him numerous questions regarding his past thirty years of ruling over Tennebris, to how he felt about having Sie as an opponent. The nervous King Lunder they aired from the stands vanished in the spotlight. He looked confident as he merely responded that the most deserving would be the king after today. He didn't comment on much else regarding the up-and-coming rank five and did a good job avoiding questions about Sie altogether.

Right before the third portion began, Effin called both males into the arena. The blood and dirt was cleared from the ground. Not a single trace remained of the fight that just took place.

"Please welcome our challenger, contestant Sie Axel Noren!"

The crowd came to life in a thunderous applause as Sie walked back into the arena. The dried blood had been cleaned off his face, leaving only a cut above one eyebrow. They didn't bother changing his clothes, leaving the once white shirt to hang off his body in visible shreds. It exposed part of his abdomen with a nasty bruise already forming on his side.

Despite some of his injuries on display, he seemed fine. He wasn't limping or acting as if he was hurt in any way. He held his head high and stood tall as he strode toward the center of the arena again.

"Sie is a known rank five," Effin continued. "His abilities are teleportation, compulsion, and total mind control."

"What does total mind control mean?" Vallie asked with her red brows furrowed together.

"Is it like mind readers? Where they can read your thoughts or tell if you're lying?" Yuri asked.

I had no idea. I'd never heard of it before. I'd heard of compulsion where someone could force you to do something against your will. I'd even heard of mind readers, although they were extremely rare. But total mind control seemed like something else, something more. I said, "I think it's something we hope to never find out."

Miles startled us by saying, "Isn't having compulsion going to be pointless during this fight?"

"How so?" one of Yuri's friends asked.

I answered for her, realizing for myself that Sie had a disadvantage yet again, "Because compulsion doesn't work on our own kind. You can't compel someone of Tennebris unless they have no powers—"

Yuri interrupted me, "You mean unless they are a nix like you. Only nixes have weak minds that can be compelled."

I ignored her and turned back to the other girl. "Basically, Sie or anyone that has compulsion can only compel someone who is Luxian, human, or a rank zero Tennebrisian. Since King Lunder is none of those things, Sie's compulsion won't work on him."

"We all know a nix like you can be compelled by anyone," Yuri snapped again as if I didn't hear her the first time. She quieted once she saw Miles' stone-cold gaze directed at her.

"I wonder what makes Sie a rank five over a four then? Teleporting is a rare ability, but compulsion amongst our kind is fairly common. I wouldn't think it would be enough to make him a five," Vallie said.

"Hmm, I don't know. It must be whatever his total mind control thing does," Miles responded.

It was scary to think about Sie having compulsion and what a king could do with those abilities. He would be an asset to Tennebris, but to Lux, my true kingdom, he would be something to fear. He could compel anyone there, even the Lux King. Although I was sure the King of Lux would never go anywhere without a Luxian Alluse user by his side—someone with the ability to nullify anyone's powers. Alluse or a force shield from a Luxian air user would be Lux's only defense against Sie, against any compulsion user of Tennebris. Not that they would ever find out with the Peace Treaties.

I longed to know what abilities of Lux I possessed. I knew I wasn't blessed with the ability Alluse because Kole, a boy in my guard class, compelled me all the time.

I remembered the first time I was compelled by him. He forced me to eat dirt on my first week at LakeWood after months of seclusion with my counselor. I would never forget the words he spat at me as he laughed in my face. *"You filthy nix. You should be dead like your family. You don't belong with us. You're nothing but dirt."*

When the other little boys around us laughed with him, laughed at me, his smile broadened as he compelled me, *"I heard you're not eating. Too scared over a stupid fire. Let me help you to a meal only worthy for a nix like you. Eat it. Eat the dirt at my feet."*

It was the first time I had ever been compelled. I shivered, thinking back to that memory, to the horror of not understanding why I was listening to him. Why my hands acted on their own accord even though I knew I didn't want to do it. I still remembered the dry taste of the dirt as I tried to force it down my throat. Swallowing it was hard as it consolidated in my esophagus. Kole didn't release his compulsion until I was vomiting on the ground next to him, my knees soaking into the wet earth. I washed my mouth out ten times that night and swore I tasted dirt for the months that followed.

It took a good year and many detentions later before Kole finally learned that compulsion wasn't allowed at LakeWood. Kole alone was the reason for my tainted school record. I used to fight back, but I'd since learned it was better to just take whatever he threw at me than to continuously get in trouble with our professors. He became craftier as we grew older. Now, he only compelled me when he was certain he could get away with it.

Drawing me from my thoughts, the announcer chimed in again, "Everyone, please rise and welcome our precious king to the arena. All hail King Lunder!"

The announcer spoke in a louder voice than when he had previously announced Sie. Everyone fell silent as they bowed in respect for the king. A round of applause, cheers, and whistles broke the silence a moment later as King Lunder came into view.

"King Lunder is a known rank four and has been our gracious king for the past thirty years. His abilities are energy weaponry and projection." I shuddered. Such horrible powers the Advenians of Tennebris possessed. Projection could be turned into a savage ability. I'd read enough about King Lunder's previous King's Tournament to know that his projection type was more common. He created clones of himself, but the deadly ability could go as far as fear illusion, where someone could trick you into thinking you were somewhere you weren't. People have died thinking their worst fears were coming to life. When in reality, they were just standing idly, with no one around them understanding what torments were happening inside their minds.

I heard a few Advenians from the crowd on the screen shout, "Hail, King Lunder," as he confidently closed the gap across the arena to stand before Sie. Sie bowed low in front of the king, receiving an upward tilt of the king's head in return.

Both males stared at each other as Effin went into a long speech regarding the tournament's significance. Once he finished, he animated, "Let it be known. There are no rules in this final round, except that the challenger, being Sie, may not kill the current king. The winner will be announced when one male can no longer fight.

That can happen in many ways; if one is knocked to the ground and cannot get back up, if one becomes unconscious, surrenders, or if the challenger dies. Abilities are encouraged. That is all. Best of luck, and let the fight begin!"

As his last words rang across the arena, an air user from Lux, who was stationed to work in Tennebris, generated a force shield, engulfing around the arena's dome. It separated King Lunder and Sie from the onlookers observing them, creating a faint silvery glow where it shimmered.

"It's to protect the crowd from any abilities they might use during the match," Miles remarked, noting one of the girl's confusion.

King Lunder's markings immediately took shape on his skin as large, golden circles materialized over his arms and hands. Three King Lunders stood before Sie. It happened in the blink of an eye. I couldn't make out which one was the real king and which were his projection clones.

Without a second of hesitation, all three Lunders lunged forward to attack. Before they reached Sie, his body flared up in golden swirls of his own, spiraling up his extremities. His markings reached and circled around his entire neck. One moment Sie was standing before the clones, about to get pummeled. The next, he was gone. He teleported behind the king and threw a punch to the back of one of the Lunders' heads, causing it to vanish back into the real one.

The announcer chimed in, "It looks like a hit to one of Lunder's clones makes them disappear! Sie used his teleportation to his advantage. The real question is, who has more stamina? Who will drain their abilities' reserve first? Rank fives are known to have the highest ability reserve on record. And according to Sie's ranking Trials from when he graduated, his are off the charts. However, teleportation is taxing to one's reserve and can deplete it quickly."

As the announcer continued speaking about strategies and advantages, King Lunder created five more clones before Sie. Amid the fight, the king and his clones started producing daggers out of thin air.

"Oh, would you look at that," Effin exclaimed. "As you know, weapons aren't allowed into the arena, but abilities are, and King

Lunder's ability can produce any weapon that he has previously held. This will surely make it more challenging for Sie to land a hit."

Sie kept his distance, dodging the daggers, axes, and knives thrown his way. He was the only one who could die during this battle, and with Lunder using weapons, it just got more complicated for him. The current king didn't falter in creating clones to go with each deadly blade. More and more of them kept appearing out of thin air, all attacking Sie immediately.

"Truly amazing," Effin cheered as all seven of the clones in the arena held a dagger in their hand, "that the king's energy weaponry ability is transferred to his clones as well."

Sie tumbled into a forward roll to avoid being penetrated by the current daggers all seven of the Lunders were throwing at him. He came to a halt before a fallen blade and bent forward to pick the knife up, but it disappeared before he could reach it.

"Well, well," Effin dictated, seeming to find the need to narrate every minute detail of the fight. "It looks like Sie won't be able to use one of Lunder's blades against him. This is exactly what makes our current king so powerful, and the reason he has won the last three King's Tournaments. Just as freely as he can produce a weapon, he can make them disappear."

The fight continued on. King Lunder seemed to have the advantage of using both of his abilities, while Sie could only use his teleportation to get out of the way and physical strength to counterattack. Lunder stayed out of Sie's range as he fought against all the weapons and clones he continued to pour upon him.

The clock by Effin flashed, indicating twenty minutes had passed. King Lunder's reserve seemed to be diminishing as his clone creation started to slow. He went from making dozens of clones at a time to only one or two. His markings faded from his skin, then completely disappeared.

Then began the brutal combat style of fighting. In physical strength, Sie seemed to have the advantage. The two only fought for minutes before Sie had King Lunder lying on the ground. Was this what Sie was waiting for? Was he just toying with Lunder, letting him tire by using up all his reserve so he could no longer use his ability? Sie really only used his tele-portation to dodge attacks. He hadn't made a move on the king until now.

Sie was towering over him, ready to land another hit, when the king's hand frantically flew up in the air, as if surrendering. Sie immediately teleported off of him, his chest rising and falling rapidly as he watched King Lunder continue to lie on the ground, defeated.

Moments passed as the buzzer ticked by. Sie waited as Lunder was sprawled on the ground with his arms raised for the official amount of time to surrender. The announcer's voice boasted through the arena, "And our winner is Sie Axel Noren!"

Sie's golden markings disappeared as he turned his back to Lunder and started to walk out of the arena. But Lunder's markings reap-peared as he used his abilities to produce a clone holding a short short directly behind Sie.

Sie attempted to dodge once he realized what was happening. His own markings flared to life, maybe to teleport away, but it was too late. The clone took the sword and threw it forward, executing its mark with precision, directly into the right side of Sie's back.

A grunt escaped Sie's lips as the sword glided further in, the tip piercing out the other side. Lunder finally stood. The camera panned over the audience, taking the attention away from the king and Sie for a second. Everyone in the stands shared the same shocked expression. Most of them clasped their hands over their mouths, eyes widened at what just happened. The fight should have been over. Effin was just announcing Sie as the winner.

A few audible gasps and murmurs were heard before the camera circled and flicked back to the two males in the arena. One with a pool of blood now forming under his feet, the other with a smirk plastered on his face.

The clone disappeared, but Lunder kept the sword in Sie's back as he sneered at him, "Never turn your back to the enemy, and never assume a fight is over."

Lunder sauntered toward Sie, closing the distance between them like a predator stalking a wounded prey, ready to pounce. He now held another short sword in his hand, twin to the one still in Sie's back. The king twirled the blade readying to wield it again, to finish Sie off. A groan escaped Sie's lips as he spat blood onto the ground. Vallie clasped her twin's hands so tight that her knuckles turned white as she murmured, "No, no, no," over and over.

Sie, finally seeming to come to his senses, whipped around to face Lunder. Through all the blood staining his shirt, I could see his skin beginning to shape into intricate, golden spirals again. Only this time, there were more.

The spirals started at his fingertips, looping around the palms of his hands and up his arms. They formed broad double bands around his biceps that circled up to his neck. A thick golden coil bobbed in rhythm with his Adam's apple. The golden markings stopped just short of his face. And through the rip in his shirt, I could glimpse the delicate markings expanding over his bloody abdomen too.

They were everywhere, covering him entirely until the mix of skin and gold meshed together. I couldn't tell where one started and the other stopped. He glowed as he began using his mind ability for the first time. His hand, now raised in the air, stopped Lunder in his tracks. The king stood frozen in place, his eyes fixed on Sie.

"Is this Sie's total mind control?" Vallie barely breathed, still clutching hands with Miles.

"I don't know," Miles replied as he tried to shrug Vallie off of him. "I think this is just compulsion. But it doesn't make sense."

"I... I thought he couldn't use compulsion," Vallie said, her eyes glued to the screen. "On someone that was ranked from Tennebris, I mean. I thought he could only compel someone like Scottie."

"Yeah. Shit." Miles let out a breath. "He's fucking powerful."

I ignored the jab, I knew Vallie didn't mean any offense. She had a habit of being brutally honest, and she was right. I'd never seen anyone use compulsion on another ranked Tennebrisian before. From everyone's reaction in the Hall and at the tournament itself, I didn't think anyone had ever seen this in their lifetime. This truly made Sie dangerous if he could compel anyone in the entire kingdom. I swallowed hard. I didn't want to think about what his total mind control ability could do.

Time seemed to freeze around Sie and Lunder. Sie's body remained mostly golden, the only indication that Lunder was still being compelled. The king's eyes seemed to be the only thing Sie relinquished control of. They widened, almost bulging out of his head, showing more of the whites than I thought possible. Sie still hadn't moved. He didn't advance as the sword was still pierced through his flank, the tip of it jutting out of his abdomen. Sie just stared at him as if an unspoken conversation was going on between them inside their minds.

The rage from Sie and fear from Lunder was palpable as the announcer, Effin, broke the silence, "Well this is a wonderful turn of events! Sie has the gift of compulsion against our own kind. It seems he can use compulsion on the ranked Advenians of Tennebris. This power has not been seen since our ancestors lived on Allium. Our kind has long believed this ability to be... well, extinct. Lost like our beautiful planet. What a true gift we have witnessed tonight. A well deserving rank five indeed."

I didn't think I would call having a sword coming out of my back a gift, but Sie didn't seem to notice Effin's words.

"I hope he's okay. I can't believe King Lunder stabbed him," Yuri mumbled, and for the first time ever, I agreed with her.

With King Lunder still frozen before him, Sie twisted and began to pull out the sword from his back.

Slowly.

Painfully.

It was hard to watch. His face was growing paler, a sharp contrast to the golden designs over his skin. But other than scrunched eyebrows, he kept his expression placid while doing so. The blade seemed so much longer now as he drew it out of his own flesh.

I was in awe of him that he didn't cry or make a sound, other than a small wince as the tip of the blade finally broke free. The once silver sword, now red, glistened in the sun through the air shield. With

Lunder frozen, he couldn't retract his creation. The sword was tangible in Sie's hand as he pointed it at the king's chest.

The pool of blood under Sie's feet grew significantly. He was bleeding out fast, yet he made no move to strike or advance further. According to the rules of the tournament, Sie couldn't kill Lunder. But he could still attack or do something to make this fight end sooner. Yet he didn't. He was taking his time, letting his fury fester.

"Why isn't he attacking King Lunder? He's dying," Vallie said with worry lingering in her voice.

Some of Sie's golden markings started to disappear from his left arm. It looked as though he was letting off some of the compulsion just as King Lunder was able to move his head. But he still didn't seem to have full control over his body yet.

"You can't kill me," Lunder spat, speaking for the first time since Sie began compelling him.

Had Sie's compulsion prevented Lunder from talking until now? The thought was horrifying to have someone take away your basic actions. My throat felt dry as I swallowed down the lump. Thoughts of what else Sie might be able to compel someone to do whirled inside me. Could he use his compulsion to force someone to stop breathing? Would their traitorous body have to obey? Would they die, or would their subconscious take over? Could someone fight against the compulsion and force their body to breathe? Deep down, I knew the answer. I knew his abilities could kill. I knew our bodies, my body, would obey him. His compulsion would win out over my own will just like it had when Kole forced me to eat the dirt beneath his feet.

"I know that," Sie said cooly, still holding the sword out in front of him, "but there aren't any rules about cutting off your feet. You can still rule without legs."

The king paled as real terror flashed across his face. Sie's markings faded faster. I couldn't tell if it was intentional or if Sie was in worse shape than he realized.

The king threw his hands up, staggering backward, away from Sie. A look of sheer panic flashed in his eyes as he murmured, barely audible through the silent arena, "I surrender."

Lunder tried to kill our kingdom's only rank five. I think everyone was shocked and confused by that. Lunder had killed a competitor in the past, but even if Sie didn't win the tournament, he would have received a high-up career in the kingdom. Even I couldn't deny that he would be an amazing asset for the Dark Kingdom, an essential weapon against Lux if they ever decided to break our peace. An eerie thought, but it was true.

"Do you mean it?" Sie said, still pointing the bloodied, red blade in his direction.

"What?" Lunder whimpered, his eyes locked on the sword Sie was still wielding.

"Do you really surrender or"—Sie narrowed his eyes at the sword Lunder held frozen in his hand—"are you going to throw another blade in my back as soon as I turn around?" Sie advanced. The tip of the sword poked Lunder's neck, making a trickle of blood drip down his collar bone.

"No, I mean it. I mean it. I surrender," Lunder replied, barely audible.

"Louder." The voice that came out of Sie was cold and menacing. A chill ran up my spine, even though we were a screen away, watching from the Hall.

Lunder's face showed pure hatred at the challenge from Sie. I almost thought he wasn't going to repeat himself. Not many King's Tournaments ended in surrender. Most Adevenians fought until they were unconscious or dying. To surrender was a show of weakness and power was everything here.

The audience seemed to be holding their collective breath as if they didn't want to miss a second of it. But then Lunder finally said, loud enough to be heard across the stands, "I surrender."

The crowd cheered as Effin's voice echoed for the second time, "The winner is Sie Axel Noren. All hail our future king. Today will start the six-month orientation Sie will go under until he is deemed fit to rule. He will be supervised and guided under King Lunder, learning the ropes of our kingdom, until King Lunder steps down. Then,

Tennebris will host Sie's coronation to the throne, officially marking the end of King Lunder's reign."

It wasn't until Effin was done spouting his words that Sie threw the sword at King Lunder's feet. Lunder shuddered before collapsing to the ground as Sie released his hold on him. The golden markings completely faded from Sie's body, leaving only blood. A group, whom I presumed were Luxian healers, rushed out to meet him halfway, guiding him through the doorway under the arena.

"Why didn't he just use his compulsion in the beginning?" Yuri asked once the tournament was officially over. "The fight would have been over within seconds, and then Sie never would have gotten stabbed." Everyone paused, letting Yuri's words sink in.

"Maybe Sie didn't want everyone to know about his true power?" Miles suggested. I nodded in agreement. But I felt like Sie was still holding back, that he still didn't show his true, full, raw power today, and that terrified me even more.

Everyone's abilities in Tennebris were placed into an official record at the time of their rankings during the Trials. The rankings were public knowledge since they burned the number into your own flesh, forcing you to wear it like it was jewelry. But abilities weren't so publicly known. Only the High Council and current and past royals had complete access to those records. An ordinary Advenian would have to fill out a form to get approval from the Council to look up someone's abilities. Most of the time, the request would be denied.

I was told by Vallie that all the records were kept in a book. How Vallie knew that was beyond me, but we were both certain that it was heavily guarded at the castle.

The book was believed to hold records dating back to before Advenians even came to Earth, going as far back to our time on Allium. I would have given anything to be able to read it, to see all the powers that had and have existed. It wasn't uncommon for Advenians to want to keep their abilities a secret. Most bragged about whatever ranking they possessed, but if someone had a special ability, the less known about it, the fewer weaknesses could exist. Most Advenians kept small parts of their abilities to themselves.

"I wonder if he's going to make it. That looked really bad. He lost so much blood," Vallie whispered. I looked over at her and she now traded Miles' hand for the table's edge.

"Of course he will," Yuri exclaimed. "After all, he is our prince now, and will be king in half a year with Lunder's training. He has to make it. Plus, they probably have tons of Luxian healers here on work visas that will tend to him."

I gave Vallie a half-smile to try to reassure her, but Sie had taken a beating. I was surprised he'd been able to continue using his ability while being so injured. My mind still whirled, trying to comprehend why he hadn't used compulsion from the beginning of the fight and what else he might be hiding about his powers.

# SIX
# SCOTLIND

Vallie rushed to find me after our classes ended the following day. There had been constant talk about what had happened after the tournament with Sie—or the prince now.

During our morning lecture, our professor announced that we had a mandatory meeting in the auditorium at the end of the day. Everyone was gossiping about what it meant and if he had recovered.

As we filed into the auditorium, I looked around and realized that only the year twelve students that were graduating filled the seats, not the entire school. Chairs were grounded into the floor, all facing a raised platform. The room itself had no windows. It was one of the few rooms that had electricity in it. An overhead light hummed above us as Vallie and I claimed two empty seats near the back.

There was a buzz flying around as all the students were chatting amongst themselves until our Principal broke the noise by clearing his throat.

"I know you are all probably wondering why we brought you here today, but rest assured, this is an exciting time. As you all know, Sie Axel Noren won the King's Tournament yesterday, making him the Prince of Tennebris. After his coronation this winter, he will be our king over the next ten years. He is doing well and recovering just fine, but that's not why you are here today. As the tradition stands, King Lunder will mentor Prince Noren over the next six months, teaching him everything he needs to know about ruling our great kingdom. As is custom, we cannot have a king without a queen. Many of you are aware that the prince is not yet married and has claimed no significant other he wishes to pursue."

A small hum of excited murmurs filled the auditorium.

"So it's true. He lived and will really be the king."

"He's so scary."

"I hope I get to be his wife."

"When he was fighting…"

"Silence!" Principal Myers shouted as everyone stopped talking. "The High Council has decided to consider any female from the ages of eighteen to fifty." Principal Myers paused for a moment, surveying the room.

With an Advenians' average lifespan lasting well into the thousands, it wasn't uncommon for a marriage age gap. Most Advenians' aging drastically slowed sometime in their mid twenties.

Principal Myers continued, "That is why you are all here. Every female graduating this year over the age of eighteen will be included as a potential suitress. This goes for all of the six schools in our kingdom, not just LakeWood. That being said, there is potential, however slim, that essentially any of you sitting in this very room could be selected. Any of you could potentially be the future Queen of Tennebris. After your examinations in two days and your Trials and rankings the third day, we will be sending your scores to the High Council for review, as well as every other female who has graduated within the past thirty-two years.

"There will be a banquet held the day after your Trials in Addler once the High Council has reviewed everyone's files. Every female from the six villages who is being considered is required to attend. Professor Hale will also be selecting five guard students to attend as a training exercise. At the banquet, the High Council will announce who will be the future queen. Since your graduation was supposed to be held that day, it will be pushed back to the following day.

Everyone will leave their dorms by the sixth night following graduation."

Vallie and I exchanged glances at each other as another uproar of screams and cheers rang across the auditorium. Every single female practically jumped out of their seats with excitement and exhilaration. I thought I heard a few groans under the cheers from the males in our class.

I didn't hear anything our Principal said after that as he rambled on about the logistics of how the banquet would proceed and how it would affect our Trials and graduation weekend.

My mouth felt dry as I momentarily freaked out about what would happen if I was selected. I wouldn't be able to hide that I was Luxian from a husband. I thought that trying out for the guard meant I was safe, that I wouldn't have to take a spouse. A guard wasn't encouraged to get married. That didn't stop them from sleeping around, but they never actually committed to anyone.

Of course, I wasn't a guard yet. I wouldn't know until after my Trials, and they could still fail me. But still, why would I even be considered for this? Wasn't just trying out for the guard enough to show devotion toward the profession, enough to not have to be considered for marriage? It must be a mistake.

I took an uneven breath, then another and another, until I started to calm down. The likelihood of me being selected was slim, practically non-existent. There were six villages among the Tennebrisian Kingdom, and of that, they included every female who wasn't yet married and had graduated within the past thirty-two years.

I was already a laughing stock at my school for being a female with no abilities and trying out for the guard. A nix would never be queen. The High Council would make its decision after reviewing everyone's rankings and Trials. I let out another steadying breath. Once they saw my file and realized I was a rank zero, they would pass right over me.

I tried not to dwell on the fact that my chances of being selected for the guard were just as slim. There were rarely high-ranked females that were guards and there definitely has never been a rank zero one before.

Principal Myers said our guard teacher would be picking his top five students to attend the banquet. Maybe I could convince Professor Hale to select me for that. It would look good in my folder and be an opportunity for me to show my determination to be a guard. Plus, on the bright side, this banquet would give me an extra day with my best friend.

———

THE NEXT DAY, only one class sat between me and my guard training. I just had to get through my Human Relations lecture, which was dragging on more slowly than usual. I planned to talk to my guard professor about the banquet after this class. I practiced what I would ask Professor Hale over and over in my head until it became second nature. I was so focused on reciting my thought-out speech that I didn't realize I was being asked a question. Everyone in the class turned to look at me.

"I'm sorry, Professor, I didn't catch that," I said softly, shifting uncomfortably in my seat from all the gawking eyes on me.

Professor Madick gave me a stern look before he said, "Scotlind Rumor, it would be wise for you to pay attention in my class. I asked for you to tell me about the physical differences between our kind and the mortals of Earth."

My cheeks heated as some of my classmates snickered at me. "Yes, sir. Um, physically we look the same as humans. Our only physical differences are our markings and that our kind is typically taller and more slender than them."

"Very good," Professor Madick said as he paced to the front of the room. "Now, what are the major differences?"

"The major differences are our abilities and how we age. Humans don't have any powers."

Someone mumbled from the back of the class, "Just like you, nix."

I ignored the taunt as I continued. "Humans age extremely quickly and die easily—"

The guy sitting next to me cut me off, "Hence *mortal*." A few people in the class laughed as Professor Madick looked at me to continue.

I cleared my throat. "We don't age like them. Most of our kind will taper off aging in their twenties. As diseases do not kill us, we can live for a long time."

"That is correct, Scotlind. Don't forget, another major difference is reproduction. Humans reproduce quickly and often, making it so their kind outnumbers us greatly. Most Advenians are not able to reproduce. A baby is considered a gift from our Goddesses. Some Advenians go their entire lifespan without bearing an offspring. However, every five hundred years, our Highest Goddess, Pylemo, blesses us with Lakimi. Can you tell me what Lakimi is, and what makes these next few years so special to our kind?" Professor Madick asked, still maintaining eye contact with me.

I hated his class because he always pinpointed a single student and drilled them with question after question. Usually it was a student who wasn't paying attention. I should have known better than to zone out during his lecture.

"Lakimi is a reproduction ceremony that, if the rites are performed, will make our kind more fertile over the next decade. It occurs when Allium's two pink moons align in the sky."

"Very good, Scotlind. On top of making our kind more fertile, the two moons usually give Advenians more *urges* toward one another. If you have a desire for someone, it would be difficult to stay away from them during that time period."

"It's basically a decade-long fuck fest," someone from the back of the room smirked.

Professor Madick glared at the student, but didn't deny it. "Since this planet only has one moon, the effects of Lakimi haven't been as strong. That is until the last one that just occurred eighteen years ago. It's why our current class is so large. No one knows for sure why Pylemo blessed us generously with the last Lakimi, but we don't question the work of the Goddesses. It's the first time that all six schools have been filled with students," Professor Madick beamed. "Reproduction is the one thing the mortals exceed our kind in. Because of humans' enhanced reproductive systems, we decided to stay hidden when we first discovered Earth, as we were vastly outnumbered." He paused to pull down a map of the planet we now live on, right next to a map of Allium. "Miles, why don't you tell the class about how we came to Earth and why we decided to stay hidden."

Miles cleared his throat from behind me. "After the Ability War between Tennebris and Lux that destroyed our planet, Allium, our kind was forced into space, confined by small steel walls, unable to use our powers on the craft. It took centuries before our ancestors finally found a planet that was hospitable for our bodies. When they came across Earth and realized that it was inhabited by humans, they feared that a battle against them could destroy this planet as well. While in space, the two Advenian Kingdoms had finally agreed upon a Peace Treaty and didn't want to throw it off balance. They didn't want more years stranded with the Luxian air users' artificial gravity. They wanted to breathe real air. In the process, they developed AASP, the Allium Advenian Space Program, with the goal to someday find our own planet. Tennebris oversees the space program, researching new potential planets, while Lux monitors the mortals on Earth. Overtime, both kingdoms have adapted some mortal customs, even though it's illegal to interact with one. Our time here was only meant to be temporary, but somehow, we've been here for—"

Vallie groaned next to me and whispered as Miles kept rambling, "Of course he would ask this question to my brother who could talk about space and the Ability War for *hours.* Professor Madick didn't even ask about AASP and somehow he finds a way to bring it up."

I laughed as Professor Madick whipped his head in our direction, ceasing our giggles. "Quiet, ladies, or I'll assign extra homework to the class," Professor Madick challenged. "Now Miles, can you show us on the map where each kingdom went into hiding?"

The chair groaned behind us as Miles stood. He flashed Vallie a glare as he passed us which she matched with a wink. Miles pointed to an area on the water. "This is what the mortals call the Bermuda Triangle. There is a large island positioned in the middle of it, and it's where the Kingdom of Lux went into hiding when they first arrived here." His long fingers trailed over the map of Earth. It was fascinating to me the vast expanse the mortals occupied while the Advenians were confined to two small areas. "Our kingdom made its roots here." His fingers stopped over the word Antarctica on the map.

"Wonderful," Professor Madick boasted. "And how have we been able to successfully hide?"

"As part of the Treaty, Luxian air users generated shields when we first arrived. They worked in tandem with illusion and compulsion users from Tennebris. It gives a blind eye to the mortals. They are unable to see us through the shields, but instead, they see what the Tennebrisian illusion user projects on them. And if any mortal still manages to come across us, a compulsion user will wipe their memories. It took a while to get the system down. At first, many humans came across Lux more due to their proximity to one of the mortal continents, and numerous compulsion users had to be stationed on the island with work visas, but now the system is flawless."

"Excellent. You may take your seat," Professor Madick grinned before turning to someone else in the room to ask them the differences between technologies.

It was an effort to pay attention to whatever humans called cell phones as their means of communication. Monitors, speakers, and lights were the only things Tennebris adapted since coming to Earth. The Dark Kingdom preferred harnessing the mortal synthetic energy over utilizing Luxian electric users. But from what we learned in our classes, the mortals were obsessive over it and used electricity in almost every avenue of their lives. I didn't really care for it, but Vallie, on the other hand, was soaking in every second of the lecture. She was fascinated with everything mortal related, especially technology.

I flung out of my chair the moment the bell rang and sprinted over to the NorthEnd of campus. My plan was to get to class early enough to speak with Professor Hale in private.

When I arrived at the gym six minutes later, panting heavily, I let out a sigh of relief when I saw Professor Hale in his office. He was basically a giant walking muscle that trained us without many rules. Even though I was the only female in the class and the only guard student without any abilities, he didn't treat me differently. He considered me an equal among my peers. It made me respect him, look up to him. It gave me hope that not every Advenian was obsessive about rankings.

I did have to prove myself over the years. No one in my class thought I belonged there. They believed the notion that a female guard was ridiculous, a nix female guard even worse.

Most of my guard classmates had warmed up to me, or at least learned to tolerate me. Especially since I could now hold my own against them. I won most of my sparring matches, except when I was up against Kole Sanders. He was relentless when we fought. Kole never let me forget that most nix females in our society ended up as servants.

"Scottie, what are you doing here so early?" Professor Hale asked, startled to see me. "Class doesn't start for another fifteen minutes."

"I know, sir. I was really hoping I could have a minute to speak with you." Regardless of how much I had rehearsed this conversation, my nerves were getting the best of me. I tried to recover my breathing and willed my heart rate to slow. Sprinting here wasn't the best decision.

"Sure, take a seat," he suggested as he held out his hand toward the empty chair positioned in front of his large desk.

"Thank you, sir." I cleared my throat before I continued. *Deep breath, Scottie.* It was just a simple question. *You can do this.* "You know I have been training really hard in the hopes of becoming a guard."

"Yes, I know. You're one of my best students as far as determination goes, and you're a great fighter during non-ability combat training," he replied matter-of-factly.

Professor Hale tended to favor critiquing what we could improve upon. I was taken aback by his half compliment, but it gave me the confidence I needed. The final push to ask him if I could guard the banquet.

"Th-thank you, sir," I stuttered. "I was... I was wondering, since it's known that I want to be a guard, and a guard cannot take a husband or wife, if I could, um, attend the banquet not as an *option,* but as a guard." My cheeks heated as I honestly didn't know how to word it. Potential bride, potential queen, potential wife? It made me feel like we were cattle to be lined up for the High Council to choose the fattest one.

He remained silent as his gaze found mine. Whatever long speech I had rehearsed wholly left my brain as I kept rambling, "It would be a good way for me to prove how serious I am about this profession. I can show my dedication, and I will be on the lookout the entire time. I won't socialize or talk to anyone. I'll be on my best behavior and represent your guard class well. You won't be—"

He held up his palm to cut me off, and I realized that I hadn't taken a breath the entire time I'd talked.

"Scottie, I figured you would ask me. I know you are very dedicated and want to be a guard. I don't doubt you would do a fine job guarding the banquet." I leaned forward in my seat, practically off the edge of it. "Unfortunately, we cannot allow that. It's mandated that every female attend. We cannot go against the High Council's request. It was not a mistake that your name was included. Every single female must go."

I slumped back into my seat, defeated.

"However, it's unlikely someone like you would even be considered," he continued. I ignored the insult since it was what I wanted to hear anyway. I didn't want to be selected. "You may wear your guard uniform instead of a ball gown if you wish. You can take on responsibilities as a guard, but you won't be included in the five students I select. You must still attend the ceremony, but before and after the banquet, you may work with your five fellow students if that pleases you."

Well, it was better than nothing. "Thank you, sir," I said.

I rose from my seat on shaky legs. Professor Hale let out a long sigh that echoed across his office. "Scottie, I know you chose to try out for the guard for your Trial, but you are aware that you may not be selected, right? No matter how well you place in the Trial itself, your ranking has a huge weight on where you get placed."

"I know that, sir. That's why I've been training really hard, and I want to use this banquet to prove how serious I am about this."

"I guess what I'm trying to say is that it might not matter. Even though you're an excellent fighter, they might look at your ranking and disregard how well you do in the Trials. There is a chance, I'm afraid, higher than I'd like to admit, that they might make you a servant instead. So it's important to do your best on your examination. You can't afford one slip up in your Trials the following day. Unlike the other students, you don't have any room for mistakes."

I gritted my teeth. The last statement was like a jab through my heart. It was what everyone always told me when they found out I was trying out to be a guard. That I wouldn't make it. That a female could never make it. That a nix could never make it.

"Yes, sir," was all I replied as I left his office with the door slamming shut behind me.

———

I OCCUPIED the remaining time I had before class by waiting in the female locker room—if you could call it that. Professor Hale had to remodel an old cleaning closet to give me a place to change. Lake-Wood hasn't had a female try out for the guard in decades, which was why I got stuck with a four by four space, but I didn't care. I was the only Advenian who used it, so the closet became a sanctuary to me. I quickly changed out of my uniform and into my guard outfit, trying to let out my frustration before everyone else showed up.

"Listen up," Professor Hale called out once everyone filed into the gym. "Today, we'll be sparring with abilities. You will spar using any powers you possess on top of your regular combat skills. A successful guard will learn to master both and incorporate each into your fighting. It's weak to rely on only one. I will pair you off in twos. You will spar for thirty seconds on, thirty seconds off, for a total of thirty minutes. At the end of class, we will review fighting strategies for your final exam. Then I will explain how the Trials will proceed. Take this sparring session very seriously. It will be your last practice before the

Trials. I will also be picking my top five students to attend the banquet based on your performance today."

I patiently waited for my name to be called as Professor Hale started pairing us off in twos.

"Scotlind Rumor and Kole Sanders."

Ugh, this day was getting worse and worse. I looked over at Kole, who flashed me a cocky grin. I made my way over to the mats where Professor Hale directed us to stand.

Kole glided over to me. The top of my head came to his chest as he peered down at me, glaring from under the bridge of his nose. I was smaller than most Advenians, not having the blessed genes for height like most of my kind. It was something to add to the long list of reasons why I was an outcast. It was also another comparison Kole often used to compare me to the mortals.

Kole's awful smirk never faltered as he said, "I heard they're allowing you to attend the banquet on Sunday. What a joke to give a nix like you false hope, but at least you'll get to see who you will be working for as a servant."

His laugh stopped short as I kicked him in the ribs, hard. Grunting, he glanced toward Professor Hale, who, mercifully, was looking the other way.

"You bitch," he sneered as he took a step toward me and leaned down so that our faces were inches apart. I could practically smell his breath on mine. His brown eyes darkened. "You wanna play dirty, nix? I'll gladly oblige."

I didn't want to give him the satisfaction of backing away. I didn't want to give him any indication that I was afraid of him, so I stayed planted in place, narrowing my eyes at him.

"Kneel," he compelled as his skin flashed golden markings the second the command left his lips. He casually placed his hand in his pocket so Professor Hale wouldn't see his markings flare to life as he held his compulsion over me. Kole's markings were only visible on his right hand and forearm, and since we trained in our guard outfit which consisted of a long-sleeve shirt, it made it easy for him to compel me in public.

It was banned to use compulsion on other students at LakeWood as it was considered far superior to the other powers of the Dark Kingdom. Many teachers argued and fought the rule, but ultimately it was decided that a student didn't need practice commanding others to do things. But after school, once Kole graduates, he wouldn't have the restriction placed on him. He'd be able to use as much compulsion as he pleased.

Cursing under my breath, I sank to the ground in front of him. I knew I shouldn't have kicked him, shouldn't have provoked him. I was usually better at controlling my temper, but Kole had an obsession with getting under my skin, and he knew all my triggers.

He grinned down at me. "There. I just thought you should get comfortable with where you'll be spending all of your time after you graduate."

I spat on his shoes before I quickly jumped to my feet as soon as his compulsion wore off. The classmate standing next to us laughed softly, having overheard the whole thing. I shook off the humiliation and gritted my teeth.

Professor Hale blew the whistle hanging around his neck, indicating the start of our first thirty-second round. I started bouncing lightly on my toes as we circled each other.

Kole, not finished with our conversation, taunted, "Get used to that view, little nix. When you're a servant, you'll provide a lot of services to males from that position."

I cringed. I hated when he called me *little nix*, but I hated what he implied even more. I wouldn't let that happen. I wouldn't become a servant. I knew how they were treated here, and depending on the household you served, Kole wasn't far off in his assumption. It was illegal, but the high ranks got away with it all the time. No one ever believed a rank zero.

Anger rose in me as I threw a hook in his direction, aiming for his jaw. But Kole, seeing through the move, grabbed my wrist and threw me off balance. I needed to calm down. He was getting a rise out of me on purpose. He knew me well enough to know that I lost focus when I was angry. I made mistakes, and right now, I was enraged. At him, at my current situation, at everything.

I recovered my footing and blew out a breath before stepping into the circle with him again.

I managed to get in a few more kicks and punches, landing some as Kole blocked or dodged all the others. As much as I hated him and knew how much of a prick he was, he was the best fighter in our class. On top of being skilled in combat fighting, he was expected to be a rank three or four, although we wouldn't know for sure until the Trials.

I knew he possessed telekinesis and compulsion, as he had used both on me numerous times. And since compulsion was banned, Kole was only allowed to use his telekinesis when he sparred in class, not that he followed the rules. Kole stole a glance at Professor Hale, and I knew what was coming next. His smile turned malicious as he said, "Don't move, little nix." He kept his golden hand down, hiding it from view.

Instantly my feet leadened, gluing me to the floor. My arm froze midair as my gaze locked onto his. Only my hair moved as my braids fell down against my back. Kole prowled around me slowly, "You see, this is why you're worthless. I can make you do anything I want."

A growl escaped my mouth. I was about to snap a retort at him when he spun around to face me. With his fingers pressed against my lips, he whispered, "Shh. Don't speak either." He paused to look at my face before adding, "You see, I can do anything I want to you, and you wouldn't even be able to cry for help. I could compel you to never speak of it—"

Professor Hale turned around, and I instantly fell to the floor as his compulsion lifted. Kole grinned down at me as I scrambled to my feet and resumed my fighting stance.

"Maybe I'll be nice to you and let you be my servant when we graduate. I think we could have some fun together."

I finally managed to land a front kick to his face. He stopped his taunting as he rubbed his jaw, baring his teeth at me.

I offered him a fake, plastered smile in return. "That will never happen."

A punching bag and a heavy kettlebell from the corner of the room came flying toward me. The punching bag came first, and I made the mistake of dodging the bag as the weight connected with my left upper arm.

I cried out as the pain pulsated through my body, the bones in my upper arm screaming in agony. Before I could recover, Kole took a step toward me and landed a jab just above my eye. I staggered back in an attempt to regain my balance, but tripped over the bag, landing flat on my back.

Professor Hale's whistle blew, indicating the thirty-second round was up, and everyone stopped fighting. "What did I tell you, Kole? No objects over fifty pounds. I don't want to call a healer in for Scottie."

"Sorry, sir. Honest mistake," Kole said in his fake apologetic voice. He held his hands up in the air, feigning innocence. Then he offered one to me. I didn't take it as I swatted him away and jumped to my feet.

"Prick," I mumbled under my breath, but I knew his answering smile meant he'd heard me.

Two massive bruises formed on my arm and above my eye by the time the sparring portion of the class was over. Smaller black and blue flecks took over my olive skin tone throughout the rest of my body.

"Get out your notebooks and pay attention. I want to go over what you can expect to see at your Guard Trials this weekend," Professor Hale stated as we sat down on the mats. "The first part of your morning will be your rankings. After that, I want everyone to arrive at the Guard Trial thirty minutes before it starts, so you can warm up. There will be three sections of the Trial itself. This will give you ample opportunity to show off your abilities and prove yourself in combat. The first portion will be combat skills only. You will be fighting amongst yourselves without any abilities." A groan echoed throughout the class, but I sat up a little straighter as he continued.

"The second portion will be weapons. You will not know ahead of time what weapons will be selected. It could range from target practice with axes to sword fighting. So make sure you are practicing all your skills. The final section of your Trial will be abilities-combat, where you will combine your ability with fighting like we did today. Members of the High Council and Prince Noren himself will be attending your Trial."

A murmur at the mention of the prince's name went out across the gym. It was expected for the High Council members to watch the Trials, specifically the Guard Trial, as the King's Guards were hand selected. But to have *him* watch, to have him analyze us... I gulped.

"I wish all of you the best of luck on your examination tomorrow morning and your Trials the next day." Professor Hale finished, then he called out the five names he selected to attend the banquet.

Kole was among them.

To my horror, Professor Hale added as everyone began filing out of the gym, "Scottie will be attending as a suitress. However, I gave her permission before and after the banquet to guard amongst the five selected, so please include her." I could feel Kole's eyes on me, but ignored it.

I remained seated on the sweat-covered royal blue mats long after class ended. My mind spinning in circles, processing what Professor Hale had just said. I should do well in the first two stages of the Trial with regular combat and weapons. I'd made myself good. It was why I woke up early—what I trained for every morning. But the abilities-combat fight was going to hurt me, and that was what the High Council would be watching for. The High Council and the prince.

## SEVEN
# SCOTLIND

Everyone filed into the Hall to take their examination the next morning. It took me the entire eight hours they allotted to finish the test. I kept second guessing my answers and doubting myself. As soon as I finished, I sprinted to the nearest bathing room and hurled up my guts. Thankfully, it was mostly bile as I barely managed to eat breakfast earlier and skipped out on lunch.

Vallie and Miles tried to cheer me up afterward, understanding that I needed to score well to make up for what I would lack in the ranking portion of the Trial. They both reassured me a million times that I would get a good score.

"You've studied your whole life for that test, Scottie. I know you aced it," Vallie said over and over again. "Now come celebrate one-third of our Trials being done and get a drink with us!"

That was only half true. I studied all the time, but I detested it. My studying mostly consisted of looking over my notes for a few minutes, then reading one of the novels I got from the library. I was envious of Vallie's ability of knowledge absorption. She could skim anything once and retain it, making her the top student in our class.

"Vallie, I'm not drinking the night before my Trial. I have to fight tomorrow."

"Come on, Scottie-cat. Just one drink. We won't be out late, and it will help your nerves," Vallie insisted.

Miles seemed to grasp my logic and turned to his sister. "Vallie, you know Scottie has never had a drink before. It's not the best idea for her to have one tonight. She's going to be fighting Kole tomorrow afternoon."

I would be fighting a lot more Advenians than just Kole, but I didn't push the issue. Vallie hated that I was Trialing for the guard. Growing up, she had tried to talk me out of it numerous times. Vallie was a social butterfly even before the two of them started drinking, and although Miles didn't like many Advenians, he never turned down an opportunity to drink with his twin.

*If you tried out for any other career, you wouldn't have to train every day. You could go out partying with us. You could talk to cute boys, be a normal Advenian for once,* she would plead. Eventually, she stopped trying.

"Ugh, fine. But you aren't getting out of it this weekend. I'm having a drink with my best friend before you leave me forever to be a famous guard!"

I gave her a weak smile. Once Vallie realized I was serious about it, she was always so confident that I would pass my Guard Trial. Miles seemed to air more on the side of realism and understood that I had a slim shot. I didn't know which one I preferred.

I turned to them both. "Fine, one drink, but not until after the Trials."

Vallie's smile broadened from ear to ear as she gave me a kiss on the cheek. Then she grabbed Miles by the hand and dragged him out to whatever party they were attending tonight. "Great. You heard it here first, Scotlind Rumor will be a normal Advenian this weekend and will finally attend her first party."

"I said one drink, not a party, Vallie!" I called after her, but she was already walking out the door. Miles turned around to look at me before the door closed behind him, leaving me alone for the night. I sighed, locked the door, and then went straight to the bathing room to fill the tub. I waited the allotted time it took to heat the water over the coals, then soaked in the warm fluid until my hands turned to prunes.

———

I DIDN'T REMEMBER FALLING asleep, but when I awoke the morning of the Trials, my roommate was sleeping half off her twin bed, still in her dress from the night before. Two pink heels had been tossed haphazardly onto the floor and light snores echoed throughout our small room.

Quietly, I dressed in my gym gear, leaving my workout bag. I opted for just a run this morning. I knew with my fights later on today, I didn't want to exhaust myself now. So I ran just long enough to clear my head, to calm myself down a bit, but not enough to tire my muscles.

When I got back to our dorm room thirty minutes later, Vallie was awake and getting ready.

"Good morning," she smiled at me. "Hurry up and bathe. You stink. Miles is going to meet us in fifteen minutes to walk over to the Trials together."

It always amazed me how easily Vallie recovered after a night of drinking. I didn't know what a hangover felt like, but I had seen it on Miles. He would complain of headaches all day and beg me to make him some sort of fatty, greasy breakfast. Vallie, on the other hand, would be ready to go, cooking alongside me.

"Okay," I said, rushing toward the bathing room. Knowing Miles was headed over here was enough motivation to move quickly. I wanted to be dressed before he showed up.

Banners and decorations were scattered all around the school grounds for graduation, covering every single brick building as the three of us walked in silence to the Trials. I hadn't noticed them until Miles pointed it out. Little details seemed to lapse my attention when I got distracted. My mind would wander and it was like I became oblivious to my surroundings. I hated that about myself. It definitely wasn't a trait for someone who wanted to be a guard.

All six schools in Tennebris conducted their Trials similarly, according to the standards placed by the Council. LakeWood, being the furthest village from the castle, was always held last. The makeshift arena they created for the event was at the NorthEnd of campus on one of the vacant fields.

The chilly summer breeze blew the free strands of my brown hair that fell from my braids. A small trickle of sweat crept down my neck as we walked down the path, navigating through the brick buildings. Not from the heat, which was nonexistent in Tennebris, but from nerves. I was instructed to wear my training outfit instead of my school uniform, and even though it was thicker than the usual button down and dark gray plaid skirt I wore to class, I was thankful that I grabbed a coat to throw over it. Even if I'd sweat through it, the fabric was a thick, warm, non-transparent material that protected my back from being exposed.

The Light Kingdom's constant protective shields did more than just block the mortals' view of potentially seeing us. It kept the extreme temperatures at bay. The air was frigid, despite being summer in Tennebris, but I knew without the protective shields of Lux, it wouldn't be survivable. The precipitation was left out when designing it. And mercifully, it held up most days of the year. Only remnants of seldom storms that occurred outside the shield would sprinkle in.

I tried to enjoy our slow walk to the NorthEnd. I tried to savor every second of it, but my nerves prevented me from embracing the moment. It would be my last walk to NorthEnd—the training grounds that became my second home. My last walk with my friends.

After today, our rankings and Trials would be over with. This would be my last weekend at LakeWood, where I'd spent most of my life. I looked over at Vallie and Miles. They were the closest thing to a real family I would get here. I pushed the fact from my mind that I wouldn't see them again after this.

Vallie was the first person in Tennebris who made me feel like I would survive. Back when I cried all the time, randomly breaking down in fits of rage and sobs over my parents, over my counselor not believing me. I'd felt insane, confused, and scared.

One day, Vallie found me quietly crying to myself over some awful thing Kole had made me do. I'd never felt so alone until that day. This red-headed girl with the warmest smile walked over to me and handed me a lollipop. I didn't even know what it was until she explained that it was a mortal sweet. How she got it, I still didn't know.

"Don't cry," she said. "You'll have better days." I took the lollipop, and we'd been inseparable ever since.

A couple weeks later, Vallie introduced me to Miles. Twins were rare in our society. In general, having children was considered extraordinary as it could take years, decades even, to conceive. Once Vallie found out I was an orphan, she forced me to tag along with her during the holidays.

Spending time with her family, laughing by the fireplace on Yule or having a picnic outside on Allium Day, would always be my most cherished memories. Probably my only elated memories of Tennebris. Vallie's kindness was the only reason I didn't fall apart entirely.

After graduation, everyone would go their separate ways. I didn't want my life here without my red-headed friend, but we would be forced to part after this weekend. Dread filled my solemn steps as I realized I would be alone again.

When we finally arrived at the arena, my hands were throbbing. Looking down, tiny half-moon cuts were now embedded into my skin from clenching my fists too tightly. I shook my hands out and wiped the small amount of blood off on my long coat as I looked around. It was amazing what they had put together in such a short time. There were two pop-up buildings that were labeled "Rank Evaluations." I looked closer and saw an "A-M" on one building and an "N-Z" on the other.

Someone standing at the entrance forced a pamphlet into my already shaky hands. I quickly mumbled a thank you as I opened it up. It was bare with nothing fancy written on it, like in true Tennebrisian fashion, but it contained the list of times for the day.

The first time listed didn't start until midday. It read, *"Twelve pm: Ranking Evaluations. Go to the building that correlates with your last name."*

The next few times listed were the various Trials that were being held. *"Arena One: One pm: Mending Trials. Two pm: Culinary Trials."* I kept skimming the page until I saw arena five with the Guard Trials. It wasn't until three. Being only eleven now, I had an hour before the rank evaluations would begin.

Taking a deep breath, I turned toward Miles and Vallie. "I'm going to walk around for a bit, scope out where my Trial will be held."

Vallie embraced me with a warm hug. "Good luck." As much as I was going to miss them and wanted to spend every second together, I needed to be alone right now. I had to clear my head and focus on passing my Trials. After tonight, the Trials would be done, then I could spend the remaining two days with them.

"You too. The both of you." I smiled at them before walking away. I thought I heard Miles murmur something, but I couldn't make it out over the thunder in my chest.

Further past the buildings, there were five other ample sections of the field divided by tall gates. I walked closer to the first one and skimmed the large sign hanging from the wooden gate. It wasn't the Guard Trial. I looked up, taking in the full height of it. It was massive, completely blocking the view from whatever was held inside. The only thing I could tell was there wasn't a roof, leaving it open to the outside elements.

I kept walking until I found the fifth arena located in the back. The sign read, *"One pm: Human Relations Trials,"* then under it, *"Three pm: Guard Trials."* This sign contained the shortest list of Trials. The Guard Trials were infamous for taking the longest since there were three separate sections. It wouldn't be surprising if they went into the night.

Satisfied with knowing where I had to go later, I turned to walk back toward the entrance. Out of the corner of my eye, I saw Sie Noren in the distance surrounded by males in the official guard uniform. I knew they belonged to the King's Guard by their dark leather attire with twin pink moons engraved on the chest. The symbol of Tennebris, whereas Luxian guards wore the Allium sun.

Something about his presence and demeanor made me stop. I found myself unable to pull my gaze from him. He kept his facial expression placid and emotionless as he stood tall, towering over everyone surrounding him. The guards were discussing something. I couldn't tell if the prince was ignoring them or if he was listening intently.

He looked very much like the king he would soon be. I studied him for a few more moments, aware that I was gawking. He looked healthy. Other than a faint cut and bruise to his lower jawline, you wouldn't have known he'd been injured just days prior. His black clothes covered his body, hiding any lingering injuries he might still possess. Probably none, since Lux had healers stationed in Tennebris, they most likely healed any wound he earned during his fights.

I finally dragged my gaze away from the prince as I looked at the guards that surrounded him. They seemed nervous, shifting uncomfortably from foot to foot, not daring to meet the prince in the eye.

A male with shaggy blonde hair standing next to him noticed my stare. He wasn't wearing the official uniform, but he stood among them like he belonged. His vibrant green eyes found mine. He wore a devilish grin and didn't seem intimidated or threatened by the Advenians he surrounded himself with. I quickly glanced away, my heart beating faster, as I continued making my way back to the main entrance. By the time I got there, it was almost time to enter the building to get my rank.

I joined the end of the line for the building that read, *"Rank Evaluations N-Z."* I found Vallie in the crowd. She was standing next to Miles in the middle of the line for the other building. Miles and Vallie Hartlin. At that moment, I wished my name wasn't Rumor. I wanted to stand with my friends, to walk through the doors together.

Vallie looked as nervous as I felt, which was unlike her. Her radiating confidence dimmed as she curled her body against her twin. I gave her a small smile before we both walked into our separate buildings.

I was greeted with a chill as my nerves completely overtook me. The building wasn't a sanctuary against the cold. I knew this day would come, but watching Vallie walk into a different building, disappearing behind the big black doors, made reality set in. I took a steadying breath, then another.

*Breathe Scottie. Just breathe.*

"Everyone, listen up. When I call your name, step forward and get in your assigned line. We will be organizing you alphabetically," a woman ordered. I recognized her as a LakeWood professor, even though I had never been in any of her classes.

The students inside the building started moving and shifting to where they were directed. "Rumor," I finally heard. "Line to the left."

The cold air peppered my body with goosebumps. With nothing else to do but wait, I hugged my chest, frantically moving my hands up and down my arms.

Finally, a teacher I recognized, Professor Alfitini, came to explain what was about to happen. She studied the paper in her hands before she began to ramble, "You will go in one at a time to be evaluated. One student will be in the waiting room where you will remove your clothes. The judges need to examine your markings and it's imperative as everyone's markings are on different areas of their bodies. The judges are made up of the High Council and your teachers. So relax, as they are not there to critique your body, but merely to look at the golden markings that appear as you use your powers.

"Each judge will have a folder detailing your entire life up until this point. It will include but is not limited to family history, medical history, academic history, and your known abilities throughout your years of training here at LakeWood. They are allowed to ask any questions they want. Please answer honestly and quickly so we can keep things moving. Each evaluation will be different lengths of time depending on how long you need to showcase all of your abilities. Some of you have none or only one ability, while others have two or three. The max amount of time you can take is ten minutes. I need everyone to pay attention and move swiftly. We have limited time here as you all need to attend your designated Trials.

"If the judges feel that they need more time to determine your ranking, you will be notified and sent to another waiting room for a second appraisal. Please take this seriously. Whatever rank you are given today will be yours for life. I know this can be a long day, so there will be complementary drink stations and some light refreshments throughout the grounds.

"No one is allowed to leave NorthEnd until all the Trials are finished. Dinner will be provided promptly at five and will last one hour. You were instructed to have already eaten breakfast, so seek out the different refreshment stands if you are hungry. You will not be given your ranking until graduation. More information will be provided regarding your ceremony and the burning of your rankings, which will take place in two days.

"That is it for now. When your name is called, go into the waiting room and remove your clothes. When it is your time to be evaluated, the doors to the other side will open, and you will step forward into the room with the judges. Your clothes will be removed by our staff and placed in the exit room. Once your clothes are removed from the waiting room, we will call the next person in line to enter and so forth. Good luck."

After she finished her long speech of instructions, she turned on her heels and walked away, leaving the room silent with anxiety-ridden students. I slowly moved up step by step as my classmates before me were called to enter the waiting room.

I tried to focus on my breathing. *In through my nose, out through my mouth.* I couldn't help but fidget as they began calling the last names that began with the letter *R*. Only two stood between me and the waiting room.

I needed to calm down. No one told us what the rankings entailed before. It was meant to be kept a secret. Anyone that had abilities were encouraged to practice and learn about their powers to be able to showcase them for this moment. Our school even had special ability classes that we were mandated to take. I dreaded them since I always sat in the back awkwardly with nothing to do.

What went on beyond those doors was private information, but I never imagined we would have to be naked in front of the judges. I thought we could just expose the area on our bodies where our markings appeared, and since I had none, as far as the Tennebrisian abilities went, I figured that meant I didn't have to show anything. I should have been in and out in a matter of seconds. With my Guard Trials constantly on my mind, I never really gave much thought to the rank evaluations.

But after hearing that speech, I couldn't help feeling this was worse than I thought. Even with the cool draft and the goosebumps peppering my skin, I was starting to feel flushed. The tiniest drop of sweat dripping down my back could expose me. Then what would happen? Would they believe me if I told them the truth, or would they kill me on the spot?

I took a deep breath, filling my lungs as the Advenian in front of me entered the waiting room. I was next.

"Scotlind Mae Rumor," I heard called as the doors automatically opened in front of me. For Tennebris not favoring excessive electricity, they sure didn't hold back when constructing this building.

Lux provided the Dark Kingdom with light. Either from their electricity users or from the mimicked, synthetic kind from the mortal world. Tennebris usually looked at electricity with disdain. It reminded the kingdom of their former enemy, so most buildings were lit by firelight or the sun's natural rays from the windows. Only the wealthy and the schools received any electricity at all.

I hated using candles, torches, and fireplaces to see. I loved any room that had any resemblance to electricity. Anytime I saw open flames, it brought me back to that day, and I was in that fire again, my leg burning, the screams of my family fading. But right now, I would take the dim light of a candle over this.

The lights were glittering as I walked into the waiting room. It was small. Only a square stool stood in the corner. I quickly stripped out of my guard uniform and checked my skin, craning my neck to see my back.

Sweat lingered in the palms of my hands, but that was it. Alright. I could work with that. I was thankful for the cool air that seemed to be pumping through the walls. Even though it felt glacial and caused all of the hairs on my body to rise, it calmed me a little, keeping any nervous sweat at bay.

The most amount of time this could be was ten minutes. That was it. Ten minutes of my life. Then things would go back to normal. Well, not really normal, as I had my Guard Trials this afternoon and I would be fighting the strongest males in my class, but I was prepared for that.

Just then, the doors opened on the other side, widening into a larger, much brighter room. I was blinded as I stepped forward into the fluorescent glow. Under this illumination, I was sure the judges could make out every grainy detail of my skin. That they could count every mole and connect every freckle. They could see the various stages of healed bruises I earned from my guard class. Every scar. Every cut. They could see *everything*.

No. Not everything. My Luxian markings only appeared when they made contact with fluid. I would be fine.

I blew out a breath and attempted to wipe my sweaty palms on my bare thighs. All it did was shift my sweat onto my skin and made me hyper aware of how utterly naked I was.

The five judges were separated from me by a thick, sleek desk. I spotted my name written on the paperwork scattered in front of them. To my surprise, I saw full, detailed pages written. I wanted to lean forward and read them, but I couldn't get a good look without making it obvious.

I knew what it would say anyway. It was shoved down my throat every time I fought against my counselor as a child. Hector and Elaine Rumor, parents of Scotlind, died in a terrible fire when Scotlind was seven. Elaine, a rank zero, a nix like her daughter. Hector, a rank two. His ability of illusion landed him a job in the psychiatric field like my counselor. He would enter the minds of the disturbed and alter their visions, usually dealing and healing with terrors and traumas.

Lies. All of it was lies. I frowned at the paperwork before shifting my gaze up toward the Advenians who would judge me.

Among my group of judges, there was only one professor from my school. She had been my Literary teacher in year nine. She gave me a small, encouraging smile and gestured for me to walk toward the center of the room. My legs followed where her eyes led as I finally looked up at the other four judges.

I didn't recognize any of them, but I knew they were from the High Council based on their uniforms. I wanted to cover myself with my arms and shield my body as best as I could, but I knew that wasn't allowed. So I held my chin high, met each of them in the eye, and waited.

The male seated at the center of the desk spoke first. His uniform seemed more refined than the rest—more extravagant.

His eyes were so dark I couldn't pinpoint where his irises met his pupils. His hair was slicked back, exposing a sneer on his oily face as he looked me up and down. Then slowly, his eyes trailed back up. When his lips parted to begin speaking, I noticed two slightly crooked teeth. Otherwise, he possessed an unfittingly straight smile for his face.

"What abilities do you have to present for us today, Miss Rumor? Your school records do not hold anything of significance." His voice sent chills down my spine. I tried to hide the fact that it caused me to shudder.

The gazes of the other three males were still raking my body as the first one spoke. I unclenched my fists, stretching my fingers out slowly by my sides. *I won't get nervous. I won't sweat. I can do this. Breathe in and out.*

"I don't have any abilities to show."

"None?" another judge asked, bewildered. "It says on your paperwork you are trying out to be a guard. A female, nonetheless, yet you have no abilities?" He scoffed at me as if that was the most bizarre thing he had ever heard.

"A female nix as a guard?" another one grumbled under his breath, so soft that I almost missed it. Almost.

"I've trained in combat," I replied. *Simple answers, just reply with simple answers.*

"And you believe that a female with no abilities has what it takes to get placed as a guard?" the creepy male sitting in the middle asked as he folded his hands out in front of him. I noticed his name tag then as I turned to him. *Synder Phillips.* I knew they chose this panel for a reason. The High Council was all made up of powerful rank threes and fours. It wouldn't surprise me if one of them possessed the lie detection ability or had the rare gift to read minds. I struggled to keep my mind void of anything that could destroy me.

"Yes, I have trained very hard for this," I replied to Synder's question. I immediately regretted my response after seeing the look of disgust on his face.

It was true. I despised the ranking system. It was cruel and sadistic to measure one's worth based on a number, and then brand it onto them. I had many reasons for trying out for the guard. The main one being I couldn't take the risk of having a husband. But some part of me knew I was doing this to prove that rank didn't matter.

"So why try at all? If you've had to train so hard, why not go for being a servant? In the end, that's probably what will be decided anyway. You could have at least enjoyed your school years. Much more fitting for a rank zero, wouldn't you say?"

"I believe I can make it as a guard without abilities," I bristled.

"We will see about that shortly during your Trials." One of them chuckled. The sound of papers flipping and turning filled my ears as the judges looked through my files.

My teacher spoke quietly, "I don't see any point in hooking her up to the machine if she has no abilities." My mouth dried as I followed their gazes to where a large monitor with wires stood in the corner of the room.

Synder responded as if noting my unspoken question on what exactly the machine did. "It's called Akula. It was developed by Lux to measure someone's ability reserve. It's a tool to see how much power an Advenian may use before they drain themselves and need to rest to regenerate their powers. It's good for someone to know their limits since it will weaken them if they use too much of their ability at once. It also contributes to someone's ranking. If your reserves are weak, you are more likely to get a lower ranking, and the same can be said about higher rankings for much stronger reserves, so everyone is required to get it done."

I felt like my heart stopped beating. Would this machine show how much Luxian reserves I have? If they forced me to take it, would it give away that I'm not really a rank zero? Since I have no golden markings, they'd find out I was from the Light Kingdom.

Synder nodded to my teacher. "But you're right. There is no sense in wasting the energy on her." I let out a breath.

"Turn around," the third judge spoke before I even had time to be relieved. I did as he asked and slowly spun in a circle. Feeling a drop of sweat start to roll down the back of my neck, I instinctively raised my hand in an attempt to wipe it away.

"Hands at your sides," Synder snapped as I turned back around to face the judges. My heart was beating out of my chest.

"Very interesting," Synder purred as he looked up to meet my eyes. Shivers shot down my spine again as he looked me over with that same haunting gaze. There was something about him that didn't sit well with me. He reminded me of a scarier, more lethal, and much more powerful version of Kole.

I didn't realize I was holding my breath until he finally said, "Leave us."

The exit doors swung open as soon as he spoke the words. I bolted toward them as fast as I could. Grabbing my clothes, I quickly shrugged them on with trembling hands, trying not to hyperventilate. Someone who was a known zero should not be this nervous coming out of the evaluations. I needed to calm down.

I headed outside and started pacing around the grounds, weaving through the five arenas. It didn't really matter where I was going as long as it was far away from that evaluation. The rapid movement mixed with fresh air helped to calm my nerves so I wouldn't break down completely.

I made ten laps before the shaking subsided and my reality set in. It was over with. I would be a rank zero, I expected that, but now it was officially done. I took one more lap around the grounds before deciding to make my way over to Vallie's Trials since I had some time before mine began.

I was mad at myself for almost missing it. Vallie was trying out for education, even though I knew she wished she was Trialing in human relations. But those jobs required frequent travel to Lux with a work visa. *I don't want to be separated from Miles*, she'd told me when I tried to convince her to Trial for what she actually wanted.

The large wooden sign out front of the arena read, "Astronomy Trials" following hers. Funny how both of them had Trials in the same area. If Miles succeeded, he would be considered a member of the high class. Getting a job in the AASP was sought after and hard to be accepted into. Miles would be able to provide well for his family if he passed.

The AASP was constantly searching the universe for a different planet for us to live on. One that wasn't inhabited by humans or other creatures. One where we could live freely and not have to hide. We wanted a planet of our own, one like Allium once was to us, but the few planets they had discovered so far had too harsh a climate.

Earth was the only one suitable for us as we were similar to the human race. We survived and thrived in the same environment and possessed similar biological make-ups.

Many Advenians feared that living among the mortals was the reason nixes had evolved. Non-ability people hadn't existed on our home planet. Many theorized it was because our ancestors reproduced with humans. Now, laws forbade any relationship with the mortals, but nixes were still looked at with disgust. Advenians feared that if we stayed here, our abilities would continue to dwindle, eventually becoming non-existent.

Miles used to tell us stories when we were young that he would find a planet for me, Vallie, and him to live on. There, we could be together forever. I used to fantasize about it as a little girl, but now I knew it was only ever a dream.

I sat on the empty raised bleachers inside the arena. Spectators were encouraged. Some Advenians even invited their families to watch their Trials. I sat alone watching Vallie, embracing the calm around me. They questioned her relentlessly, forcing her to retell every grueling detail about our kind and the fall of our planet. Vallie's ability of knowledge absorption didn't disappoint her as she answered each question without hesitation. I smiled at my friend as her Trial continued. She was a living, breathing, walking textbook and I knew there wasn't anything she couldn't do.

When it was almost three, I headed to the far end of the grounds toward the last arena.

I was ready.

# EIGHT
## SIE

I sat down next to Peter to watch the Guard Trials at LakeWood. I was thankful for my friend's presence. I declared him my second the moment I won the tournament, which meant that we had to travel to every damn village to watch the end-of-the-year Trials. The High Council insisted on parading us around. I was already regretting the juvenile tasks of being the prince. The purpose, supposedly, was to select the new guards I wanted for my rule. It felt like a joke. I had yet to see anyone fight that I thought could actually protect me. Nonetheless, Peter and I had been agonizingly picking the lucky few to join the King's Guard.

LakeWood was the last of the schools I needed to visit. The only good thing about watching all the Trials was the distraction it provided for what would happen tomorrow—the banquet. Only one more day separated me from the High Council choosing who I'd have to marry, who I would have to spend the rest of my life with. The thought made my stomach turn.

I wasn't lying in my interview when I said I had no one in mind. No one I'd met had interested me enough. Reagan, the girl Peter and I knew growing up, was furious when she found out I didn't pick her. She even made it a point not to talk to me all week. I really didn't care. I wasn't blind. She only wanted me for my title. To be queen.

I couldn't stand the thought of having to pick someone myself, so the High Council doing it for me was just fine. I just didn't expect it to happen so soon. Synder Phillips seemed especially elated when he found out I wasn't claiming a bride.

If it was up to me, I wouldn't get married at all. Having a wife or someone to care about only created a weakness. On the other side, maybe it would stop all the females from throwing themselves at me. I was growing sick of constantly being approached by them, trying to woo me in hopes I would change my mind and select them.

Peter interrupted me from my thoughts. "There's a female competing at this school," he said, staring at the arena.

"Really?" I asked, looking down to see where his gaze fell. A female hadn't tried out for the guard since I'd been alive. They were so rare to come by. Since Advenians could die by weapons, most females weren't signing up for a potential death sentence to their otherwise long lives. Only males went out for the guard. Males who later hoped to participate in the King's Tournament, not that it was a requirement, but the training gave an Advenian an edge in the competition.

"Yeah. Give me a sec, and I'll find her files," Peter said, sorting through the stacks of folders we'd received on every student at LakeWood.

My eyes were fixated on her as I watched her go through her warmup routine alone. She was beautiful in a unique sort of way and stuck out amongst all the males. With her petite frame and short height, I wouldn't pin her as a fighter. She was at least a head smaller than everyone she was going up against, but she didn't seem nervous. She looked focused, determined. Her brown hair swayed in the wind, causing a few strands to fall from her long braids.

Her sapphire eyes were gleaming so vividly that I couldn't miss them, even from this distance. She bent over to stretch, and I caught a good glimpse of her—

"Wow. How strange," Peter said, pulling my gaze from the girl as he held up her folder. "She was declared a rank zero today at her evaluation. Her name is Scotlind Rumor. Orphaned at seven, but her parents weren't impressive either."

"What?" I grabbed the folder from him and quickly glanced over it. For the first time during these Trials, it felt like an invasion of privacy to read the papers that were given to us. They included a picture of her, zoomed in on her face. She was beautiful. Up close, I could make out all the freckles scattered across her pointed nose and the way her bottom lip pouted. Her eyelashes were dark and heavily framed her wide eyes, drawing even more attention to the beautiful coloring.

I had to force myself to look away from the photo to read what was enclosed. They had listed everything about her: her age, birthday, weight, and height. They had her entire school records, which portrayed her as an average student. I was surprised to see she had a long list of hindrances and seemed to get in trouble a lot. She wasn't that impressive on paper.

I looked down at her again. Now, a tall, brown-haired male was looming over her. She snapped her head quickly in his direction, rolled her eyes, and stormed away from him. He just laughed as he watched her go, paying attention to her ass, no doubt.

Professor Hale, who delivered the files to Peter hours earlier, walked out onto the arena, ushering his students to follow. I did my best to watch everyone in the tournament and evaluate them fairly, but I'd be lying if I said I didn't focus on Scotlind more. I was impressed by her. Shocked that she was even competing, especially with no abilities. She had nothing to gain from being a guard. Regardless, she was surprisingly good.

The first round of the Trial was combat-only fighting. She annihilated it, coming in second only to the brown-haired male who had been taunting her earlier. The moment the buzzer sounded, it was as if a switch in her flipped. She transformed, and I was transfixed.

Her eyes narrowed and honed in on whatever poor male she was fighting, solely fixating on them. I could see the determination and focus etched onto her face. I could see she worked hard for every win, with each drop of sweat that glistened off her body. She left the world around her behind, engulfing herself in each round. Like the fight was the only important thing on this Goddess-forsaken planet. I was watching a huntress toying with her prey, and she was about to make the kill. She passed with flying colors and only had a few black and blues to show for it.

After the first round, they began to transform the arena for the weapons portion. Staff set up targets for archery and a knife combat section to the left.

"Kole Sanders is good. Really good," Peter said as the brown-haired boy stepped up to the target. He hit the bullseye every time. The arrows were practically splitting down the middle from being embedded on top of one another. "He was in the lead for the first section of the Trials, and according to his file, he will be declared a rank four at his graduation ceremony."

"What are his abilities?" I asked, my eyes still glued to Scotlind. I watched as she took the sleeve of her shirt and wiped the sweat from her forehead.

"His abilities are telekinesis and compulsion. We could use him at the castle."

"Yeah, we can take him," I said quickly, not too keen on having another asshole around, but I couldn't deny that he was damn talented. "The girl is good too," I added.

Peter flashed his famous smile at me, exposing all his too-white teeth. "That she is," he said. "But you know we can't take her."

"I know that," I admitted. "I wasn't saying to hire her for the King's Guard, but she should be a guard regardless of her ranking. She's impressive."

Peter sighed. "It doesn't matter how skilled she is. They are planning on making her a servant because of her ranking. Synder was at her evaluations earlier this morning and already made note of it."

I ground my teeth together. I hated Synder as much as I hated my father. The two of them lived and breathed for the ranking system. If it was up to them, they would make every rank zero a slave and take away all their rights.

"She deserves more than being a servant," I growled.

Peter tore his eyes from the arena to look at me and smirked. "You have a soft spot for her."

"I do not," I said way too quickly judging by the smile still beaming on his face. "Fine," I added. "I just don't want her to become a servant. Just get her a different job."

Peter nodded, but didn't say anything else as we continued to watch student after student come up to the target range.

He knew better than to bring up why I didn't want her to be a servant. He'd been to my house numerous times to see how my father treated them. The thought of her talents wasted on doting on people like my father made me sick. With her looks, I knew she would be abused in more ways than one.

I also knew better than to assume my request would be granted. It didn't matter what I wanted, not until my six months of training were up and I became king. I didn't plan to abolish the ranking system. I knew that was impossible, but I at least wanted to make things more fair. I didn't want to give in to people like my father. I didn't want them taking advantage of lesser rank Advenians just because they could. This girl would end up a servant if that's what Synder wanted, and there would be nothing I could do about it.

As they finished up with the weapons portion, the staff cleared the arena once more for the last section of the Trials.

"Your girl didn't miss a single target," Peter teased.

"Shut up," I snapped but couldn't hide the smile creeping up my face. "She's not my girl. Just because I don't want her to end up being a servant doesn't mean I like her."

"Okay. Okay." He laughed as he threw his hands up in the air. "You know, though, she's going to struggle in this portion if she has no abilities."

"I know." I didn't want to think about all the ways she could get injured fighting without powers. I honestly didn't know why she was even competing or why it bothered me. I decided to read Kole's folder to focus on something else.

The last part of the Guard Trials allowed only two students to fight at a time instead of everyone sparring in pairs at once. It allowed me to evaluate them better. I could see who relied heavily on their abilities and who had learned to incorporate their powers with their combat skills.

Peter and I made notes of the ones we liked and the ones we didn't as they fought again. Each fight lasted two minutes with the winner continuing on. They won by getting the most points on their opponent, knocking them out, or earning a surrender. The loser of the match was eliminated immediately, and their Trial was over.

So far, it was a mix of all three, and I found myself hoping that it wasn't a knockout whenever the girl fought.

# NINE
## SCOTLIND

I was forced to watch ten rounds of sparring before my name was called. Good. It was about time. I took a deep breath as I made my way toward the center of the arena. I purposely avoided looking in the stands. I didn't want to know who was watching me. I couldn't afford any distractions.

I looked to see who I would be up against. It was Hardan Georges. I tried to recall his abilities as I looked him over. Was it compulsion? No. Paralysis? No. Hyperspeed? No. My mind raced with the possibilities. I had to remember what power he possessed. If I could recall it, I would know what to avoid, what to watch out for.

Fighting strategically was my only saving grace when it came to sparring against the Dark abilities. That, and the fact that I was generally more agile than my classmates.

Kole hadn't been called to fight yet, so at least I could continue on for a few rounds if I fought smart. I knew from all my years at practice that I couldn't win against him. He was too strong and powerful and made it his goal to learn my fighting style and how to beat me.

I blocked everything out as I heard the buzzer go off, letting me know my two minutes had begun. Right before the fight, I recalled that x-ray vision was Hardan's ability. It was a remarkable ability to have, but didn't help in a fight with no weapons. He could detect in an instant if anyone was concealing anything. X-ray users were usually utilized at the annual meeting the High Council had with Lux. The only thing he could use it for now was to look through my clothes, which I think would just be a distraction to him.

I almost felt bad for him. He didn't land a single hit on me as I mercilessly took all my stress out on him. The buzzer went off again in the blink of an eye.

"Fifteen to zero. Scotlind moves on," Professor Hale announced at the end of the match. I found myself glancing up at the bleachers, even though I told myself I wouldn't, and I froze.

Prince Noren and the blonde-haired boy from earlier were both staring down at me. The blonde was smiling, but the prince's expression was void of emotions as his gaze found mine. His eyes lingered for a few seconds before he shook his head and looked back at the folders splayed out in front of him. Was there a folder on me? I didn't have any time to analyze or think about him reading about my life as my next fight started.

The next six matches were similar to the first. Most of my other classmates landed hits on me, but I won each round. My body was throbbing and aching all over to show for each victory. A male named Kirt, who I last fought, shared the same ability as King Lunder. He possessed weapon energy and drew a dagger out in the middle of our fight, leaving me with a bleeding gash down my forearm.

Luckily, it was shallow and small, maybe only an inch or two long, but the pain around the area felt like it was on fire, leaving a sharp, agonizing sensation shooting up my arm. Blood was slowly trickling down my wrist, covering my hand and embedding itself under my fingernails. I ground my teeth together as I wiped off as much of the blood as I could. It would be a weakness now. Weapons were supposed to be banned during the final round of Trials, but abilities weren't, so Professor Hale allowed it.

There were only two more Advenians left to fight—Grady and Kole. I listened for who Professor Hale would call next. I knew Kole was impatiently waiting to fight me.

I saw him grin as his name was the one called.

The buzzer went off, and Kole didn't hold back. He immediately threw a front kick and landed it on my face—the same tender spot above my eye he'd hit only days before. I stumbled backward before regaining my footing.

We paced around each other as I lightly bounced on the balls of my feet, ready to dodge his next move. I knew from years of sparring with Kole that he was impatient and wouldn't wait. He was an offensive fighter to a fault. He came forward with another kick. I jerked to my left, extending my arm out to block it. Blood from my gash sprayed onto him as I rebounded with a sidekick. His nostrils flared as Professor Hale called the score from the sidelines. I internally smiled.

It was one to one. He attacked again. I dodged his kick, but he landed a punch immediately after. A grunt escaped my lips as I felt the full power of his blow.

Another jab. Kick. Dodge. Punch. I groaned as Professor Hale called out three more points for Kole. I knew I had to stop fighting defensively. I didn't have the time to wait for counter-attacks. I stepped toward him, lifted my leg, and extended it into another kick.

I didn't notice him using his telekinesis until it was too late. Kole managed to pull an empty bleacher from the stands and sent it flying toward me. I didn't have time to react as the bleacher slammed me back, pinning me against the wall of the arena. Kole's smile turned malicious as he strode over toward me, taking his damn time.

I glanced at the clock. Dread filled my stomach as I saw we still had a minute left. Kole could do a lot of damage in one minute. He knew he had won as he stopped right before me.

He leaned in and whispered in my ear, "I was trying to go easy on you at first, little nix, but I guess you needed a reminder of your place. This is what happens to nixes. You're powerless and completely in my hands now."

His smile was playful as I struggled to break free of the bleacher. The golden markings on his hand shimmered against the sun as he continued to wield his power. I didn't move an inch.

Kole laughed as he caressed my cheek. "You can always surrender, little nix. You don't have to put yourself through this."

His smile wiped off his face as I spat at him, leaving a glare that could kill. He grabbed my forearm and pressed down hard against the open wound from Kirt's blade. I cried out in agony, hating myself for letting the pain overtake my body. My scream echoed into the now silent arena.

He didn't hesitate after that as he used the remaining time on the clock to land blow after blow. Over and over again. I was defenseless until the buzzer sounded. I knew I could surrender. I knew I should. I'd lost. Letting him beat me up didn't prove anything. But I didn't want to give Kole the satisfaction. I couldn't let him win, not in that regard. Instead, I stood there, trapped between the wall and the torn bleacher as I braced for each painful blow.

The arena was quiet long after the buzzer sounded. Kole wiped away the blood that was running down my face with the back of his palm. "Don't worry, I won't beat you up when you're my servant."

"You're a prick," I cursed at him, trying my best for my voice to sound strong. It didn't. I could barely catch my breath.

He smiled before letting go of his hold on the bleacher. I fell forward as my hips became free and stumbled over it.

"Forty-seven to two. Kole wins," Professor Hale called.

Kole grabbed me by the arm and forced me up.

"Don't touch me," I snapped at him as I tried and failed to pull away from his grip. I was at his mercy and he knew it. Everything hurt, and I felt weak. My body ignited in pain as he grasped me tighter along the gash on my forearm, giving it a good squeeze. I cried out again as Professor Hale yelled something to Kole about our match being over.

"That was low," I mumbled under my breath to him as I started to stumble off the arena, trying my best to stand up straight. Dizziness washed over me. I didn't want to look down to find out how much of me was covered in red. I was already tasting blood in my mouth. I ran my tongue along my teeth, checking to make sure none were loose.

"Gotta do what you gotta do, little nix," Kole shouted after me. "In the real world, I would have demolished you within seconds if I was allowed to use compulsion on you. I wouldn't have needed to use the bleacher to hold you in place."

I tried not to let his words sink in. I hated that he was right. I would have been defenseless against his compulsion. He could have compelled me to walk right into his fist and I would have obeyed. I had obeyed in the past.

Professor Hale called out Grady's name. He was the last one to spar. I took a seat among the students who had already been eliminated.

Grabbing a sip of water, I tried to cool off as I watched the final round.

An unsettling feeling washed over me, like I was being watched. I looked up toward the stands and saw Prince Noren glancing my way before he drew his attention back to the fight.

Grady surrendered to Kole within forty-five seconds of the next match.

# TEN
# SCOTLIND

The next day, I let out a sob as I rolled over in my bed. Bruises were scattered across my body like splattered paint from where Kole had landed his blows. Cradling my left rib, I slowly peeled myself off the bed, making my way toward the bathing room. I groaned as I lit a candle on my way in, hating even the small flame it produced.

I'd heard rumors that the Luxian City was flourishing with electricity. That every building lit up the sky, constantly humming with enough power that you couldn't tell if it was day or night. I wished I could remember it, just to have been able to see what a golden city looked like.

Inspecting myself in the mirror, I let out a heavy sigh. My bottom lip was split open, leaving a bloody scab. The swelling around the cut made my lip almost twice the normal size and it looked ridiculous. The sight of me was laughable.

Last night, I opted to just listen to Vallie and Miles talk about how their own Trials went. They didn't need to ask about mine. It was written all over my face and body how horribly it had gone. The previous bruise I had over my eye had now turned from purple to black.

Anytime I did chime in, my lip would burst open again from the tension, dripping blood down my chin. It was better to keep my mouth shut, and Vallie was sick of me getting blood on our carpet.

My ribs ached and throbbed the most. They were entirely bruised. I couldn't take a full breath without wincing in pain.

I pulled my gaze from the mirror. After latching the lock on the door, which I always did when I bathed, I started filling the tub. Not bothering to wait for the water to warm, I slowly eased myself in. The cold water stung my body, especially the gash on my forearm, as I submerged myself into its embrace. I ignored the burn as I fully sank into it. The water always had a way of relaxing me, of making me feel at ease. I leaned my back against the cold marble and closed my eyes.

I was done. It was done. I would find out tomorrow at graduation if I'd passed. I just had to get through the banquet first, but my Trials were finished. My fate was out of my hands.

I soaked in the tub until the dried blood from my body merged with the water, turning it murky. I really should have washed last night, but I couldn't get myself to do it. I could barely get myself to move.

Once I was dressed, Vallie greeted me from her desk chair as I exited the bathing room. "How are you feeling?" she asked, her eyes raking over my body. She had been doting on me like a concerned mother since my fight with Kole.

"I'm fine." I gave her a wink. "You should see the other guy."

Her warm smile faded as she said, "Miles and I came to your Trial after ours finished. We watched the ability-combat fight. We saw what Kole did to you at the end. It wasn't right."

We hadn't talked about it last night, and I wanted to keep it that way. We'd spent the evening laughing and enjoying each other's company. Happy. I wanted our last few memories together to be happy, not wasting our time talking about how miserably I'd failed.

"Vallie, I'm fine, really." When she wasn't buying it, I added, "We only have two more days together, Valerina, and I would like to make them good ones. Now let's get you ready for this banquet."

She smiled at that. "You're right," she replied as she shifted in her chair to look at me. "And I'm going to make us look so beautiful that even the prince won't be able to take his eyes off of us." She sucked in her teeth as she scanned me. "Don't worry, I'll use some foundation to cover up your eye."

*Us.* Crap. I didn't tell Vallie yet that I wasn't dressing up. I'd evaded the topic because I didn't want to face her wrath or disappointment, but seeing as the banquet was in a few hours, I couldn't avoid it any longer.

She loved dressing up as much as I loved being in the sparring ring, outside with a book, or soaking in the tub. I cleared my throat as she sprang up from her chair to open her closet door. "Um, Vallie, I forgot to tell you, but I'm not dressing up. Professor Hale gave me permission to go as a guard, so I'll be wearing my guard uniform tonight."

"You aren't being considered as a match for tonight? Does that mean you passed your Trial? That you're officially a guard?" she asked, stopping in her tracks.

The excitement on her face stung as I said, "No. I won't find out if I got it until tomorrow at the graduation ceremony just like everyone else. So technically, I'm not one of the five students he selected, but I can at least practice guarding at the same time, and I don't have to wear a dress."

"What?" Vallie fumed, her doe-like eyes popping out of her head. "Scottie, come on. You promised me I could dress you up. What do you mean you aren't wearing a dress? You can't wear your guard uniform. It's ghastly and awful!"

We continued bickering like sisters. Vallie was desperately trying to convince me to wear a dress, which resulted in her showing me each and every single one she had stuffed into her small closet. It was twenty minutes before we finally compromised. She would do my hair and makeup, but I was still dressing for the guard.

After I threw on my uniform, which took me longer than usual with my stiff body, I sat on my bed and talked with Vallie as she did her own hair and makeup.

"You look gorgeous, Vallie," I said, taking her in as she placed the final pin in her hair.

Her shoulder length hair looked more orange than red today as she twisted and twirled the heavy locks up on the top of her head. She complemented her vibrant hair with the same bright, red smear she always applied to her lips.

"Oh, hush. Just wait until you see how you'll look." She brushed off my compliment and started to undo the curlers she'd positioned in my hair. She ushered me over to the window before she began coating my eyelashes with something sticky.

"There. All finished," she said as she looked at me. "Now go look in the mirror. Who said you can't make even that dreadful uniform look pretty?"

I was shocked when I saw myself. She wasn't wrong about either statement. The guard uniform at LakeWood was awful. The pants were a dull green, and too loose and baggy around my legs. It didn't help that I was a head smaller than most of the males they were designed for. The shirt was a thin, white material that thankfully hid much of my bruised body.

Vallie styled my light brown hair in loose curls that fell down my back. I was surprised by how much I loved my hair down. I usually wore it in two long braids to keep the inevitable falling strands out of my face.

Despite my busted lip and bruised eye, which was almost completely covered with an unnatural amount of powder, I felt pretty. I never bothered before with caring about my looks. I was always too focused on training and studying to be able to give it much thought, and I knew I never could have dated a Tennebrisian.

"I did loose curls so that it looks more natural," Vallie commented proudly, coming up behind me in the mirror. "If only you would let me put a smear on you to cover up that busted lip."

"No, Vallie. I told you I'm not wearing anything on my lips. It's only going to make the scab worse, and I need it to heal. This is enough, more than enough. Thank you."

"It's such a shame that someone as gorgeous as you would rather fight with boys than dress up and be a normal female for once. Such a waste of a pretty face." She audibly sighed, making it known she was disappointed in not getting to completely dress me up.

"Our kind needs more female guards," I said.

"Our kind would have no idea what to do with your badass self."

I stuck my tongue out at her before glancing at myself once more in the mirror. It felt like I was looking at someone else, someone I didn't know—a stranger.

The freckles scattered across my nose were still visible through whatever layers of makeup she'd caked on me. And whatever she coated on my lashes made my sapphire eyes glisten and stand out even more than usual. It was not something I usually drew attention to, as blue eyes were known to be more of a Luxian or human feature. They weren't unheard of here in Tennebris, but they were rare. To me, they were just another reminder that I didn't belong here.

"Well, do you love it?" she teased, noting me gawking at myself.

"Yes. Thank you, Vallie. You seriously have a talent for this."

She beamed at me, clearly pleased with my answer. "See, I told you I was amazing. I mean, come on, Scottie. I can't take my eyes off you. If I was a dude, you would so be my type."

"Ha. Ha. Hilarious, Vallie." She laughed as I pushed her to the side, the effort hurting my stiff muscles more than her.

I was still staring at my appearance in the mirror that I didn't notice Vallie put on her gown. A pink strapless dress clung to her curvy figure so tightly that I was in awe at how swiftly she was able to move around, nonetheless sit down. Even though the gown didn't expose much of her skin, it was still scandalous for Tennebrisian fashion.

I turned away from the mirror to face Vallie, who now took up a spot on the edge of her bed, smiling. The dress had a thin line of lace around the bottom trim that reached her calves, exposing some of her tanned ankles, but was otherwise plain. She adorned it with a beautiful pair of gold drop earrings.

Vallie didn't need much. A simple gown suited her because she would always stand out in a crowd with her bright hair, warm smile, and feminine figure. Males gawked at her everywhere we went, and she was never one to shy away from harmless flirting.

"Wow, Vallie."

"Is it too much?"

"No, you look stunning. It's perfect, just like you."

I gave Vallie a confused look as a knock sounded on our door.

"Can you get that?" she asked as she hopped off the bed and strode over to our mirror. She then added another layer of red to her lips.

"Are we expecting anyone?"

"Yes, I asked Miles to stop by. I left my favorite pair of heels in his dorm room last weekend when we went out drinking. He's dropping them off for me," she said, leaning forward to get a better view of her reflection.

I opened the door, and Miles nearly dropped the tan, strappy heels as he looked me up and down. "Wow, Scottie," he murmured. "You look... You look..."

"Beautiful, stunning, drop-dead gorgeous," Vallie finished for him from behind me.

"Come in," I said awkwardly, ignoring them both. I stepped aside, allowing him to stride into our room as I tucked a loose curl behind my ear.

"Miles, thank you so much!" Vallie said as she rushed over to her twin, giving him a small peck. "You're a lifesaver."

Miles made a point to look disgusted as he swiped off the red stain left on his cheek from her kiss before he glanced at me again.

Vallie purred, now talking to the pair of heels she was clinging to her chest, "I missed you, my babies."

"I can't believe they are making everyone go to this banquet to parade all the females around. It's barbaric." Miles grumbled as Vallie leaned over her desk, buckling her heels to her feet.

"What are you talking about, Miles?" Vallie remarked. "I believe everyone, and I mean *everyone*, wants to be Sie's wife."

"Not everyone," he said under his breath.

"Ah, okay, come on now." She smiled, pulling me by the shoulders.

"Scottie and I don't want to be late to be in the presence of the hottest guy ever."

"Okay, I'm coming," I laughed. She'd emphasized the word *hottest* a little too much just to annoy her brother.

I looked over at Miles and gave him a smile. He frowned as I grabbed my favorite pair of white, flat boots and ran after Vallie.

"I'll come back to your dorm later so we can go out and drink," Miles said before the door shut in his face. Right, because I'd promised them both, days earlier, that I would drink with them tonight. I pushed the thought away for now as I followed my best friend toward the Hub of campus.

There were a total of four large, black vans that were leaving Lake-Wood. I'd never been in one before as they were exclusively saved for the higher ranks and rarely ever utilized in LakeWood. Vallie and I managed to grab seats on the second one.

As I sat down next to her, I never felt more out of place. I was the only female not dressed up, and although five others were wearing the same uniform as me, they were all males, and none were in this vehicle. Lace, silk, ruffles, beads, diamonds, jewels, and beautiful gowns surrounded me.

I was slightly relieved Vallie had done my hair and makeup, just to help me blend in more. I thought wearing my uniform would let me go unnoticed, but I quickly realized it was doing the opposite. Among so many stunning gowns and dolled up smiling, jittering faces, I stuck out like a dark cloud on a gorgeous day.

Everyone was cheerful and giddy, excited for what the night would bring. I heard the prince's name brought up too many times to count during the ride over as I tried my best to block out all the conversations stirring around.

Mostly the girls just gossiped about how muscular he looked, how mysterious he was, or how good in bed they thought he'd be. Not one person talked about his rule, what kind of a king he would make, or how this would affect our kingdom.

"Did you see his abs when his shirt ripped?" the female in front of me asked her friend.

"Yes! Seriously, he has like an eight-pack, and I've never seen calves that large before," her friend responded. "Imagine him picking you up..."

I rolled my eyes, managing to block them out.

Vallie was busy gossiping with someone who had taken a seat across from us, so I decided to look out the window during the ride. A rush of excitement jolted through me as I realized this would be the first time I left LakeWood.

The banquet was being held in Addler, the village closest to our school, but still a long ride away. I found myself searching for bodies of water, hoping to see an ocean whiz by the window. I soon discovered that if I had managed to climb those mountains, it would have been futile.

We passed by a few lakes and rivers, more mountain ranges, most with snow-capped tops, and—to my surprise—extensive forests, but never an ocean. The closer our drive got to Addler, the denser the world around us became. I knew Luxian ground users had added various vegetation throughout the kingdom inside our borders, but I'd never seen it before. The trees were glorious, and I realized that I loved the forest. I wanted to explore it, to see what wonders were kept inside. But to my disappointment, our van maintained its path on the long road of Laten.

When we finally arrived in Addler, the sun was shifting in the sky. Hues of orange and yellow scattered across the horizon, casting everything with light. I was so thankful that this was happening during the summer months, that I'd be able to see everything. I looked around, scanning the village with a new kind of excitement. There were a few mountain peaks, but not as many as LakeWood had.

The few ranges were pretty to admire. It was nice to not feel trapped by them. I already liked Addler a lot more than LakeWood for that reason alone, but what really caught my eye was the green.

The deep forest we passed on the drive seemed to surround the village. I saw the timber and wood and leaves through the tinted windows of the van, but to see it in person, with clear eyes, was something else. Trees, large and small, were scattered across Addler. Moss and vines traveled up the bark, masking the thickness of the trunks. The trees weren't as dense as the ones in the forest, but were still just as beautiful. I inhaled deeply as scents of pine and cedar filled my nostrils. It was refreshing and clean.

As we made our way through the crowd toward the grand building, I couldn't help but shiver as the wind stung my face, sweeping my hair into a flowing cascade behind me. The air was colder here. Even though LakeWood was the closest village to the shield, it had more mild temperatures because it sat at a lower elevation. The frigid air only worsened the farther inward you traveled.

I was thankful for my shirt's long sleeves, even though it was thin. Most of the females were wearing dresses that left their entire arms exposed. I didn't know how they were managing.

The building we arrived at was massive. Beautiful, white clay scaled its length with full windows framed in flowers and greenery. A garden stretched around the perimeter. It was so peaceful and serene that I could hear different birds chirping that lived within the shield.

Once we were ushered inside through the opulent front doors, I was greeted by a wave of heat that hugged my body. I embraced it as I frantically rubbed my hands up and down my arms, willing warmth into them. Being from Lux, the cold affected my body more fervently and faster than someone from Tennebris.

"Wow, it's so…" I struggled to find the right word to describe what I was seeing as I craned my head to look around. "Lavish," I finally settled on.

"I know," Vallie breathed as she gaped around the room.

The inside of the building was just as luxurious and unique as the outside. I couldn't hide my shock as I took in the green-carpeted floors and the cream-colored walls. Any part of the wall that wasn't exposed to the massive windows overlooking the gardens was decorated with thick oil paintings in gold-trimmed frames. It was such a contrast to the nondescript buildings at LakeWood, where bricks lined every single wall. Addler was a wealthier, more affluent village and it showed through this one building alone.

We were directed into a large ballroom. White chairs backed with sheer ribbons were positioned to face a stage. It was raised above everything else, making it the focal point in the massive room. Six green, carpeted steps led toward the top of the platform where there were five Advenians already seated, who I presumed were members of the High Council.

The councilmen talked amongst themselves, not bothering to notice the swarm of females that flocked into the room. The center of the stage held one bulkier, more luxurious seat that was left vacant. I wondered if it was replicated to resemble a throne. A podium stood next to it, barely visible from where I stood. The far right of the room was the only area not covered by chairs, presumably for dancing. Whimsical music sang through the room as if begging us to dance, so soft and light, I couldn't tell where it was coming from.

"Wow," Vallie and I both breathed in unison, taking everything in.

"I didn't think it would be this beautiful. Imagine what the actual castle looks like if this is only a conference center in Addler," Vallie continued.

I was so immersed in admiring the room and taking in the shining chandeliers hanging from the high-volted ceiling that I didn't notice the sharp tug on my shoulders until it was too late. I stumbled and crashed right into Vallie. We both caught ourselves before we landed on the floor. A huffed moan escaped my lips as I shifted away from my friend.

I turned to see who had pushed me and was greeted by Kole's smirking face. His brown eyes burned into mine. They were the same muddy brown as the dirt he'd forced me to eat all those years ago. His eyes were a constant reminder of his hatred for me. I wanted to punch him and knock that grin right off. But instead, I gritted my teeth. "What do you want?"

He tsked. "You're clumsy and rude."

Vallie took a tentative step closer to me. "Leave her alone, Kole."

"Relax, Valerina. I just wanted to see how good of a job she did at covering up the bruise. Not bad, little nix. Too bad you couldn't do anything to hide that lip." He said as he bent down to examine my face, pressing his thumb hard into the bruise over my eye. "If it wasn't for the guard outfit, you might have actually passed for a female. It's sad they don't even let you play dress up for a day. Oh well."

He laughed as I swatted his hand away. I was not about to admit to him that I asked to guard tonight. He could think whatever he wanted.

"Anyway, Professor Hale wants you to patrol the outer rim, not inside the ballroom. So get going, little nix," he straightened, reaching his full height. He walked away, but glanced over his shoulder once, his eyes roaming over Vallie, before gowns, jewels, and smiling females blocked him from my view.

"That jerk. If he wasn't such a complete asshole to everyone, I would think he picks on you because he likes you," Vallie growled.

"I don't think it's possible for Kole to like anything, except maybe himself." I gave her a reassuring smile as she patted my outfit down to make sure I didn't have any marks on my white shirt. I tried not to grimace as she rubbed off the dust from my left side. "Have fun at the banquet, Vallie. I'll catch up with you later," I said as I gave her a hug and started making my way toward the outer rim.

I took the small steps that lead out into the hall two at a time. It took me about ten minutes before realizing that the outer rim made a complete circle around the ballroom and the outside. Other than one set of stairs that lead to the floors above us, the first floor only held the sunken ballroom and a few bathing rooms. There were benches for sitting throughout the hall, but otherwise, it was bare.

Once I did two full laps, I decided I'd earned a break to look out the vast windows. Through cracks in the lush gardens, I could just barely see the trees and mountains in the distance.

Gazing through the window, imagining the expansiveness of the trees, I started daydreaming about what my life could have been if I really was from Tennebris and didn't have to pretend. I could have had a boyfriend and tried out for any career I wanted. Would I still have wanted to be a guard? The reasons that led me toward learning to fight were because of my past. I wanted to avoid getting a husband, and I wanted to learn to fight back so that the night I was kidnapped could never be repeated. If I lived a normal, peaceful life, would I still have wanted that?

Would I be excited about tonight if things were different? I didn't think I would be interested in marrying the future king either way. I didn't care how attractive someone was. I would have wanted a husband who was kind and loving, not cold and intimidating. I pictured myself in a ball gown, being giddy with Vallie, actually acting like a normal Advenian youth for once.

Would I want to give up any abilities I might possess of Lux to be an Advenian of Tennebris? If I was truly a nix, I probably still wouldn't have the freedoms I yearned for. I would wind up as a servant no matter what I did, no matter where I originated.

But I would be free to love, free to have children, free to have a family. Perhaps that was the only thing I could ever gain if I wasn't Luxian. Maybe I would go out with Miles. I shook my head a little too forcefully at that, causing my temples to pound. The thought left me as quickly as it came. He was my best friend's twin and entirely off limits. Miles was nice, some might say attractive even, but he would only ever be like a brother to me.

Flustered, I quickly turned around, with the intent of making yet another boring lap around the halls, when I bumped into something firm and strong. Whatever hard, solid surface I'd crashed into, I did it forcefully enough, causing my feet to go off balance that I fell forward. Under my breath, I cursed at myself for being so clumsy, for yet again tumbling into something, further injuring my bruised ribs.

I braced myself for the hard landing, but it never came. When I opened my eyes, clearing my thoughts, I realized that I landed directly on top of a male.

# ELEVEN
## SCOTLIND

His black hair was a messy mop on top of his head, completely obscuring his eyes. One of my hands was pressed flat against his chest, making it impossible not to realize how sculpted he was beneath it.

The male shook his head, pushing his hair out of his eyes to gaze up at me. Dread and humiliation crept in as I realized I was still lying on top of him. My deceitful body betrayed me by deciding now that it didn't want to move. I just laid there, frozen, as every inch of me was pressed into every inch of him. I had never been this close to a male before, besides perhaps kicking or punching one. I didn't know how to act. I knew I should get up. I should move. I should say sorry, say anything, do something other than just lie there.

I stopped breathing as his hand came up from the floor and wrapped around my waist. My heart fluttered as a different kind of fear and excitement pulsed through me.

It took me a good second to realize that he'd grabbed me to push my body off of his. Heat rose in my cheeks as I flushed harder.

"I'm sorry," I finally stuttered as I took the hint and stood. He followed suit, reaching his full height. I had to crane my neck up to see his face.

He cleared his throat. I thought I saw a glimmer of a smile on his face, but I whipped my head to the ground before I could be certain. My own gaze narrowed in on my white boots. I was going to burn a hole right through them.

My fingers nervously reached for a long strand of my hair. But the curl became knotted and tangled on my finger, probably from whatever product Vallie put in it to maintain the waves. I put my hands back down, pressing them against my thighs.

"What's your name?" His voice was deep, rougher than I expected.

"What? Mine? It's um…" I paused. Why was I so nervous? I was acting as if I'd never spoken to the opposite sex before. Which was stupid because I had, numerous times. I was practically surrounded by them during class. "It's Scottie."

"Okay, Scottie. May I ask what exactly you are doing in the hall alone, staring out a window, may I add, when the banquet is going on in there?" he gestured toward the ballroom. I could feel his stare bore into me as he looked me up and down.

I refused to meet his gaze.

When I didn't answer, he added, "Based on the fact that your left wrist isn't branded and your lack of attention to your surroundings, I would not presume you're here to guard."

Right. I was in my guard uniform. I tried to not bare my teeth at him as anger rose up inside me.

"I'm not a guard, not yet anyway. I'm in training, or I was in training. I just had my Trials."

"That doesn't answer why you are in the hall alone."

"I was told to guard the outer rim," I seethed, not knowing why any of this was his business.

"Goddess save us if this is the person protecting us tonight. She can't even walk straight," a voice sounded from behind me. I spun around only to realize that three other males loomed behind me, who had all witnessed this fiasco. Great.

They all wore the black leather uniform of the King's Guard. Tennebris' twin pink moons seal glimmering on each of their chests. The dark-haired male that I fell on ignored the comment. I had a weird sensation that he recognized me from somewhere with how thoroughly he was assessing me.

"I can tell that you're training to be a guard by your uniform. Are you not qualified to be considered for queen then?"

Something about his tone of voice, the question, and his stare unsettled me. Like he was mocking me. "I'm qualified," I said slowly, my voice almost a growl. "I just don't want to."

The other males gasped as their eyes went wide in shock, but the dark-haired male just smirked, or I thought he smirked. I still refused to look at him.

A guard behind me questioned, "Why the hell not?" He was balding and was unusually large for our kind. He sneered at me, revealing stained, yellow teeth. "Every female was told that they have to attend by the king's request. That is the law. You have no choice if you are selected. You can't just decide it's not for you." I could smell the reek of his breath from where I stood as his words shot at me.

"You are correct. Every female has to attend, and here I am—attending. As far as I'm aware, it isn't the law to have to dress up and parade myself around for some arrogant male I don't know, nor someone I have no intention of marrying. Now, if you will excuse me, I have to go."

The dark-haired male let out a low laugh. I just wanted to get away from them. I started to leave, but the bald guard grabbed me by my waist before I even took a step, holding me taut in place. He was faster than I thought he'd be.

"You need to show more respect," he breathed as he pressed his body against my back. Then he grabbed my neck with one thick hand and my waist with the other, forcing me into a deep, low bow. "You cannot talk to your future king that way. You should be bowing, showing your fealty."

I reacted without thinking. Taking the guard by surprise, I elbowed his sternum as I twisted out of his grasp and kicked him as hard as I could between his legs. The guard toppled to the floor, one hand clutching his chest, the other his groin. His breaths were raspy as he glared up at me.

Then his words sunk in.

*Future king.*

He said future king. That would mean that the handsome, dark-haired male was… Goddess above. I swallowed the lump rising in my throat.

"Enough. Leave us," the prince said, not taking his gaze off of me. "I'd like to speak with her alone."

The other two males did as he requested and immediately left us. The one on the ground hesitated for a moment before wobbling off. He casted one last glare at me over his shoulder before he disappeared behind the corner.

I shifted awkwardly on my feet, finally daring to meet his gaze. My face reddened even deeper as I saw it was very obviously Prince Noren standing before me. With his height, the way he held himself, his lithe body that I'd just had my hands on moments ago. He wore a dark suit that obscured the muscles beneath. One button was left undone on his shirt that revealed pale skin, a striking contrast to his dark features. He was even more handsome and captivating up close.

I took in his sharp appearance, now settled on me. His strong jaw fashioned in a half-smile, his dark hair that had a slight wave to it as it curled over his ears and fell to the middle of his neck. If only I'd actually made eye contact with him before and hadn't been so nervous, I might have saved myself from this embarrassment.

"Are you alright?" he asked, his eyes narrowing on me.

"I…" I started, then stopped. He should not be asking me if I was fine. I was the one who fell on him. I fell on the *prince*. "I am truly sorry for falling on you. I wasn't looking where I was going. I will be more careful," I said as I tried to walk away for a second time.

I managed to take all but three steps past him when he said, "What? You can't have a conversation with the guy you so adamantly don't want to marry, or as you said, *parade yourself around for?*"

I stopped dead in my tracks. My breathing rose, coming out in heavy, uneven pants.

"I'm sorry," I half mumbled, completely mortified, still facing away from him. "I didn't know. I mean… I didn't know who you were. I never would have said that to your face."

"But you did, and now you can't even look at me?" he laughed, amusement lingering in his voice.

Taking one long breath, I slowly turned around to face him. "I'm really sorry, your majesty. I didn't mean to insult you… or fall on you."

"*Your majesty?*" he huffed. "Just moments ago, I was arrogant. Now you want to give me a title?"

I didn't know what to say. I cursed myself for using the word *arrogant*. I didn't know him. The only time I'd even heard him speak was during his interview at the King's Tournament. Then it dawned on me. He was injured just days before, stabbed in his back through to his abdomen. My entire weight had been crushing his body when I refused to get off him.

"Did I hurt your wound?" I asked as I instinctively reached out to touch him. My fingers lingered on his stomach. The comment one of the girls on the van said about his abs came back to me, and I immediately drew my hand back. I wrapped them around my elbows so I couldn't do anything else that I'd regret later.

Did I really just reach out to touch him, and I called him *your majesty*?

"So you were watching me?" he remarked with a cocky grin.

"What? No… I… I mean…" I let out a breath. "The whole school was watching the tournament. Not watching you. Just in general, watching. We had to."

"Last I checked, it wasn't mandatory to watch the tournament. Encouraged maybe, but not mandated."

My cheeks burned as I felt the temperature in the room rising. I shifted my weight from side to side, unsure of what to say back to him. I didn't even know what I was saying and I was making this so much worse for myself. I had to go back to patrolling the rim. If Professor Hale, or worse Kole, saw me talking to him, I would be in so much trouble.

"Tell me," he purred, "why do you want to be a guard?"

Such a simple question, but I couldn't give him my real answer. I couldn't tell him that I was only doing this so that I never had to take a husband. I could never let someone get to know me. I could never be intimate with someone and risk exposing my back, exposing what I truly was.

I couldn't say that I wanted to be a guard for myself. I wanted to be strong and be able to defend myself. I never wanted to repeat that night eleven years ago when I was kidnapped, abducted against my will. I didn't want to admit that my past still haunted me, clinging to me like a shadow.

So instead of answering his question, I deflected, "Why do you want to know?"

"I find you curious."

"My father was a guard," I lied. I didn't even know who my father was. I also realized my mistake as he'd probably seen my folder during the Trials yesterday, not that he would even remember me.

"I see." He seemed to know I wasn't telling the truth. "What was your father's name?"

Again, he asked a straightforward, innocent question.

"I would rather not talk about it," I said as I straightened, standing a little taller. "And I really have to get going."

Liar. I was such a liar, and he knew it. He gave me a knowing smile, but let me go.

———

I WAS STILL FLUSTERED when I ran into Professor Hale. "Scottie, what are you doing in the rim? The ceremony is about to start. They are going to announce the future queen. Come, you should be in the ballroom already."

"It's starting now? But Kole told me..." I started and stopped, realizing that Professor Hale had never assigned me to watch the halls. Why would he give me an assignment when I was only here as a guest?

I reluctantly followed Professor Hale back into the ballroom. He directed me to the only empty chair. A small white card that read, *S.*

*Rumor*, laid across it. I withered into the seat, glancing up at the stage just in time to see Prince Noren doing the same.

The same announcer from the tournament, Effin, pranced to the podium to start the ceremony. I tried and failed to calm myself down as Effin introduced the prince to the crowd. I blocked out the rest of Effin's welcome speech as I replayed my own conversation with him.

I sank lower into my chair as the humiliation set in. I reflected on every single word I'd spoken to him.

Suddenly, the room fell silent—so eerily quiet that you could hear a pin drop as everyone turned in their chair to stare in my direction. I turned my head too, to see if someone was entering the room, but no one was behind me.

Me. They were looking at me. I gave the girl sitting next to me a puzzled look as she nudged me in the arm. "What?" I whispered.

"It's you," she said as everyone's gazes burned a hole through me. "They called your name."

As if I didn't hear her right, Effin repeated, "Scotlind Mae Rumor. Please come to the stage."

The girl next to me pushed me up, practically forcing me out of my seat. What did I miss? Was I in trouble? I slowly made my way toward the stage. I saw Kole out of the corner of my eye, glaring at me along with everyone else. If looks could kill, I would have died a thousand times.

I finally reached the edge of the stage and ascended the carpeted stairs leading up to the podium. Prince Noren was pointedly looking out toward the crowd, his nostrils flaring. He was probably the only person in this room not gawking at me.

Effin took me by the hand. "Do you, Scotlind Mae Rumor, accept the High Council's demand to take Prince Sie Axel Noren, not only as your future king, but as your future husband? Do you accept to be the Princess of Tennebris, and once his coronation happens six months from now, become the queen?" The announcer's voice echoed across the entire room.

*I'm dreaming. I must be dreaming.* But I could feel Effin's touch. I noticed his warmth seeping into me as he squeezed my hand, encouraging me to answer. This wasn't a dream. It was a nightmare.

"No," I blurted, the words flying past my lips before I could stop myself. Gasps fluttered through the crowd. I swallowed, glancing up toward the High Council, not having enough courage to look at *him*. I could make out every wrinkle and frown animated on their faces as they flared with disgust.

I tried to recover. "What I mean is, I'm sure there is someone else more suited."

Effin barked out an awkward, fake chuckle, but didn't say anything. One of the males from the High Council rose to face me. My gut twisted as I noticed him immediately. He had the same slicked-back, greasy hair from my ranking evaluations.

"Surely, miss, we heard you wrong," Synder suggested. His voice was harsh, sending chills down my spine. "To refuse a demand from the High Council is to refuse the kingdom and King Lunder himself. Welcomed or not, you were lucky enough to be chosen as the future Queen of Tennebris. Mind your words, as I'm sure you aren't trying to commit treason right now before this gathering." He smiled at me, but it was anything but warm and welcoming.

Why were they asking if it wasn't a choice? I gritted my teeth as I answered, "Yes."

"Yes to what exactly, Miss Rumor?" Synder sneered.

My heart pounded in my chest as I realized he would force me to say it. The reality of my situation was sinking in. My breath hitched as I managed to say, "I accept the engagement."

Synder gestured lazily toward the announcer to continue. Effin didn't miss a beat as he turned toward where the prince was still sitting. I finally found the courage to glance in his direction. He hoisted himself up from the elaborate throne-like chair. Would he reject me? Would he say no? Would he have any sway in the matter if he changed his mind? He had a choice on who he could marry before, but did he give up his rights after winning the tournament?

Judging from the frown plastered on his face, it was safe to assume that he was just as disappointed in this arrangement as I was.

Moments before, when we'd talked on the rim, his gaze had been unfaltering, but now he wouldn't even look at me. Was he only being nice then because he didn't think I stood a chance of being selected?

"Do you, Prince Noren, take Scotlind Mae Rumor to be your fiancé?"

*Please say no, please say no,* I silently begged in my head, but Prince Noren responded with a resounding, "Yes."

The announcer, finally pleased, stepped away from me, and walked toward the podium with his hands spread wide. "Please join hands," he began, his voice booming. "There will be a full engagement ceremony later to come, but we must make sure your alignment is Goddess blessed." He looked far too theatrical to take seriously, but Prince Noren stepped forward, filling the space between us.

Effin started reciting some prayer, but his words were lost on me as the prince reached for my hands. His were rough and calloused, but his grip was light, barely touching my skin. This couldn't be real. I couldn't get married, and I certainly couldn't get married to *him*. This wasn't the plan.

I started breathing heavily as the panic sunk in. My biggest fear was coming true. This was what I'd worked so hard to avoid, and now it was happening. He would discover what I was. He was bound to see the Luxian markings on my back. Or worse, what if I fell pregnant and we had a child mixed with both abilities? What markings would an offspring have from both kingdoms? It didn't matter—any child we conceived would die immediately, and we'd both be sentenced to death for treason. Our schoolings taught us that back on Allium, an interbred child wouldn't survive their first breath. That was why our kingdoms lived separately—why we were never allowed to mix. That and the fear of what the collide of Light and Dark abilities could conjure.

Effin turned and faced the crowd as he spoke, "I present to you the Prince and Princess of Tennebris."

Prince Noren immediately dropped his hold of me. The crowd clapped quietly, but not in cheer or celebration. It was the kind of pathetic, soft clap where no one was really excited or happy about what was happening, but you had to proceed anyway. Before I could say anything, he stormed off the stage and disappeared. I guess that answered my question as to whether he was disappointed.

After that, the world around me blurred as everyone moved, making their way toward the exit. I knew if I focused my vision, if I blinked away the blur, I would be able to see the glares of jealousy and hatred.

But I couldn't bring myself to move. I stood glued to the center of the now empty stage. The weight of what had just happened was anchoring me down.

Distantly, I heard the gossip starting. I heard the females around me muttering, but I didn't care. My breathing increased, becoming faster and faster as I continued to suck in air, not able to get enough. I was going to die on the stage from lack of oxygen.

*It was just a dream. It was just a dream. It was just a dream*, I repeated to myself over and over again. But the muttering only got louder the more I pleaded.

"Can you believe it? The prince is so hot. I feel so bad for him that he has to marry *her*."

"She has nice eyes."

"Who is she?"

"What was she wearing?"

"Is this even allowed?"

"I can't believe she said no."

"How rude is she?"

"Our future queen is a bitch."

A voice came over the microphone, announcing that the banquet had officially ended and instructed everyone to go home.

That got me moving. Home. I would go home. I would sleep it off, wake up, and then this day would start all over again, the banquet not yet started. I walked back to the van like the dead walking to the grave. Once in the familiar vehicle, I found Vallie with swollen, red-rimmed eyes.

"Vallie, I…" I didn't know what to say, but I wanted to say something. I knew she wanted this. This was Vallie's dream, not mine.

"Congratulations." She smiled, but it didn't reach her eyes. Her signature large grin was diminished. "Let's talk when we get back to our dorm," she said as she moved to the seat across from me.

We rode the rest of the way in silence. This time, I didn't glance out the window or notice a single tree. It wouldn't matter anyway. I would never get to explore the forest or see the world.

I would be dead as soon as Prince Noren was crowned and we were forced to marry.

# TWELVE
## SCOTLIND

THE LONG RIDE TO LAKEWOOD GAVE ME TIME TO PROCESS the panic of what had just happened. Once we were back in our dorm, I told Vallie everything—about falling on the prince earlier that night to our conversation before I got called up on stage.

"I still can't believe you said no, Scottie," she laughed. The warmth had returned to her smile. "You should have seen the look on Yuri's face when your name was called, and you said *no*."

I laughed with her as I dodged the pillow she chucked at me. "I would of loved to see that." I paused, our laughter fading out together. "Vallie, what am I going to do?"

"What do you mean? You are going to marry the hottest, most badass guy in our kingdom and get to live life as an effing princess, and then a queen. I'm so jealous of you. In fact, I think every female in Tennebris is jealous of you."

"Vallie, I don't want this—any of it. I don't want to marry him. I can't."

She gave me a puzzling look. Vallie had always accepted that it was my life's dream to be a guard, but she never knew the real reason why. She never understood why I never took an interest in dating.

No one knew my secret. Not even her, although I'd wanted to tell

Vallie countless times. I thought about it over and over again and decided that she would likely react well to it. She wouldn't hand me over or think I was crazy. She would listen, understand even, but I also knew that telling her would put her in danger. One look into her head from a mind reader and they would mark her as a traitor just for knowing my secret and not coming forward with it. I couldn't do that to her. There had been countless times when I swore to myself that I was going to tell her. I opened my mouth to speak the words, but they never came out. I could never put her in that situation no matter how badly I wanted to confide in her.

"Look, Scottie, I know that you were never interested in guys before, for reasons I don't pretend to understand, but wow. You know that we don't get to decide what we want to be in this world. It's not always fair, but that's life. I know you worked really hard to get into the King's Guard and trained your butt off every day, but sometimes your path leads you in a different direction. And you are going to have to deal with it. I kind of don't want to hear you complain about having to marry the most attractive guy in the kingdom. Not to mention, the only rank five alive in Tennebris, which means you will go down in history. Our children and our children's children are going to read about you, study you, learn from you."

"I know, but—"

Vallie cut me off. "I know it hasn't always been easy for you, Scottie. I know how people treat you just because you don't have any abilities. But now you can change that. You can change everything. I know you've dreamed of showing the world what a badass female guard could do, but now, just show the world that you are a badass queen."

"I'm sorry," I whispered to her. I knew it was wrong to try to vent to Vallie. She wanted this so badly—to be chosen. And I was sitting here complaining about it. Guilt formed in my chest and embedded itself in every nook and cranny of my heart. I'd let my fear overtake me. Besides, it wouldn't change the outcome. Even if it felt like a death sentence, I had been chosen, and I would have to marry him whether I liked it or not.

And maybe Vallie had a point. Perhaps being the queen would give me the power to change what was wrong with our society. Maybe I could make a difference in how females and rank zeroes were treated. I could at least try until I was discovered, however long that may be.

Who was I kidding though? I was pretty sure being a princess or queen would grant me no power, no freedom to do as I pleased. I didn't think they even let the royals dress alone. There were servants for everything, and I would be monitored everywhere I went.

Would I be able to bathe by myself? Would they allow it if I asked? What would the prince expect of me when we were alone? I knew nothing about that kind of relationship.

*When* I was found out, I realized, because they would find out and discover my secret. I was a ticking time bomb with the fuse lit.

Vallie drew me from my thoughts as she clapped her hands together. "Come on, Scottie. Let's go to a party! You promised us a drink, and I think after tonight, we both need one."

"What?" I asked, surprised by the sudden change in conversation. I'd forgotten about the drink I had promised. I was so tired from the whirlwind of emotions.

"Tomorrow is our graduation, and this is our last full night together. Let's go out and celebrate before we are both stuck in lives we don't want. Let's just forget about everything and have fun tonight. Come on, please," she begged, giving me her biggest smile and puppy dog eyes. "You promised."

"Fine," I agreed reluctantly. "But only one drink."

"Good, because I already told Miles we are going, and he is on his way over here." She smiled as she hopped off her bed and reached for the bottle she was stashing under it. "And I already got the alcohol."

I grabbed the bottle from Vallie's hand and dragged it to my lips. Tipping my head back, I drank down a few gulps of the contents and almost gagged. "Ugh, it's awful," I coughed as I yanked the bottle away. Some of the clear liquid sloshed off the top. The strong scent of it filled my nostrils. It smelled like the cleaner the servants used in the public bathing rooms. "Why do you and Miles drink this all the time?"

She laughed. "I was going to suggest that we mix it with something first, but you grabbed it from me before I could say anything. Plus, I kind of wanted to see your reaction."

A knock on the door made me jump. More of the disgusting liquid from the bottle spilled over onto my hands. Vallie made her way over to the cabinet as I got up and opened the door, wiping my sticky palms on my thighs.

"Hi," I said, cracking the door and moving aside, allowing Miles room to come in.

"Hey," he replied as he plunked down on my bed. "I'm really going to miss this place."

"You're going to miss hanging out in a girl's dorm room?" Vallie teased as she poured out three drinks.

Our two sides of the room were opposites. Vallie's half was decked out in shades of pinks and reds. Floral sheets covered her bed, and beautiful paintings hung on the walls. Vallie loved to paint and had an eye for color. It was why she loved doing makeup so much. *The face is just an empty canvas meant to be filled with color and life,* she would always say when I complained about her taking too long to get ready.

My half of the room was bare with only a thin, gray comforter, an inflatable punching bag, and my gym gear. The only decoration was a lone painting hung above my bed that Vallie had gifted to me for Yulemas one year. She'd painted the three of us. Vallie hugging me from behind, wrapping her full arms across my bony collarbone. Miles was painted standing to the right of us and looked out of place. He had complained for days when Vallie gave it to me. He'd begged me to take it down, claiming he looked awkward. It only made us laugh and want to keep it up all the more.

I took my drink from Vallie as I settled down on the floor, not wanting to sit on my bed with Miles.

He broke the silence first, "So, how did it go? Anyone we know?" When none of us answered, he added, looking between the two of us, "The banquet, I mean. How was it? I can presume from your lack of excitement that you didn't win the prince's heart, sis. So who's the unlucky girl?"

I took a long, slow gulp from my drink, giving me time to think about how I could answer. I'd forgotten that Miles didn't know yet, that he wasn't at the banquet. The incident seemed like days ago, not hours. I was sure the news spread that a nix was chosen, but Miles came right to our dorm room. He didn't get the chance to hear the growing gossip.

Vallie looked over at me and gave me a small smile. As if reading my mind, she saved me from answering. "It's Scottie."

Miles spit his drink across the room as he went into a laughing fit so hard he was clutching his abdomen. He stopped once he realized we weren't joining in. He took in the grave seriousness of our faces. "Wait, really?" he asked, his voice coming out an octave higher than normal.

"Yes," Vallie whispered. "We aren't joking."

I didn't say anything. I couldn't. I opened my mouth to explain, but nothing came out. I turned away, but still felt Miles' stare boring through the back of my head. I took another long sip of my drink, this time finishing it.

A few awkward moments of silence passed. The stillness was heavy against my chest. Then Miles chucked his cup across the room as he cursed a slew of words. Pink fluid dripped down the brick wall.

"It's not right," he finally spoke, "to force you to marry him when you want nothing to do with—"

"Miles, stop." I cut him off as I twisted from where I sat on the floor. I looked up to meet his stare. "Please stop. This is one of our last nights together. Can we just not talk about it and have fun? Please," I pleaded, my voice breaking a bit. I could feel tears pooling in my eyes, threatening to spill out. I knew I sounded desperate, but I didn't care. I wanted to enjoy tonight with my friends.

He sighed loudly before looking down at me. "Fine," was all he replied before grabbing the bottle of alcohol from where Vallie had placed it on my nightstand and drank heavily from it.

I think alcohol might have been what I needed tonight. Vallie always said it helped her calm down and relax. That didn't sound so bad. The twins were both huge partiers, always trying to convince me to join them. I embraced the burn and flutters in my stomach as the pink, bubbling contents slipped down my throat. I giggled to myself, wishing I had joined them sooner.

I never had in the past because I wanted to wake up early and train. What a joke that was now. My old self would laugh at the sight of me, the situation I was in, betrothed and utterly tipsy. Two things I never thought I would be. But I wanted to forget about everything, just for tonight, so I continued to drink.

I didn't want to be stuck in my dorm room alone thinking about the prince and what marriage to him would be like. And I especially didn't want to think about what was going to happen once I arrived at the castle. *It's not like anyone would know I was from Lux just by looking at me,* my drunk self thought. My biggest concern should really *only* be the prince, and that's *only* if he sees me naked, and *only* if he looks at my back, and *only* if I was covered in water—or sweat.

I could avoid that. Easily. Just no baths with the hot prince, and I would be fine. I giggled at myself for being concerned earlier, for thinking this meant it would be my death.

But what about the figure in my dreams? The male on the beach with the lavender eyes eleven years ago. He knew about me. He knew the truth.

I took another long sip, finishing my second cup. Then I grabbed the bottle from Miles and drank more, this time not shuddering as it slid down my throat. "Okay," I smiled at my friends. "Let's drink."

———

As soon as we arrived at the party on the WestEnd of campus, I regretted my decision to come. I should have just convinced Vallie and Miles to drink with me in the dorm room. The place Vallie took us to was packed with Advenians, so tight I could barely move without pressing my body against strangers. I cringed every time someone's slick sweat grazed my arm. The music was blaring in my ears as the song vibrated in my bones.

And what was worse was that everyone was staring at us, at *me*.

The news of the prince's engagement—our engagement—had traveled like fire.

Vallie shrieked as she spotted a group of Advenians in the kitchen of the home. Grabbing my hand, with Miles tagging along behind us, she navigated us through the crowded room.

Miles whispered in my ear, "We could make it a drinking game, one sip for every girl that gives you the death stare."

I whirled on him, giving him that same death stare, and he laughed.

Vallie released my hand once we reached the group. She spoke in a rushed state with a girl I didn't recognize. Vallie was friends with everyone and I usually couldn't keep up with all their names, but this girl was beautiful. Her black coiled hair was tied in an updo revealing the dark, silky skin of her face. Her smile was dazzling and almost as infectious as Vallie's. I could see why they were friends. I couldn't make out anything the two of them were saying over the roar of the music.

One of Vallie's friends grabbed my hand and slipped the smallest cup I'd ever seen into my palm.

"A shot!" Vallie screamed over the music as everyone around us gathered in a semicircle, each holding a similar glass. "Let's toast to Scottie landing the hottest male ever!"

I wished Vallie hadn't said that because everyone in the group turned their attention to where I stood. There was a pause, long enough to make me think no one would agree to the toast, but then, slowly, everyone raised their small cups to meet their lips.

I internally groaned as I realized Yuri was among them. She gave me a nasty glare before throwing down the contents of her own drink and then turned her attention to the male next to her. I looked up at Miles. His jaw was clenched as he tipped his head back and drained his.

Vallie rotated, noticing my still full shot. "Come on, Scottie-cat, take it!" she said as she lifted the glass up to my lips.

"Okay, okay." I swatted her hand away, but took the shot. It was just as disgusting as the bottle we had in our room. I needed Vallie's drink-making skills to mask the bitter, gross taste of it.

I was about to tell her just that when a male I didn't recognize came up to Vallie and consumed her attention. She was laughing and smiling as she leaned heavily into his chest. I realized I wouldn't be hanging out with her tonight. My friend had a different life outside of our dorm room. Everywhere she went she became the life of the party. It suited her.

I took in my friend, her hair and makeup was still the same from the banquet, but she'd changed out of her long, pink dress and now wore a red one. It was simpler, more casual than the banquet attire, but she still looked absolutely stunning. I looked down at myself and huffed.

I anxiously pulled at the top of the black strapless dress Vallie had forced me into, which didn't take nearly as much convincing after all the drinks. Since I didn't have money, all I owned were Lakewood's required clothing—my school uniforms and my guard outfit—which Vallie protested over and over that I couldn't go to a party in either of them.

The more Advenians that filled the room, dancing against one another, the more claustrophobic I became. One person became two, and the floor was rising up. I couldn't tell if someone was casting their illusion projection ability on me or if it was a result of the drinks. Either way, I had to get out of here. I started to make my way through the house, each room just as crowded as the last.

Once outside, I let out a small, almost inaudible sigh of relief. The music still played, but it was softer and no longer pounded against my chest. I stretched my arms, rejoicing in the fact that I didn't hit another person.

Outside was much better. I looked around at where I was. I recognized the backyard through my foggy memory. I'd been here before. It had a beautiful high white fence, surrounding the vibrant, green grass and an artificial hot spring where steam constantly stirred above the surface. I imagined they paid a fortune to have a Luxian fire user heat the water to the perfect, non-scalding boil.

The spring was filled with people, most of them sitting and talking while sipping their drinks, but there were a few couples who melted into one another. Sitting on each other's laps with their tongues shoved down the other's throat. I didn't know where one body stopped and the other started. Realizing I was staring, I quickly looked away.

Even if my friends didn't tell me beforehand that this was Yuri's house, I would have known. I recognized that spring from the first time I met her. During year nine, Vallie told me she made a new friend and wanted me to tag along to go to her home. It started Yuri's feud with me when I refused to get into the water and swim with all the other girls. I had a panic attack when she tried to push me into the steamy liquid, which ended with a punch to Yuri's face. A broken nose later, I couldn't really blame her for hating me. It also caused a rift in Vallie's friendship with her, because ever since that night, Yuri loathed me with all her being. And as much as Vallie loved gossip and knew everything about everyone—partly because her ability of knowledge absorption never let her forget any meticulous detail—she hated drama and couldn't stand when someone spoke ill of someone else.

Most of the students at our school lived in the dorms. However, if someone was lucky enough to come from wealth like Yuri, they usually opted to reside at their parents' home.

Most wealthy Advenians found it difficult to adjust to the lack of electricity on campus. The residents of this side of the village were associated with the school in some way. It was a smaller section, but the richest in LakeWood, which explained the excessive access to electricity.

I was looking around the yard for so long that I didn't see Miles making his way toward me. I turned toward his sharpening figure and found him already staring at me, watching.

"So you're going to go through with it?" he questioned once he closed the gap between us.

"Go through with what?" I asked as I took the drink he offered me.

"Marrying him. You're going to marry that asshole."

I coughed, choking on the liquid as he openly called the prince an asshole in public. "Miles, what do you expect me to do? I have no choice in the matter. This wasn't my decision."

"Well, I just thought you were the only one who wasn't obsessed with him. When I found out it was you, I thought you would have found it difficult."

"And what makes you think I'm not struggling with this? What gives you the delusion that this is the best thing that has happened to me? Because it's not. I don't want this," I seethed, my voice growing louder. A few people turned to stare at us.

"It didn't seem like that earlier when Vallie told me. You didn't have anything to say except that you wanted to have fun tonight."

"I don't want this, Miles. I don't want to marry him. I just don't know what I can do about it," I whispered, fully aware of the attention we were amassing. I turned my back to the growing crowd and faced the wall as a tear slid down my cheek.

Miles let out a long sigh before grabbing my arm and leading me behind a tree I was sure Yuri's father paid a fortune for. Once we were alone, he turned to face me, positioning his body to block my view of the hot spring. Only inches apart now, he spoke softly, "Then don't, Scottie. Don't marry him. Don't go." He wiped away a single tear. His fingers were soft against my cheek, nothing like my own callused hands.

"You know I don't get to decide. I don't have a choice. None of us have a choice once the High Council declares our future," I said as the tears continued to flow.

"Please, Scottie. You must know how I feel about you. This is torture for me." He wiped more tears away before cupping my face with his hands. "Please don't marry him."

"What are you saying, Miles?" I blurted as I pried his hands away from my face and stepped back.

"If things were different, if you didn't have to marry him, would you be with me?"

"Miles, if I didn't have to marry him, I would be trying out for the guard and wouldn't be able to take a husband."

He let out a frustrated grunt. "Scottie, come on. You know what I'm trying to ask you. Would you be with me?"

"Miles, Vallie is my best friend, and you are her brother. I could never be with you." I couldn't believe what he was saying, what he was asking me. Some part of me guessed that he had feelings for me, but I never believed he would act upon them. I always thought they would be tucked away in a chest, buried deep in the ground, and never opened.

"I don't care about anyone else. That's not what I'm asking you. I'm asking you to think about just you and me. Forget about Vallie. Forget about everything." He bent down, leaning forward so that his lips were inches from mine. I could feel his breath against my cheek. I could smell the alcohol lingering on his lips, giving him courage. "Kiss me, Scottie. Just once," he breathed, his voice soft as he leaned forward, closing the small distance between us.

I jerked my knee up to meet his gut, and staggered out of his grasp.

"What are you doing?" I rasped. "You can't. We can't." I couldn't find the words to tell him that I didn't—*couldn't*—think of him like that. It didn't matter that I was now engaged or that he was Vallie's brother. I would never be with him. I could never be with anyone. I could never date someone in Tennebris. I tried to speak, to open my mouth to explain, but words left me.

Miles took a hesitant step toward me, still clutching his abdomen. "Scottie, please. Just this once. No one has to know."

"No." I didn't look to see his reaction as I stormed away from him. I had to get out of there before he could say anything else. Before he could do anything else. He was my best friend's twin. How could he think that was okay? Frustration rose up inside me, swirling around my chest like an angry storm brewing, ready to be let out. I sprinted toward the house, the crowd not seeming as daunting now. I wanted to get lost in it.

I didn't mind when someone shoved another drink in my hand. I didn't mind as I downed it. I didn't want to think about what Miles just said or what almost just happened.

A few drinks later, my mind was warm and fuzzy again. The

alcohol rushing through my veins making me loopy. I realized quickly that I already had a love-hate relationship with the liquid. I didn't like feeling out of control. I couldn't keep one thought straight in my head, but as a result, it made me forget about Miles. And the prince. And the banquet. And every other worry I had.

This was why people drank. It made you forget about everything. It took away your nervousness, your fears, your worries, and just made you feel happy and free. Laughing. I was laughing.

I didn't last very long inside and eventually found myself outside again. I leaned against the home's outside brick to support myself as the ground started to sway.

An unsettling feeling washed over me, like eyes were locked on me. I looked up and saw a male was watching me from across the yard. His shaggy, blonde hair and green eyes stuck out against the crowd. He looked familiar, but I couldn't pinpoint from where.

He crossed his arms over his lean build as his gaze was fixed solely on me. I didn't think much of it. People had been staring nonstop since the banquet. And I definitely didn't want to talk to another male tonight. I gave him a crude gesture, making it known that I knew he was staring. I thought he would turn away, but he just smiled and... kept staring.

I was about to march over to the blonde and give him a piece of my mind when a figure approached me from the side. I turned, expecting to see Miles again. "I'm sorry—" I started to say to him, but stopped when I realized who it was.

Kole.

He grabbed my wrist and dragged me across the lawn. "What are you doing? Let go of me." I think I slurred, but I honestly wasn't sure if I spoke the words at all. He kept dragging me along, causing me to trip and stumble over my own feet as he walked twice as fast.

"Shut up," he grumbled as he led me to the far corner of the yard, behind the same massive, secluded tree. The same tree Miles had taken me to earlier tonight. I decided that I now hated trees, at least this one in particular.

He threw me up against the trunk and pressed his body against mine, pinning me so I couldn't move.

"What are you doing? Get off..." I tried to yell, but it came out more in a slurred mumble. He covered my mouth with his fingers before I could say anything else. His hands were too large for my face —only my eyes were left out of his grasp. Gold circles flowed up his arm as a wave of nausea came over me. *No, no, no.*

"Don't scream, don't fight. You aren't allowed to leave my side until I say so," he compelled. His voice came out lighter, softer, almost musical. I didn't want to listen, but my brain, though dazed from the alcohol, was drawn to his compulsion.

I stopped fighting underneath his grip. My body went limp in his arms, waiting on the strings he held, waiting to obey.

"Good," he smiled. "Now look at me." My eyes moved on their own accord, darting up at him like shooting stars. His hips were still pressed against mine as he leaned his upper body back to peer down at me. I couldn't make out his expression. Frustration, maybe. Confusion and anger definitely.

"I don't know what game you are playing or what you're trying to do, but there is no fucking way someone like you is going to be the queen. You're nobody. You're not even worthy of being an Advenian. You're nothing but a nix. A mortal. A fucking human. You have no abilities, no fucking talent other than that pretty little face of yours. So tell me, how did you do it? Did you sleep your way to the top? Did you sleep with everyone on the whole fucking Council? What's your secret?"

He was still compelling me. I was about to answer him, the compulsion running through my veins, working its way up to my mouth when I heard footsteps approaching.

"Shit," he grunted before quickly releasing me and sprinted off. My body sagged as the weight of his left mine. His hold on me died with his fleeting figure.

I started trembling as I slid down the tree trunk, the bark digging into my back, causing my dress to ride up until I hit the ground.

He knew something was off about me. Did he suspect that I was not from the Dark Kingdom? No, he couldn't. I had been careful. There was no way he could have seen my back.

This was a mistake. I shouldn't have come. I wasn't friends with anyone here but Vallie and Miles. I didn't know where Vallie ran off to, and I didn't want to face Miles again tonight.

Two strong hands pulled me up off the ground, stopping my thoughts. I gasped as I looked into Prince Noren's rugged eyes. I couldn't turn my gaze from his, but this time it was from my own free will. His eyes were beautiful. Not only the color, which was so dark they were almost black, but the shape of them. Elongated and sharp. They were striking.

His eyes narrowed on mine as if he was staring right through me, analyzing everything about me. His expression was taut as he held me up. His arm wrapped around my waist to steady my uneven gait. Then everything spiraled. I started seeing four eyes. I looked at him, puzzled, "Why are there two of you?" A squeak of a giggle followed my question.

"Are you okay?" he asked, genuinely seeming concerned, or was it just the alcohol making it seem that way? "Did he hurt you?"

Kole. Oh yeah—he was just here. My thoughts were getting more jumbled as the time ticked on.

When I didn't answer he scanned me from head to toe, his eyes raking over my body. Then, "How much did you drink?"

"I haven't... I mean, yeah."

His eyebrows furrowed as I giggled louder.

I shuffled forward, but my foot caught on a root, causing me to stumble headfirst into him. I really hated this tree. My hands landed on his chest to keep myself from falling. His arm tightened around my waist, steadying me further. My fingers pulsed against his muscles, trailing down his abdomen before I realized what I was doing.

"How are you here? Is someone casting an illusion on me?" I asked, more to myself than to him.

"It's not an illusion. I was sent here after the banquet. Once you were announced as my bride, the High Council thought it best that I attended your graduation. I'm staying at one of the inns in LakeWood."

Not an illusion. He was here, in LakeWood, at this party, holding me up.

"Why are you at this party?" I slurred into his chest as my hands continued to roam.

"My friend, Peter, was watching you. He said you had too many drinks and that some males were giving you a hard time," the prince said with a seriousness that had taken over his features.

"Well… I had everything handled with…" I mumbled as I moved my hands up his chest. "Why are there two of you?"

"Why do you think?" he smirked.

"I think…. I think that the girl was right."

"What girl?" he asked, amused.

"The one from the van who said you had nice abs," I giggled, leaning into his chest. I told myself it was just for support. I inhaled, taking in his strong scent. Cedarwood and something else, something muskier. My mind whirled as I watched his four eyes focus on me. The liquid stirred as my stomach clenched in response.

Spinning. Everything was spinning. Faster and faster until I became so dizzy that I thought I was going to faint.

"Come on. Let's go," he said as he repositioned his hold on me, grabbing my wrist in his hand as he started walking back toward the door. I thought I saw Miles out of the corner of my eye, a sullen look on his face.

"Where?" I tried to protest as I stomped my foot on the ground. The motion made me trip—again. He caught me in one swoop, bending over to scoop me up. The last thing I remembered was listening to his heartbeat against my ear and smelling his neck.

# THIRTEEN
## SCOTLIND

I WOKE UP THE NEXT MORNING WITH MY GUT WRENCHING and my head feeling like it was about to explode. Tiny nails were being hammered into my skull while acid filled my insides, threatening to spill out. Still curled on my side, I slowly peeled my eyes open. I only managed to pry them to slits before I clamped down and rubbed my temples. The sun was too bright through the window.

"Morning, sleeping beauty," Vallie laughed as images from last night came flashing before me in broken bits. It was like putting together a puzzle with only half the pieces. Fragments of Miles trying to kiss me, Kole threatening me, and the prince carrying me in his arms.

*The prince.*

*Carrying me.*

Goddess above. But then what? My mind was blank. How did I get back here? Did he carry me all the way across campus back to my dorm? Was he still here? With that horror, I pried my eyes open and bolted straight up in my bed.

Scanning the room with newfound vigor, I let out a sigh when only Vallie's amber eyes were staring back at me.

I slumped back into my bed, nausea creeping its way up my throat from the movement. I leaned back, hoping to land on my pillows, but instead, my head slammed into the wall. I groaned, rubbing the new bump until my fingers became entangled with the knots in my hair.

Vallie skipped over to me and plopped down on my bed. I didn't know how she could be so lively. "So, tell me everything!"

"What happened last night? How did I get back here?" was all I could muster.

"What? You don't remember? How lame. I wanted to hear all about it," she frowned, pouting her gloriously red lips. "I was looking for you all over the party and couldn't find you. Then Miles told me that you left with the prince. I didn't even know he was in LakeWood, but everyone was talking about it. I'm dying to know what happened."

I recoiled deeper into my pillow as the volume of her voice escalated with each word. "You and me both," I winced. "I didn't know he was here either. I barely remember any of it, and I definitely don't remember coming back to our dorm."

Vallie's dress I had on last night was folded neatly on my chair. My eyes shot to what I was wearing now. A black shirt that barely reached my mid-thigh was in its place.

My gut curdled, and I really thought I was going to vomit. This wasn't my shirt. I tried to sort out my thoughts, to remember what happened. An image of me leaning against something black and touching a muscular abdomen was now stirring front and center.

*No, no, no.* This couldn't be happening.

Vallie seemed to come to the same conclusion I had. "It's okay, calm down," she said, but it was no use. I started hyperventilating.

I still had my undergarments on, so nothing could have happened, right? But then the thought of him even seeing me in my underwear made me go red. I couldn't decide if I was more embarrassed or enraged. I threw my hands over my head, flopping back down against the mattress as I groaned, not even caring that I landed on my sore ribs. "I hate alcohol."

Vallie pried softly as if aware I was treading water, "You really don't remember anything?" When I shook my head, she added,

"Relax. I'm sure nothing happened, and even if it did, he will be your husband soon, right?"

She gently rose from my bed to finish getting herself ready. "Come on. You overslept, and our graduation is soon. We have to start getting ready."

"Right," I said as I followed suit and agonizingly lifted myself from the comfort of my bed.

Vallie was right. We were getting married, so it wouldn't be a big deal to anyone else, but it was to me. I wanted to remember my first time. I never thought I would even get a first time, but now that it was an unavoidable reality for me, I wanted to remember it. Maybe even enjoy it. Because the first time I had sex with someone from Tennebris, it would probably be my last.

———

WHEN WE FINALLY REACHED THE Great Hall where our graduation was being held, I couldn't help but notice the decorations and lights hung up for the celebration. Sparkling, twinkling strings hung low from the ceiling. It was beautiful. It was like looking at the night sky while still being indoors. I knew that LakeWood only splurged with the lights because Prince Noren was here. They just wanted to make a good impression for the future King of Tennebris. Normally, the only light was the dingy overhead one that hung in the center of the room. The Hall usually required many candles and torches on the walls to make it visible during the winter months or when the sun was blocked by clouds, but now it was blinding.

The front of the Hall had plastic chairs lined up facing the stage, similar to the banquet, just without the overly large ribbons. The back was filled with tables of different arrays of foods and drinks. My stomach growled in response, and I wanted nothing more than to stuff my face with whatever cheese and meat platters were on display.

As we were ushered to sit down in the chairs that corresponded with our names, I realized that the food would have to come later.

Our principal stepped toward the microphone directly in the center of the stage—another luxury in honor of Prince Noren.

He began addressing the room, "Congratulations to this year's graduating class. It has truly been a blessing to teach each and every one of you here at LakeWood. With one hundred and eleven students here today, this is the largest class LakeWood has ever seen. You should all be proud. I urge you to remember your fundamentals as you begin to navigate your way through your wonderful new careers. Take the life path given to you with pride as you officially join the Tennebrisian society. But know that LakeWood will always be a home to you."

He paused, glancing around the room. "Now without further ado, we will continue with what I know you have all been patiently waiting for. You want to know your official rankings and how you placed in the Trials. Let me explain how this will proceed. I will call you up one at a time to announce your official ranking. You will be given a folder by one of your former professors, detailing your ranking and what it means within your specialties.

"If you have a career path that requires higher education, there will be information provided about one of the two universities you must attend. Not everyone has been granted what they Trialed for. However, I think many will be pleased with how you placed. What is detailed in your folder is permanent. Whatever the High Council deemed as your job is final. There is no changing it.

"Before you walk off the stage, you will sit in the chair over there and get your ranking burned onto the back of your left wrist. Remember to wear your rankings proudly from this day forward. Every rank is crucial and important to ensure our society continues to blossom. Each number comes together to make a whole."

Principal Myers continued to ramble, but all my attention was directed at the man standing to the side of the stage. A boiling iron cauldron with six different pokers to brand us with stood waiting, labeled from zero to five.

Everyone seemed antsy. I knew I would feel the same—anxious to find out my fate if I didn't already know what my future held. I knew my ranking would be a zero. And I was sure my folder consisted of information on the kingdom and the duties of being a princess.

I zoned out for the remainder of the speeches that I didn't realize when the ceremony officially started. With the seats alphabetically arranged, my last name landed me a spot in the second row to the back.

"Miles Acker Hartlin. Rank three." I couldn't help but smile as Miles strode toward the stage.

"Valerina Alice Hartlin. Rank two," Principal Myers continued. Good. Vallie could get an excellent job with a rank two. I would have to ask both of them what was listed in their folders.

Miles barely flinched as he got his *three* burned into his flesh. Vallie didn't handle hers as well when the male burned a *two* into hers right after. She wasn't used to pain and let out an audible cry. As she made her way back down the steps, I saw a few tears streaking down her cheeks as she cradled her wrist. I seethed. It was barbaric, forcing everyone to be burned. I wanted to walk up and punch the man for hurting her.

The row before me was filing out one by one, going up the stairs, having their rankings declared, receiving their folders, and proceeding to the chair where they would get their number permanently burned into their flesh. Branding them. Labeling them. Making their worth to the society known. Most students let out a wince, a few flinched, some cried.

It was finally my turn as the person before me, Ali Kern Rabbe, had already gone across the stage.

"Scotlind Mae Rumor." As I stood and walked through the now empty aisle toward the stage, I noticed the prince sitting on one of the chairs along the side of the Hall. Great.

The same shaggy blonde-haired male with the striking green eyes filled the seat next to him. They looked funny sitting next to each other, a complete contrast. The male from the party seemed happy and warm. He had an infectious smile that seemed permanently plastered to his beautiful face. While the prince gave off the persona of someone you wouldn't want to be alone with.

"Rank zero," Principal Myers declared.

I tore my eyes away from the two of them and continued up the stage. The word zero seemed to clang through the Hall as I walked, echoing with each footstep that took me closer and closer to the stage, sealing my fate.

No one clapped for me as I ascended the stairs to shake the hands of the professors standing before me. Professor Hale handed me my folder, which was surprisingly thicker than I thought it would be, then ushered me to the other side of the stage. The side with the chair.

Ali had just finished with her burning. She was holding her left wrist so tight that I thought it would fall off as she walked down the stairs.

I took the now empty seat as the male performing the burnings stalked over to the cast iron cauldron. He pulled out the poker with the large zero on it and swung it out.

My eyes were drawn to the bright, red ash falling to the ground around the poker as he sauntered over to me. Steam radiated off the iron. Embers trailed in his wake on the floor beneath him, indicating the path he took each time to dip the pokers in the flaming hot coals. I couldn't stop reliving my nightmare. I was going to get burned again, but this time I had to sit still and wait for it to happen. It took everything in me not to freak out in front of all these people, to try to act like this wasn't killing me on the inside.

I held my breath as I positioned my left wrist for him to burn and closed my eyes. But the pain never came to my outstretched hand.

Cold fingers clamped down around my other side, then I gasped as he adhered the poker to my right wrist. An intense ache radiated up my arm as the iron lingered on my skin much longer than it should have.

Everyone halted and looked at me. Principal Myers stopped calling out names and turned his gaze over to see what was happening. I was still stunned, frozen in place, with my left arm stretched out to brand. But instead, a big, red zero was seared on the skin of my right.

"Why did you do that?" Professor Gibs yelled as she took a step toward us, her cane thudding on the stage. "She was holding her left wrist out. It has to be the left. Now you have to burn the poor girl again."

I looked up at the male as he walked back to the burning cauldron to reheat the zero iron poker. "I'm so sorry. An honest mistake. It's been such a long day. I wasn't paying attention."

"Wasn't paying attention?" Professor Gibs howled. "Are you telling me that you aren't paying attention as you burn our students? Do we need to get someone else in here to do your job?"

"No. It won't happen again," he promised.

I was sure it wouldn't.

I continued holding my left arm out. It was far worse knowing the pain to come, but I didn't have a choice. Everyone must have their rankings burned on their left wrist. They wouldn't let me leave the stage without it.

A few seconds later, he came back with the same zero iron, freshly steaming, as he pressed it into my left wrist. This time I didn't close my eyes, and I could have sworn there was a glimmer of a smile on his face.

Principal Myers collected himself enough to continue with the ceremony. As the poker left my flesh for the second time, Professor Gibs gave me a weary look before hobbling back to her spot on the stage. I stood up from the chair and narrowed my eyes at the male, my legs shaking. He chuckled.

*Chuckled.*

Like he wanted to hurt me. Like his actions were intentional. Was he mad that a nix was going to be the queen? Was this some sick reminder of what I was? Because now, every time I looked down at my hands, angry zeroes would greet me, always reminding me what I was to these people. Reminding me that my worth to them was nothing.

Movement from the corner of the room caught my eye as I made my way back to my seat. The prince was standing up, his fists clenched at his sides, his sights set on the male performing the burnings. The blonde next to him tugged his shoulder and forced him back down, whispering something into his ear.

Then his green eyes glanced at me, offering a small smile. The pity was worse than the nasty glares I received from everyone else. I quickly looked away as Principal Myers said, "Kole Michael Sanders." Kole stood, then stalked toward the stage. "Rank four."

Everyone clapped as Kole's smug face crossed the stage. He didn't flinch as the number four was burned into his wrist. The hot iron lingered on Kole's flesh for one heartbeat, leaving his skin pink and only slightly raised.

I looked down at my own throbbing wrists. My left wrist was similar to those around me. Pink with minimal flesh gone, but enough to make out the number. My right wrist was angry and raw, painful and fuming red, indicating he'd left the iron on for too long. Some of my skin was sloughing off and fell onto my clothing as the throbbing made it hard to focus on the rest of the ceremony.

I knew deep down I wasn't a zero. I had Luxian abilities of some kind. Even though I'd been too scared to test them out and see what they were. My markings on my back told me otherwise. I wasn't nothing. I wasn't a zero. The burns on my wrists shouldn't matter to me, but I tugged the sleeves of my shirt down to hide as much of the numbers as possible.

I couldn't help feeling for the people who were truly rank zeroes. It made me furious that our society publicly ranked us to show who was better than the others. It made me feel small and insignificant. It shouldn't be this way. People shouldn't be made to feel inferior to others based on a number. And that number shouldn't determine the outcome of our entire lives, but it did. I looked down at my wrists, the top of the zeroes poking out from beneath my clothes.

For my entire life, two zeroes would be staring back at me anytime I did anything. Anytime I threw a punch, or took a sip of water, or braided my hair. I would see them. A reminder that I was a nix.

That I was nothing.

# FOURTEEN
## SCOTLIND

AFTER EVERYONE'S NAMES WERE CALLED, PRINCIPAL MYERS gave his final words before leaving us to enjoy our last night at Lake-Wood. Tomorrow, we would no longer be students, we would be essential members of our society.

A light hum stirred around the room as everyone was full into celebrating. A large number of students and faculty members gathered around the refreshments, chatting amongst themselves. And that was exactly where I planned to go after I found Vallie and Miles to congratulate them on their rankings.

I started to search for Vallie in the crowd, scanning the room for vibrant, red hair as the blonde guy from the party walked over to me.

"You were watching me, *stalking* me," I blurted when he was close enough to hear me.

He laughed lightly as he held out his hand for me to shake. "I'm Peter. I'll be Sie's second." He flashed a half smile, exposing deep dimples on his silken cheeks. "And," he added, "I would call it *protecting* you, not stalking."

"So you followed me to a party, watched me the entire night, and call that protection? Last I heard, that's not in the job description of a future second to the king. Some title you've got there."

His smirk turned wide, revealing straight, white teeth. "Sie's my friend. I would be happy to do whatever he asks."

"So he asked you to watch me?"

"Yes. He knew you were drinking for the first time and wanted to make sure you didn't get into any trouble."

"How did he know it was my first time or that I was even drinking?" I snapped. My voice was getting louder as I narrowed my eyes. "And I don't need a babysitter."

"It didn't seem that way last night," he teased softly, pointedly ignoring my first question. I jerked myself into standing taller, straighter, even though it barely made a difference. He was average height for an Advenian male, but I still only reached his chin.

"So was it you that told him to come?"

"Yes."

"I didn't need your help, or his for that matter."

"I beg to differ." His smile sent any ounce of patience and reserve I had out the window.

I half growled as I stepped toward him, closing the gap. "I don't need you watching me and acting all noble like you came to my rescue. Leave me alone. I can take care of myself, and I prefer to not have some pretty boy stalking me."

His light demeanor faltered, his lips went taut, forming a straight line. "I had to watch not one, but two different males approach you last night. One of which tried to kiss you, and the other had you pinned against a tree. On top of that, you could barely walk straight. So I would think again before you yell at me saying you can handle yourself."

I huffed, not bothering to try to hide how angry I was. "So what? You're just going to follow me around everywhere I go?"

I tried to mask how mortified I was about his admission to everything he'd witnessed. I willed my face into a calm expression. The thought of this stranger seeing Miles and Kole with me at the party was unsettling, and I had a sinking feeling that he relayed everything he saw to the prince.

"I will if you insist on acting like a child and go around getting drunk around asshole males who can't control themselves. But no, Scotlind, I'm not going to follow you everywhere you go. I'm one of the few Advenians Sie trusts. I hope you can learn to trust me too. I'm not here to make your life more difficult, but to look out for you." He paused. "I am happy to hear that you find me pretty, though."

I went to open my mouth to snap some retort back at him, but he cut me off. "We can discuss my good looks later. For now, we have to go."

"Go where?" I asked as my glaring expression changed to confusion.

He looked at me curiously, as if I should have known the answer. "To the monorail. We're heading back to the castle tonight, and you need to pack if you haven't already."

"Tonight…" I started to say. "But the graduation just started. I thought I wasn't leaving until the morning. The monorail—it's closed at night, isn't it? It shouldn't even be running now." I was unable to keep the pathetic pleading sound from my voice.

"The monorail is closed to the general public overnight, but not for the High Council and future king. I'm sorry, but it's an order that we leave tonight. We have a strict schedule to follow. Your belongings will be taken there by our guards. We will have our own transportation to take us to the rail, so you have to get ready. Sie will meet you outside your dorm in an hour."

He looked toward me sympathetically. That pitying expression again creeping over his face, but it wouldn't change anything. Not if it was ordered for us to leave. I wanted to spend tonight with Vallie. I thought I had one more night with her.

"Can I at least say goodbye?" I wasn't opposed to fighting him if he said no. I would go kicking and screaming before leaving here without giving Vallie a hug.

"Sure," he replied. "Just make it quick."

I found Vallie and Miles standing by one of the food tables. Miles noticed me first and had the decency to look slightly embarrassed.

When I reached them, Vallie's smile brightened. "Scottie-cat! Yay, you found us. You have to try this," she commanded delightfully as she wolfed down whatever food was on the table. I'd never seen such an assortment at LakeWood before. I couldn't tell if whatever Vallie was moaning over was meat, cheese, or something else entirely.

My eyes started tearing up as I realized this would probably be the last time I saw her. My carefree, wild, loving best friend.

Vallie noticed my mood and stopped eating, her food still pocketed in her cheeks. She took my hands in hers and leaned in to whisper in between chewing, "Scottie, are you okay? It was so cruel to burn both of your wrists. Do they still hurt?"

She turned my wrists over to inspect them. Out of the corner of my eye, I saw Miles staring at the right one before I pulled away. "No, I'm fine. Congratulations. What's in your folder?"

She swallowed her remaining food, then smiled broadly. "You are now looking at the new Human Relations professor of LakeWood Elementary, and..."—she gestured to Miles—"the newest recruit of the AASP of Tennebris."

My smile was genuine. I beamed at both of my friends. "Congratulations, that's amazing, and for your rankings too."

Vallie would make a fantastic teacher. She loved children and had always been fascinated by the mortals that dwelled on Earth. I couldn't think of a better career for her.

I turned toward Miles. "Maybe you could still fulfill our childhood fantasy of finding us a planet to live on." I meant it as a joke, but my words came out in a choking sound, catching in my throat.

"Anything for you," he replied.

"Yeah, yeah. Enough talk about our future. Tonight we are stuffing our faces with whatever this amazing gooey stuff is and stealing the champagne from the professors' table." Vallie laughed lightheartedly as she pointed to the nearest assortment of food.

I took a step toward her, wanting to follow, wanting to celebrate, and spend the entire evening with her. We both agreed to not go to bed tonight so we wouldn't miss a minute of our last night together. My eyes filled with tears, and this time I couldn't stop them from falling.

"Scottie, what's wrong?" she asked delicately as Miles took a tentative step toward me, then hesitated.

"I want to… I want to spend tonight with you, with both of you," I choked out, the words catching in my throat. I meant it. I didn't care what happened with Miles last night. I was going to miss both of them. "But I'm leaving. I have to go to the castle."

Vallie's eyes bulged. "What? I thought we still had tonight."

I shook my head as more salty tracks broke free and rushed down my face. "I thought so too, but I have to leave now."

She engulfed me in a big hug. "I love you," she cried into my shoulder, soaking my shirt. "I love you so much, Scottie-cat. Don't you ever forget it."

"I love you too, Vallie. You're my family."

We hugged each other tighter, not wanting to let go, not caring about who was watching. I didn't know how I got so lucky throughout my time here for Vallie to befriend me. To have her welcome me into her family, practically kidnapping me on the holidays and forcing me to come with her because she knew—she knew I would have otherwise spent them alone. Vallie was the reason for me not falling apart on numerous occasions. She was the glue that held me together. I didn't know who I would be without her.

Vallie reached inside her pant pocket and fished out a small blue box with a white ribbon on it. "Don't open it now," she smiled in between tears, a bit of her red lipstick smeared onto her chin. "Or it'll make me cry more."

Once I pulled away from her, Miles stepped forward and embraced me. "Be careful," he murmured into my ear.

I gave him a small smile as I whispered back, "You too, and take care of Vallie for me."

"Always," he responded. This could be the last time I would ever see them.

I stepped back. "Thank you for everything," I said to them both as I made my way back to where I had left Peter. I couldn't look at Vallie's crying face as I turned around. The muffled sobs I heard coming from my friend were enough to break me.

Once I trekked back through the Hub to our dorm room, I packed up the few belongings I owned. I was careful to place the painting Vallie gave me in one of my bags. That was coming with me no matter what. It only took me a few minutes to pack. Then I sat on my bed one last time and looked around the small dorm.

The multiple candles we'd light during winter were still spread across our room. Various remnants of wax remained. This room had been my home for the past eleven years. I peeled my eyes away from Vallie's bright, floral side. I didn't want to cry anymore. Everything was sinking in and felt too real.

I reached in my pack and pulled out the box Vallie gave me, mad at myself for not thinking of getting her a gift. That was what made Vallie so wonderful. She was so nurturing and thoughtful and brightened everyone's day. Her positivity was contagious as she spread those warm wings to me when I first arrived here, making me smile when no one else could. Making me feel alive when I wanted to die.

Inside the box was a lollipop, similar to the one she first gave me when I came to Tennebris. A handwritten letter was folded four times over. I smiled through glossy eyes as I opened the letter with shaky hands.

*SR,*

*I hope this letter finds you well. You will forever be my Scottie-cat. Words can't begin to describe how much you mean to me, and even though he won't admit it, you mean the world to my brother too. I feel so blessed to have you as my best friend. I'm honored to have watched you grow into the female you were meant to become. I know the idea of being queen scares you, but trust me, Scottie, you are going to make one hell of a queen! How, you may ask, do I know that? Well, because I practically raised you! If only I could come with you and do your makeup all the time, you would even look the part too. Jokes aside, I know you are meant for this. Stop worrying so much about life and finally start living it. I know you never talk about them, but it's what your parents would have wanted. I'm sure of it. I love you so much, SR! You won't ever be alone in this world as long as you have me. Don't forget about me when you are all famous and important.*

*Love forever and always, Vallie*

*P.S. You have to let me know if the sex is good!*

Vallie was the only person who could make me bawl my eyes out and laugh at the same time. I held her letter over my heart and sobbed, staying curled on my side until I heard a knock on my door.

"One second," I said through the thick wooden frame. Wiping the tears from my cheeks, I rushed over to the mirror and glanced at myself before heading out. My eyes were still slightly swollen and puffy from crying, but at least they weren't red anymore.

I put Vallie's letter back in the blue box with the lollipop and tucked it into my pack. I took one last look at our dorm and then walked away from the only life I'd known. I walked to go meet the prince.

To become the future queen.

# FIFTEEN
## SCOTLIND

WHEN I EXITED MY DORM, PRINCE NOREN WAS LEANING against a black, shiny car. The windows were tinted, blocking the inside from view. He took a step toward me and grabbed my bags before placing them in the back of the vehicle. I felt like a walking corpse as I silently followed him inside, neither of us saying a word to each other.

Inside the vehicle, the blonde from earlier, Peter, flashed me a grin. He was sitting next to two Tennebrisian guards who both bore the twin pink moons on their chests. The car was ghastly smaller than the vans we took to the banquet. I wouldn't be able to escape into myself throughout the ride.

I felt myself shrivel up as a sickly feeling of being trapped overtook my body. I pressed my thighs together as tightly as I could to avoid touching the guards sitting next to me. Peter had moved to sit next to the prince who took up the seat behind me, and even though I couldn't see them, I felt like their eyes were burning a hole through my skull.

Once the car finally came to a halt in front of the monorail, I stepped outside and was greeted by crisp, cold air. It was harsher, colder, and rougher than the air in LakeWood. The wind was potent as it whipped my long brown hair over my face and loosened my braids. I could feel the knots starting to form as I briskly tried to gather it back.

I started shivering immediately, my long gray coat not nearly thick enough. Once my hair was tucked behind me in a tangled mess, I crossed my arms across my chest in an attempt to keep warm. Snow peppered the ground, and white flurries were still falling. I tilted my head up to gaze at the sky. Everything felt different here. I couldn't tell if it was actually snowing or if the wind was so strong that it made it seem like it was from sweeping the snow off the ground.

Peter noticed me peering up and casually walked over to my side. "We are at the border of our territory, so the shield is weaker here. Around the perimeters, it's impossible to keep the frigid temperature out. That's why it feels colder and why you see the snow. It's also why all the villages and towns are scattered around the center."

I nodded in response, too cold to say anything back. Once my teeth started chattering, they didn't stop.

Every time I opened my mouth, I saw my breath leave me in a puff of air. It would linger there for a moment before it was swallowed by the wind. I took a few long, slow breaths and tried not to think about the last time I was this cold. Memories resurfaced from the time I was first brought here. It took another moment to realize that the beach I was left on must have been on the border of the Dark Kingdom's territory. That even if I'd climbed those mountains, I never would have lasted long enough to find it.

I squinted through the wind gusts, seeing black and white specks in the distance as a low squealing sounded. It looked like small animals in tuxedos. "What is that?" I puffed through the frigid air.

Peter grinned. "They're penguins and so freaking adorable. There are thousands of them on the border of the territory." Despite how numb I felt inside, I found myself melting as I watched some of the little creatures waddle only to fall on each other.

I wanted to stay and admire the penguins, but I was ushered onto the monorail by a guard. Heat engulfed me immediately, and I embraced it like a hug from the sun. I gawked down the beautiful aisles, feeling like there was an entire world beyond LakeWood. Electricity hummed throughout the long snake-like contraption, and soft lights lined every creamy, white wall.

The monorail was divided into little compartments with doors for privacy. Someone directed me into one, and I blindly followed. Inside the box-shaped chamber, a large row of cushions lined the walls, almost like a mini scrunched up sofa on each side. A woven wool blanket and a pillow were laid out before me—my only indication that this trip would take all night. A frosted window stretched from floor to ceiling, exposing the outside.

I sighed, disappointed that the temperatures were too cold that it froze over the windows. I couldn't look out at the scenery as we passed. After only seeing Addler once, I was curious about what differences existed between the six villages.

Were there more forests and wildlife? Would the monorail pass by that frozen, rocky beach? I frowned at my reflection in the ice frosted window as I took a seat along the wall of cushions, wondering how long the ride would be.

The door to my compartment slammed shut, leaving me alone with nothing but my pack. I wrapped myself in the wool blanket and tried to warm up as I opened up my bag and removed the folder I'd received during the graduation.

I stared at the shiny, black material. It was thicker than I'd imagined. I hadn't dared to open it yet, but I figured now was as good a time as any. There would be no way I could sleep with all the nerves stirring inside me. Careful to avoid putting pressure on my burned wrists, I started sorting through the papers.

Sure enough, it was filled with information regarding the duties expected of me as the princess and then the queen. The bold lettering of the word *queen* was enough to make me want to vomit. Every painstaking detail about the castle and the royals were listed below it.

I had no idea how they expected me to process and retain all this information. I glanced through files of every member of the High Council, not only detailed with their abilities and backgrounds, but their names, rankings, pictures, and job descriptions. They even had information of each member of the guard and every servant, all of whom I realized were rank zeroes. I had to go over a passage five times before my brain could process what I was reading, and even then, it was half the words at best. I was envious of Vallie's ability of knowledge absorption right about now.

My fingers halted over a picture of one of the Council members. I knew without reading the name that it was the male from my rank evaluations. Synder Phillips. His oily skin, slick hair, bent nose, and crooked sneer unsettled me. I cringed as I read his job description as the king's second, making him the head of the High Council. It was the highest ranking one could receive after being the king.

Amongst the paperwork was a detailed layout of the castle grounds. "It's massive," I breathed to myself as I scanned through the map. It spanned across multiple pages. I was surely going to get lost. A lot.

Hours later, I sighed heavily as I glanced up, my brain unable to retain any more information. I pulled the blanket closer around my shoulders, clasping to the warmth it brought. The sun started peeping through the frosted window, melting the ice on the glass. We must have been traveling more inland, away from the freezing borders of the shield. We were passing by more varying degrees of Advenian-made vegetation.

The door to my compartment shifted open, making me jump. My head slammed against the glass as I looked up and saw the prince standing in the frame.

He closed the door behind him and silently took the seat across from me. He couldn't stop talking to me before I was picked, and now that I was going to be his wife, the silence was infuriating. I didn't know what he was thinking. Did he know that I was the girl who fell on him before the banquet? Did he even remember?

He started to examine the raw zeroes that were now forever burned into each of my wrists. The blanket slid off my shoulders as he took my hands in his, completely engulfing mine. I tried not to wince as his fingers inspected the burns. It took every ounce of self-control I had to not pull them away.

The prince turned my hands over so that my palms were facing up. The burn on my right was far worse than my left. Angry, red, raw flesh stared back at me. It was missing skin and was still bleeding around the raised zero. I couldn't help but notice the five branded into his left, completely healed and forcing me into self-consciousness. The male that branded me did a good job planting self-doubt into me yet again.

Fury about this whole situation started boiling through me. Rage and frustration about being ripped from my home, about my family being burned alive. About my counselor not believing me when I pleaded with her as a child. How after I joined LakeWood, I was denied seeing her again when I asked for her. The way I was treated by everyone in Tennebris because they thought I was a nix. How all nixes were treated. And now, as if it was some cruel, sick joke, I would be forced to become the Dark Prince's bride when there had never been a rank zero queen before. So why me? Why now?

"He shouldn't have done that," he finally spoke. His voice was low and rough. He noted my confusion and added, "Burned both of your wrists. We questioned him after the ceremony. It wasn't until I used compulsion on him that we found out his ulterior motives for hurting you were because of me. I'm sorry."

I studied him for a moment, trying to process this newfound kindness from him as he smeared healing ointment over my wrists. Pity. He was only doing this out of pity. Not because I was going to be his future wife. Not because he cared. I'd seen the disgusted look on his face when my name was announced. I tried to pull my wrists away, but his grip on me only tightened.

"What were his reasons?" I asked.

He stopped bandaging my wrists for just a moment to meet my gaze. "His son was one of the males I fought during the tournament. Apparently, he suffered greatly on my behalf and hasn't recovered yet. I broke his femur. He won't be able to walk right again. He lost his position as a guard, and once he recovers, he will become a servant for the remainder of his life. That's why he did that to you, vengeance for his son." He started to bandage my wrists again, but his voice was laced with a cold sorrow he couldn't hide.

"I don't understand. Why won't he be able to walk again? Lux has healers. I thought they used them after the fight?"

"They do have healers, but Tennebris refuses to use their services for the King's Tournament. They claim it is a sacrifice you have to make if you want to compete. You must accept whatever outcome you get."

"Why isn't that talked about?"

"It's not meant to be public knowledge. It's a tactic to wean out some of the men. A ruler shouldn't back down out of fear and he should be willing to sacrifice himself for the greater good of the kingdom. There were a few males who dropped out once the document was in front of them. It's also a custom that has continued from when they held the King's Tournament on Allium. It's been around since the first ever tournament, and Tennebris likes to keep with their traditions."

"But you were stabbed."

"Still healing." His lips formed a taut line as he lifted up the bottom of his shirt and revealed his abdomen. "Luckily, the king didn't hit any vital organs. I just needed a few stitches."

A few stitches seemed like an understatement. The white linen wrapped around his stomach was stained red from blood that had seeped through the fabric. The small amount of skin exposed through the wrap was bruised so heavily it was pure black. But it explained why they never healed the cuts and bruises on his face.

He noticed my prolonged, wide-eyed gaze, and pulled his shirt back down to resume examining my damaged wrists.

We sat in silence as he continued to work. I didn't know what to say. I never knew that was the sacrifice for the tournament; that healers weren't allowed afterward. A shudder ran through me, thinking back to some of the horrific injuries I'd read about in past tournaments.

Pressure pulsed through the wrist he was bandaging, and I flinched.

"Sorry, are you okay?" he asked, bringing me back to the moment.

"Yes," I replied softly. Heat rose to my cheeks. It was foolish how trivial my wounds were compared to his many. He was still injured and far worse than I was. His wound made my burns seem like nothing. Yet, he was here taking care of me.

"Thank you," I said once both my wrists were wrapped in fresh, white cloth.

"Don't thank me when it's my fault." There was something in his voice that had me leaning closer.

"It's not your fault," I gulped, aware of every inch of his body and how close he now was to me. He gave me a defeated look, so I added, "You didn't make him burn both of my wrists. And besides, everyone gets branded."

"I don't want you to get hurt because of me." He leaned forward, whispering in my ear. Our lips were a breath apart.

Slowly, he trailed his hands up my arms, causing the hairs on my arms to raise. His rough calluses scraped against my skin as they moved higher and higher. His one hand glided over my collar bone before wrapping his fingers around the base of my neck, and pulled.

I leaned forward so slightly as a small gasp of air escaped my parted lips. He didn't miss it. His lips formed a half-smile as my body reacted to his. I stilled, waiting for what he would do next.

Black eyes seared into me, his gaze unwavering and full of longing. My own blue eyes traveled down to his soft, full lips as I leaned closer and closer. I wanted to know what it felt like to kiss someone. To kiss *him*, which was crazy. He was a stranger to me, and one that had ignored me almost as long as I'd known him.

Any rational thought I had left me as I gave into the pure desire of him. I took in his scent, his broad posture, the feel of his hands around my neck. My core tightened in anticipation. I wanted this. I wanted him.

My heartbeat was the only sound, echoing against my ears, threatening to burst out of me. He leaned forward, his lips alarmingly close to mine as they curved into another half-smile. The expression so set on his face, like he would continue to smirk into mine.

The door to our compartment swung open, causing us both to jump back.

Peter coughed awkwardly, knowing full well what he had just walked in on. His smile widened as he took in my reddened face. "I'm sorry to interrupt what I'm sure would have been rather enjoyable, but Synder requested to speak with you, Sie."

His expression darkened at the name. The smirk-like smile from moments ago was gone. "Tell him I'll be right there," he said to Peter, his gaze never leaving mine.

Peter looked between us both, still grinning like a child. He nodded his head once before closing the door behind him.

The silence that followed was endless. I scrambled for something to talk about. For anything to say. "Isn't it a waste of time for you to ride the monorail when you can just teleport to the castle?"

I instantly regretted the question. What a stupid thing to ask him after we almost kissed. I should have asked him if he remembered me. What he thought of me being selected. I should have tried to find out his stance on rank zeroes. Instead, my brain went right to his ability.

He leaned back in his seat, stretching out his long legs as he let out a small laugh. "Is this really what you want to talk about?"

I bit my lip. I had about a million other questions I wanted to ask, but I couldn't bring myself to say anything. The prince's eyes trailed to my lips, my teeth nervously gnawing on them. Blood trailed down my chin. Great. I'd reopened my scab from my Trials. He chuckled as he passed me a cloth to wipe up the blood.

"Teleportation doesn't quite work like that. There are limits to how far you can travel at once. Besides, my teleportation ability is my weakest power. It drains my reserve fast."

"Isn't teleportation the same ability as portal users from Lux?" I asked.

He eyed me for a moment. His gaze went from the cloth I was dabbing against my lower lip to my eyes. I shifted in my seat. Maybe I shouldn't have brought up Lux.

"It's similar to those of Lux that can use portals, except nothing opens up between them. Luxian portal users have to have set up a portal prior. They need to create a portal at a starting point and an ending point. They can't travel on a whim. But, once a portal is established, they can travel within it for however long they want. Portal users also rarely have limits to how far they can travel. They could transport themselves across the planet if they wanted to. Teleport users are different. They can't travel far distances, but one minute they are standing there, the next they are gone. All you need with teleportation is to know where you want to end up, and you will go there. It's more of a whim whereas portal users have to plan."

"And how far can you travel?" I asked. The more I knew about him, the better, and I knew absolutely nothing. Plus, my curiosity was getting the best of me.

"I can only teleport as far as I can see. Several miles at best, and that will drain my reserve fast, forcing me to rest in between jumps. If I use little movements, teleporting only a few feet at a time like in a battle, it's fine. My main abilities lie in compulsion and mind control."

I wasn't ready to ask him about that. I wasn't prepared to hear how dangerous he was, what horrible things he possessed behind that beautiful face of his. I didn't want to fear him. And he probably wouldn't even answer me if I asked, so I blinked away the question and turned to look out of the window.

"Here," he said as he passed me a necklace. It sparkled as the sun shimmered against the small, white pendant on a long golden chain. I held the chain closer to my face to examine the circular design. The golden sun of Lux was etched in the center with Tennebris' twin moons surrounding either side in waning and waxing crescents. It was as if the pink moons were a blanket for the sun, like they were always meant to fit together. It was beautiful. I was in awe admiring the necklace, at a loss for something that seemed designed from both kingdoms, that I didn't realize he was still speaking to me.

"What?" I asked.

"I said I want you to wear this and never take it off."

"Why?" I asked as I took the necklace from his outstretched hand and examined it.

"I'm not the only one at the castle who can use compulsion. This will protect you from being compelled by anyone, including me. It will protect you from any abilities being used against you. It is infused with the blood of an Alluse user from Lux. You can't trust anyone at the castle, Scotlind. And now, because of that"—he pointed to my wrists as he leaned back into his seat again—"everyone in the kingdom will know that you can be compelled."

I looked down at my wrapped wrists and sucked in a breath. He was right. There would be no hiding that I was a nix. I was basically labeled as weak and asking to be compelled, or worse.

I took a shaky breath as I looked down at the necklace again. I'd heard rumors about the horrible methods Lux used to make devices like this. That they developed ways to drain Advenians' blood and fuse their abilities with objects. I hated the thought of wearing someone's blood around my neck. It was worse knowing that it was most likely taken by force. Alluse users were known to be mistreated amongst our kind, worse than nixes even, as their abilities nullified anyone's around them. But with Alluse infused in an object, it could block powers being used on me.

"Thank you, Prince Noren," I said and meant it. The thought of being protected trumped my hesitancy about the necklace. My heart leapt, knowing that I would never have to worry about being compelled. That I could be my own person. I wouldn't have to fear someone forcing me to do anything against my own will. This was freedom, maybe the first thing in Tennebris that I could decide for myself.

"Don't ever call me Prince Noren again," he smirked, still leaning back in his seat. "You can call me Sie."

"Thank you, *Sie*," I said again, unable to stop my own smile from forming.

He nodded, then gestured toward the necklace. "If someone does compel you, though, I need you to play along. Do whatever they are telling you to do. Don't tell anyone about the necklace, and never let anyone know that you can't be compelled."

"What?" I snapped sharply. "What's the point of me wearing this if I still have to act like I'm being compelled?"

His eyes narrowed as he stared darkly at me. "Because you aren't safe. Some people would rather see someone like you dead than rule our kingdom. Many Advenians support having rank zeroes' rights being taken away. To them, seeing one on the throne is unthinkable. They want to take them out of schools, which would mean they wouldn't get a Trial. All of them would automatically become servants. There are numerous members of the Council who support this. It hasn't passed yet, and I don't intend for it to. However, a lot can happen in six months. It doesn't add up that they selected you as my bride. Most matches are more..." he paused, searching for the right word, "ostentatious."

I seethed as he continued. "If someone uses compulsion on you, they could force you to kill yourself. They could get rid of you without ever laying a finger on you. So, I want you to agree to any trivial compulsion someone might use on you. Don't reveal that you have an Alluse object unless the situation is life or death. If that happens, I want you to run and come find me right away."

Well, that answered some of my questions about him. I swallowed the lump that was now in my throat. I knew what he was saying was true. I wouldn't be safe at the castle. I knew it the moment they called my name, but there was something about hearing it out loud that made it feel more real—scarier.

The meaning of his words didn't get past me either. People would rather have no queen than be ruled by a nix. I had to fight against my growing anger, thinking about how some wanted to make things worse for rank zeroes. To take away their rights and not allow them a Trial...

"So, I'm to wear this necklace," I hissed, my voice rising an octave, "and still do whatever anyone compels me to do, except kill myself?"

"More or less, yes."

He knew I was fuming as he studied me, gauging my reaction. I wasn't good at keeping my emotions in check and was practically wearing them on my sleeve for him to analyze.

I willed my anger down enough to say, "If Tennebrisians won't approve of a queen who is a rank zero, then why have me at all? There are plenty of girls who would be better suited than me as you said. Plenty who actually want this. Surely you could have found someone better."

"You're right. I think any other female in this kingdom would have been a better pick than you."

My jaw dropped at his words. Not that they weren't true, but because he flat out agreed to it.

He ignored my gaping mouth and said, "Especially since they didn't even deem you worthy of being a guard."

"What?" I practically screamed. My rage twisted in my gut like a dagger.

He paused as if unsure if he should continue. My glare made it known I wouldn't let him leave without further explanation.

He sighed and ran his long fingers through his black waves. "They were going to make you a servant. The High Council members who were at your ranking evaluation put it on your record before they even saw you fight. It didn't matter how you performed. It didn't matter how good of a fighter you were or how well you trained your body. It didn't even matter that you knocked out half of your male classmates. You were going to become a servant."

His words stripped me, leaving me raw inside until there was nothing left. I felt bare. It was like I was naked despite being covered in more clothes and blankets than I owned.

I ignored the fact that he remembered me, not only from the outer rim at the banquet, but from watching me fight. He remembered my Trial. A more unnerving truth came crashing down.

None of it had mattered.

All those days of waking up early to train before class, all the bruises and cuts that turned to scars on my body, were pointless. All the times I had to suck down my urge to fight back whenever someone abused me because I couldn't risk *tarnishing* my record for the Trials. None of that mattered. They were going to make me a servant without ever seeing me fight. Just because of the two zeroes that are now forever on my wrists like shackles. The burns were chains holding me down.

I would have been a servant. And they wanted to do this to every rank zero. They didn't want to give them a chance at the Trials. They didn't want to give them any opportunities to become something better.

Sie studied me before saying, "I'm sorry, Scotlind, but I don't think it was random that you were selected. The Council is planning something and I want to use you to find out what."

His words were laced with ice. I processed them over and over again in my head, unable to muster a response, unable to grasp this reality. My stomach turned in on itself as I realized three hard truths.

The first was that Sie wasn't a nice male. He wasn't trying to protect me by giving me this necklace. He wanted to use me. The fact that I almost let him kiss me just moments ago made me sick as I recalled all the rumors about him. He was a flirt. He could be with any female he wanted. He didn't like me. He would use me, whether it be my body like he almost just did, or for some greater agenda like finding out what the High Council was up to.

The second thing I gleaned was that I was in trouble. Someone picked me for a reason, and I had a sinking feeling that it had nothing to do with changing our world for the better or how we treat nixes. It couldn't be a coincidence that the first nix to be picked for the future queen wasn't really a nix. Maybe whoever was behind this knew I was Luxian. Was it the lavender-eyed male from the beach? Was this the plan all along? Was I a part of some bigger scheme?

The third thing I realized was that I was done playing along. I would not allow them to change the ranking system. I would not allow them to make things worse for rank zeroes. If they tried, I'd dedicate my life to demolishing the court from the inside out. I would do whatever I could to prevent that from happening until I was discovered or killed.

"You want to use me?" I finally said. "How?"

"Yes." He replied truthfully, not bothering to hold back or lie about it. At least he was blunt and honest. "I want you to be my spy. If you hear something or if someone tells you anything, then compels you to forget, I want to know about it."

I shook my head in confusion. "I still don't understand. Why would you agree to this? You didn't have to accept me. All you had to do was say you had another person in mind. You could have picked anyone to be your wife. Why me?" It was the question that had been on my mind ever since the banquet, but I had been too afraid of the answer to ask it.

"Something else, something bigger than whatever future is between you and me, is going on with the High Council. I realized it as soon as they called your name. I intend to know why they selected you, and I need you to play along in order to do that. If I picked someone else to marry, the High Council would still attempt whatever they are planning. Something will happen, Scotlind. It's only a matter of time, and it will be to our advantage that everyone thinks you are weak. They won't be worried about masking things from you because you are a known zero."

"So you don't plan on marrying me then? You just want me to play along with the engagement long enough until you can figure out what is going on? Then I'm free? To do what exactly? You said yourself I can't be a guard, and now I missed the placement for careers."

He shook his head. "The High Council is planning something whether or not I decline you for a wife. Like I said before, I don't care who my wife is. I will marry you. Just help me figure out what they are planning and come to me when anything happens. I want to know right away when and who tries to compel you."

"Why are you telling me any of this? For all you know, I could be working with the High Council."

"You're not. I saw the expression on your face when your name was called," he said. "And I'm telling you this because I want you to know what you are getting yourself into. You will be in danger."

"I'm not getting myself into anything," I sneered, unable to hide the anger from my voice. "I have no choice in this. I can't say no to this, unlike you. If you accept me, I *have* to marry you."

His lips went into a straight line. Realizing this conversation wasn't going to change anything, I clarified, "So basically, if people compel me, I have to do whatever awful thing they want me to do, except kill myself? Is that what you are telling me?"

"Not if, but *when* people compel you. And yes, that's exactly what I'm telling you. There is a button on the back of the pendant. If you're in danger, press it, and I'll find you right away."

"I thought you told me not to trust anyone, but you want me to trust you?" I pried, not bothering to mask my disgust.

He gave me a dark look before answering, "No. You can't trust me. But at least trust me enough with this. I have no intention of harming you. I had a tracker placed in the necklace. If you press it, I will come for you. It's technology developed by Lux that will give me the location of where you are. Help me find out what the High Council is planning, Scotlind, and I will protect you. After that, I won't bother you, except for when martial duties are called upon."

I cringed at *marital duties* and what that would entail. He still didn't know I was from Lux. He had no idea that I could never act upon those duties and have a child with him. Thankfully, Lakimi wouldn't happen for another four hundred and eighty-some years, so the chances of us conceiving were slim.

"Lucky me," I sarcastically hissed. "Just what I always wanted. To live in a castle where everyone wants me dead and marry an asshole prick of a prince who wants nothing to do with me except warm his bed." The words flew out of my mouth before I even had the chance to regret them, but I guess it didn't matter what he thought of me. To him, this was a transaction. There would be no relationship.

"I don't *need* you to warm my bed. Although, I certainly wouldn't protest," he said as he stood. He looked me up and down before sauntering out of the compartment.

I chucked the necklace against the closed door. Then, thinking better of it, I stalked over to it and angrily picked it up. Any happiness I felt about being protected against compulsion had vanished. It was replaced with pure rage, fear, and dread about the notion of having to pretend to be compelled. I was sick of being forced to do things against my will, things I didn't want to do.

Maybe being the princess, Advenians wouldn't pick on me. Perhaps everyone would just leave me alone for fear of the wrath of my now horrendous and very intimidating betrothed. And if I pushed my luck, maybe it could help me find the answers as to why I was brought here all those years ago. And if I did find anything out, he would be the last person I told.

I clasped the golden chain, fastening it around my neck.

# SIXTEEN
## SCOTLIND

When we finally arrived at the castle, I was at a loss for words. The detailed map in my folder portrayed the grounds to be massive, but it was something else entirely to see it in person. Large stone gates groaned against the gravel as they slithered open, revealing an ancient, beautiful, daunting castle.

I raised my hand, shielding my eyes as I squinted past the bright sun peeking through the force shield. Tilting my head back to get a better view, I tried to make out the castle's full mass, but it stretched beyond what I could see.

Well-kept gardens surrounded the perimeter. Red roses bloomed throughout the trimmed bushes and I knew it was from the work of a Luxian ground user. A few snow-capped mountains flashed in the distance behind the castle. Other than that, the landscape was flat. Trees of varying sizes were scattered throughout, and to my back laid a thick forest, one I knew I wouldn't be allowed to explore.

I looked up at the sandstone walls and looming pillars. It was a different kind of enclosure from the mountains surrounding Lake-Wood. It would now be my new home—at least until the next King's Tournament, or whenever I was discovered.

Fortunately, I hadn't seen Sie since our conversation on the monorail. It was a good thing because I still wasn't sure if I wanted to hit him or kiss him. What he had said on the monorail unnerved me—how he wanted to use me. I was just a pawn in whatever larger game he was playing.

I was still gazing up at the castle when Peter strode toward me. I turned to look at him when he stood a foot away. His blonde hair was messy atop his head like he'd just rolled out of bed. He wore a loose gray button-up lined with silver stitching that probably cost a fortune, but he somehow made it seem casual.

His hands were hidden in the pockets of his black pants. His usual playful demeanor had changed to a mask of calmness. The seriousness of his features seemed unsettling, as if being here took away his youthfulness. "Morning, princess."

"That. Is. Not. My. Name." I seethed.

"Okay, then. Scotlind." He smiled lightly.

"It's Scottie."

"Good morning, *Scottie*," he taunted. "Come with me. Sie has meetings all day with the High Council and the king. He will be busy until your engagement banquet tonight. I'll give you a quick tour of the grounds before you need to get ready."

"Engagement banquet?" I repeated as Peter guided me up the vast stone stairs leading into the castle.

He laughed. "Did you not read through your packet?"

"Some of it," I admitted. Though I'd purposely avoided anything labeled *Princess Duties*.

"Well, you might want to read it. They are throwing both of you into a full schedule starting tomorrow, but yes, you have a banquet tonight."

"A banquet?" I pressed, hoping he would fill me in so I didn't have to open the folder again.

"It's a tradition to have a banquet honoring the new prince and princess. It serves as a way to welcome you and Sie into the kingdom. After the banquet, there will be a brief ceremony where the priest will officially declare you both the Prince and Princess of Tennebris. You will meet King Lunder and everyone serving on the High Council. A reception, open to the public, will follow the ceremony with drinks and dancing. They should also be assigning your guards tonight."

"I have guards?" I asked, annoyed at the thought of needing someone looking after me. I trained for eleven years. I knew most Advenians trained for centuries, but still, I could look after myself.

"Yes," he replied coldly. The warmth in his tone vanished as his voice turned serious. "You aren't safe in the castle. I will stay with you until it's time for you to get ready for the banquet. Your servants will take you to the Grand Hall after they dress you. But Scottie, after tonight, everyone will know who you are. It's important that you remain with your guards."

"But—"

"Don't even start," he cut me off. "You will have guards with you at all times. All it would take is one mind user to get inside your head and control you. It doesn't matter what physical training you've put your body through over the years."

I could tell there was no talking him out of it. Clearly, him and Sie had discussed the fact that they thought there would be attempts made on my life. Could Advenians really hate rank zeroes that badly that they would murder just to not have one on the throne?

I swallowed. The answer to that became blatantly obvious as everyone that passed me glared in disgust. I knew what they said was true. Guards were strategic. Sie wouldn't be able to use me to figure out what the High Council was planning if I ended up dead. Just a pawn in a mind-altering game… I just never thought I would need them. It gave me an idea. "I want to train while I'm here."

"I'm sure you do," he laughed softly. The lightness returned to his voice as we walked past the entrance. Two imposing curved staircases wrapped around the walls to meet in the middle of a second landing. Peter ignored the stairs and headed straight toward a darkened hall.

The castle had a few chandeliers dangling from the arched ceilings, but I was surprised to see more torches, candles, and fireplaces used to light the palace. I always imagined that the castle would be exploding with electricity, but so far it was contained to small amounts here and there.

"You really don't know what you're getting yourself into," he chuckled. I rolled my eyes. I wasn't voluntarily getting myself into this, but I decided it wasn't worth arguing over. "I suggest that you read through your folder today, Scottie. You already have a full schedule, and training is not on the list."

I halted. "What am I going to be doing?"

"Oh, they will keep you busy with lessons and etiquette classes."

I scoffed. The idea of being cooped up in classes all day long without moving my body sounded absolutely miserable. I would go crazy if I couldn't kick something.

"I propose a compromise."

Peter arched his brow. "I didn't realize you had a choice."

I ignored him. "I will agree to your guards and these classes if I can keep up with my training. If the castle is as dangerous to me as you and Sie say, then I want to be able to defend myself. And frankly, training would be more useful to me than whatever my lessons and etiquette classes entail."

He crossed his arms across his chest, making a show of looking me up and down. "Fine." He turned to start walking again, and I had to hurry to keep pace with him. "I'll talk to Sie about it. We'll get your schedule changed. But trust me, Scottie, I can guarantee you that your lessons are more important than training. You *need* all the etiquette classes you can get."

"Jerk," I mumbled under my breath, but from his lingering grin, I was pretty sure he heard it.

Peter was a breath of fresh air, despite the insults, as he finished showing me around. He talked to me like Vallie did and made me feel like a person.

He only showed me a portion of the grounds on the first level, but I honestly couldn't remember anything. Everything was blending into one another—Council rooms, offices, a dining hall, the central kitchen, three smaller cafes, the Hall where our engagement banquet would be held.

Finally, we reached the back of the castle. A stone patio opened up into an extensive garden. A beautiful but dark lake was hidden behind the wide hedges of the path. The water was static, begging to be disturbed. There was a quiet stillness to it that made me believe no creatures lurked below, or if they did, they were hidden well beneath the depths of the surface. I had the urge to jump in. I wanted to feel the water surrounding me, clinging to my existence. I wanted to explore the bottom, see what sulked beneath, but I never could. Even if it was an acceptable thing to do, my markings would show.

Peter took me back inside through a different door. I couldn't hide my excitement as we toured the library. It was massive. I had to crane my neck to see the top of the stained glass ceiling. The sunlight glinted through the red and orange depictions, casting a fiery glow over the books. A slim black stairway spiraled upward, leading to each level.

"What kind of books are here?" I asked.

"All genres," he replied, seeming bored.

"More than a school would keep?"

Peter crossed his arms over his chest as he leaned against a pillar. "Not the scandalous sort."

"That is *not* what I meant." I squealed as I turned away from him in an attempt to hide the heat from my cheeks. I wanted to know if they contained books on Lux. Not that I could correct him and admit to that.

"Uh-huh," he laughed. "Come on. I'll take you to your room now. You should read over what is expected of you so you don't look like such a lost puppy."

I stuck my tongue out, but followed him anyway. He was effortless to talk to and instantly made me feel at ease—unlike how I felt with Sie. How Peter was friends with someone so emotionless was beyond me. They were complete opposites. I wondered if people thought the same about me and Vallie. One light, warm, and welcoming, the other dark and closed off.

"This will be your room," he said as he opened a set of double doors.

"Wow," I breathed. The floor was solid oak, with walls painted dark to match. Small, circular tables were situated beside a black leather sofa and singular chair, the material looking stiff and uncomfortable.

A massive bed took up the opposite space. From the sheer size of it, the bed looked like it would swallow me whole. The comforter was white, fluffy, and soft, perhaps the only light thing in the entire room. It took every ounce of my self-control to not surrender myself to it now.

Three sets of floor-to-ceiling windows aligned the far wall. Red velvet curtains hung open, letting the natural light spill into the space. A massive fireplace was already roaring to life, making the room feel toasty. Unlit candles and torches hung from the walls for when the sky turned permanently dark in winter. I guess that meant no electricity in the bed quarters then.

"This is where you will be staying until your wedding night. There is a private bathing room over there," Peter said as he gestured toward a closed door.

I sighed when I saw it. No latch for a lock was visible, but at least there would be some privacy.

"I'll let you rest for now. I'll be back in a couple of hours to take you to your fitting room so you can get ready for tonight, but until then, don't leave this room. You don't have any guards yet."

"Thank you, Peter," I said as he turned to leave. He nodded as he shut the door behind him.

I was surprised to see my bags had already been brought up. I hadn't thought about them since they were loaded into the vehicle before the monorail. It only took me a few minutes to unpack all my belongings. My fingers lingered on the blue box that Vallie gave me. I tucked the box with her note under my pillow, hung the painting of us up over my nightstand, then flopped on the bed, not bothering to close the curtains.

My eyelids grew heavy with exhaustion as I sank into the deep mattress. I thought about listening to Peter and opening my packet, but sleep won out in the end. The warmth from the sheets and blankets engulfed me as I drifted off into a soundless rest.

A KNOCK on my door woke me from my nap too soon. I wanted to keep sleeping. My eyes fluttered open by the third heavy pound. I stretched, looking out the large windows as the sun was sinking lower in the sky. Even though it would never fully set in summer, I'd long since learned to read the positions of it as it moved through the sky.

"I'm coming," I grumbled by the sixth urgent knock. The wood doors were heavier than I thought they would be, and it took both hands to yank one of them open.

Peter stood on the other side of the door. "Shit, Scottie, I'm sorry. I was held up in a meeting with the guards. You are twenty minutes late for your fitting. We have to leave now," he said as he rushed me out the door.

He navigated us through the dim halls of the castle. I was almost jogging to keep up with his quick-paced strides. He weaved and guided us through multiple different turns and long halls before we arrived. Three females in similar plain dresses waited for me behind open doors. One of them was tapping her foot on the ground, her thin arms crossed over her chest, perking her cleavage up.

I glanced around the room and realized that it was a dressing chamber. Full length mirrors aligned the back walls with racks and racks of beautiful gowns laid out before me.

"This will be where you'll be getting dressed for now. Once you are married, your belongings will be moved. You and Sie will have a fitting room inside your royal chamber," Peter remarked.

I gaped at the room. Vallie would love this. I'd never seen so many gowns in my life. They put Vallie's closet to shame. Each one was uniquely stitched with varying beads, lace, and silks. No two were the same, and there was enough for me to wear a different dress for an entire year.

I looked down at my own pants and shirt of my guard uniform. Unless Peter managed to get me into training, I would be saying goodbye to my current wardrobe, which really wasn't much of anything, but I hated the idea of only wearing dresses.

"You're late," the female with her arms crossed snapped. Her beautiful ashy brown hair was curled around her slim shoulders.

"My fault, Rosie," Peter said as he flashed his knowing grin at the girl. It worked. Her frown softened as she fluttered her eyes.

"Scottie, these will be your personal servants," he said as he gestured toward the three females. I gave them a smile of my own, two of them returned the favor. The other female continued to gawk at Peter like he was a prize to be won. "This is Roslyn," Peter continued.

"And this is Ashley," he said as he gestured toward a heavier set female with dark, frizzy hair. Her eyes were a deep brown, and so wide they reminded me of a doe. Ashley gave a curtsy.

"And this is Annabel," Peter said as he pointed to the last girl. Annabel's short, sleek hair covered her pointed nose as she bent down into a low curtsy beside Ashley. She smiled widely, revealing crooked teeth through her full lips.

"She's all yours, ladies." Peter patted my shoulder. "Good luck," he added to my servants before walking out of the room.

"Hi," I said by way of greeting once he was gone.

"No time for small talk. We have to get you ready," Roslyn said as she pulled me deep into the fitting room, her ash hair bouncing behind her.

They worked in silence as they dressed me in a fitted, black gown. Ashley told me Sie had selected it himself for tonight before she threw it over my head and tugged it down my body.

The dress pressed against my chest tightly, leaving nothing of my upper body to the imagination. The constriction caused my sore ribs to ache just by breathing. The tight, silken bodice stopped once it reached my navel and cascaded down in flowing waves until it reached the floor. The material that made up the lower half of the dress was so sheer that depending on how the torches illuminated it, I looked naked beneath.

Gold stitching was etched throughout the gown in heavy, thick spirals that tapered off as it hit the floor. The design reminded me of Sie's Tennebrisian markings. There were no sleeves, exposing my jutted collar bones, thin arms, and bandaged wrists.

I glanced around at the other dresses in the room. Most of the gowns' sleeves never reached the forearms. It seemed no matter what they dressed me in, my wrists would always be exposed.

Annabel redressed my bloody bandages before ushering me over to the mirror. Her crooked smile came up behind me as I gazed at my reflection. The gown fell to the floor, dragging slightly whenever I walked.

Roslyn pulled out a pair of tall heels as I protested, "No, please. I can barely walk straight as it is. I'll fall in those heels." The amount of times I tripped over my own two feet in my guard boots made those shiny heels look like death traps on straps.

"You have to wear heels," Roslyn scoffed. "You're the princess."

"It's fine, Rosie," Annabel spoke lightly. "Her dress is long enough. No one will see her shoes." She stole a glance at me and gave me a wink. "I have shoes you can wear for now, but you must learn to walk in heels in your free time. We'll put a pair in your room so you can practice." Her smile was warm as she handed me a pair of small boots. They were nothing like the clunky ones that I usually wore. "The black will blend in with the dress."

"Thank you," I said to Annabel, grateful that at least for tonight, my feet wouldn't have to suffer.

Ashley broke the silence, "Now for your hair and makeup, princess." She gestured toward a wooden chair.

"Please call me Scottie," I said as I took the seat. The three of them got to work fixing and pulling my hair. Then they smudged a line of coal over my eyes, coated my lashes with that same sticky substance Vallie had used, and smeared red over my lips.

Once they were done, they started to make their way out of the room. I didn't move. I needed a minute.

Ashley paused as her wide, brown eyes found mine in the mirror. "I will be waiting just outside the door. Come out once you're ready." She bowed slightly before following the other two into the hall, allowing me a moment to myself.

Picking up the ends of my gown, I took a step closer to the mirror. A small gasp escaped my lips at what stared back at me. I thought

Vallie had done an amazing job with my hair and makeup before, but this was something else. I didn't recognize myself.

My hair was in perfect curls, cascading down my lower back. Golden pins held the strands out of my face, revealing black drop earrings that dangled to my shoulders. They were heavy with dried blood caked around the metal points where they pierced holes through my ears.

For the amount of time they spent doing my makeup, it was lightly done. The red on my lips was just enough to completely mask the scab that was still there. They highlighted all my features, focusing heavily on my eyes. The sapphire outshined any lingering gray that sometimes sparkled through the blue. With the black dress and the lined coal, my eyes were unavoidable. It was like I was staring into that depthless lake behind the castle. So deep, they'd swallow you up and drown you if you stared for too long. For the first time in my life, I felt beautiful.

I *was* beautiful.

I took one last glance at myself before meeting Ashley out in the hall. "You look magnificent," she beamed at me. "Prince Noren will be delighted to see you."

"Thank you," I responded, not wanting to comment on Sie. I didn't miss the lingering admiration that crossed her face at the mention of him. It left me riddled with guilt that so many girls would have switched spots with me in a heartbeat, especially Vallie. But I felt the opposite of lucky. Me being connected to him was just forcing my inevitable doom. And no amount of unholy attractiveness was worth that. Besides, it was washed away by the fact that he was an emotionless jerk. I almost told Ashley just that but thought better of it.

Ashley and Annabel seemed sweet. Maybe they could be my friends. I could really use some. My heart was left hollow without Vallie's comforting presence.

So far, everyone I had met at the castle had been cordial to me, which was not something I was used to or expecting. Minus a few unpleasant glares, maybe Sie was wrong about the threats. Maybe people would be happy to see a nix as queen. Even if I desperately wished that the nix wasn't me, perhaps I could change things for the future. I could try to soften the ranking system and advocate for treating the Advenians who are rank zeroes with respect. Even if I had no clue where to start, I'd try, as long as I didn't get myself discovered or killed in the process…

"This is it," Ashley halted as she gestured toward the looming doors of the Grand Hall. She gave me a low curtsy, her brown doe-like eyes never leaving mine.

"Please, don't bow for me."

"What would you rather me do?" she asked, startled, as she straightened.

"I would rather you treat me like a friend. I could use one here."

"I can do that," she smiled.

I returned it before walking through the doors, to start the first night of whatever was left of the rest of my life.

# SEVENTEEN
## SCOTLIND

The conversation halted as soon as I entered through the doors. It was like the energy was sucked dry, the door I came through a vortex, leaving nothing behind. My cheeks flooded with heat as every eye in the room turned their attention on me, making me utterly aware of how tight and revealing my dress was.

The room was filled with males seated around a large rectangle table. King Lunder took up the head, with the only other female in the room seated straight-back beside him. The current queen. She looked imposing amongst the sea of men. Her coppery crown, smaller than her husband's, looked just as regal. Her hands were folded into one another and laid flat across her beige beaded gown as she offered me a small smile.

I would never be like that. I would never complement the king, wouldn't complement Sie. I looked as out of place as I felt. Still covered in bruises and scabs, I was a fool in a pretty dress.

The males at the table weren't as kind. All of them remained seated, not moving on my account. I bowed awkwardly, lowering my head at the table before me. I honestly had no clue how to act. Maybe Peter was right, that I desperately needed etiquette classes or whatever other lessons they'd shove down my throat.

Sie was staring coldly in my direction. His eyes never leaving mine until Peter stood to save me. He walked over to me casually, his hands in his pockets as he flashed his dimpled smile. The silence in the room grew, all eyes watching our movements. I took Peter's outstretched arm as I let him lead me toward an empty seat across from Sie.

Then he stalked around the table and slumped into the chair next to his friend. He seemed so out of place amongst the High Council. He was too casual amongst the stiff backs and placid stares.

Conversations started again, numerous light gossip and small talk spread across the table. Slowly, the males seated around me began to introduce themselves. I recognized several from my packet, but I couldn't remember a single name, even as they told me again and again.

I didn't utter a word to the prince but found his gaze lingering on mine as it swept over the room. No, he wasn't watching me, but more how the males were interacting with me. His eyes trailed to which ones spoke to me, who gawked at my dress, and who ignored me wholly.

Was this all a setup? Did Sie select this outfit on purpose? As a test to see who would approach me? Was this to gauge who might be in favor of me being here and who wasn't?

The dinner portion of the night dragged on and was made worse when I discovered it was a five-course meal. I never ate so much food in one day, nevertheless in one meal. The servants took their time in between each dish. Slowly clearing every plate, replacing every cloth. They tended to the grand fireplace behind King Lunder three times. Adding more wood so that the flames danced angrily as they roared back to life, warming my bare arms from across the room.

I was thankful whenever one of them brought out more food. Even though I was full, it saved me from having to make small talk. Anytime anyone tried to ask me about my life at LakeWood, why a female nix would train to be a guard, or about my family, I stuffed my mouth with food.

The judge from my evaluation was seated in the chair next to the king. Peter noticed my gaze and leaned forward to whisper, "That's

Synder Phillips. He is King Lunder's second and leader of the Tennebrisian Guard. All thirty members of the High Council report to him."

I nodded, remembering reading about his status in the packet. "And who does he report to?" I asked softly.

"Only Lunder. He has a lot of… influence here." I couldn't help but notice how his voice turned cold. I nodded as I forced another bite of stew down.

After dinner, we were ushered from the dining hall toward the private chapel off the ballroom. The room was dark, with only the sun lighting it through the cracks of the stained glass windows. Hues of red, orange, and gold bounced along the wooden pews and velvet plush cushions. The glass seemed to be a staple in almost every grand room in the castle.

An altar was centered in the middle of the room, placed directly in front of the statue of Pylemo. The twelve lesser goddesses were erected around her, bowing in her presence. All were made entirely of glass, allowing the light to swirl through them.

The dinner party filed into the cushioned pews. The king, queen, Synder, and Peter took up the first row. I looked to Peter, trying to gauge what would happen next as the priest came forth in a deep set of purple robes, the color of Pylemo. The twisted knot symbol of our Goddess was etched onto his chest like twin corded snakes, wrapping around one another. His expression was hard and hinted at nothing of what was to come. I always thought the king's priest would be warm and welcoming, but he was austere and closed off.

The priest stopped before the altar, and my heart skipped a beat as I realized it was where Sie and I were being positioned. I swallowed hard as I finally looked up at him. He was already staring down at me. We still hadn't spoken since our conversation on the monorail. The necklace he gave me was visible through my dress's low cut. The pendant felt heavy between my breasts.

"We are gathered here today to welcome the union that has begun between Sie Axel Noren and Scotlind Mae Rumor." The priest's voice was rhythmic. "After tonight, they will officially become our Prince and Princess of Tennebris. After tonight, they will officially be betrothed before our Goddess, and their future marriage set in stone."

There was no going back after this. My chest rose to match my rapid breathing. Sie's fixed gaze made everything feel worse.

"Please join hands," the priest continued. Sie didn't react as his callused hands found my sweaty ones. "Do you both pledge your betrothal to one another before Pylemo? Do you pledge to accept one another as husband and wife until the end of your time?"

"I do," Sie said.

The entire room shifted their attention to me, surveying me. They were waiting for me to speak. "I do," I whispered, my voice shaky.

The priest smiled slightly at our joined hands. "Let us pray to Pylemo that she may accept your engagement. May she bless your souls with an offspring during your consummation of marriage just as she does every five hundred years at Lakimi. Let us pray that Sie's reign will correlate with an advantageous rule over Tennebris and that you both may bring our kingdom wealth and prosperity."

I swore the light halted and stopped dancing through the Goddesses' statues as I sent a silent prayer to Pylemo that she *wouldn't* bless our marriage. After the deafening silence, the priest looked over the crowd as he raised his arms in the air. "May I present to you our Prince and Princess of Tennebris. Their betrothal is blessed by the Goddess herself."

The priest bowed his head, closing his eyes. The rest of the room followed suit.

As the prayers were spoken, I dropped Sie's hands, leaving mine cold and empty without his touch. I was going to marry him. This was going to be the rest of my life, however long that may be. My breathing turned ragged. The necklace felt like a heavy weight, chaining me to a future I didn't want.

I needed to breathe, to be alone, to have a minute to myself. I bolted down the narrow aisle, picking up the hem of my long dress, not caring that my boots were visible to anyone that looked, not caring if the ceremony wasn't finished.

As soon as I pushed open the doors to the chapel, I realized my mistake. The ballroom had been completely transformed. The emptiness just before we entered the chapel now bloomed with life. A dance floor was erected over the alabaster flooring, tables were scattered throughout the perimeter. Soft music echoed off the stone walls. I had no idea how I couldn't hear the beautiful melody through the chapel because now it was all consuming.

I stood frozen inside the frame of the door. The room was filled with Advenians anxious to see the newly engaged couple, and there was me, dress hiked to my knees, wide-eyed and panting.

I bit down my nausea. All the food I forced myself to eat earlier was stirring and threatening to come up. This was going to be a long, long night.

I made my way toward the back of the room, awkwardly watching the few brave Advenians who swept over the dance floor. Most just chatted amongst themselves, filling their stomachs with wine.

I hated crowds. I hated dancing. I hated that everyone's gaze was focused on me, stealing glances when they thought I wasn't looking. Some stared even when I returned their gaze. Most of the males didn't pay heed to my narrowed eyes and furrowed brows as their focus drifted toward my low neckline. I knew it wasn't the golden pendant they were staring at. I was going to curse Sie for selecting this dress for me.

Everyone wanted to see for themselves what was so special about me. Why a rank zero was selected for their prince, and this dress played right into the part that I was only meant to be arm candy.

To make things worse, everyone wore their branding like jewelry, exposing their left wrist to display their rank. I was the only one in the room with a rank lower than a three. Only the servants shared the same zero that was burned into me.

I could feel the silent judgment radiating off of everyone. The mean sneers of the females dressed in radiant, flowing gowns, wondering how I was chosen to be the princess. You and me both, I thought.

Synder approached me like a cat. He was so quiet that I didn't realize he was before me until he spoke, "I'm here to inform you about your guards, Miss Rumor."

"Um, thank you," I said.

"You will have three guards in total. You'll get briefed and acquainted with them tomorrow morning."

"Three guards?" I blurted before I remembered who I was talking to. Peter mentioned that I would have a guard with me, but I didn't think I needed three.

An amused look crossed his face. "For someone who wanted to be a guard herself, you know nothing of the position. I would have thought you would have done your research, Miss Rumor."

I tried to maintain my composure and not bristle at his insult.

He sneered, a cruel smile lingering on his thin lips. "You will have a guard with you at all times. Two of the guards will rotate between shifts. One will be with you throughout the night, the other during the day. The third guard will be your backup guard, he will be in charge of other duties around the kingdom. However, if one of your guards gets injured on the job, your backup guard will fill in. You will be spending a lot of time together, so I recommend that you make yourself comfortable with them."

"Gets injured on the job," I repeated, letting his words sink in. He made it sound like that was a common occurrence.

"Yes," Synder said, noting my words. "Contrary to what you may have believed, being a guard is not glamorous. Especially protecting someone as weak as yourself. If people want to get to Prince Noren, it will be a lot easier going through you. Your betrothed is a rank five. I think Advenians will find it impossible to attack him directly."

"However," he continued, "his princess, a rank zero, makes you a *very* easy target. You should always be on high alert. Your school's training was child's play compared to the real thing, so it would be wise to stay close to your guards. The use of abilities like compulsion are not monitored within our walls."

He didn't wait for me to respond before walking away. Chills continued through my spine long after he left me.

I hadn't thought about it. That Advenians could use me as leverage to get to Sie. Sie mentioned people may want to kill me, but it didn't cross my mind that I might be used in that way too. Well, they would be disappointed if they tried. I didn't mean anything to him. Besides, I was not helpless. I'd trained as a guard my whole life. I knew how to fight, and Peter agreed to more training.

A tall head of black hair stood above everyone else. I stole a glance across the hall and instantly regretted it. Sie was surrounded by females, all flirting with him and fighting for his attention.

Didn't they know he was going to be married now? I was literally standing across the dance floor, and this stupid banquet was supposed to be celebrating our engagement. Maybe they hoped to become one of his mistresses or just wanted to be with the only rank five for a night. I couldn't deny that he was attractive.

Tall, dark, and handsome was an understatement.

I found myself unable to stop staring as one of the girls leaned into his chest, giggling. She was beautiful with silky golden hair falling past her shoulders and light brown eyes that shone against her pale complexion.

Sie didn't push her away as she pressed every curve of hers into him. By the way the two of them were talking, they appeared to be well acquainted. He finally turned to look at her, smiling at something she said.

"How are you doing?" a voice asked, startling me. I turned to find a familiar face. Peter. I was relieved to stop thinking about Sie. I hated how seeing him with other girls bothered me.

"I'm good," I spoke flatly. Peter's face lit up with amusement, taunting me.

"Really?" he questioned with a smirk as he followed my stare over to Sie. "Don't worry, he won't do anything with them."

My mouth dropped at his words, that he thought I was thinking *that*. It had been on my mind, but was it that obvious?

"The blonde over there," Peter continued, pointing to the beautiful girl still leaning into Sie, "is Reagan. We've known her since childhood. Sie's never been interested in her, no matter how hard she tries. As for the other girls, they are her little minions. They follow her around like a bee to honey."

Flustered, I tried to recover, "Oh, no. That's not what I—"

He cut me off. "You don't have to explain yourself to me. Come. Let's get a drink. You need one."

He was still smiling as he led me over to a beautiful tower of champagne glasses. I wanted to try it—to taste it—as I stared at the bubbles floating around in the golden flutes. I could see why Vallie loved to drink. When it came to guys, it was nice to have a distraction, but I wasn't sure if that was a good idea right now.

"I don't really drink," I started.

"Funny. If I recall, I clearly remember you getting drunk and seeming to like alcohol very much."

"And I recall a *stalker* following me around the entire night."

He shrugged. "You needed help, and I was happy to oblige. I'm curious though, does this newfound phase of not wanting to drink alcohol have something to do with the fact that you like to take your clothes off afterward? Something about being too hot…"

I whipped around to face him. "What?" I gasped.

He laughed at me, clearly amused with himself as the tips of my ears heated. "I was staying with Sie at LakeWood for your graduation. I knew he walked you back to your dorm that night, and when he came back to the inn, shirtless might I add, and grinning from ear to ear, I forced it out of him. He'd seen tons of naked girls before, but I guess there was something about you that—"

"I was naked?" I asked, my voice catching in my throat. My eyes felt like they were going to pop out of my head. With everything that had happened, I forgot to ask him why I woke up in his shirt the next day. Goddess above, what did I do?

Peter seemed to note my rising panic. "You don't remember what happened?"

Words couldn't form in my mouth as I turned the brightest shade of red and shook my head no.

"After I sent word to Sie to come get you, he carried you back to your dorm. He said that once you were there, you kept complaining about how hot it was. Before he could stop you, you apparently started stripping down. That was right before you vomited everywhere."

He laughed as my mortification grew. "Relax, nothing else

happened. He cleaned you up and gave you fresh clothes. You fell asleep before you could embarrass yourself more."

I couldn't believe this was happening. My hand instinctively grabbed my neck as I swallowed. I couldn't decide what bothered me more. The fact that Sie carried me home—*carried* for crying out loud—or the fact that I had taken off my dress in front of him, and then vomited while being *naked*. Sie telling Peter was just the cherry on top.

I also couldn't shake the comment about Sie seeing tons of naked girls. It shouldn't bother me, so why did it? It did, however, answer my question about the rumors of Sie being experienced in that regard.

Of course he had been with tons of people. He had been a known rank five ever since he was little, making him famous in Tennebris. That, along with his annoyingly handsome face and tall lithe body, must make females throw themselves at him.

"I've never seen Sie so dopey before. I guess he saw before everyone else did that you have a nice body underneath all the guard gear and male clothing you usually wear. I can see now why he was so happy."

Peter pointed toward the thin material of my dress. I shifted on my feet. "Are you mocking me?"

"Only a little," he said, grinning, exposing his two deep dimples as he placed a glass of champagne in my hand. "Don't worry, Scottie. I'll make sure you don't drink too much, and I'll make sure your clothes stay on, even though I'm sure half the males in this room wouldn't mind if they didn't," he added.

I gave Peter the nastiest glare I could muster, but it dropped as my mind started to race.

I couldn't stop replaying Sie's words, *I don't want you to get hurt because of me,* and how his lips were so close to mine on the monorail ride. Then remembering how he told me he didn't care about a wife. How he thought that me being chosen was a setup, that I wasn't an appropriate match for him.

Then my traitorous mind went to all the females throwing themselves at him right now, even though this banquet was supposed to celebrate our betrothal. Sick of my thoughts being consumed by him, I put the champagne glass to my lips and drank deeply.

The liquid fizzed as it went down my throat. It was sweet—nothing like the vodka and beer I had at the party.

"You better keep your word," I said as I finished my drink. "I'm sure your prince wouldn't be happy to have his future wife embarrassing him."

Peter returned my words with a smile, and despite myself, I found myself smiling back at him. He went to open his mouth to say something when someone came up behind him.

"Peter," the male purred as he placed a hand on his shoulder. "And this lovely female must be Princess Rumor?"

"It's Scottie," I said to the male. He smiled at me as he shook out his coppery hair. He wasn't built like a fighter, not in the way Peter and Sie were. But even though he was more lanky than lean, he had an aggressive arrogance to him. I couldn't tell if it was cockiness or confidence. The four branded on his wrist told me enough, that even if he didn't physically train, he was powerful.

"Nice to meet you, Scottie. I'm Alec. Friend of Sie, Peter, and our dear Reagan. I'm sure I'll be seeing a lot of you now."

Peter stiffened next to me. The gesture suggesting they weren't friends. Alec assessed me as he drank from his glass. There was a gleam in his eyes as his gaze raked over my body.

Out of the corner of my eye, I saw Sie stalking straight toward us, his eyes more narrow than usual. The girls he'd left behind all looked disappointed. Especially Reagan, who was now glaring at me as she tossed her blonde hair over her shoulders.

"Peter. Alec." Sie sneered under his breath, voice low and raw. Some silent conversation must have gone on between them because Peter and Alec both looked at Sie, nodded, then left without saying a word.

Once the two of them walked off, Sie turned his attention to me. "Don't talk to Alec."

"Excuse me?"

"You heard me," he said, taking a step closer. "Don't talk to him."

"I don't take orders from you." I crossed my arms as I looked up at him, my empty glass now dangling from my hand.

He huffed and I couldn't tell if it was in amusement or irritation, maybe both. "I'm surprised to see you drinking again."

My eyes narrowed at the audacity of him. "Like I said, I don't take orders from you. If that's what you wanted, you should have picked someone else to marry."

"I wasn't trying to tell you not to drink. I was just surprised." When I didn't answer, he added, "On the contrary, I find you quite amusing when you drink. You're not so uptight." He almost smiled, taking me in. "I don't mind the less-clothing thing too." It was as if he'd heard the conversation Peter and I had moments before. "I like the dress," he added.

"I bet you do. I was told you picked it out, so I guess I have you to thank for all the stares not directed at my face tonight."

I shifted uncomfortably as his own gaze briefly drifted to what I'd implied.

He turned serious, the half smile dropped from his face as he said, "You shouldn't let your guard down, not yet. I don't trust anyone here, and neither should you."

That was not what I expected him to say. "Should I not trust your friends either? Is that the reason I'm not allowed to talk to them?"

"You can trust Peter, but not the others," he said matter-of-factly as he gestured toward where Reagan and Alec were both standing. "Come, dance with me. It's tradition that the engaged couple dances at least once at their own party."

"I don't want to," I deadpanned. He ignored me, tossed my empty glass to the side, and grabbed my arm, careful to avoid the wrappings still on my wrist. "Sie, stop. I don't want to dance."

He pulled me out onto the dance floor and swung me around. My hand splayed flat against his chest as I crashed into him.

"You're going to find, Scotlind Rumor, that it doesn't matter what either of us want anymore. We are both going to have to do things we don't like."

"I hardly see how dancing is something we have to do."

"There are a lot of old traditions Tennebris has kept, and there will be a lot that is expected of us."

I didn't want to know what other things we would be forced into, not now. I gritted my teeth. "What I meant is, I can't dance. It's not about not wanting to… I don't know how."

His eyebrows scrunched up as he assessed me, but he didn't laugh. "I'll guide you. You just have to get close to me."

"What? No—"

"You can learn to dance later, but for now, just follow my lead. Like you said, I don't want a wife who will embarrass me."

I rolled my eyes as I looked up to meet his gaze.

"Come on, Scotlind. One dance won't kill you."

Hesitantly, I stepped closer to him, filling the gap between us. He placed his hand firmly on my back, drawing me in closer. My breathing quickened as my breasts lightly touched his chest with each movement. A soft, quiet melody began playing from the musicians. I couldn't tell where the music was coming from or where the musicians stood, but their song carried across the room as he guided me further onto the dance floor.

"You look beautiful tonight. Wearing a dress suits you," he whispered into my ear, his breath hot on my neck.

"Th-thank you," I stuttered, feeling flushed. Had he noticed? By the smirk he was giving me, I would think so. I looked away from his gaze and stared at his chest, which wasn't much better.

I hated how my body reacted to him. How I felt dizzy in his presence. I couldn't catch my breath, and my stomach twirled in knots. I didn't want to be like the other doting girls that followed him around everywhere he went. I hated him, even if my body disagreed. My mind hated him.

Sie swept me down, leaning into me as my hair brushed against the floor. I caught Reagan scowling. Alec was leaning against the wall with his arms crossed over his chest. Amusement flickered in his gaze as he watched us like a hawk. I scanned the room for Peter, but he was nowhere to be found.

"Try not to look so frightened," Sie said as he leaned into me, whispering in my ear. "Right now, every single High Council member is watching your movements, seeing how you react, so look like you belong."

"And do I belong here?"

"It doesn't matter if you do or don't. You have to now. You don't have a choice."

I couldn't tell if he was helping me out of concern or for his own benefit. Synder's words haunted me as I scanned the crowd. Sie was right. Every member had their eyes glued to me, watching our every movement as Sie twirled me around the now empty floor.

"Chin up. Just look at me," he whispered. I did. His dark eyes lightened. It was just a dance. Why did it bother me so much?

*His princess, a rank zero, makes you a very easy target.*

*It would be wise to stay close to your guards.*

*If people want to get to Prince Noren, it will be a lot easier going through you.*

*The use of abilities like compulsion are not monitored within our walls.*

The music finally faded out, and I was thankful Sie kept true to his word and only requested one song. We both took a step back. Sie stared at me like he was waiting for something, but I didn't stay to find out as I turned in the other direction, storming out of the Hall before anyone could stop me.

I didn't care that I was alone in a foreign castle where people might want me dead. Or at least, I didn't care enough.

# EIGHTEEN
## SCOTLIND

T HE  BANQUET  WASN'T  OVER,  AND  I  KNEW  THERE  WAS probably more expected of me during the night. But I needed to be alone.

I focused on my breathing as I leaned against a stone wall. I was in a deserted hallway with only a torch as company. The embers slowly fading and dying off, making the room dimmer as the minutes ticked on.

The music was faintly playing in the distance. The only indication that the banquet was still going on. I listened to it until it grew softer, using the melody as a map to guide myself further from that room full of Advenians. I didn't stop walking until the sound faded into silence, and I was left with nothing but my panting, ragged breaths.

I wanted my bed. I wanted to curl up inside the warm sheets and forget about everything. It would be my last night of peace. My last night before a guard would be stationed at my side. The problem was, I had no idea where my room was. Each hall looked identical to the next, each passageway a maze. I embraced the silence of the empty halls, but the more I roamed through the castle, the more I realized I had absolutely no idea where I was going.

I wandered into a wide, oval corridor with an arched, glass ceiling I didn't recognize. Light was shining through the dome-like window, but it was impossible to tell how much time had passed since I'd left the banquet.

I was still looking up, searching for the position of the sun through the stained patterns on the glass, when I heard a light, whimsical voice sound from behind me.

"You look lost."

I spun around. It was the beautiful blonde from the party. "Is it that obvious?" I asked. She laughed, it was warm and sweet and nothing like I expected. "I'm Scottie," I added.

"I know." She cocked her head to the side. "Reagan. Come, I'll help you find where you are trying to go."

"Back to my room," I admitted.

She reached out and clasped her warm fingers over my wrist. I held back a wince as the cloth wrapping dug into my charred flesh.

"The castle is huge. We know it well now because we have been coming here since we were young, but Sie, Alec, Peter, and I got lost numerous times as children. I can imagine how overwhelming it is to you. You've been here for how long again?"

"Only today. We arrived this morning."

"I'll walk you back," was all she replied.

She started leading me through the castle. I happily followed, knowing my bed waited for me. Sie said I couldn't trust her. Frankly, I didn't trust anyone, but that didn't mean I couldn't accept her kindness, and I needed sleep.

Reagan halted in front of a tall black door studded with metal spikes.

"This isn't my room," I started. I could, at least, remember what my door looked like.

"I know. They had to change your sleeping chamber. Some remodeling of yours needed to be done. Sie sent me to come find you once you left the banquet since they didn't get to tell you about the change." She smiled. "You will be able to pick your belongings up tomorrow. There's some shirts in the top drawer that you can sleep in for tonight. I hope you don't mind. I know it's not fit for a princess but—"

"No, it's fine. Thank you so much. It was lovely meeting you."

"Pleasure is all mine," she said over her shoulder as she stalked off. "I'm sure we'll get along just fine, Scottie."

The room was larger than the one Peter showed me earlier. Torches hung on the slick walls, and candles were scattered throughout, already lit and half melted. Black silk sheets were spread across the bed. It was just as grand and just as pointless of a waste of space as the rest of the room. No one person could take up that much room while sleeping. Unless it wasn't meant for just one person.

I shook off the thought and walked over to the black leather sofa, facing the crackling fireplace. Stone surrounded the relentless fire, taking up a substantial portion of the wall. I usually wouldn't sit so close to open flames, but my body felt numb. It didn't help that my dress barely covered my skin.

Red wine was poured into a crystal glass. The bottle was left open as if someone had been drinking from it moments prior. I didn't care. I grabbed the glass and sank into the cool seat, the leather biting against the slit in my dress.

A thud sounded from the next room as I went to lift the glass to my lips. I jerked, and the red liquid spilled down my chest and onto the very expensive, very sheer material, staining my dress. Goddess above.

I walked toward what I presumed was the bathing room, praying to Pylemo this stain would come out with water.

I pushed the door open and slammed into something hard and wet. My feet gave out from under me, and I tumbled with whatever I'd hit coming down with me.

A shriek escaped my lips when I opened my eyes. I was lying right on top of Sie... again.

I quickly jumped off of him. He chuckled softly as he propped himself up onto his elbows and looked up at me through his wet, wavy locks. I tried not to notice how his legs were slightly spread, or the fact that he was only wearing a towel that hung dangerously low around his waist. He shook his head slightly, causing his hair to flip and move away from his eyes.

The water clung to his still-bruised body, making his skin glisten. I couldn't help but watch the droplets trail down his broad shoulders, down to his defined chest and lithe abdomen. His biceps bulged as he adjusted himself and propped himself up a little higher. My eyes traced down over his stomach where his wound from Lunder was starting to crust over. A little bit of dark hair started below, forming a thin line, leading down to his towel.

"Like what you see?" he asked as he looked up at me, smiling. I didn't realize I was staring, but his low voice brought me out of my trance.

"What? No!" I said, whipping my head away to stare at the wall.

"You know," he purred, "we really have to stop meeting like this. You have a knack for falling on me."

"I wouldn't have bumped into you if you weren't in my bathing room. What are you doing here?" I asked. I was thankful for the steam collecting on the mirrors, blocking my view of my face. I didn't want to see how flushed I was yet again.

"You mean, what am I doing getting out of *my* bath in *my* room?"

I looked around. "Your room?"

"Yes, my room, Scotlind. Now I should ask you the same question. What exactly are you doing in my room, barging in on me while I'm bathing?" he asked as he slowly, so slowly, peeled himself off the floor. His hand rested on the top of his towel, careful to not lose it as he advanced closer to me.

I stepped back, trying to maintain our distance, but my back met with the cold marble wall. I flinched. I couldn't go back any further, and he didn't stop moving closer. I was utterly aware of every inch he took as he closed the distance between us.

I bit down on my bottom lip nervously. "I don't know. Reagan— she found me in the halls. I was lost and couldn't find my room. She told me they moved me here because of the remodeling."

"Remodeling?" At his laugh, I realized how foolish it all sounded. "Right, they are remodeling your bedroom in the middle of the night.

Are you sure about that?" His chest brushed up against mine, leaving watermarks over my dress. "To me, it looks like you came to my room late at night, without your guards, might I add. And now, here you are, standing in a very revealing dress, barging in on me while I bathe."

I followed Sie's gaze and looked down at my gown. The top of my dress had fallen lower, revealing more cleavage than I would have liked. I quickly tugged on it, trying to pull it higher, but it barely moved.

"What is a male supposed to think?" he breathed into my mouth as he planted his hand next to my face, pinning me between the wall and him so I couldn't move. His other hand slid to my chin, forcing me to look up at him. I could smell the alcohol on his breath as he leaned in, completely closing any gap between us.

He was going to kiss me. Except this time, Peter wasn't here to interrupt us. No one would come. This was his private chamber. I closed my eyes, waiting for it, wanting it. My brain couldn't think past my body's desire, couldn't process that I should hate him. All I could think about was how his lips would feel against mine. How his hands felt as they touched my face, rough and calloused. Every place he touched sent a jolt through my system, waking me up.

I wanted him. Needed him on me. My breath hitched, and I let out a small noise as his lips finally met mine.

At first, he just barely grazed against me, lightly, lingering, teasing. Testing me. His lips were soft, still wet from his bath. He pulled away slightly. His eyes met mine, allowing me the chance to back out of this if I wanted.

I didn't.

"Please," my voice came out ragged and breathless. It was more of a plea than a statement. I wanted to taste him. He didn't hesitate as he leaned forward again, this time crashing into me.

My lips parted for him, allowing him in, giving him full access to me. My hands fell to my sides. I gave up trying to pull on the fabric of the sheer dress. He slowly—but strongly—moved his lips against mine as he ground his hips into my stomach. I felt him harden against me as an ache began to form between my thighs. I wanted him. I pulled him closer to me, my own hands slipping against his wet back.

"Scotlind," he groaned low into my mouth as he pushed the fabric away to cup the underside of my breast. "Fuck," he whispered so softly, I thought I imagined it.

I knew I should hate this. I should have stopped him, but I didn't. I found my lips matching his, moving slowly, exploring the taste of him. I couldn't get enough. His hands caressed my body, exploring each of my curves.

I moaned into his mouth as my back arched. He took that as an invitation to move his lips faster and harder against mine. He moved like he couldn't get enough. One of his hands found its way into my hair. He grabbed, tangling his fingers into my curls, tugging softly so that my head tilted up for him. I obeyed. His other hand trailed down my back, pulling me against him.

I didn't know what had come over me, but it felt good. I forgot about who I was kissing. I forgot about everything but what was happening right now. I was lost in the moment. My mind a blank canvas, only wanting to be painted by him.

I placed my hands on his arms, not caring that they were getting wet, that my dress was slowly becoming soaked with each movement. I slowly traced them down his body, taking my time feeling him beneath me. Feeling each muscle bulging below my fingertips as I traveled down and down.

When I didn't think it was possible to get any closer to him, he continued to kiss me as he pulled me deeper into him, grabbing me by my hips.

He moaned as my lips parted for his tongue. His kisses became more fervent, more aggressive. I felt his need as strongly as I felt mine. I wanted more. I *needed* more.

My body grew sticky as the steam lingered in the air, collecting on us like morning dew—an invisible cord, entangling us into one another until we became one. The cedarwood fragrance from his soap filled my nostrils as he lifted me off the ground. His lips broke from mine as he pinned me, my back flattening against the cold wall.

Without thinking, I wrapped my legs around his waist, locking him onto me.

He leaned his head down, his forehead resting against mine, teasing me with his closeness. I felt the absence of his lips. His eyes met mine. He was panting into my mouth as his hands gently worked their way up my legs. He grazed his fingers over my calves, my knees. He was pulling my dress up with his touch, the material bunched around my thighs.

He stroked his fingers idly, lazily, making caressing circles on my inner thighs, slowly working his way up higher and higher as my ache for him became all consuming. I needed him to kiss me again, but he didn't. The tightness in my core grew and grew until it became unbearable.

"Please," I panted.

"Please, what?" he murmured into my neck. My eyes fluttered shut as I leaned my head back against the wall. I could feel his smile against my throat as his lips formed soft kisses over my neck, not meeting mine again until I moaned, loudly.

"Shh," he breathed in between kisses. I didn't know why I had to be quiet, but I was too distracted to ask.

My breath became shallow. Water droplets dripped down from his wet locks, landing on my face, but I didn't care. He was overpowering all my senses. I didn't have room left in me for the water to scare me like it should. I couldn't think about anything but wanting him, needing him.

My hands worked their way to his chest, feeling his muscles tense under my touch. I grinned into his mouth, gliding my way down his abdomen, feeling everything as I went. His reaction made me feel powerful, a feeling I wasn't used to. I felt in control as my body went out of it.

My fingers lingered briefly over the cut where King Lunder had stabbed him before moving down to meet his towel. Without thinking, I curled my fingers under the fabric, wanting to feel him on my bare skin. My breathing was ragged, my heart racing as he moaned my name into my mouth.

Something snapped inside me. Reality came flooding in as I realized what I was about to do—what we were about to do. Sie noticed my hesitation and stopped kissing me. He looked me over, scanning my face. I quickly pulled my hands off his towel and raised them up in the air. It was a mistake. My fingers caught the edge of the white fabric, causing it to drop to the floor.

I gasped, my eyes flaring wide. He was still holding me up against the wall. But without his towel, I felt every inch of him pressed against the bareness of my upper thighs, my dress still bunched over my hips.

He gently set me back down on the ground. My hands flung up to cover my mouth. As if I could take back what just happened.

The world stilled as I came back to myself. What we did and what we still hadn't done racing through my mind. The euphoria of the moment washing away with each passing second, leaving me with an emptiness.

I couldn't read his expression. Sie's face was again a blank mask. I looked anywhere around the room, but down. His eyes never left mine as he stood there, naked, not bothering to pick up his fallen towel. His breathing was heavier than normal, his chest rose and fell with every inhale. I knew mine was worse, coming out in raspy waves like I'd just run for hours.

I didn't know what to do or what to say to him. I turned to get out of the bathroom as fast as I could, but I slipped. A pool of water had collected over where we were just kissing.

Sie stepped forward to catch me, but his foot landed on the extra material of my gown, flooding at my feet, causing it to pull and rip in the back. Before I could catch myself, I landed hard into the puddle, face up on the bathing room floor.

My cheeks were burning as Sie stood over me, the thing I was trying so hard to avoid, directly in view.

A half smile crept over his face as he bent down and reached out a hand toward me. "You okay?"

I swatted his outstretched hand and ignored his question as I pushed him off. Gathering the bottom section of my dress in one hand while holding the top that was threatening to come off with the other, I sprinted as fast as my feet allowed.

Once in the hall, I took a deep, uneven breath. I just had my first kiss, and what was more, I liked it. I'd wanted to do more than kiss, and I might have let him. My mind kept replaying the images of his lips moving over mine, claiming me. The feel of his hands roaming over my bare skin. How he'd moaned my name and kissed my throat. I was furious at myself for letting him. That I'd leaned into him. That I'd *begged* him to continue.

He probably would have done that with any girl who came into his room. It had meant nothing to him. I was just another girl he could add to his long list of conquests.

I shook my head, forcing myself to snap out of it. I swore and cursed myself that I would never let that happen again as I began marching down the hall.

It seemed like I had been roaming the castle forever, looking ridiculous, before I finally came across the familiar oak doors to my room.

I stripped out of my torn dress and screamed into my pillow.

# NINETEEN
## SCOTLIND



"It's time to get up, princess. You have to get ready for breakfast," Annabel said with a smile as she opened the curtains, letting the rays shine through. "Quickly jump in the bath, then put this on." She pointed to a simple tan dress that hung over the sofa. I wished it were my usual pants and shirt, but at least it wasn't as revealing as last night's attire.

"It's just Scottie," I told her again. I couldn't stand being called princess or whatever other names they had for me. "Thank you." I gestured to the dress as I made my way to the bathing room.

After I bathed and dressed, Annabel walked me toward the smallest of the three cafeterias in silence. I briefly recalled Peter telling me it was only available to the royals, council members, and their families.

As Annabel held the door open for me, I couldn't help but notice the zero burned and healed on her left wrist. Would my life have been like hers if I hadn't been chosen to be the princess? Did she know it? I wasn't any different from them. According to Sie, I was supposed to be one of them. Waiting and doting on the upper rank. Maybe that's why Roslyn didn't like me.

Synder found me the moment I finished with breakfast. He

directed me into the hall where three males in guard uniforms waited. Their arms were neatly folded across their stomachs, all the same unmoving statues.

Synder waved his arms out, gesturing to the males. "Miss Rumor, I have been given permission for you to be late to your lessons this morning since you're being introduced to your guards. You are not to go anywhere without one of them by your side."

*Lessons.* Goddess above. I never read through my packet. I had no idea what my day was supposed to entail. I should have listened to Peter and studied the information they provided me.

Synder's lip curled up in the corner. "I took the liberty of selecting them myself. I thought it would make you happy to have someone you are familiar with guard you. A friend from school to make your adjustment to the castle more comfortable."

That was when I looked up. My jaw dropped as I saw Kole standing among them. Just as still, just as professional as the other two. The twin pink moons were etched into his black uniform, making him look older, colder, and more scarier than before.

*No, no, no, no.*

"Are you not pleased?" Synder challenged. Was this a test? I willed my face into neutrality.

"Yes, I am. Thank you. That is very kind of you," I said placidly. Internally I wanted to scream.

"Has anyone ever told you about my abilities, Miss Rumor?" Synder asked, taking me by surprise. I read in my packet his title and standing, but I couldn't recall his abilities. Most members of the High Council liked to keep the full extent of their abilities a secret.

"No, I'm not aware of them."

"As you probably know, there are many variations of mind control. It's not only limited to compulsion." I nodded my head, waiting for him to continue, not daring to breathe.

"Well, I was gifted with being able to determine whenever someone is telling the truth and when someone is lying." I swallowed the lump back in my throat. Images flashed through my mind of him at my evaluation. Did I say anything that wasn't truthful then? The day was a blur and I couldn't remember, but an uneasy feeling swept over me. Did he have a hunch about me? About the side of me that was Luxian?

"That is a very useful ability," I remarked carefully. Kole smirked despite his bowed head.

"Indeed, it is." Synder's smile turned mischievous. "Kole will be your guard throughout the night. And this is Abherham. He will be your guard during the day."

I turned my attention away from Synder to meet Abherham's gaze. He seemed older, not in his appearance, since every Advenian looked young, but in his demeanor, in how he presented himself.

His brown hair was kept short, his skin a rich chestnut. He wasn't as tall as Kole's looming figure, but stood straight, proud, silent. His facial features were fixed as he gave me a subtle nod.

Synder turned my attention toward the third male standing before me, "This is Alexander. He will be your substitute guard."

Alexander gave me a grim smile. "I hope you won't be seeing much of me, princess, but it is nice to make your acquaintance."

I cringed as I remembered what Synder had told me during the banquet. Alexander would only be filling in if one of my main guards became injured on the job.

As much as I wouldn't mind that happening to Kole, I said, "I hope that you don't need to step in. It is nice to meet you all."

Synder clasped his hands together. "Well, now that you all know each other, Abherham will take you to your lessons. Kole will take over at night."

I caught a glance of Kole before Abherham guided me toward wherever my lessons would be. My stomach turned in on itself at the smug, brooding grin. I bit the inside of my cheek. I wanted to punch that grin off his face. How was I going to be able to sleep when Kole would be guarding me throughout the night?

———

THE ONLY GOOD thing about my new schedule was that it was a distraction. Despite how dreadful the lessons were, they kept me engrossed. I didn't have time to think about Sie or our kiss. I didn't have time to worry about Kole spending every night with me. About how I probably wouldn't be able to sleep again.

The first half of the day was slow, painfully slow. I was almost thankful I had never looked at my schedule beforehand because I would have dreaded it. Abherham remained by my side the entire time. He never spoke to me but would offer an occasional smile or nod as he directed me through the halls in between lessons. My only break was a prolonged lunch spent with females of the high rank. I was surprised to see the current queen among them. Although she kept too busy with a handful of people to even notice me. I assumed they were wives of the High Council. Reagan was among the group, but she avoided me too. I didn't know what I dreaded more—the classes or the forced gossip.

The lessons were a mixture of general knowledge and etiquette. My entire morning was spent relearning the ranking system and how each rank was categorized. I stared at the paper before me for hours until my eyes hurt.

- **Rank 0:** No abilities, no magical reserve
- **Rank 1:** One common ability, small magical reserve
- **Rank 2:** One strong ability, small magical reserve; or one common ability, large magical reserve
- **Rank 3:** Two common abilities, large magical reserve
- **Rank 4:** Two strong abilities, large magical reserve
- **Rank 5:** Two or more strong abilities with one ability considered rare, large magical reserve

MY CLASSES after lunch were worse—etiquette training. Lady Applebee was overseeing my studies. She was a scarier, younger version of Professor Gibs, but without the hunchback and an even stricter sneer.

By the end of her lessons, I had bruises already developing across my breasts and arms. She had smacked me across the chest with a book every time my posture drifted into my normal slouched stance. I'd never been insulted so many times within a few hours as she grumbled under her breath that I sat like a male or walked like a penguin. She'd grumbled that the task of making me a lady was impossible too many times to count.

I was rubbing my chest when Abherham spoke for the first time. "You have one more lesson, milady."

I groaned. This was a new sort of nightmare. If I had to sit through one more class, I was going to lose it. I struggled with remaining calm during my normal classes back in LakeWood, but this was worse, so much worse.

"What more could they possibly want me to learn in one day?" I mumbled under my breath, unable to keep my composure. All I wanted was to curl up in my bed, fall asleep, and not have to talk to anyone. Except that wouldn't happen, not with Kole as my night guard.

My guard cleared his throat. "It is the training you requested, milady."

Oh—OH. Heat flushed my cheeks, and I felt guilty for snapping. "I'm sorry, Abherham."

"No apologies needed, milady," he said as he led me toward the gym. I quickened my pace. I wanted to spar someone. I wanted to hit something, to let my frustration out with each punch.

"Please call me Scottie," I told Abherham. I was getting sick of repeating the same phrase over and over, but every time I heard any variation of a title, I cringed.

Abherham's lips curved into a slight upward tilt, barely passable for a smile, and I knew that he wouldn't oblige. But it didn't matter, not right now at least. I was going to be able to train. I would be able to get out of this awful dress and put on pants and a shirt.

We had just rounded another corner when I ran into Peter. Three females surrounded him. One was clutching her belly, doubled over at something he said. The other two smiled shyly, covering their mouths to muffle their laughter. I clicked my tongue. The fact that it was lady-like to mask your emotions, hide your laugh—at least one of the girls was living right. His smile broadened as he saw me approach. Abherham took a step back, lingering a safe distance behind me.

"Ladies." Peter nodded toward his entourage as they took the cue and dispersed.

"Hi." I smiled as he came up beside me.

"Hi back," he grinned. "How was your first day? Are you a lady yet?"

I rolled my eyes. "My day will be a lot better once I get to the gym and I can finally spar someone. Thank you for adding training to my schedule."

His smile faltered. "I did the best I could. Sie could only get the Council to agree to a *controlled workout*. It won't be the training you are used to. You aren't allowed to fight anyone."

"What? Why can't I spar?"

He arched his brow. "You really need me to tell you the answer to that?" When I didn't say anything, he sighed before adding, "It's not forbidden for a girl to fight, but it is still frowned upon. Why do you think there are no female King's Guards? They expect you to act the part of a princess, and a princess wouldn't show up to functions with a black and blue eye and a split lip."

"I'm just as likely to get a bruise from Lady Applebee," I tried.

He shrugged. "Rules are rules. I don't make them, I just follow them. Sometimes."

I ignored his wink. "And what exactly does a *controlled workout* entail?"

"Well, the punching bag will be very frightened of you."

His tone became serious as he added, "Scottie, just lay low for a little bit. This is new for everyone. You will have a lot of eyes on you, especially because of your rank. It will be hard for Sie to make any changes until he is king. You don't want to draw any more attention to yourself."

I nodded because I agreed with him about the attention part. I just didn't see how fighting anyone would be an issue.

"Speaking of which," he elongated his words. "I did hear that you stirred a bit of attention already."

"What do you mean?"

"Reagan found me earlier today and was uncharacteristically chipper. She told me that you two became friends. What happened?"

It definitely didn't seem that way by how she pointedly avoided me at lunch today. "I talked to her once. She tried to help me find my room last night after the banquet. I was lost."

"That was nice of her," he drawled slowly as if he was surprised by it.

"Yes," I admitted but couldn't keep the heat from rising in my face thinking back to last night. "Although she took me to the wrong room."

"What?" he laughed, genuinely seeming confused. "We have all been visiting the castle together since we were little kids. She knows her way around this place better than anyone. Where did she take you?"

"I think she just mistook Sie's room for my room. She told me my room was being renovated," I said. Peter stopped laughing. "What is it?"

"First off, this castle is old as balls and hasn't been remodeled in Goddess knows how long. Secondly, she did not mistake the rooms. She knows exactly which room is Sie's." He paused for a moment, thinking something over. "She was banking on Sie not being able to control himself around you. She must have thought you two would sleep together."

"I'm not following," I started to say, even more confused now.

"Reagan insisted on waking Sie up today with a handful of members from the High Council. She thought you would be there and that they would reject your engagement if you broke the rules."

"Broke what rules?"

"Your betrothal was Goddess approved. You two aren't allowed to consummate anything until your wedding night. If the High

Council thought you two slept together, it would have ended very badly."

"And they would have revoked our engagement if they thought that?"

He puzzled that for a moment. "It's hard to say. They certainly could have, but either way, you and Sie would have gotten in a lot of trouble. It's good you left without doing anything."

I blushed harder. I wished I'd left without doing anything. I was thankful I hadn't seen Sie since it happened. How far would we have gone if my nerves didn't ruin the moment? Would Sie have stopped it?

"Does Sie know about the rule?" I asked.

Peter nodded his head, his shaggy, blonde hair landing over his green eyes. "Yes, everyone in the castle knows about it, except clearly you. It goes against Pylemo's blessing to do so."

"Why would Reagan do that then?"

"Reagan has always had a crush on Sie. She believed that he was going to pick her as his queen. As you can imagine, she was livid when he didn't. She probably thought that if she could take you out of the picture, Sie would finally choose her."

"And finding me in Sie's room would be enough to end everything?" I questioned, wanting to know if I heard him right.

Peter looked at me. "Scottie, have you still not read through the rules? I know for a fact that you got them in your folder at graduation."

I bit my bottom lip, then stopped when my teeth scraped against my almost healed scab. It probably would have been fully healed by now if I hadn't aggravated it by kissing Sie last night. If it wasn't for the throbbing on my lower lip, I would have thought I imagined the whole encounter.

"I um… skimmed some of it," I admitted, remembering that I barely retained anything I read on the monorail. And even when Peter reminded me yesterday to familiarize myself with it, I just couldn't be bothered.

"Whether they would actually call off the engagement is hard to say, but you would definitely have been punished."

"Oh," I said flatly. "And if that happened, if our engagement ended, I mean, could I try out for the guard again?"

The words vomited out of my mouth as soon as the idea popped in my head. I knew I shouldn't admit it to Peter, but the idea of being able to get out of this was overwhelming. All I would have to do was spend one night with Sie, then I could be free. I could go back to my regular life.

"If that happened, Scottie, it wouldn't end well for you. No one can try out for Trials a second time. As for Sie, they would just select a different female for him to marry, which I think is what Reagan was hoping for. But you have to be careful. They won't hold you to the same standards as everyone else. You would be lucky if they made you a servant after an incident like that."

I swallow hard, taking in his warning. I was replaceable. Expendable. Nothing. I was a nix.

Peter took a step closer to me, leaning in to whisper in my ear, "I'll make you a deal."

My eyes snapped to his gaze, startled by the way he was speaking so softly. I could barely make out what he was saying.

"I'll train you."

"Really?" My voice spiked.

"Shh," he hushed. "Before your classes. I know how to hold back punches, so I'll be careful not to bruise your delicate skin."

I crossed my arms. "I'm not delicate."

He chuckled. "I guess you aren't. Okay then, I'll be careful not to bruise anywhere noticeable, but no one can know about it. We could get in a lot of trouble."

"Why would you do that for me?" I asked.

"Because you are in danger, more than Sie is letting on. I want to give you any fighting chance you can get."

"Thank you," I smiled.

He smiled back, noting my excitement. "I won't go easy on you. I don't think you will be thanking me afterward."

"I'll hold you to that," I said as he started to walk away.

He grinned. "Tomorrow, then."

# TWENTY
## SCOTLIND



I DIDN'T REALIZE I HAD FALLEN ASLEEP EARLY UNTIL I heard a knock on the door.

"Come in," I yawned as I stretched my arms over my head. Abherham strode into my room with Kole behind him. Dread crept up inside me as I knew what Abherham was going to say.

"Have a good night, milady." He bowed deeply. "I am off shift now. I will see you at five."

I wanted to beg him to stay but instead said, "Have a good night, Abherham." I could do nothing as he walked out the door, leaving me alone with Kole.

Kole waited until the door shut behind him before strolling over to an empty chair adjacent to the bed. "Well, well. Look at you, little nix. You look like a female for once with all the makeup and gowns." He looked me up and down slowly, and I pulled my sheets over my chest.

"Go away, Kole," I snapped.

"I can't. In case you don't remember, I will be with you *every single night* from now on. So you better get used to me." I winced at his enunciated words like it was a purr on his lips. Like I had forgotten what Synder had said this morning.

"You should ask for a reassignment."

"Oh? Why would I do that when I get to spend my time watching you sleep, making sure no one hurts you?" He sprung from the chair and lunged toward me. "It would be a shame if someone were to bruise your pretty face."

I bucked backward, my back slamming against the wooden post of the bed. I revolted at his nearness as he hovered over me. His fingers just grazed my lips as he reached out to touch me.

"Why don't you do us both a favor, and at least leave my bedroom so we can pretend the other doesn't exist."

He laughed, the sound dark and haunting as he walked back to the chair.

"No. I don't think I will do that either," he said, leaning back further into the seat, making himself comfortable. "You see, this is my job now, to protect you. So like it or not, I'll be staying right here."

"You don't have to stay in my room, though," I pleaded. I knew I sounded desperate, and I hated begging, but there was no way I would be able to rest with him here. "You don't need to watch me sleep. Can't you sit on the chair out in the hall?"

He smiled, showing all his teeth, knowing full well how uncomfortable he was making me. I was thankful that I hadn't changed into my nightgown yet. Annabel, Roslyn, and Ashley seemed to think a nightgown meant the smallest silk dress—if you could even call it a dress. It barely covered my thighs. The flimsy thing was so thin my nipples peeked through even when I wasn't cold.

"You think you can order me around now? Do you think you can tell me what to do?" he spat. "Just because you have a title now doesn't mean anything has changed between us. I am better than you. I'm a rank four, and all you will ever be is a nix with a pretty face. It would be wise for you not to forget your rank. I can make you do whatever I want behind these doors. I could compel you to obey me, then compel you to forget. Or better yet, I could let you remember *everything*. Maybe I would just compel you to never speak of it. It could be our little secret."

Sweat clung to me, dripping into every crevice of my body. He really would compel me. Then what? If I didn't do as he compelled, Kole would know I had an object of Alluse. It would ruin Sie's plans. I also didn't doubt that Kole wouldn't stop until he found whatever object I possessed and ripped it from my body, then compel me anyway.

My fingers clung around the long clasp, the cold pendant biting into my sweaty palm. I couldn't part with the necklace. Even if I hated the reason Sie gave it to me, I felt protected for once in my life. I didn't walk around wondering what someone would force me to do. I had a choice. I didn't have a choice in my situation—of being Sie's future wife—but I at least had a choice with my free will.

"My future husband is a rank five. I think it would be wise for you not to forget that," I said carefully as I pushed off from the bed. I tried to mask my terror as I stalked over to him. I tried to hide any ounce of fear Kole held over me. This felt different than when he messed with me at LakeWood. At school, we were never alone together. Now, there was no buffer, no professor looming over our shoulders.

"Wow," Kole blew out a breath. "The nix I used to know wouldn't have hid behind someone. I never once thought that you'd cower behind a male's protection. Interesting how a title changes people." Kole rose from the chair. I didn't flinch as he towered over me. "You're pathetic," he spat before storming out of the room, slamming the door behind him.

His words hit a nerve. He was right. I wasn't one to hide behind someone. I didn't want anyone to come to my rescue. I wanted to be competent on my own. I wanted to protect and defend myself.

I locked the door and sprinted under the covers, but as soon as I was lying in the bed, I realized the lock was pointless. I knew it didn't matter. Kole could turn the lock with his mind by controlling his telekinetic ability.

I didn't fall asleep.

———

THREE WEEKS HAD PASSED since I first arrived at the castle and the days were starting to blur together. To my surprise, I still hadn't seen Sie since our kiss. Peter informed me that he was engrossed in learning from Lunder. I wondered how that was going for him, having to learn from the male who tried to murder him during the tournament. Although it felt like Lady Applebee wanted to kill me on numerous occasions, he probably was having a harder time than me.

I was kept busy during the day with lesson after lesson. Various instructors were brought in to teach me some trivial knowledge about the kingdom, the villages, and the rule. It was hard to act like I cared.

The only teacher that remained the same was Lady Applebee, and she hated me. *Hated me.* Her classes were the longest part of my day, or at least it felt that way. She was all too aware that I would rather be running outside in pants than sitting with a stick taped to my back, sipping tea.

The only part of my day that I looked forward to was the early morning. Not only was it when Abherham replaced Kole, but Peter would wake me up every morning to train.

And he kept true to his word, his training was brutal. I left every morning groaning and limping in pain. My muscles were stiff and sore on the inside, but he was a controlled fighter. My bruises were confined beneath my dresses and never anywhere my skin was exposed.

It felt so good to finally be doing something I was familiar with. Every morning Peter started our session off with a long run. It felt so similar to my days at LakeWood, only now I had an attractive blonde smiling next to me.

I was convinced that he never stopped smiling. Even when we were sparring, both drenched in sweat, even when I kicked him in the face, or if I pinned him to the ground, he was smiling.

I, however, did not smile. My breathing was ragged by the time we were done each day. I could barely hold our conversation, but Peter would listen as I complained about my classes in breathless pants. I would vent about how ridiculous it was that there were five different ways to bow, or how unfair it was that everyone was required to learn them all except for Sie.

Once a male won the King's Tournament, it was considered beneath them to bow. Even a slight nod of the head was offensive. A king bowed for no one.

After my final lesson today, Abherham brought me to my fitting room. Beautiful travel bags were scattered across the room, and my three servants were running frantically about.

"What is all of this?" I asked Ashley.

"We are packing for your trip," Ashley said as she tucked a lavender gown into a leather bag.

"What trip?"

Annabel was the one to answer, "You and Sie have your tour this week. You will be gone for a couple of days in order to see each village, so we are making sure you have enough gowns. We are going to find the most perfect dresses for you."

"Tour? What tour?" I asked.

"Do you know anything that goes on around here?" Roslyn sneered. "You're always so clueless."

"Rosie, stop that," Ashley hushed. "She is being told all about it tonight at her dinner. You know she didn't grow up in this lifestyle."

Roslyn clicked her tongue as she moved toward the dresses laid out before her. "That's for sure," she mumbled under her breath.

The next hour was spent trying on an assortment of different gowns and long coats. Most of which were thick and made of wool since the majority of the tour would be outside, or so I was told. My body was so sore from training that Ashley and Annabel had to help me in and out of each one, making sure they fit perfectly. Mercifully, they didn't comment on it. I was thankful they never dressed me in anything revealing again, besides the first night when Sie had picked my dress. Tennebris favored modest clothes and all the gowns they selected for me seemed to follow their customs.

"It's your time to make them believe that rank zeroes have a voice," Annabel whispered to me as she helped me out of the last dress. I'd never thought of it in that way—that other zeroes might be happy that I was selected.

"You can change things," she added. "Hopefully, we can all be treated better."

I smiled at her, wishing it was true. "I promise I'll try," I said to her and meant it. I would try for all the rank zeroes that had similar stories, who were treated like me or worse. I would use this tour to try to sway the Advenians of Tennebris that a rank zero could do this job. That we were more than the number burned onto our wrists.

Ashley's eyes brimmed with tears as she gave my upper arm a tight squeeze. I realized now why they fussed so much about my appearance.

Once the three of them were satisfied with all the outfits they had selected for me, they dressed me for dinner. It would be the first royal dinner since the engagement banquet. All the other nights, I'd been able to eat dinner alone in my room. Despite my growling stomach, I wanted nothing more than to go straight to bed.

The full-length gown they put me in was a deep green. It was simple yet elegant, nothing like the extravagant dresses I would wear during the tour. The dress covered all my skin, except for the long sleeves stopping just above my wrists, exposing my rank.

Even though it was conservative with no high slits or plunging necklines, it clung to my figure, hugging my ribs.

They applied the usual amount of makeup to my face and curled my hair. Other than when I was training with Peter, I was always forced to wear it down. My previous braids were not up to par for the look of a princess. Tonight though, Ashley took the strands sweeping my face and twined them into small braids, pinning them back with a beautiful, gold barrette.

"You ready?" she asked as she fastened the final barrette into position.

I nodded, attempting to give my best smile. I just didn't know what I was ready for yet.

Soft classical music was steady beneath the constant chatter radiating from the royal dining hall. Abherham halted just outside the door.

"I will wait for you here, milady," he said with a nod of his head.

"Thank you, Abherham." I'd been relying on him less and less for directions as I was slowly forming a map inside my head of the grounds, but his constant presence wasn't as bad as I thought it would be. He was quiet and serious and barely sparked conversation with me, but he never ratted me and Peter out for training. He didn't make me uncomfortable the way Kole did. I was growing to really like having him around.

Taking a deep breath, I pushed open the large wooden door. A long table expanded the entire length of the room. Seats were filled with more Advenians than the first night at the banquet. Various members of the High Council, and some of the ladies the queen insisted on dining with during our luncheons, were already wine deep and chatting amongst themselves. The king and queen's chairs were still vacant. I scanned the room for black hair and dark eyes but found none.

I spotted an empty chair beside Alec, Reagan, and Peter that I assumed was saved for Sie. So I sat down in a seat on the other side of the table, wanting to be farthest from Sie and his friends.

Peter smiled as he stared at someone next to me.

I whipped my head around and jumped as Sie lowered himself into the adjacent chair, our arms almost brushing against one another. I shifted uncomfortably in my seat and leaned into the opposite armrest, pushing myself further away from him.

A half smile formed over his lips as he took in my movements. My eyes lingered on his soft, very kissable lips. Vivid flashes of us in his bathroom raced through my mind. How it felt to have his lips against mine, on my neck, my throat. I tore my gaze away from his and stared into my empty place setting.

"You look nice," he leaned in and murmured into my ear so only I could hear. His breath was cool against my neck. I turned to meet his gaze and was about to open my mouth to speak when Synder stalked into the room with the king following behind. Everyone stood in

Lunder's presence. I glanced over to Sie, gauging his reaction to the male who tried to kill him. The male he was forced to learn from, but his expression was blank and unreadable.

Everyone bowed at the waist except Sie. I curtseyed along with the group, my lessons crashing into me.

Queen Lasindra followed a few steps behind her husband. She was gorgeous and elegant and a queen in every way, reminding me how out of place I was. My eyes lingered on her beautiful, ornate crown resting on top of her luscious, golden curls. Her heavy dress matched her crown and had intricate gold pieces scattered throughout the ecru material.

Despite being forced to have lunch in the same room with her every day, she paid me no heed. I wondered what her thoughts of me were. If she was upset that soon she would no longer be the queen.

King Lunder clasped his hands together as he took his place at the head of the table, the only seats that were assigned. His gaze found Sie and me further down the table.

"Welcome. Please take a seat," he gestured at everyone's still-bowed form. "Tonight, we dine together. In the morning, Prince Noren and Princess Rumor will embark on their tour of the kingdom. The first of many royal festivities to begin now that we are one month into our six month celebration of Sie's rise to the throne." He raised his glass toward us. Everyone else followed suit.

Sie picked up his own wine and took a long sip.

Across the table, Peter looked at me. "The tour is a tradition for every future king. It's a way for the new royals to meet their people and for them to gaze upon you as well. You will travel to every village of Tennebris. There will be a scheduled visit at each one. We leave first thing in the morning."

I understood what he didn't say, no training. I smiled, and mouthed *thank you* to him. He flashed his dimple filled grin back, then resumed conversation with Alec and Reagan. I stayed silent throughout most of dinner and only spoke when someone asked me a direct question, which to my relief, wasn't often.

Sie, on the other hand, seemed to be relishing in my discomfort.

Halfway through dinner, he leaned into me and whispered, "I missed you these past couple of weeks. No more bathroom visits?"

I choked on my water and tried to recover by wiping my doily over my mouth. "I told you I thought it was my room."

"Don't look so upset. From what I recall, you seemed to enjoy the visit."

I ground my teeth so hard that my jaw hurt. "It won't happen again."

"Until our wedding day then, huh?" Sie looked at me, noting my tense jaw, my knuckles white from clasping my silverware. "Damn, Scotlind. I'm just joking. Relax."

He didn't talk to me the rest of the meal.

Reagan glared at us from across the table, visibly upset that Sie sat next to me and not the empty seat still beside her. I knew from the little training I received from Lady Applebee that the way she was stabbing her meat was not proper etiquette. She visibly tensed every time Sie turned his head to glance my way.

Alec placed a possessive hand on her and murmured something into her ear. She looked up and our eyes met as she smiled. I swallowed and tried to avoid their glances the rest of the evening.

Finally, after everyone was done eating and the king explained the tour for the tenth time, we filed out of the dining hall.

Alec stopped me. "Princess, wait up a second."

I paused at the door, allowing the others to pass. Alec caught up to me with a smile on his face. "Sie asked me to give this to you," he said as he discreetly placed a piece of paper in my palm.

"Thank you," I replied, crumbling the paper in my hand. I forced myself not to look at it until I was alone in my room.

I glanced around the dining hall, but Sie was already gone.

———

I WAS PACING back and forth in my room with the note in my hand, contemplating if I should go. Sie asked me to meet with him tonight.

The message was simple. A time and a place to meet with clear instructions to come alone. *It's important,* the note emphasized.

I didn't trust myself alone with him. I didn't want to repeat the night in the bathroom, but he said it was important. What couldn't wait until I saw him for the tour tomorrow morning? Did he discover the reason I was selected? Did he know what the High Council was planning? Did he know the truth about me? Why I was brought here?

My curiosity or anxiety got the best of me, the two emotions were blending together. I took a deep breath, crumbled the note back up into my hand, and walked over to the door.

I pushed open the heavy wood, only a crack, careful not to alarm Kole. Mercifully, he was lax with his guard duty. He hadn't entered my room since the first night and waited out in the hall. Once his shift started, I remained locked in my room. Any chance of avoiding him, I took.

Lately, I'd been having Abherham escort me to the royal library before his shift would end. I loved books and the escape they provided. I loved becoming invested in made-up characters and engulfed in an unrealistic world. Along with training, books were the one thing to settle my mind. But I didn't read for enjoyment, not anymore.

I scavenged the library for any texts on Lux. I read history book after history book until my eyes bled and my brain hurt. I hated history. I hated boring texts, and I absolutely hated documents, but I needed to know. Any bit of information I gleaned could help me. I searched for answers, for any indications of what Luxian powers I could possess. For any reason as to why I might be here. I read texts dated back to when our kind lived on Allium, scanning to see what documents existed between the two kingdoms. The necklace around my neck made me question everything I had learned. I started to doubt that the Advenian Kingdoms always lived separately. I stared down at the design etched on the pendant. The Tennebrisian symbol of the twin pink moons surrounded the Luxian sun, making it seem like they belonged together.

But every night, I was left disappointed. I found no proof of

Luxians and Tennebrisians living together. I barely found any information on Lux. Whatever texts were in that library were factual and just as bland on the inside as the cover suggested on the outside. But I wouldn't be reading tonight.

I sent a silent prayer to the Goddess that Kole wouldn't see me as I slipped past the door. Luckily, he made just about the worst guard ever. He was resting his head back against the wall. An echoing snore escaping his open mouth.

I smiled as I easily crept past him.

# TWENTY-ONE
## SCOTLIND

With the note still in my shaky palm, I took a deep breath and opened the door to where I was supposed to meet Sie. Music drifted toward me, along with the warmth of a roaring fireplace. I stepped into the room only to halt as soon as I noticed a crowd of drunken Advenians.

A party. I walked straight into a party.

This note wasn't from Sie that much was certain based on the two females clinging to his side. How could I have been so stupid to think he would want to meet with me?

One chandelier illuminated the packed room. Champagne and wine glasses, full and empty, filled every table. Most of the crowd had hazy eyes, either talking or swaying their hips to the melody.

Reagan smiled as she scooted closer to Sie on the red leather sofa. Another female I didn't recognize took up his other side. She had silky, black hair that flowed over her shoulder as she bent down to graze his neck. Goddess above, what did I walk in on?

I bit down nervously on my lower lip as I retreated a step back to the door.

Sie remained lounged on the sofa, his legs spread wide, his left knee bent while his other leg was stretched out in front of him. He looked regal. Regal and daunting and alluring and utterly unaware of my presence. He definitely was not expecting me.

Peter, who was in the corner of the room refilling his drink, noticed me right away. His eyes flared wide, and he shook his head, but it was too late. Alec, who seemed to be the only one expecting me, acknowledged me standing there awkwardly by the door.

"Ah, princess. How nice of you to join us. We are having a farewell revel for Sie as you both will be leaving tomorrow for your tour," he exclaimed over the loud, pounding music. "I see you brought my note." He smirked as he took a step closer to where I stood.

Sie looked up at me then, as if just noticing me for the first time. He didn't move from the sofa or stop the black haired girl from leaning into him, but his eyes intensified, his gaze never leaving mine. The girl wrapped her legs around his as she giggled something into his ear.

Sie narrowed his eyes at the note in my hand before moving his attention back up to my face. I quickly crumbled it up and tried to shove it behind my back. But Alec reached forward to grab it and, to my horror, started reading it out loud.

*Dear Scotlind, meet me tonight. It's important. I'll be waiting at midnight on the second landing, first room to the right. Come alone. Don't let your guard see you leave. Sie.*

The room quieted as the loud music lowered into a soft hum so Alec could be heard amongst the crowd.

I risked a glance at Sie. He sat up a little straighter, finally brushing the female off his lap. His jaw clenched, a muscle moved along the side of this cheek, but other than that, he masked whatever emotion he was feeling.

"Poor, innocent Scotlind," Reagan crooned as she leaned into Sie, making a show of rubbing her hand over his sculpted chest. The top two buttons of his shirt came undone, exposing part of his peck beneath. "She thought you actually wanted to spend time with *her* of all Advenians. Don't worry, Scotlind. We have him quite entertained for the night. You can go now."

I planned to do just that. Biting the inside of my cheek, I quickly turned on my heel, rushing out of the room. I made it to the door when Alec grabbed my upper arm, holding me in place.

"Don't leave now, princess. You came all this way. Let's have some fun first," Alec mused as he spun me around to face Sie again. He reeked of alcohol. His breath hot against my neck as he brushed my hair aside.

My cheeks heated as blood rushed to them, painting my freckles red. I wanted to go back to my room. I wished I never came.

Sie shifted uncomfortably on the sofa.

"Here, have a drink," Alec smiled as he pushed a glass of champagne in my hand.

I tried to shake it away. "I don't want to drink," I gritted between my teeth.

"You don't want to drink? Now that's not any fun. Hmm, let me think. What can we do for fun with someone who doesn't want to party with us?" His smile turned mischievous as he glanced over to Sie and Reagan, then looked me up and down slowly.

"What did you have in mind?" Reagan narrowed her eyes at Alec.

"I was thinking of playing surrender." He smirked as Reagan lit up. Sie remained silent, staring at me with heavy eyes. I swore I saw a brief flicker of worry flash over his face, but it was gone in an instant. His cold demeanor returned. I didn't know what surrender was, but I definitely did not want to stay to find out.

"I don't think that's wise," Peter said carefully, taking a step toward me. "She isn't just some female rank zero you brought to a party, Alec. She's going to be Sie's wife. You shouldn't mess with her like that."

Reagan huffed. "Well, she isn't his wife yet. There's still time for Sie to change his mind about her." She looked at me as she ran her fingers through Sie's raven-black hair, pushing back the strands from his eyes. He leaned out of her grip but only pressed himself into the other female still wrapped around him.

Peter gritted his teeth. "They said the vows before the Goddess, Reagan. Don't be delusional."

Reagan clicked her tongue.

"Relax, Peter. She is still a nix nonetheless. Even I could compel her to forget what we do with her tonight. It'll be our little secret," Alec added as he breathed into my neck. "Let's see what Scotlind has to offer Sie. It can be our engagement present to him."

"I'm not playing your stupid game," I growled at Alec as I tried to break free of his grip. But his hold only tightened, causing a wince to escape my lips. I scanned the room for anyone who might help me. But the Advenians who were paying attention to me seemed to enjoy my impending humiliation, and the few that weren't, we're too focused on each other to notice.

I turned to Peter, and my stomach curled. One look from him and I knew he couldn't help me. Worry and pity overtook his dimpled grin.

My breath came out ragged as I tried one more time to disarm Alec's threatening grip. My body was already exhausted from the lack of sleep I'd been getting since coming to the castle.

Alec spun me again, and in an instant, grabbed my chin with his other hand, forcing me to meet his gaze. The smell of liquor filled my nostrils. It was the same strong scent from the night Vallie and Miles took me drinking. I tried not to gag as Alec's breath mixed with mine.

"Such a feisty one. But you see, princess, you don't get a choice in the matter. Surrender is where we take someone that's a nix and can be compelled, and we make them do *whatever* we want for the night. Basically, that person *surrenders* to us and becomes our little plaything for the evening. Sometimes into the morning, depending on how much fun we're having," he slurred.

Bile threatened to rise in my throat as I took in the meaning of his words. My heart thumped so fast I thought it might burst out of my chest. I twisted against his grip, but he only pressed my chest into his, locking me in place.

He looked me up and down with a grin. "I have compulsion. Mine isn't as strong as Sie's. I don't have complete mind control where I can compel anyone in Tennebris, but I can compel humans, Advenians from Lux, and well, nixes like you."

"No," I snarled as his grasp on my chin tightened. His other hand made idle strokes down my face, embracing in my discomfort.

"I'm afraid you don't have a choice, princess. This is what happens when you're weak. You can't stop us. It was growing rather dull playing this game on our servants, but thanks to you, we can have some real fun." He smiled as his neck turned golden. "Now, you are going to have a drink."

I heard the slight change in his voice as he compelled me, but with the necklace Sie gave me working against his ability, I didn't feel the pull to obey. My body wasn't tethered to his like it normally would be. My hand didn't fly toward the drink. I didn't have to do what he was telling me. I could walk out. I could leave.

I looked to Sie, trying to plead with him to stop this before it started, but he remained seated. Blank, expressionless, and glaring at Alec's hold on me.

His stare was unwavering as he calculated what I would do.

*If someone does compel you, though, I need you to play along. Do what they are telling you to do. Don't tell anyone about the necklace, and never let anyone know that you can't be compelled.* His words on the monorail coursed through my head. Did he know they would do this to me? He suspected people would compel me, but did he know his own friends would do it, and right in front of him?

He knew I would have to pretend to be compelled because I couldn't let anyone find out about the necklace. A different dread filled me. I would have to obey. I would have to do whatever awful thing Alec told me to. For a brief moment, I wished I was compelled. It would have been easier to forget whatever Alec had planned.

"You are going to drink with us. Right, princess?" Alec winked.

I let out a sigh before whispering yes. Sie wasn't planning on stopping this, and I couldn't let them know about the necklace.

"Good girl. You will forget all of this by morning. You will wake up thinking that you came to meet Sie but he wasn't here, so you went back to bed," he compelled again as he stepped around me, inspecting me. Except I wouldn't forget this. How many servants had they done this to? Would they even remember?

He placed the glass of champagne in my hand. "Drink it."

I did as I was told and downed the entire cup. At least it would be easier to manage with some alcohol in my system. He grabbed my left wrist where the zero was branded into me, now completely healed, and turned it over in his hand. "Again," he murmured as he filled my glass.

I emptied the contents, my eyes never leaving Alec's. I could feel Sie's gaze burning into me, but I refused to look at him now. Alec filled my drink for the third time, and after finishing it, I felt the liquid hit my head, making everything slightly fuzzy. Alec loosened his grip on my shoulders, and I slipped, not realizing I was relying on him to hold me up. He caught me with a grin.

"Enough," Sie growled, speaking for the first time. "She's a light-weight and isn't going to be able to stand much longer if you keep making her drink."

"Excellent point, Sie. Why would we want her standing anyway? Kneel," he smirked. I stared back at Alec, my eyes wide and unmoving.

"Did you not hear me? I said *kneel.*" He repeated as he pressed down on my shoulders, forcing me onto my knees. I landed hard on the marble floor as both of my knees smacked against it. I muffled a wince as they popped. Reagan laughed.

"It's a nice view, her on her knees, wouldn't you say so Sie?" Alec chuckled darkly as I looked up at him, narrowing my gaze.

My eyebrows furrowed as anger threatened to explode out of me. How long was this going to last? Alec mentioned this could go all night. I took a staggering, uneven breath, trying to calm myself as best I could.

I refused to look at anyone but Alec. I knew Sie was watching me from my peripheral, but I didn't turn my head to see his reaction.

"Now, I want you to tell Sie how you really feel about him. You always walk around like you hate the world, but I think you secretly want him. After all, you did show up here tonight thinking you would spend the night with him."

Reagan shifted at Alec's words. Still on my knees before Alec, I finally looked up to meet Sie's stare. "I think you are a narcissistic asshole who needs better friends."

A half smile flashed on Sie's face as if he expected that. I was thankful at that moment I wasn't really compelled because I wasn't entirely sure what I would have said if I was. I hated myself for that. Because, to be honest, I didn't know how I felt about him. I probably would have said I wanted him to kiss me again or admitted I found him attractive. I hated him, yes, and he was a manipulative prick who surrounded himself with awful people. But another part of me couldn't stop thinking about him. About how it felt when he held me against the wall in the bathing room, his hands tugging my hair...

Alec tsked loudly. "We don't want Sie's future wife not adoring him. You will like him from now on." Alec's golden markings drew further up his neck.

If I was compelled, would all of my anger toward Sie disappear? Would I no longer be confused as to how I felt about him? Would I not remember why, but suddenly like him without question?

I mindlessly repeated, "I will like him." Sie shifted in his seat again, amused or uncomfortable, I couldn't tell.

"Now go over to your future husband," Alec purred. "Apologize for calling him an asshole like a good wife. Show him how sorry you truly are."

I went to stand up, but Alec shook his head. "No, crawl to him."

I gritted my teeth at his command. Reagan and the other girl snickered as they moved out of the way, leaving Sie alone on the sofa. His eyes never left mine as I awkwardly crawled over to him, cursing under my breath. Shame and humiliation swept over me as I put one arm in front of the other. There was no way of crawling gracefully, and my dress kept getting caught on my knees.

*This will be over soon. I will make them all regret this someday.* As soon as we figured out what the High Council was planning, and I didn't have the threat of someone trying to kill me...

If someone was even trying to kill me. Was it all a lie? Maybe Sie never thought someone from the High Council was out to get me. Maybe this was all some sick joke between his friends. Did they all know I couldn't be compelled with Sie's necklace? Was this part of the game to see how long I would play along?

No, it couldn't be. Someone here had to know I was from Lux. Why else would the High Council select a rank zero to marry Sie if they wanted to make things worse for nixes? I couldn't risk my chances of finding out why I was brought here just to avoid whatever Alec might throw at me tonight. No matter how awful it was.

"I'm sorry, *your majesty*," I mocked with the most sarcastic tone I could muster once I reached Sie.

"Kiss his boots," Alec called out from behind me.

I pressed my lips to his foot and then made sure to push all my weight onto his outstretched leg as I stood up, hoping it would hurt.

"I'm not done," Alec grinned as I went to walk away from Sie. "Why don't you sit on his lap, princess, and tell him what you plan to do to him on your wedding night to please him."

Reagan now stopped smiling and was looking like she wanted to murder me or Alec for suggesting it. I bit my lip, hoping that Reagan would stop Alec in my hesitation.

"And Scotlind, make sure it's something Sie will like," he added with a wink.

"Is this really necessary?" I heard Peter mumble under his breath.

I plastered a fake, innocent smile as I wrapped both of my legs around Sie and fell onto his lap. His hands flew to my hips as he tilted his head back. A small smile curved his lips as he met my gaze. He was enjoying this. Prick.

I tried not to focus on his hand placement as I whispered to him, "You're really going to make me do this."

"No one is making you do anything," was all he replied.

"We're waiting," Alec drawled.

I pressed into Sie and spoke in his ear so no one else could hear me, "I hate you. I will never stop hating you, and I don't plan on doing anything with you on our wedding night or *ever*."

His smile faltered. "Good," he said back, so softly I thought I missed it. Then he added for everyone to hear, "I look forward to that." I pushed off of him and leapt from his lap as quickly as I could.

Alec, clearly pleased, grumbled, "Now, let's see what Sie is going to get." I turned to face Alec, confused. He rubbed his hands together as he said, "Take off your clothes."

My eyes flared. My voice was breathless and weak. "What?"

"I said take off your clothes. Show Sie what he can expect on his wedding night."

I looked over at Sie, who now stood before me. I flashed him a pleading look, begging him to stop this. I didn't care how desperate I seemed. Alec was purely trying to humiliate me, and it was working. The muscle in Sie's cheek twitched, but he didn't say anything as he glanced down at me.

"Are you embarrassed of your body, princess?" Alec taunted. He knew exactly what he was asking me to do. It was taboo to show a lot of skin in Tennebris, nonetheless be completely naked.

"Or are you worried Sie won't like you anymore once he sees you?" Reagan smirked as she walked to stand next to me.

I sucked in a breath as I took a step back from Sie and unfastened the back of my dress with shaky hands. The room was silent as everyone watched. I closed my eyes, my dress falling to the floor. I imagined myself escaping the room, imagined anything else but this moment. I had never been so humiliated before in my life, even by Kole.

"Wow," Alec breathed as he closed the space between us, making a full circle around me. He looked me up and down, taking in the lacey black undergarments that Annabel selected for me. The transparentness of them left nothing to the imagination. Everything was displayed for them to gawk at with how revealing the little fabric covered. I backed myself away from the champagne tower, placing my back flat against the cold wall. In my temper, I forgot about my markings. My dress laid a good distance away.

Alec swore under his breath, "Sie, I'm not gonna lie, you are one lucky guy. Who knew all that was hidden beneath those clothes." Alec smiled as he pointed to me and then at my clothes in a bundle on the floor. Reagan scooped up my dress and threw it into the fireplace before I could even blink.

*No, no, no.*

She smiled as the flames danced over it. I watched in horror as it disappeared, turning to ash before my eyes. How the heck was I going to get out of here with no clothes?

I clenched my fists at my sides. It took everything in me not to use my hands to cover myself, but I wouldn't give them the satisfaction. So I took a few steadying breaths before lifting my chin toward Alec.

He stood before me now, casually tracing his finger up and down my bare arms, causing the hair on my skin to rise. "Why such a long face, princess? Do you need me to compel you to have a good time with us? I can. I could make you smile, laugh, drink some more, dance with us?" Alec threatened with a deep laugh. He cupped my neck between his hands, his thumbs resting beneath my chin, tilting my head back, forcing me to look up.

"Wait," I blurted as panic overtook my senses. To my surprise, Alec's golden markings disappeared for a moment, allowing me to continue. I took a step out of his grasp and walked over to Sie, whose eyes went wide in surprise. It didn't leave my mind that I was practically naked as he took in every inch of my body.

I couldn't do this anymore. I couldn't keep pretending. There was no way I could stand naked in front of all of them and smile as they laughed at me.

When I stood a foot before Sie, he let out a low breath. His eyes darted toward my breasts as I reached to unclasp my necklace. I placed the necklace in his hands, unable to hide the fact that mine were shaking as I whispered, "Now you can compel me to have a good time."

No one said anything. Sie just stared at me, necklace in his hand, face unreadable.

"Compel her already, Sie. Should we have her dance on the table? Or have her remove what little clothes she still has left on?" Alec laughed, completely unaware of the tension going on between us. I heard him chuck his cup as he finished off the drink in his hand.

"Put this back on," Sie seethed, ignoring Alec.

"No. Unless you are going to compel me to do it." I responded, the bite in my voice noticeable. He let out a loud, frustrated sigh as he ran his fingers through his hair. He didn't know what to do. Good.

"I will compel you, Scottie."

"What difference does it make," I found myself saying. "If it's you compelling me, or you watching as your friends do it?"

Peter stepped forward before Sie could say anything else. "Enough. Stop this." He said as he grabbed me by the arm and threw his jacket over my shoulders. I was so thankful my back was hidden again. "I'm taking her back to her room now."

I stormed out of the room with Peter, not bothering to look back at Sie or anyone else.

The last thing I heard before the door slammed behind me was Alec saying, "Relax Sie, she's going to forget everything by morning."

Only I wouldn't. I wouldn't forget one second of it, and Sie knew it.

I was walking at a record pace. I didn't care about the glances I was receiving from the servants still awake. Nothing could be worse than what I just endured. The humiliation. The shame. I shuddered as anger rippled through me.

Peter tried to grab my shoulders, but I shrugged him off. "Scottie, wait. I'm sorry. They shouldn't have done that."

I whirled, not bothering to mask how furious I was. "You're sorry they did it in general, or are you sorry they did it to *me*?"

He didn't respond, so I added, "Do you wish it was some other nix who walked into that party, Peter? Would you have stopped it then or played along with them?"

Disgust and disappointment washed over me that they were the Advenians Peter grew up with. The fact that they did this sort of thing to rank zeroes for fun made my blood fume. They controlled people for their own entertainment. Alec mentioned he was growing tired of playing with the servants. How many of them had faced what I went through tonight? How many endured worse but couldn't remember to even feel the shame of what was done to them the next morning? "Just leave me alone, Peter."

"Right and let you wander the castle alone, half-naked, without your necklace. I'm coming with you," he spat back.

Well, that answered my question about how much Peter knew. I tugged on the jacket he gave me, pulling it closer to my chest. It barely covered the top of my thighs.

"Fine, but I'm going back to my room." I walked, and Peter followed.

When I finally was close to my door, Peter said softly, "I don't like it, Scotlind. What they did to you, what they have done to others. I find it disgusting."

"Then why let them? Why did you just stand there and let them do that?" I bristled as tears spilled down my cheeks. My rage was melting into something worse—mortification and pure exhaustion.

"Because if we stopped Alec before he had his fun with you, he would have showed up in your bedroom tonight, and it would have been much worse."

"And how many other rank zeroes has this happened to?" I asked, not sure if I really wanted to know the answer.

"Too many."

I sucked in an unsteady breath as the tears now ran down my face. I couldn't hold it in anymore. Peter hesitantly stepped forward. He wrapped his arms around me and pulled me into a hug as I sobbed into his shoulder.

"I'm sorry," he said again.

I pulled back, wiping my eyes with the back sleeves of his jacket. "Thank you for stopping it before it got worse."

"Don't thank me," he admitted. "I should have stopped it before it even began. I am sorry, Scotlind."

"Well, I would have appreciated it if you stopped it before I had to take my clothes off. It's freezing in the halls." Peter let out a small laugh as he wiped away my remaining tears. "I'm going to bed," I said softly. "Goodnight, Peter."

"Goodnight, Scotlind."

When I closed the door behind him, I dropped to the ground and cried. The tears didn't stop as they ran down my face in constant running tracts.

Eventually, when my tears slowed, and my voice was raw, I threw Peter's jacket across the room before storming into the bathing room. I turned on the water and sank into the tub, letting the water soothe and soak into my skin until I was numb. I stayed in the water, hoping it would wash away the nightmare that was tonight, that was the rest of my life.

# TWENTY-TWO
## SIE

I WAS GOING TO MURDER ALEC. I WAS GOING TO BEAT THE shit out of him and then fucking murder him for what he forced Scottie to do tonight. I had no idea he made up some fucking note for her to meet with me. The way her innocent eyes flared when she took in the party, when she saw Reagan and Amber next to me on the sofa... She came to meet with me and instead was humiliated beyond belief.

I agreed to Alec's stupid party to act like I didn't care about her. I knew he was on to me, trying to figure out my weakness. Trying to test the waters to see if *she* was my weakness. That's what tonight was about—to gauge how I would react to him messing with her.

I'd been trying to keep my distance and stay away from her. I'd been trying to not make it public knowledge that I cared for her, that despite my efforts, she got under my skin.

If people knew that, they would use it against me, which would put her in danger. And that fucking prick, Alec, knew exactly what he was doing. He was fucking testing me to see what I would do. No doubt to report right back to his father and whoever else on the High Council wanted me out.

If I had defended Scottie, if I hadn't played along with his sick game, he would have known I cared for her. Then the whole Goddess-damn kingdom would know that if they wanted to get to me, they just had to find my rank zero fiancé. It would be so easy for anyone to manipulate me by using her.

And I had to fucking let it happen. I had to watch Scottie do those awful things with pure hatred on her face as she realized I wouldn't stop it. It killed me on the inside. I thought she would leave right away if she saw me with those girls, but she didn't.

Maybe it was for the best. If she hated me, she would stay away from me, not tempt me into giving into her. It would be better if she kept her distance from me altogether.

The less we were seen together in public, the better. It would be easier to prove to others that I didn't care for her if she outwardly hated me.

Scottie was strong. Despite having no Tennebrisian abilities and her petite frame, she made herself into a weapon. It was part of what first intrigued me about her, that she could take down men twice her size by sheer skill and will.

But without abilities, all they had to do was look at her, and she could be controlled, forced to do their bidding, becoming a slave to their mercy. All it would take was one compulsion user, and she would be rendered helpless, especially without that damn necklace around her neck.

And now, because of me, she had to walk the halls half naked with Peter, without wearing the Alluse. Fear overtook my sense of reason as I found myself making my way toward her room. I didn't care how much she despised me, she had to wear the necklace. If something happened to her because of this... If someone really compelled her tonight, I wouldn't forgive myself.

I halted outside her door. Her guard, the brown haired male that went to her school, was asleep a few feet down. I stalked over to him and woke him up with a jab to his throat.

He bolted awake, choking and hacking up a lung as he clutched his neck. I grabbed the collar of his uniform and lifted him up to me. He didn't deserve to sport the twin pink moons that were engraved on the chest.

His eyes went wide as he beheld me. "If I ever catch you sleeping on the job again, you are done for." I growled at him. "You are the guardian to my fiancé, and you better start taking this seriously. She snuck out tonight and easily got past you. If this was the other way around, and someone slipped by you and snuck into her room, you wouldn't be alive to explain yourself. Do you understand?"

He was still grasping his throat, his eyes bulging, bloodshot, and red as he nodded his head furiously.

"Now I am going in there to speak with her. If anyone else tries to enter her room, you do not allow them in. If she ever tries to sneak off again in the middle of the night, you do not allow her to. Got it?" He nodded again.

Satisfied, I dropped my hold on him and grabbed the door handle to enter Scotlind's room. It was locked. I didn't bother knocking. She wouldn't open the door to let me inside anyway, so I teleported in.

She just walked out of her bathing room, towel drying her hair, wearing a flimsy white nightgown that clung to her body when she spotted me.

The towel fell to the floor by her bare feet as she backed up a step. "What are you doing here?" Her voice was shaky. "Did you not get enough? Are you here to compel me more?"

She tried to mask her fear with rage as she moved to push past me, her shoulder brushing against mine. It caused her to fall off balance instead of moving me.

"You know that's not why I came," I said as I turned to face her.

"Right. You're better than that. It's so unlike you to force a girl to strip down to embarrass herself for a few laughs with your friends. You wouldn't do that at all," she seethed, nostrils flaring. Her cheeks were rosy pink, her eyes swollen.

I sighed and ran my fingers through my hair. She wasn't going to forgive me for what happened tonight. I couldn't blame her, and I shouldn't try to convince her to. It would be better if she hated me. It would be safer for her, but fuck, it killed me.

"I came to give this back to you." I held out the golden necklace between my fingers, the white circular pendant dangling by her face.

"There is no sense in me wearing that if I'm going to have to pretend I can be compelled anyway. I really don't see the point when you and your friends can force me to do whatever you want for your enjoyment."

"I didn't enjoy tonight."

"Right. I can see how it was a difficult night for *you*."

"Scotlind…" I started and stopped. I didn't know how to explain everything to her, and no matter how much I hated every second of that, it was far worse for her. I couldn't take back what had happened, what she had to do. "Just… just take the damn necklace. Wear it. People in the castle can make you do worse things than what happened tonight."

"So should I thank you? Was that you being noble and honorable? Trying to give me a warning or some sick reminder of how weak I am? How anyone can walk all over me?"

I stifled a wince, forcing my face blank. "It wasn't a reminder," was all I said.

"Just leave, Sie," she huffed. I wasn't going to budge, not a damn inch, not until I saw that necklace between her breasts, fastened and safe around her neck.

"I said get out," she seethed, using her body weight to push my chest.

I looked down at her. I would find her scrunched forehead and furrowed eyebrows adorable if I knew it wasn't directed at me. I blew out a breath, bracing myself for what I would have to do. She would never forgive me for it. It would only confirm her belief about me and pin me as the bad guy, and as much as I hated it, as much as I wanted her to not hate me, I needed her to be safe more.

I took a step toward her as she backed up into the wall. "You will wear the necklace, and you will not take it off again." I felt the compulsion pulse through my veins before the golden swirls worked up my arms. A surge of energy ran through me. My raw power radiated from my fingertips, begging me to use more. I hated how much enjoyment I got out of using my abilities. It was untapped ecstasy rushing through me, caressing and seducing me not to stop. I willed it back, hating the fact that I was taking away free will more than I craved the feeling it gave me.

She gasped as she reached for the necklace and placed it over her neck. The white pendant falling between her breasts.

"I thought you weren't going to compel me or was that just another one of your lies." She pleaded as a tear escaped her eye and ran down her cheek.

"I will never compel you for my amusement, Scotlind, but if it means keeping you safe, then yes, I will. I have no problem compelling you," I said as I left her shaking behind me. I saw her slump to the ground, sliding down the wall as she clutched the necklace that would now remain forever on her neck.

# TWENTY-THREE
## SCOTLIND

The next day, all three of my servants came to wake me up to get ready. I yawned loudly as I stretched my stiff body, unwilling to pry myself out from under the fluffy comforter just yet. I was exhausted from crying. I had spent the night curled up into myself until sleep finally overtook my body.

I couldn't shake off what had happened last night. I was disgusted with everything. Shame and embarrassment clung to me like sweat, hugging my skin, unwilling to wash away. I hated the high rank. I hated how they thought having abilities made them superior over others. How they abused rank zeroes, merely for their own entertainment, just because they could.

I couldn't help my lingering gaze on my three maids. Were they victims of Alec's game too and compelled to forget?

For the first time since arriving here, I wished for my regular, monotonous schedule. My gut twisted, knowing I would have to spend the day with Sie. No, not just a day, but *days* with him, as this tour was supposed to stretch out over a few nights.

Once Ashley, Annabel, and Roslyn were satisfied with how I looked, they led me toward the castle's main entrance.

To my surprise, both Kole and Abherham were waiting for us. Kole had a crazed expression on his face as he glared at me.

He pulled me aside right away. "If you ever think you can sneak off while I'm guarding you again, you will regret it," he managed to say through gritted teeth. His voice lowered so no one else could hear.

He couldn't have known about last night. I'd slipped back inside my room without him noticing. I was sure of it. Unless he was only pretending to be asleep? I grimaced at the thought, at him seeing me so vulnerable.

My cheeks heated as I gave Kole a small nod, unable to conjure up enough effort to speak. Last night left me empty, and if I was honest, I wasn't planning on leaving my room again. I started to walk back to the group that was now gathering underneath the arched stairwell.

"Damn, nix," Kole groaned under his breath. It was the first time he dropped the *little* in front of the word when addressing me. Even though I hated when he called me *little nix* and found it degrading, this was different. He wasn't taunting me like he usually did. He wasn't calling me that just to get a rise out of me. There was no smirk on his face, just a cold, deadly demeanor. He used the term and meant it for what it was—an insult.

We filed into a large black vehicle that would be taking us to the monorail. I was surprised to see Peter sitting with Sie. I didn't think he was coming along. I was grateful that, at least, Alec and Reagan wouldn't be joining us.

We rode in silence. Neither Sie nor I acknowledged one another.

The kingdom had six villages, and our tour was laid out so that we would visit two a day, making this trip a three-day and two-night venture. The first stop on our tour was the village closest to the castle, called Palm. The ride didn't take long. We arrived shortly after breakfast which wasn't nearly enough time to process what was about to happen.

Palm seemed like a small city, or at least what I thought a city would look like. I'd only seen depictions of them in textbooks. Most of the buildings were a few stories high with varying shades of colors throughout the stone. They were congested and squished together, making the air feel thick and heavy. A few mountains and trees lined the one side of the town, while the other was completely bare. Just building after building after building, all packed with Advenians.

Palm had closed their shops for the day, allowing everyone who resided there to greet us. Only the stores that lined the tour route were open and bustling with customers. Advenians bought hot drinks to warm their hands as they waited in the frigid air. Many young females held signs with Sie's face on it. I noticed many of them carrying a stick of food. Meats, potatoes, and vegetables were all crammed together on the thin wooden spike that they held vertically before bringing it into their mouths. Peter leaned in and told me that it was tuskalu, a popular dish of the village. I didn't have it in me to respond to him, so I just kept walking.

I was forced to take Sie's hand as we shuffled through the passage crammed with Advenians. It was an isle of bodies, the path only big enough to fit four across at a time. Guards stalked in front and behind us, Peter at the tail, as we walked down the city's main cobblestone street. Cheers erupted and an endless stream of shouts followed in our wake. I felt naked all over again. Sie's hand felt like a shackle. I wanted to curl into myself and disappear.

Sie stopped every so often to shake a few nobles' hands, making small talk and light, innocent gossip amongst Palm's citizens. It was known to be one of the higher rank villages. Too many eyes were honed in on me, too many faces plastered in sneers. I kept quiet as the emptiness in me grew. I couldn't concentrate on anything Sie was saying. All I could think about was last night—what Alec had forced me to do. And staring at the Advenians of Palm, seeing their nasty glares, I wondered how many others wished ill of me. How many loathed me for no reason other than for the two zeroes burned into my flesh?

The moment we filed back onto the monorail to head to the second village, I dropped Sie's hand and stormed to the back of the moving cylinder. I wanted to put as much distance between us as I could.

I was sitting in my own compartment when Peter knocked on the door. "Mind if I join you?" he asked gently.

I gave him a weak nod toward the open seat in front of me. I was still frustrated for his part last night, for being friends with them, for not stopping it sooner. But he had this way about him, making it impossible to stay mad at him, unlike Sie, who I despised to my very core.

I sighed heavily as Peter slumped onto the cushions adjacent to me. It would be easier if I was marrying him instead of Sie. He was sweet and kind. He calmed me in a way only Vallie had been able to do.

"How are you doing?" he asked.

"Fine," was all I said, crossing my arms over my chest.

"If it makes you feel better, Sie had an early morning training session with Alec before we left. He beat him to a pulp for what he did last night."

"And who is going to beat up Sie for his part in it?" I asked, not bothering to hide my disgust.

Peter grimaced. "He's not as bad as he seems, Scottie."

"Are you really going to sit there and defend him after what happened last night?"

He contemplated it for a moment before saying, "You're right. There is no excuse for what they did. I would never defend Reagan and Alec."

"I thought you both were friends with them?"

"No." Peter forced a laugh. "Sie is obligated to put up with them, but neither of us like them."

"Why does he have to put up with them?" I asked, unable to keep my curiosity down. "He didn't seem to mind their company last night, especially Reagan's."

"Sie and I are from the village of Kitlarn. It's one of the larger villages by the ocean. Growing up, Sie's father was the commander of the Guard and a member of the High Council. A very important, crucial high ranking member. He had to travel to the castle a lot for his line of work and stayed there for weeks on end. He usually brought Sie along, who usually brought me too. Everyone knew Sie had a real possibility of being the future king, so his father brought him to the castle to expose him early. We spent a lot of time there together. Reagan and Alec are from here, in Palm. Their fathers are also members of the High Council, so all of us were forced together as children."

"Who are their parents?" I realized how little I knew about these Advenians. The fact that Sie's family already came from power was a shock to me.

"Alec's father is Braven Bask. You know him. He's the guy who is always following Synder around like a lost puppy. He is the third in command on the Council after Synder. Sie's father used to be Lunder's second, but he dropped out once Sie was declared a rank five in order to devote his time to training him. The Council voted Synder into the role only after Sie's father left."

"I thought that the king always picked his second?"

"Not a second time. King Lunder selected Sie's father at his coronation, but if a second leaves or dies, the Council then votes on who will replace the spot."

"Oh," I said as I processed what knowledge he was giving me. "Does that mean you are going to be in charge of the High Council when Sie is king since you are his second?"

"Yes," Peter's brows furrowed as he gazed past me. "Synder is not thrilled about it, to say the least. He's been snaking his way into more and more power slowly throughout Lunder's rule. He isn't keen on giving it up. He will still be a member of the High Council, but not the Head High Council Member as Sie named me."

"What about the commander of the Guard? Will that fall to you also?" I asked.

"No. Only the king solely declares the second. Every other position on the Council needs to be voted in. Synder will remain the commander."

"And what is Reagan's connection?" I asked.

"Reagan's father is Heavon. He's one of the lesser men on the High Council but still on the Council nonetheless. I think Reagan believed that Sie would make her his wife after all those years, but he never did. Then, when the High Council selected you instead of her...

Well, Heavon was furious. To be honest, we were all kind of confused."

"Why…" I paused, swallowed, then forced myself to meet Peter's gaze. "Why do you think I was selected?"

"I honestly don't know. Sie and I have discussed it, but we can't figure it out. Not that I don't think you are capable and will be an amazing queen because you will, Scottie. It's just odd. Sie thought that maybe it was to appease the lower ranks. Rumors are that some have wanted to join the reb—" he stopped mid-sentence.

"Join the what?"

"Nothing. It just doesn't make sense. Sydner and Braven have been trying to pass a law eliminating the rights of rank zeroes. They don't want them to have an education or a Trial. They think from birth, if you are a rank zero, you should be a servant. It hasn't passed. It's been turned down countless times, but it doesn't add up. Why would the High Council select you to be queen if so many of them want to make things worse for rank zeroes?"

"Make them all servants," I whispered as a ragged breath left me. I still couldn't believe it. Rank zeroes were already treated poorly, and they wanted to make things worse. Sie mentioned to me that some Advenians felt that way, but I didn't realize they already tried to pass laws about it.

He sighed heavily. "I'm sorry. I know it's not what you want to hear, but I wanted you to know the truth. I want you to prove them wrong, Scottie. I know you're upset about what happened last night, but they win if you let it get to you. I don't think it was a coincidence Alec chose last night to have you come to the party. He revels almost every night and usually forces me and Sie to attend. He could have chosen any night to bring you, to do that to you, but he did it right before the tour."

He paused to look at me. "For now, don't worry about why they selected you. Sie and I will figure out their motives. Don't let it affect you. This tour is important. This is the first time our kingdom will have a rank zero princess. Don't give them a reason to not want one. Don't give them a reason to think that rank zeroes are not cut out for this. Prove that they can be more than servants. Prove that they can be *queens.*"

I thought about what he was saying, and he was right. It didn't matter if I didn't want to be the princess—I was. It didn't matter, for now, why they'd selected me. I needed to use this opportunity to prove them all wrong. I needed to be better than them. Better than Alec and Sie and Synder and Braven and every other male on the High Council making my life difficult. I needed to be better for Ashley, Annabel, and even Roslyn.

I needed to prove that a rank zero was capable of this title. Not just capable but excel at it. That rank zeroes are capable of being more than just servants. We deserve an education. We deserve a fair Trial. That we deserve to be treated to the same standards as everyone else. My conversation with Sie from the first night on the monorail popped into my mind. He told me that Synder declared me a servant before he even saw me fight.

I needed to play the role of the princess.

I didn't realize a tear had slipped down my cheek until Peter leaned forward and wiped it away. Slowly at first, then all at once as his hands cupped my face. "Be their voice, Scotlind Rumor."

"Thank you," I whispered, my voice coming out shaky. "For everything. For telling me all that and for just being... my friend. Because you are my friend, Peter."

He smiled at me. His gaze felt like it was piercing my soul and seeing through me. "You're welcome, *friend*," he said as he let go of my face and sank back into his seat. "We are heading to my hometown now. We will be spending the night in Kitlarn. Tomorrow we'll head to Addler, then LakeWood. I thought you would like to spend the second night in LakeWood so you can see your friends and family."

"I don't have any family," I said before I thought better of it. "But it would be nice to see Vallie and Miles. If they are still there."

"I will arrange for them to be there."

"Really? Thank you so much!" I beamed, unable to hide my excitement. My heart ached thinking about them. I didn't realize how much I missed them. I meant what I said about Peter being my friend, but I needed Vallie's hug and her warm smile. The thought of being able to see her again was overwhelming.

Peter seemed to notice and said, "Of course, it's the least I can do." He didn't need to add *after last night*.

"Will you be seeing your family when we arrive at Kitlarn?" I asked.

He nodded his head. "I'm actually going to be spending the night with them. I have a younger sister. Her name is Lilia. You two would absolutely love each other. She's still in school but has the mind of an Advenian over the age of a hundred. She's like you, a rank zero, or we think she will be at least since no abilities manifested yet. She adores that you are the princess. You should have seen her face when she found out someone like her was selected." He smiled broadly as he added, "However, she loves Sie and has had a crush on him ever since she could speak, so you might actually be fighting with her for his attention."

I laughed softly with him, picturing a miniature girl version of Peter that speaks her mind. I didn't doubt for a second that I would love her. It made sense now—why Peter was so kind to me, why he was talking to me today, why he wanted me to do well on the tour. He wanted a better future for his sister.

"She can have him," I said. I meant it as a joke, but it came out rougher than I had intended. "I can't wait to meet her."

"Unfortunately, you won't be able to tonight. The High Council has already selected your sleeping arrangements, and my home is way too small to host you. But someday soon, I hope."

"Where will I be going?" I asked. I never thought about the sleeping arrangements for this trip.

"You, Sie, and everyone else has accommodations at the local inn."

"Sie won't be staying with his family?" I pried, remembering Peter saying they were both from Kitlarn.

"Not if he can help it," he said with enough of a bite that I didn't dare ask him to elaborate.

The sun moved across the sky as we continued on the monorail to Kitlarn. Peter happily sat with me, telling me all about his hometown and family and what it was like growing up by the ocean. I was thankful for his company. It was like he saw the downward spiral I was heading into and pulled me out before I got to the bottom. He kept me distracted so my thoughts didn't dwell on the humiliation of last night.

I listened intently, genuinely interested in what his life was like. He was careful not to mention Sie at first, worried it would tip me back under, but my curiosity got the better of me, and I couldn't help but ask.

Peter humored me on some things about Sie's past, but he never talked about his home life. He told me how Sie had a hard time making friends as a child. All of their classmates either wanted to sleep with him, mock him, or challenge him to a fight to prove that they were better than him. Every male wanted a chance to beat a potential rank five. It put a target on his back.

When we finally arrived at Kitlarn, Peter led me out of our monorail compartment. Sie flashed Peter a glare as he took my arm, and we descended into the crowd. "You two seemed comfortable," Sie mumbled, surprising me. Was he jealous?

"So were you and Reagan last night. Oh, and that other girl too. The one who was kissing your neck. What was her name again? Right, I never was introduced since your friend had me a little preoccupied," I sneered.

He remained quiet after that and didn't talk to me again the entire time we weaved our way through the crowd. This time, I made it a point to smile at everyone, meeting the gazes of the lower rank Advenians who had come out to see us. I stopped and talked with many of them, making our parade through the town last longer than the one in Palm, but no one stopped me.

Kitlarn was different from any of the other villages I had seen so far. The monorail passed through a forest to get here, but no trees crowded the town that seemed to be stretched out wide. We walked miles to get from one end of the main square to the other. It reminded me of LakeWood, but without the mountains. In the far distance, I could make out a rocky beach with rough waves. Ice glaciers were scattered throughout the water and ice patches by the coast.

"What color is the sand?" I asked Sie, forgetting for a second who I was speaking to.

His eyes flared. "The normal color," he replied.

I squinted, trying to make out the details, but we were too far away. "Which is what?" I pried.

Sie halted, causing me to jerk back into his arm. "The sand is tan, but it's mostly covered with snow," he said slowly. "Why?"

"Nothing," I said, looking straight ahead to avoid his assessing gaze.

When we finally finished with the tour, Peter left to meet his family as the rest of us arrived at the inn. Kitlarn was the furtherest village, making it the longest we would have to travel. I knew it was late, regardless of the sun still shining in the sky.

We were just about to enter the building, the warmth it promised already gnawing at my frozen hands, when Sie stopped dead in his tracks. Two figures approached the doors, blocking the way in.

A muscle in Sie's jaw twitched as he beheld the older of the two males. But it only lasted a second before he took a step forward and focused on the younger one.

"Greyland," Sie smiled as he pulled the younger one into his arms and hugged him. I couldn't help but gasp at the vulnerability Sie was showing, at the sincerity that he genuinely seemed happy to see him.

I studied the boy he was hugging. He, luckily, was solely focused on Sie so he didn't notice my gawking. They shared similarities. They both had the same dark eyes, the same angular jaw and straight nose. Their hair was almost an identical black with soft waves, though Greyland kept his short.

Greyland was shorter with a smaller, leaner frame. Sie's shoulders were broader, blocking his lanky form from view. It made Greyland seem younger, closer to my age than Sie's.

"I missed you," the boy named Greyland mumbled into Sie's shoulder, still embracing him. The older male produced a cough, drawing the two from their hug.

"Father," Sie remarked in a bored manner. I stared at him, trying to read his emotions and gauge his reaction. All Peter had told me about the male before me was that he used to be on the High Council, and that he'd quit to train Sie, whatever that meant.

"I thought we agreed not to see each other," Sie added.

"You know your mother. Once she found out you were staying here, she insisted on having you over for dinner."

"We can't," Sie said. His fist clenched, then relaxed at his side. "We have to check into our inn and be up early tomorrow. Tell her I'm sorry."

"I'm afraid I won't be doing that. I took the liberty of canceling your rooms. You will be staying with us."

"Rooms... as in plural? Are you planning on hosting all of us at your estate tonight?" Sie remarked as he gestured to the group. "I don't think mother would appreciate so many Advenians in her home."

"No. Just you and your betrothed," Sie's father replied with a lazy grin. My mouth dropped open. I tried to quickly compose myself as I heard him say, "And where is my future daughter-in-law?"

A grave look overcame Sie as he glanced at me. But he recovered quickly and wore a stoic expression as he gestured for me to come forward.

"Hello, sir. It's a pleasure to meet you," I said, unable to hide the slight shakiness in my voice. I thought Sie was intimidating before, but he was nothing compared to his father.

I held my hand out for him to shake while giving him a bow that Lady Applebee would have been proud of. He grunted and disregarded my hand as he turned toward Sie. "Well, she's pretty for a nix. At least she won't be horrible to bed."

Sie's jaw set, and I thought if he clamped down any harder, he might break his teeth.

Greyland took my hand that was still awkwardly stretched out and shook it. "It's a pleasure to meet you, princess."

"Just Scottie, please," I said, grateful for his kindness and distraction. His father clicked his tongue.

"Greyland," the boy returned with a kind smile. "Sie's my older brother."

Sie's father ignored the rest of our greeting and stalked off toward a vehicle at the end of the road. Sie walked over to our guards and quickly briefed them before guiding me to follow his family.

"They aren't coming with us?" I whispered to Sie as I saw the guards, both Sie's and mine, file into the inn. Kole's glare sank into me before the door slammed behind him.

Sie shook his head in answer.

"Is that allowed? For us to be separated from them?"

Sie turned to look at me. "Scottie, I am stronger than any of them combined. I am capable of protecting you for one night. Besides, you won't be leaving my side."

I nodded as I followed him into the car. I didn't know what scared me more—whatever was about to happen with Sie's family or being alone with him.

# TWENTY-FOUR
## SIE

IT WAS AN AGONIZING DRIVE TO MY CHILDHOOD HOME. No one spoke as the town whizzed past us. Scottie kept her hands folded into one another and pressed against her lap. She hadn't stopped looking out the window, watching the buildings spread further and further apart. Her lips parted as we passed the glacier-filled ocean, and I couldn't help but wonder what her fascination was with the water and the sand.

A large fence blocked most of the view of the property as we rounded the corner. Ornate silver trim was etched and designed into each panel of the tall metal. I always thought the fence was unnecessary. There wasn't a soul in Kitlarn who would try to break in. The distance alone from the village was protection enough. Not many citizens could afford vehicles, at least not Advenians of the lower rank, which was precisely why my father built the home miles away from the town. Any sign of luxury, status, or wealth my father could flaunt, he took advantage of displaying as a way to show that the Noren family held power.

My mind whirled as I contemplated what game he was playing now. He loathed Scotlind. That much was made clear to me when she was first announced as my fiancé. He couldn't hide the disgust on his face when he found out I would be marrying a nix. He stormed right to Synder and demanded what the hell he was thinking. I would have liked to have Peter's ability in that moment to be able to sit in that room unnoticed and listen to what was said. Because I couldn't figure out the reasoning for them picking her.

I still didn't know what to make of my future wife. She wasn't like other females. She intrigued me. Not just her looks, and Goddess kill me, those were amazing, but there was something different about her. Some mystery to her, and damn, did I want to uncover it. I wanted to know everything about her. I wanted to know what she was thinking. What her dreams and desires were because they weren't this. What led her to try out for the guard even when she knew the odds were against her?

She was a skilled fighter in combat, but that only went so far. Most Advenian females never wanted to be in the guard because they didn't want to risk their otherwise very long life. So why did she? She had everything going against her, from her lack of abilities to her small frame. But she willed it to her advantage, taking males she fought by surprise and using calculated tactics to outmaneuver them.

Ever since the day I saw her fight in her Trials, I'd been transfixed. Consumed by her. I was shocked when they selected her for my bride. For a selfish, fleeting moment, I was happy. Then reality hit me, and I knew she would never be safe again. I knew she was just being used for some greater game.

I had tried to keep my distance from her, trying damn hard to appear like I didn't care about her. I'd even agreed to numerous amounts of Alec's revels and entertained every female he threw at me. All were tests to see how I would react. I played along in the hopes that if I was seen with other girls, it would deter them from looking Scottie's way. But that was all it ever had been—an act. Because no matter how gorgeous, sexy, or gloriously curved the girls Alec pushed on me were, I could never go through with it.

My thoughts were filled by a stubborn female with long brown hair and sapphire eyes. One whose height was laughable for an Advenian. One who, against all odds, didn't let anything stop her from attaining what she wanted. One who had a habit of biting her lip or anxiously twirled her hair around her finger when she was nervous. And now, one who was in danger because of me.

I glanced over at her. She was still staring out the window, but as if reading my thoughts, her gaze drifted toward me. The sun caught the gold in the necklace. My stomach sank, remembering how I'd compelled her, how she had looked at me after I did it. She was safe, I told myself over and over again to shake the guilty feeling that came with compulsion. I hated using it. I had one of the most powerful gifts, and I hated using it.

The driver spoke into the scanner box, breaking the silence for the first time on this horrible ride. Immediately, the doors to the gates groaned open, exposing the familiar and hated stone building. Scottie's eyes widened as she took in my family home. The sheer mass of it alone was daunting. All she'd ever known was her dorm—half a room was all that had belonged to her since she was orphaned.

We were ushered inside to the main entrance, and my gut twisted as I realized one part of my father's sick game. All the servants were present, and all with their sleeves rolled up, exposing their rank zero brands. I glanced at Scotlind to see if she noticed. Of course, she had. My father made damn sure she did. She took in all the servants' vacant stares, noticing their left wrists before she averted her eyes. Her own hands cupped over her burns as she nervously pulled at the sleeves of her dress.

As the servants stared at the tops of their shoes, refusing to look at me or my father, parts of my childhood came crashing back. The only time my father was proud of me was when he discovered my abilities. But it only lasted a fleeting moment. He was livid when he realized I refused to compel anyone. He told me I was weak minded. That I could control all minds but not my own. He would force me to use compulsion on the servants. It was either that or—

"Sie, my darling," my mother's voice released me from my trance.

She was thin, thinner than the last time I'd seen her, but she smiled at me, nonetheless. I resembled her more than my father with her long, curly hair and dark eyes. She moved with elegant grace as she gripped me in a tight hug before I shrugged her off.

"Mother, this is Scotlind Rumor, my fiancé," I said. Scottie cocked her head toward me at the mention of fiancé. It might have been the first time I referred to her as such. The first time I even said it out loud myself. It sounded both right and wrong all at once.

Scottie returned her attention to my mother and gave a bow. "It's wonderful to finally meet you. Your house is marvelous. Thank you for having us, Mrs. Noren."

My mother smiled. "Oh, this is nothing. But come, the servants are putting dinner on the table. Let's eat while it's still hot."

We walked into the grand dining room. The servants had the large fireplace roaring and adorned the table with our finest settings. The large, satin curtains on the far side of the room were pushed open, exposing the large windows and the door that lead to the patio. The ocean view was just visible through the window as the sun reflected off the water.

I took a seat next to Scottie. Greyland filled the one across from us while my parents sat on opposite ends at the head of the table. Various cheese and fruit platters were already spread out across the table, but no one touched them. My father leaned back into his chair, his eyes never leaving Scotlind. I could hear her stomach grumble as the servants brought out some variation of meat pie. I wondered if she'd eaten lunch with Peter on the monorail. Knowing Peter, he probably forgot. Unless they were serving bread, he didn't care much about eating lunch. A hearty breakfast and a good dinner was all he ever needed. His only weaknesses were croissants and warm rolls.

I served Scottie first before scooping two helpings of the pie onto my own plate. She glanced up at me in question. I gave her a nod to start eating, my father wasn't one to worship the Goddesses before a meal.

"Did they not teach you how to properly eat, girl?" my father asked, still eyeing her like a hawk. I glanced at her and noticed she was using the dessert fork. I clenched my fist and flashed him a look. He just laughed it off. "Tell me about your upbringing, Scotlind. What of your parents?"

"My family passed away when I was seven years old. LakeWood has always been my home."

"Hmm, an orphan," my father scoffed, even though I was sure he already knew everything about her past. "Interesting how you, with no power, were the only one to survive. A fire, wasn't it?"

Scottie looked up from her plate, her eyes wide, probably wondering how he knew it was a fire. But I knew Synder had shown him her files. She nodded her head.

"Were your family nixes as well?"

"Maverich," my mother interjected before I could say anything.

"What, Katherine? I'm just trying to get to know the girl better. After all, she is going to join our family," he declared as he stared directly at Scottie. "I was told that you were trying out to be a guard before you were selected for my son."

"Yes, I was," Scottie replied softly.

"You believed that was possible? Achievable, I mean, for someone like you?" he asked her with such calmness, it sounded like he was discussing the weather, not belittling her. "You didn't consider being a servant?"

The food in my mouth turned sour. I slammed my fist down on the table, rattling the dishes. My father smiled at my tension before adding, "You see, that's the problem with this arrangement. Rank zeroes should never be queen. You shouldn't have to marry my son. It's very unfair to you, Scotlind, that they are giving you a job you are incapable of succeeding in. Our High Council owes it to our society to place our people fairly among their rankings. It's the reason the Trials were established. They truly did you and Sie a disservice."

My fists clenched the arms of the chair I was sitting on. "That's enough."

"It's not too late," he ignored me. "Sie, you can help her by renouncing this marriage. You should marry someone of a high rank. Someone who is fitting of your status. Think of your future children. If you reproduce with her"—he gestured to Scottie who was frozen in her seat—"your kids will be weak. Her blood will taint their power. It's a waste of your rank five. I'll make you both a very generous deal," he said with a smile. "Son, if you agree to marry Reagan, I will welcome Miss Rumor here with open arms at our estate."

Greyland and my mother both shifted uncomfortably in their seats. Still, they didn't say anything, as if they were expecting this conversation to happen. Greyland looked at my future wife and gave her a tentative smile.

"Scotlind will not be a servant here," I said through gritted teeth as I pushed my chair back. "She will be my wife, and you will show her respect as your future queen." I turned toward her and pulled her by the arm, lifting her out of the chair. "Come on, let's go."

———

MY BLOOD WAS BOILING as I led Scottie to my old room. It took every ounce of self control I had not to go back downstairs and punch my father in the face. I couldn't believe he'd said all of those things in front of her, *to* her. This was exactly what I wanted to avoid by not coming here. I knew how much he despised rank zeroes and believed they were beneath us. My father devoted his time to making me powerful, so that one day I would be king. I was living out his dream. He sought out any opportunity for the Noren name to rise. A part of me was happy that Scotlind had no powers, that I could defy him in this. That some part of his plan wasn't going his way, but a bigger part of me was worried for her. I knew my father was serious about her working here.

Scotlind trailed wordlessly behind me as I guided her through the house. She had been incredibly calm during dinner. I stole a glance behind me to look at her. Her eyes were glued to the floor, her head down. How many times in her life was she talked down upon to be able to maintain such composure? The thought made my blood heat.

I waited until we made it to my old chamber and locked the door behind us before I said, "I'm sorry."

"It's okay," she replied quietly, still looking at the ground. "I'm used to it."

A heavy sigh escaped my lips as I ran my hands through my hair. That was what I figured she would say. I slumped down into the chair closest to me as I gestured toward the bed in the middle of the room. "Sleep," I told her.

Her eyes flared. "In here? With you?" she asked as she finally looked up at me. Those beautiful, damn eyes that made me lose my train of thought. Such a bright blue that I felt like I was drowning, and I would be happy to die if it meant I could continue to stare at her.

"What were you expecting?" I shrugged as I stretched my legs out in front of me.

"I just... I thought we weren't allowed to be together until we were... you know." She didn't finish her train of thought, but I knew what she was thinking. We weren't supposed to be alone together until our wedding, until we consummated our marriage.

I smiled, noticing her shyness on the topic. "Technically, that's true," I said, enjoying the way she fidgeted with her hair. "We aren't allowed to, *yet*."

"Then why am I in here with you?" she bit down on her bottom lip so hard I thought she might draw blood. It was an effort to force my attention away from that lip. I couldn't stop thinking about that night in my bathing room. Fuck. Staying in the same room with her was going to be harder than I thought.

"I told you that you wouldn't leave my side while you were here and I meant it." When I realized she wasn't satisfied with that answer, I added gently, "Remember when I told you that some Advenians will go to great lengths to not have a rank zero be queen?" She nodded her head. "Well, my father is one of those Advenians. He believes in the ranking system to a fault and feels that rank zeroes are beneath everyone else. I don't trust him with you, and I don't want you alone while you're here. You'll be safer with me."

"Why are you going to marry me then?" she asked, still gnawing at her lip. "I don't understand. If you were brought up to believe rank zeroes are nothing, that I am nothing, that I'm inferior to you, why would you agree to marry me?"

I looked at her, trying to gauge how much I should tell her before I settled on saying, "My father believes that. He believes rank zeroes are only good as servants. I think being a servant is a better position than he would like. He would prefer them to be slaves. He wants to take away all their rights. The people serving in this estate are not treated well, Scottie. I would never wish that upon anyone. And I don't trust him here with you. Just because my father is that way doesn't mean that I agree with him and share his beliefs."

She took a small step backward before sinking onto the bed. I noticed her hands clutching the necklace I forced her to wear. "Do you want to change things then?" she asked softly. "Will you change things? Get rid of the ranking system and let Advenians have a choice in their lives instead of being told what to do?"

The look she was giving me tore at my soul. Her eyes were wide and waiting, staring right into mine. Her chest unmoving, holding her breath, waiting for my answer. "The Trials at the end of schooling gives Advenians a fair shot, and last I checked, everyone is free to try out for whatever they want."

Her brows furrowed. "You believe that? That it's fair? You told me yourself I would have been a servant if I wasn't selected into this. That it was decided at my ranking before my Trial. You watched me fight. Was I not good enough to be a guard then?"

"That's different."

"No. No, it's not," she seethed. "Answer the question. Should I have been a servant?"

"It doesn't matter what I think."

"Yes, it does," she jumped off the bed and stormed toward me. "How can you say what *you* think doesn't matter. You will be the *king*. You can change things." I honestly couldn't tell if she was going to fight me. Her chest was rapidly rising and falling. I'd never seen her so rattled before, so unafraid to speak her mind.

"You know I can't do that, Scotlind. Even if I wanted to. You know that can't be done. It would cause a civil war, killing many people in the process, and I don't even know if it would work. I'm not going to be the king who is the cause of so many deaths for a chance at an unknown future."

She mumbled something under her breath as she turned away from me. "Just sleep," I said again. It came out more forcefully than I intended. "We have a long day tomorrow."

She turned her back to me as she crawled into my old bed. I was all too aware of her presence—just the fact alone that she was in *my bed* across the room from me was driving me insane. I wouldn't be getting any rest tonight.

I heard her tossing and turning and knew she wasn't comfortable sleeping in the same room either, but for entirely different reasons. She hated me, and I couldn't blame her after last night.

I couldn't get it out of my mind, how furious she was as she was forced to do all those things. Her murderous gaze while she took off her dress... I tried not to look at her as she did it. I knew it was wrong, but I couldn't help it. I also knew Alec was enjoying every inch of her too. I wanted to beat him right then and there for it.

I never thanked Peter for getting her out of there. As soon as she took the necklace off, I knew I had to do something to help her, but I couldn't be the one to do it. Alec was waiting for me to cave, waiting to push me to the brink so I would defend her. I entered Peter's head and spoke to him through his mind, begging him to take her away. Everyone loved Peter, so no one would think twice about him stepping in.

Some part of me hated that I couldn't be the one to do it. Instead, I was the one she blamed. I knew exactly how it looked to her—how *I* looked to her.

It bothered the hell out of me that she left with another male. Regardless of the fact that he was my friend and that I ordered him to do it. I couldn't imagine what else Alec would have made her do if she had stayed.

I trusted Peter with my life, and I knew I could trust him with Scotlind too. He cares for her. But I'd seen the way she looks at him. She likes him. I should be happy about it. Happy that she has someone at the castle, happy that she's not completely alone. But I would be lying if I said it didn't bother the hell out of me.

I stalked over to the bookshelf and picked up an old text. I didn't really care for reading, but I desperately needed to clear my head.

I needed anything to keep my thoughts from the female who was now sleeping in my bed.

# TWENTY-FIVE
## SCOTLIND

I woke up the next morning disoriented to where I
was. My eyes adjusted to the dying embers of the fireplace to find Sie
settled in a chair by the door. His head rested at an odd angle. It elongated his neck, and his feet were spread out before him. An old book
was opened across his chest as if he fell asleep reading.

Sleeping.

It was an unsettling picture. He looked so young and different fast
asleep. The intimidating male hours before was gone.

Grabbing the candle off the nearby table, I quietly tip-toed past
him toward the bathing room, careful not to wake him up.

When I re-entered the bedroom, dressed and ready to go, he was
sitting on the edge of the bed. I halted in the door as he stood. My
breath hitched, and all I could do was gawk at him as he slid past me
into the room. Neither of us saying anything, which only made the
tension palpable.

I listened for the water to start filling in the tub and tried not to
think about the last time I saw him after a bath.

I still hated him for what his friends did to me, but I couldn't help
but think he was not who I thought he was. He said he wouldn't
change the ranking system, that it would cause a civil war, but deep

down, I think he would. Maybe I could convince him. If I could come up with a way to change things that wouldn't lead to bloodshed, would he agree?

I paced, biting my lip in the process, scanning the room that must have been Sie's childhood room growing up. It was massive, but was barely decorated—bare walls just like my dorm room. I walked over to the chair he'd slept on and flipped through the book he had been reading. It was an ancient text regarding Allium.

I was so focused on the book that I didn't notice Sie walk out of the bathing room until I felt his breath against my neck. I jumped and gently put the book back down. He was freshly washed, smelling of cedarwood and some citrus scent. He was ready for the tour. He looked like a king, regal and intimidating in his outfit. Gone was the youthful male who was sleeping just minutes prior, it was as if his cold demeanor was a mask, something he put on when he dressed.

He wore all black with a cloak-like cape draped over his chest. Daggers were hidden within his formal attire that I had never noticed before.

"Come," he gestured toward the door. "The car is here to take us to the monorail." I followed him out and waited while he hugged his mother and brother goodbye. His father did not see us off.

Today we were touring Addler and LakeWood. My heart hammered against my chest, knowing that I would get to see Vallie and Miles tonight. I would have to thank Peter again for arranging that.

Even though I didn't have a family, I felt better about my upbringing. Miles and Vallie had taken me under their wings and welcomed me with open arms. I had good memories because of them. I couldn't imagine Sie's family celebrating anything. I couldn't imagine what it was like growing up in that house. His mother and brother were nice, but I didn't think anyone in that family ever stood up to his father.

———

TOURING Addler was awkward as neither of us brought up what had happened at his parents home, even as Peter relentlessly hounded us.

But the past two nights no longer bothered me. I couldn't think about Sie's father or anyone from the Council. I was giddy with anticipation of going home tonight.

Home.

It was funny that during my time in LakeWood, all I wanted was to escape it, and now that I was gone, I missed it. I couldn't wait to be among the familiar buildings and see my friends.

The tour of LakeWood was held at WestEnd. Peter told me that after the tour, he would take me back to the school where Vallie and Miles were supposed to meet us. The day dragged on, the hours ticked by too slowly until I was finally on the familiar grounds.

I'd never been so happy to see the endless brick.

Sie insisted on tagging along with us. He dismissed his own guards, something I was gathering he did often, but Kole refused to leave my side. "It's night time, nix. That means it's my shift to guard you and you're not leaving my sight." He sneered at me when I tried to brush him off.

When I finally spotted Vallie and Miles in the distance, standing outside one of the Hub's cafeterias, I sprinted toward them. Miles smiled at me, but it was washed off his face when he noticed Sie, Peter, and Kole flanking close behind.

I went to hug Vallie first, but Miles stepped in the way, sweeping me up off the ground and scooping me into a big hug before I could protest. When he finally set me down, longer than he should have, I noticed Sie's jaw was taut. I ignored his gaze as I moved toward my best friend and embraced her. She had tears streaming from her amber eyes and already flowing down her pink, rosy cheeks.

"I missed you guys so much," I breathed into Vallie's shoulder. Her flaming red hair had the same jasmine scent to it.

"I missed you more, Scottie-cat," Vallie cried, her words coming out ragged.

"What is he doing here?" Miles glared at Kole.

"I'm her personal guard, Hartlin," Kole retorted with a smug look on his face. "I get to spend every night watching her sleep, making sure no harm comes to her."

Miles shifted uncomfortably. I didn't dare look at Sie or Peter.

Vallie stepped out of my embrace, wiped her eyes, and glanced between where I stood and where Kole lingered behind. She took a step toward Kole. "You better be."

"Better be what, Val?" Kole asked, taken aback by her glare.

"Making sure no harm comes to her."

Kole's expression faltered for a moment as he looked at her, but I didn't want to wait to hear what he would say back. "What about you two. How have you been? How are your jobs?" I asked, desperate to change the subject.

Vallie's gaze softened as she turned away from Kole. "The school year won't start for another month, so I have been preparing my classes for the little nuggets I'll be teaching. LakeWood actually has a rigorous curriculum." Vallie said to me, but her eyes drifted toward where Peter stood. He was already staring at her.

"Things have been good at AASP. Although I don't get to see Vallie much since I'm stationed in Backerly," Miles told me. "We have reason to believe that our home planet of Allium may be habitable again. We are considering the risks of sending some Advenians there soon to investigate."

My head perked up. "Really? You think we might be able to go back someday?" I couldn't keep the excitement out of my voice. I'd read countless books about our old planet. Many artists depicted pictures of what it once was, and I longed to see it. The land seemed so vast and strange like you could be in a new world every few miles with the constant changing of plains, twisting rivers, and diverse landscapes. It was a far cry from the cold glacial atmosphere of Tennebris.

The depictions of the night paintings were my favorite. The two pink moons were bright in the sky, and the stars were more extensive, larger somehow, compared to what Earth offered.

Miles drew back a bit, realizing that everyone was listening to him now, not just me. "Well, it's not official yet. It's not public knowledge. But yes, there is a possibility of it. I might volunteer to go."

"Isn't that dangerous?" I asked. "Our home planet is so far away. You would be gone for so long."

"A year. It would take a year to get to and from Allium. Plus, you have to add extra time for the investigation of the planet. But think about it, Scottie, how worthwhile it would be if we had our own planet. We wouldn't have to hide from the mortals anymore. We could live freely."

The thought thrilled me. I'd always known that was the purpose of the AASP. It was what they had been working on ever since our kind descended here. Monitoring our dying planet as well as seeking out the universe in the chance there was another habitable one. But I never imagined it would be possible in our lifetime. The texts always said that the use of abilities during the war killed everything in its path. The ground no longer held any green, leaving the animals with no food. The trees were gone, depriving the air of oxygen. Advenian's lungs were giving out and our kind was dying at critical rates, shortening their long lifespan. Could it really be possible for the planet to renew itself with our absence?

"I would like to check out your research," Sie said, speaking for the first time.

Miles stood up straighter, acknowledging Sie and sizing him up. "I would be honored, Prince Noren." He then bent at the waist. Vallie tore her gaze from Peter, noting her twin's bow and followed suit. Her eyes went wide as if just realizing that Sie wasn't only my fiancé but technically royalty.

"No need for formalities unless we are in court," Peter smiled, gesturing to their bowed forms. "Any friend of Scottie's is our friend as well." Vallie gave a small smile back.

"Good. I'll make the arrangements," Sie said, taking a possessive step in front of me. His eyes never left Miles' gaze. They both stared at each other, unmoving.

"Who's hungry?" I said, too aware of Sie's closeness. How if he wanted to, he could reach out and graze my arm.

Peter answered with a wide, dimpled grin. "Me. Come on, Scottie, show me your favorite place to eat here, and they better have croissants," he said as he took me by the arm and grabbed Vallie with his other hand. Vallie's face turned red at his touch. I'd never seen her so flustered with a guy before. She was always so confident and sure of herself. Now she seemed timid and shy.

The rest of the evening was pure bliss. I'd never felt so happy being among my friends and back at LakeWood. Even Kole didn't ruin my mood. Vallie and Peter never stopped staring at each other. They talked all night, leaving me alone with Kole, Sie, and Miles.

"He's so cute," she whispered to me when Peter left to get another helping of rolls.

"He's the male version of you," I laughed. "Of course you would like him."

Miles claimed the seat next to me during dinner while Sie sat across from me. He wordlessly ate his meal, but I was aware that he was listening to everything Miles said to me. Every now and then, I would meet his gaze, and our eyes would lock. I had to ask Miles to repeat himself more than once.

I was sad to leave Lakewood the next morning. I found it much harder to say goodbye to Vallie and Miles the second time, but the trip wasn't over.

We had two more villages to tour today, Narway and Backerly, both of which I'd never been to before. I was thankful that we would at least be arriving back at the castle tonight, so I wouldn't have to worry about sleeping in the same room as Sie again.

That was, until our wedding night.

# TWENTY-SIX
## SCOTLIND

I COULD BARELY KEEP MY EYES OPEN BY THE TIME WE finally arrived at the castle. Pure exhaustion overtook me as I pushed open the heavy doors to my chamber with the intention of plopping down onto my bed.

But the doors didn't shut behind me.

I turned around slowly. Kole stood in the middle of the frame with one long arm outstretched to prop the door open. He stared at me before taking a step forward into the threshold.

"What are you doing?" I asked when the door clicked shut, locking us in my room together.

"That one night alone with your prince must have gotten to your head, nix. You know why I'm here."

"That's not what I meant," I said slowly, cautiously. "I know you are my night guard, but why are you in my room?"

He kicked off the door he was leaning on, closing the gap between us in two long strides. My hand instinctively clutched my necklace as I backed up a step. Then another and another, until I was pressed against the wall.

He breathed hot air into my ear. "If you think I'm going to let you out of my sight again, you're an idiot. You will not make me look incompetent in my job ever again. Do you understand?"

He shifted to grab my arm, holding me in place. I tried to shake him off, to escape his grasp, but his hold on me only tightened, causing pain where his fingers pressed against my skin. My head was level with his neck, and beneath his guard uniform, a glimmer of a bruise spread across it, bobbing in time with his Adam's apple.

I let out a gasp as he growled, "You will never leave my side while I'm on guard, and you will never fucking sneak off again without me knowing." He then pushed me away, causing my back to slam against the wall.

"Get out, Kole. This isn't funny."

"Oh, I'm not laughing," he sneered as he dragged one of the leather armchairs across the floor. A horrible scraping sound filled the room as it scratched over the oak floor. To my horror, he positioned the chair at the foot of my bed and sank down into it. Slouching low, he crossed his arms over his chest and looked up at me triumphantly.

Dread filled my stomach as I realized he wasn't planning on leaving. He really would stay in my room all night. By the smirk plastered on his face, he knew how uncomfortable he was making me. I was sick of everyone walking all over me. I was sick of not having a choice. And beyond that, I was tired. I just wanted to sleep alone.

I stormed to his chair and swung my fist at his face before I could think better of it. His smile broadened as he easily dodged it. I tried again and again and again.

I knew I was fighting carelessly thanks to a mixture of lack of sleep and the headache that was now pounding in my temples. I never fought well when rage overtook me. Kole knew it too, but I didn't care. It felt good to move my body, to take my anger out. And there wasn't anyone I wanted to beat up more than Kole. Well, maybe Alec.

The next punch I threw, he caught my fist in his large hand and didn't let go, making it seem like up until now, he'd been humoring me and decided it was enough. He dragged me by my arm, pulling me into him.

"What are you doing, Kole? Stop," I pleaded as he pulled me into his lap. "I won't sneak out again, I promise. Please," I added when he looked into my eyes.

"Since when did you get manners? I like it. Beg me, and maybe I'll go."

I attempted and failed to shrug out of his arms. He pushed me harder against his lap for emphasis as I said through gritted teeth, "Please, leave my room, Kole. I just want to sleep alone."

"Hmm, I don't think so," he smiled. I started to protest when the arm holding me began to turn gold. "You will not fight me. Stay still, nix."

My eyes widened as I looked at him, then his arm. He was compelling me. His voice sounded different, softer, almost lyrical, even though it had no real effect on me.

I swallowed the lump in my throat as I hoarsely replied, "Yes." I wanted so badly to push away from him. I wanted to reach for my necklace and press the button to alert Sie, but Kole kept both of my wrists taut against his chest. Any movement I made would tip him off that I wasn't really being compelled.

He was smiling at me now, a full grin exposing all his teeth. Amusement filled his gaze. "Now, you won't tell anyone about this. You won't fight me anymore, and you will do as I say. Understand?"

"I won't tell anyone. I won't fight you," I repeated softly, trying to mimic what my body would be forced to do without the necklace.

I struggled to keep my breathing slow, to hide my panic. I couldn't take another night of this. Another night of being someone else's entertainment. Of being at their mercy.

"Good. Now go to bed and sleep. Don't mind my presence. Act as if I weren't here." He finally let go of my wrists as I fumbled off of him. I started to make my way toward the bed before he said, "Don't tell me you sleep in your dress?"

I looked down and knew he was compelling me to act as if he wasn't here. And I would put on a nightgown. I silently walked over to my dresser and pulled out a white slip. As I made my way to the bathing room, he smirked, "You normally change in there?"

"Yes," I said through gritted teeth.

"Pity," I heard him say as I slammed the door shut between us. I wasn't about to change in front of him.

His eyes roamed over my body as I emerged from the bathing room and made my way toward the bed. I clutched my necklace tightly, staring up at the ceiling. Should I press it? All Kole had ordered me to do was sleep. I was only supposed to use it for an emergency. I doubted Sie would be pleased when he came to find out that I was just sleeping and Kole was just doing his job. Was he really only concerned that I would sneak off again and wanted to make sure I didn't? Did he get in trouble when I left that night? I thought back to the new bruise over his throat, how Kole wore the collar of his uniform high to hide it.

I pulled the heavy comforter over my head, knowing full well he was staring at me. What was the point of him being in the same room as me? He could just compel me to not sneak off. He didn't have to watch me like a hawk.

The next few nights were similar. Kole didn't talk to me. He just followed me into my room, dragged the chair across the floor, and watched me sleep. Or he thought he watched me sleep as I never could drift off with him there.

I knew the underside of my eyes were turning purple from the lack of rest. I tried to take naps between my lessons and after dinner while Abherham was still with me until Kole's shift started, but it wasn't enough. Something in me never let myself fully rest. I didn't trust Kole, and my body refused to sleep while he was watching me.

Peter said as much during our training sessions one morning. "You look like shit."

"I can't sleep."

"I can see that," he said as we ran together through the gardens and around the lake.

"Can you train me in self-defense? Like how to break out of holds and stuff if someone is holding me down?" I was a good fighter only because I was agile and quick. My motto during school was to never get caught, but now...

Peter looked over at me through his sweaty hair, eyeing me carefully. "Yes, we can add that to your training. I can incorporate that into our combat fighting, but my best advice would be to run. You are fast and can probably outrun most of our kind. If you do get caught, it will be more difficult for you to break out of holds since almost everyone is larger than you."

"But not impossible? Can you show me? Like today?" I asked.

"Yes," he said. "Is everything okay, Scottie?"

"Mhmm," I lied. I wanted to tell him. I wanted to beg for a new guard, but I knew that was just me being weak. The only reason I wanted someone else was because he made me uncomfortable. I also knew that if I told Peter, Kole would know that I hadn't been compelled.

A week of restless nights weighed heavily on me. My eyes waned as I slumped into my bed. I started to relax about Kole's intentions. I figured a couple more nights of this, and he would grow tired of just watching me sleep. He would trust that I wouldn't sneak off again and then go back to his usual spot outside my door. I just had to hold off until then.

But exhaustion overtook me. Peter had trained me harder this morning, and my body ached for rest. I tried to silently shake my head and bite the inside of my cheek to stay awake, but I couldn't. I thought I saw Kole lift off from his chair and come to my side of the bed. I thought I saw him smile over my body, but I couldn't tell as the room around me turned black, and sleep finally came.

# TWENTY-SEVEN
## SCOTLIND

Hot breath caressed my face at the same time a crushing weight came down on my chest. Then my neck tightened, restricting my air flow. I couldn't breathe. My eyes fluttered open in an instant, adjusting to the dimly lit room. Two solid brown eyes bored down into mine. I knew those eyes.

I tried to push Kole off of me, but it was too late. His knees were digging into my arms, holding them in place as he straddled me on my bed. His hands were wrapped around my neck. Unable to move any other part of me, I kicked my legs furiously, trying to shake my body out from under him. His fingers loosened their grip enough for me to fling my head forward, connecting his with mine.

Throbbing instantly greeted me as my vision blurred and I saw stars. I tried to focus, knowing I only had a second to act. Kole sat up as he cried out in pain from the collision, shifting off of my chest. I flung my left arm free at the same time I lifted my knee into his groin. Hard. He collapsed on his side, cradling the tender area with his hands. I didn't look back at him as I sprinted toward the door. My breathing was raspy and uneven, slowing me down, as my lungs greedily took in the air around me.

The lock clicked into place before I touched it. I unlocked it and reached for the handle, only for it to click again. Quickly, I glanced behind my shoulder and saw Kole's body covered in golden markings. He was using his telekinetic ability to keep the lock latched. I cursed under my breath before slamming my body into the large door, again and again, hoping it would budge.

"There's no use," Kole said as he managed to peel himself off the bed. "You know a nix like yourself can't stop me."

"What do you want?" I said, my voice quivering, still breathless. He smiled at me, really smiled. He took his time stalking toward me. A hunter circling and toying with his prey.

"You see, little nix, I'm not the only one here in the castle who despises Advenians like you. Nixes are nothing more than vessels for people with power to control. You are nothing. You will always be nothing. You should have been a servant, but look at you," he sneered as he threw his hands in the air gesturing to the room around us. "Here you are living with the grand notion that you are actually meant to be the queen. You think you actually deserve this? That the people of Tennebris will live to see a nix on the throne? That they will follow you? We made ourselves into a laughing stock for the Luxians. It's time we start rivaling their power and we can't do that with a zero on the throne."

"The High Council appointed me. You and I both know I didn't have a say in this," I said slowly, scanning the room for anything I could use to my advantage against him. I tried to move the doorknob one more time, but it wouldn't budge.

Kole noticed. His smile grew as he took another step closer to me. His eyes went to my breasts—the straps to my gown fell off my shoulders, exposing the top of them right where the chain of my necklace rested.

My necklace.

I quickly grabbed it and pressed the button on the back, praying that Sie would stay true to his word.

"That's bullshit," he spat in my direction. "Don't try to fool me. Don't pretend that you were just thrown into this position. You think just because you have a pretty face and nice body, you can seduce any male you want. You might have seduced Sie and even some members of the Council to get yourself here, but trust me, it ends now."

He drew a dagger from the sheath on his hip and looked ready to devour me as he compelled, his voice softening, "You will not move. You will not scream."

I tried my best not to fidget or even breathe as Kole came up before me. I needed him to believe that his compulsion worked. I needed him to believe that I wouldn't fight back, that I *couldn't* fight back.

"Look at me." I slowly shifted my gaze to meet his. He was only inches away now. "I have to keep you alive, *for now*, but when the time comes, I'm going to make this slow. Slow and painful, and as you die, I want you to remember that you are nothing. You deserve nothing. That this is what you and all the nixes will face when you walk among our kind, tainting it with your bad blood. First, we will take care of our own nix problem in Tennebris, making our kingdom strong once again, then we will handle the mortals."

"Who is *we*?" I asked. My breath came out in ragged pants as my eyes never left his blade.

"Wouldn't you like to know?" His smile turned cruel. "Right now all you need to know is that I'm taking you with me. I need you alive, but..." he paused as he lifted his blade to my arm, grazing it slowly over my skin. He didn't press it down hard enough to draw blood. He was teasing me, taunting me. He wanted me to fear him. He meant it when he said he would take his time with me. "They didn't say anything about bringing you in unscratched. I am still allowed to have my fun with you," he finished.

I had to act now. Twisting my hips, I drove my knee into his ribcage as hard as I could. My arm swung out to swat the tip of the blade away as my other arm went to his face.

He leaned back just enough to escape my fingers from clawing into his eye as he pushed me against the door. "You bitch," he seethed. I felt pain shoot against my upper thigh as he dragged the blade down my leg. I grabbed his wrist and twisted it away from me. A bone cracked, and he bent down to cradle his arm as the dagger clattered to the floor. I kicked my uninjured leg as hard as I could up toward his face. Another snap of bone sounded as blood gushed out of his nose.

I sprinted across the room toward the three large windows. My room sat on the second floor, and bushes blanketed the ground beneath it. I could jump. I tried all three windows, pushing frantically at each one, begging them to unlock, but they didn't budge. I heard Kole pick up the dagger from the floor. His steps were heavy as they made their way toward me. He spat what I presumed was his blood onto the floor.

I tried to turn as he fisted a chunk of my hair from behind. He pinned me against his chest just as the door to my bedroom rattled. I stared at the lock with dread before Sie teleported into the room. I sagged a bit into Kole once I saw him. He came.

Sie scanned my face, his eyes wide with worry. He trailed every inch of my skin, examining me for injuries. His gaze lingered on the gash on my thigh—my entire leg was red. His gaze then shifted to Kole and the dagger now pressed against my throat.

Sie slowly stalked closer. Kole pushed the blade further against my neck, blood starting to trickle down. "Move, and she dies."

Sie halted. His eyes found mine. "Let her go."

Kole backed up further into the room with me in tow. "Here is how this is going to work. You're going to go to the far corner of the room, away from the door." I watched as the lock clicked open from Kole's ability. "If you so much as move toward us, I'll drive this dagger into her throat. And don't even attempt to use your compulsion on me or teleport to us. The moment I see any bit of gold on your skin, she's dead."

Sie obeyed. His eyes never left me or the dagger pressed into my neck. Kole relaxed his death grip enough that the blade no longer pierced my skin. "Let's go," he said as he pushed me toward the door.

I glanced at Sie. He stood motionless as he mouthed one word to me. *Two.*

Two. The defensive move Peter had taught me this week. I'd learned eight moves so far, but number two was to escape a hold from behind. Peter must have told Sie about my training and my progress. I didn't hesitate.

Kole swore profusely as I rolled out of his grip, executing the maneuver and tumbling onto the floor.

Before I even blinked, Sie was on him. The dagger was thrown across the room, and Kole was brought down. Sie didn't use any abilities—he didn't need to. I couldn't watch. The sounds escaping Kole's mouth made me queasy. I vomited on the floor. Once. Twice.

Guards poured into my room once Kole was pinned. Sie didn't look at them as he spoke, "Take him to the dungeons, now. Don't tell anyone what you saw tonight. I'm taking Scotlind to my room." The guards wordlessly clasped shackles over Kole's wrist. He swore profusely as they clamped the metal over his broken bone before dragging him away.

Sie was instantly at my side, his hand hovering over my lower back. He didn't say anything as he looped an arm under my knees and scooped me into his arms. I didn't protest as he carried me through the halls of the castle. I didn't notice anything or anyone. I didn't know if Sie was walking or running or if he teleported us there, but it felt like a lifetime. I curled into his neck, smelling the same cedarwood scent and instantly felt safe in his arms. Shaken still, but safe.

The two guards outside Sie's door stiffened at my appearance. I was nestled against him. My thin, white nightgown clung to my sweaty skin. My blood, and maybe some of Kole's, engulfed both of us. Tears streamed down my face from the pain in my leg and the shock of what just happened. Despite being drained, my body wouldn't stop shaking. Sie tightened his grip around my body as he nodded for them to open the doors.

Candles lit the room, illuminating Peter's green, wide-eyed shock as he took in the sight of me. He rushed over to us, but Sie pressed past him.

"Scottie, you're bleeding! Are you okay?"

I pressed further into Sie's chest as the heat from the fireplace reached me. I didn't realize how badly I was shivering until he set me down on the leather sofa. Sie didn't so much as look at Peter as he ordered, "Call a Luxian healer, now." Peter left immediately, leaving us alone in his room.

In one swoop, Sie reached his hand over his head and pulled his shirt off. He ripped the fabric, tearing off a long piece, and pulled my ruined thigh toward him. His knees slammed into the marble floor as he knelt beside me and started hiking my thin nightgown up even higher. I swatted his hand away.

"What are you doing?" I gasped.

He looked up at me through thick lashes. His black eyes were endless. "Trying to save your life. You've lost too much blood."

Despite the pain and the numbness coursing through my body, my cheeks heated as his rough, callused hand traced up my thigh, pulling my bloody gown with it. I winced at the pain as he wrapped the shredded piece of his shirt over my bleeding leg, making a tourniquet to stop the blood flow. I dared a glance at my thigh and felt nauseous all over again. The wound was long and deep, starting at the base of my hip and extending down to my knee. Blood leaked from the gash, hiding any skin that was once my leg. Everything was bright red.

Sie gently cupped my chin, the pad of his thumb tracing over my jaw as he pushed my head to the side to examine the cut on my neck. "At least this one isn't deep. Are you okay?"

I couldn't respond. He held my face in his hands for a few more seconds. Then, noticing my shivering, he pulled away to get a blanket.

A few minutes later, the doors opened again as Peter and a healer rushed into the room. I barely took her in before she bolted to my side and started fussing over me. I was tired and numb, and all I wanted to do was close my eyes. I tilted my head back against the soft cushion as my vision started to blur.

Sie cupped the nape of my neck. "Don't sleep. Not yet."

The healer didn't ask any questions as she took in the blood dripping from my neck onto my breast and then my thigh. I was pretty sure there was blood matted in my hair too from the break in Kole's nose when he pressed me against him. The healer's eyes lingered on the strips of Sie's soaked shirt. The white material was a flaming red. Blood started oozing out of the wound as she peeled the makeshift tourniquet off. Peter looked away as the healer moved her hands up my thigh to my hip.

"This is going to hurt," was the only warning I got before blue light radiated off her hand, searing into my leg. I screamed as Sie pushed my hair back, soothing me.

"It's too deep to completely heal," she finally said to Sie. "My work will allow the wound to heal faster, but it will still take time to recover. She must rest her leg and take it easy."

"How long?" Sie's voice was rough.

The healer didn't look at him as she answered, "A month, maybe two. With the length of the cut, I'm worried about her reopening the stitches."

I bit the inside of my cheek to keep from crying out as she began stitching up my leg. I didn't know how much time had passed as the healer worked her way higher and higher up my thigh.

I jumped as the door to Sie's room swung open, causing the needle to pierce into the gash. The healer glared at me before grabbing my thigh and continuing.

One of the guards stepped before Sie. "He is ready whenever you are, Prince Noren." Sie nodded, and the guard bowed low before leaving the room again.

I looked up at Sie, who remained with me, standing to the side of the sofa. He met my gaze. Peter stood a few feet away, watching everything. No one said anything.

"Tilt your head back," the healer instructed as she finished the last stitch on my thigh. Her fingers moved to my neck. I couldn't help but notice they were caked in blood—my blood. Blue light palpitated off her fingertips again, tingling my neck as they swept across the cut. I winced as I felt the sting of Kole's blade all over again.

"This one is shallow and should be healed in a day or two," she said. "It will leave a faint scar, but that's it. An inch deeper into your neck, and you wouldn't be with us now. Your thigh will take a lot longer to heal. You shouldn't be putting much weight on it, or you could tear open the stitches."

"Thank you," I said to her as she wrapped my neck with fresh linens. She nodded once and walked out of the room.

Sie moved, refusing to look at me now that I was healed. His fists were clenched at his sides as he stalked toward the corner of his room. He strapped a sword across his still bare back and sheathed more daggers into his attire than I thought possible. He turned toward Peter, a muscle quivering in his jaw. "Don't let her leave this room, and don't let her out of your sight."

"What are you going to do?" I winced as I sat up on the sofa. Sie didn't bother looking at me before he stormed out of the room, armed to the teeth.

# TWENTY-EIGHT
## SIE

I MADE MY WAY TOWARD THE DUNGEONS WHERE THE guards had dragged Kole. I saw Advenians flinch as I stormed past, but I didn't care. All I could see was Scottie's body flush against Kole's as he held her there. Her revealing nightgown hiked up her leg, drenched in blood. The knife pressed against her throat as red leaked from it, and her beautiful eyes were wide. Terrified. I'd never seen her so terrified before. I knew the two had a history, but I never questioned who Synder had selected for her guards. I knew it had all been a test. Synder was watching the Trials when Kole beat Scottie. He was probably watching me, seeing how I interacted with Scottie even then. I knew if I showed too much interest in her, he would have used it against me.

Stupid. I was so fucking stupid for leaving her alone with him.

A few servants yelped as I passed them. They were frightened of me. Good. Let them be scared. Let everyone know not to mess with Scottie. Let the whole Goddess-damn court know not to fucking touch her again. I was done acting like I didn't care. I wouldn't risk losing her again.

And in the end, it didn't matter. All the times I ignored her in public, all the times I was purposely seen with other girls, all the efforts I'd made to avoid her, did nothing but kill me on the inside.

I knew it was only a matter of time before the High Council made a move on her, but I didn't think they would use her guard to do it.

The smell of rot and urine filled my nostrils as I finally reached the dungeons. I stopped in front of Kole's cell, turned toward the two guards stationed outside, and growled, "Leave us." They bowed their heads and wordlessly left us alone. Smart.

I crouched down low so I was eye level with Kole as I braced my hands on the rusty bars. Blood still crusted my fingers. I'd have to bathe after this to get Scotlind's and Kole's blood off me, along with the dirt from this putrid place.

"We can do this the hard way or the easy way," I said, my voice low and hoarse. "Tell me who you are working for. Who hired you, and what do they want with Scottie?"

"You're going to have to do a lot better than that, *prince*." The prick rested his head back against the stone wall, meeting my gaze. The way he mocked my title, making it known he didn't believe I would hold it long.

"And if you think whatever you are about to do is going to stop with me, you're sorely wrong," he added. "No one is going to stand to see a nix on the throne. It's only a matter of time before she turns up dead."

I took a deep breath, stopping myself from murdering him right here. I needed to relax enough to get answers out of him. Who had hired Kole and why? It had to be more than them not wanting a nix on the throne, seeing as the High Council selected Scottie themselves. I knew it was a setup, but to what advantage?

I felt my power turn and swell inside me as the golden spirals appeared on my arms, legs, chest, and neck. I hated the feeling of using it because deep down I craved it. I knew it was wrong to take away someone's free will so I always pushed that part of my power down, but I could care less with him. I let the energizing rush consume me as it flowed through my veins, building and building. "Who hired you, and what do they want with Scottie?" I compelled.

Kole smiled up at me. "You think whoever hired me doesn't know about you? You think they aren't aware of your abilities? You can't compel me, so give up." His face was smug, begging me to wipe the expression off of it.

I called the guards back. "Search him," I ordered as I stood up. "He must be wearing some object of Alluse, preventing me from compelling him. Strip him down for all I care but make sure he has no Alluse on him by the time I come back."

I stepped outside the dungeon door, needing a moment to collect my thoughts and breathe fresh air. This was bigger than I thought if Kole had Alluse. Whoever he was working for must be connected with Lux somehow. Alluse users were common knowledge among both of our kingdoms. However, objects that contained Alluse were rare and hard to get. The methods wielding them were unorthodox. Typically, Lux only forged Alluse into their shackles and the walls within their prison cells. An object like the one I gave Scottie was hard to come by, and would have been impossible to get without Peter's help. For Kole to possess one too meant he had to be working for someone of power.

"Prince Noren," one of the guards stuttered, "everything was removed from the prisoner. No objects of Alluse were found. He only had the clothes on his back."

"Burn the clothes," I said as I strode back to Kole's cell. Maybe Alluse was woven into the fabric he wore. Odd, but possible.

I compelled the same question to Kole, who had the audacity to laugh at me, even though he was the one chained and naked. He laughed at me as he said, "Alluse doesn't just have to be wielded into objects." His smile was bloody, showing no white in his teeth. "We have an alchemist who can wield it into serums. You won't be able to compel me, *prince*."

Shit. Shit. Shit. This was so much worse than I thought.

"Fine. We'll do it the hard way then," I sneered, making sure to mask my emotions at what he'd just revealed to me. I didn't want to give him the satisfaction that what he just said was fucking terrifying. "There are other ways to get you to talk." I opened his cell door and flashed him a wicked grin. Kole stiffened.

Good.

He was finally scared.

————

MORNING WAS FAST APPROACHING by the time I finally threw Kole back in his cell. No matter what I did to him, the bastard didn't budge.

It didn't matter. Every male would talk eventually. I just had to figure out what Kole's breaking point was. And picturing what he did with Scottie, I had absolutely no fucking quarrels trying. I didn't mind taking my time torturing him. I reveled in his screams, wanting him to pay for hurting her. The only thing that bothered me was that the longer it took to get him to talk, the more danger she was in.

I started by doing exactly what he did to Scottie, cutting his thigh from knee to hip, over and over again until he screamed. I made the cut so many times that I didn't think there would be any flesh left.

I wanted to keep going, but the healers strongly suggested he needed a break. "He will surely die at this rate before you glean whatever you need from him if you don't stop, Prince Noren," a firm-spoken healer said to me. "Give us a few hours and come back later."

"Fine," I ground out. "Heal him enough so that I can continue to question him."

I was covered in blood and filth. I needed a bath, and I needed to clean and sharpen my blades. And most importantly, I needed to check on Scotlind. I had to make sure she was okay.

Using my telepathy, I spoke with Peter while I was working on Kole. Asking for updates on how she was doing. If she slept or ate anything. He'd assured me that she was fine, but I wanted to see for myself.

I came back to my chambers to find her still on my leather sofa. A wool blanket was thrown over her. Peter was stretched out in a chair a few feet away, watching her sleep.

At the sound of the door shutting, she woke up and scanned me. Her eyes went wide, taking in my face. Then her gaze drifted to my sword and daggers. They were dripping in blood, and a good layer of dirt was covering me from the dungeons.

While she studied me, I did the same to her. We stayed silent as we searched each other. The bandages on her neck were turning pink as blood started to soak through them. Her leg was covered by the blanket, but it looked like she hadn't yet bathed or changed from her nightgown. She was still caked in blood.

"What happened to Kole?" she whispered as I threw my sword down. "Did you kill him?"

I ran my fingers through my hair and regretted it once I remembered how bloody they were. I moved to take a seat next to her. "No, but I will. He will be kept in the dungeons until we can figure out his motives and who was behind it."

Peter gave me a puzzling look, no doubt wondering why I didn't just compel the answers from him. Growing up, Peter and my family were the only Advenians who knew I had the power to compel everyone from Tennebris. I spoke to him mind to mind, letting him know that Kole had Alluse. I'd fill him in on everything else later. I didn't want to scare Scottie more than she already was.

"Oh," was all she said, the floor now commanding her attention.

"He will die," I said to her. "For what he did to you, he will die." When she didn't answer, I asked, "Are you okay?"

"Yes. Thank you for coming and um... for your help," she said softly as her eyes hesitantly met mine.

I ignored how that made me feel, how she looked at me without hatred. "You should bathe. Wash the blood off. Put on fresh clothes. We can redress your bandages afterward."

Her hand pressed hard into the side of the sofa, her fingernails embedding into the leather. Her body shook with effort as she tried and failed to stand. I was immediately there, catching her from the fall.

"I can get help," I said, "or I can call for a female servant to help you bathe."

"No," she snapped. "Just give me a minute and then... I just need help walking to the bathing room. I can do the rest myself."

We stayed there for a moment, unmoving. My hand still rested on the small of her back. The other was pressed flat against her stomach, holding her up. I gently set her back down on the sofa.

"You lost a lot of blood. You really shouldn't bathe by yourself. You could pass out in the water," Peter added.

"No," she interjected quickly.

"I don't feel like having you drown on us tonight," Peter deadpanned, trying to convince her otherwise.

"I think I can manage to wash alone, thank you very much," she glared daggers Peter's way, "I'm not going to die from a bath tub." He held his hands up in the air as if giving up.

"Fine, you can bathe alone, but we're staying here while you do. Just call out if you need us or a female's assistance. You'll be staying here tonight so that I know you will be safe," I said.

"I'm fine—" she started to protest.

"Scottie, you were seriously injured and almost murdered. You aren't leaving my side. Not when I know for sure that someone in this castle wants you dead."

"Kole said he didn't want me dead, not yet anyway," she admitted. I glanced at Peter who shared the same panicked expression as I felt. "But didn't you already know that?" she pressed. "That someone wanted me dead? And besides, you caught Kole, and he is in the dungeons, so I'm fine. I will be fine."

I bent over the sofa and grabbed her chin, forcing her to look at me. "I didn't know for sure someone wanted you dead. It was only a guess, and one I hoped wasn't true. But Kole isn't the one behind this."

"What do you mean?" she whispered. She tried to jerk her head out of my grasp, but I tightened my grip. Not enough to hurt her, but enough for her to meet my stare. I needed her to know how dangerous this was for her. How this changes everything. How seeing her like that... it couldn't happen again.

"Kole is from your school, and as much as he may not like you, his hatred for you and anyone without abilities is not enough to drive someone to murder. I believe he is working for someone. There will be more attempts on your life. It won't stop with Kole. And I'm not leaving you alone, especially when you're injured. So you are going to be staying here from now on, where I can watch you."

"I feel safer alone. I don't need someone watching over me."

"Yes, you do," I said sternly.

"And look at how that turned out. The person who was watching me tried to kill me in my sleep, so please forgive me if I don't trust you." This time she managed to pull her face free of my hand. Blood marks from my fingers were left on her chin from where I'd cupped it. Slowly, painfully, she pulled away from me and rose from the sofa. Her entire body shook with effort as she awkwardly limped alone to the bathing room.

"Scottie, please," my voice was so hoarse that she stopped in her tracks. "I know you don't trust anyone now, and that's good. You shouldn't. And I know you have no reason to trust me, but please just this once trust me. I don't want you to be alone."

"Peter," she said, whirling around to him. "I trust Peter. If you don't want me alone, I'll stay with him."

I winced at her words, the meaning behind them.

As much as I hated the thought of Peter spending his nights with her, it was better than nothing. He was probably the only one I could trust with her, besides myself. He cared for her as much as I did. And after the night with Alec, I knew I would never get her trust back. I knew I didn't deserve it, so I nodded my head.

*Protect her with your life,* I said into Peter's mind. *I'll keep our pathways open. Alert me immediately if anything happens.*

I briefly looked at her before settling my gaze on Peter. "You two can stay here for the rest of the night while her room is being repaired and cleaned. Very few in the castle are aware of what happened tonight, and I want to keep it that way. Make sure she bathes, rests, and eats. I'll be back later. Let me know if anything happens." I didn't bother to wait for him to respond. I knew he would do as I asked. I didn't look at Scottie again as I left them alone in my room.

Once the door shut behind me, I heard her say to Peter, "I'm sorry to make you stay with me. I just don't want to be alone with him, not yet."

Her voice broke, then I heard her soft sobs. Then footsteps.

"Come here," Peter said. "Don't apologize, Scottie. You have nothing to be sorry for."

I left, not able to stomach anymore. Not caring that I still had dried blood caked me, I headed for the dungeons again.

---

I WORKED on Kole until the healers begged me to stop again. I didn't want to head back to my own chambers. I didn't want Scottie to see me coated in more blood, so I headed to Peter's room.

I washed three times, scrubbing Kole's blood off that had dried on me like another layer of skin. The prick hadn't admitted to a single thing, no matter how much agony I'd put him through. I rubbed my temples, trying to press on the headache that was now forming from lack of sleep.

I pulled on a pair of black pants and a shirt from Peter's wardrobe. They were slightly tighter than my usual clothing, hugging my thighs, but they would work. The door to his room burst open as I threw the charcoal shirt over my shoulders.

"Where have you been?" Peter yelled at me.

"I was in the dungeons all day, trying to get the prick to talk. I came up here to bathe." I said to him. "What's wrong?"

"Kole is gone."

"What?" I spat. "What do you mean he's gone?"

"I mean, he escaped. He isn't in his cell."

"That's impossible. I was with him all day," I seethed. "I only left the dungeons an hour ago."

"Well, within the hour you were gone, someone worked to release him, and now he is nowhere to be seen."

I could feel my blood boiling over as his words sank in.

"Does Scotlind know?" I asked because I had seen the look of terror on her face. This would affect her, even if she denied it.

"No."

"Where is she then? You should be with her," I snapped, furious that he disobeyed my order to protect her. "If Kole is gone, she is the first person he will come after."

"I know," Peter said, letting out a frustrated sigh. "She insisted on going back to her own room to bathe, but she is with Abherham and two of your personal guards. They know not to leave her side. But our connection wasn't working and when I couldn't find you... I had to make sure that Kole didn't come after you—"

That's when I realized just how breathless Peter sounded.

I cursed. My headache and lack of concentration must have dropped the pathway between Peter's mind. "I will be fine, Peter. I can take care of myself, but I told you to protect her. No, I gave you an order to protect her." I pushed Peter aside and started sprinting toward Scottie's room.

Peter followed closely behind. "You know she isn't going to like that," he said through pants. "She doesn't like to be watched."

*I don't give a damn about what she wants until we get Kole. He can't be compelled. He is using Alluse in the form of some sort of serum that is running through his fucking veins, making him dangerous. No abilities will work on him and whoever he is working for is probably using it too. I don't trust the guards. And I don't give a fuck if Scottie is mad about us watching her. It's better than her being dead. We need to assume that everyone in the castle could be immune to abilities now, that their blood could be flowing with Alluse. And now, Scottie is wounded and completely fucking defenseless,* I seethed into his mind, not wanting to alert anyone to how weak she was right now as we sprinted past.

"Shit, shit, shit," was all Peter said as he kept his pace to match mine.

Half way to her room, I remembered my abilities and teleported the rest of the way, leaving Peter behind.

I let out a sigh of relief as I emerged in front of Scottie. The servants had done a good job cleaning her room. All the blood and pieces of broken furniture were cleared. Scottie was curled up on the thick leather sofa facing the empty, unlit fireplace, reading a book. A blanket was thrown over her, but it fell slightly off her uninjured leg, revealing her bare skin. I noticed a burn scar on the back of her calf. Her gaze went to where mine was fixed, and she immediately covered the scar. "What is going on?" she said slowly. Her sapphire eyes met my dark ones.

"Leave us for a minute," I ordered Abherham and my two guards, Bradwick and Danes. They all nodded and stepped out of her room without question. The next moment, Peter burst through the doors. "Thank Pylemo," he panted when he saw her.

Scottie closed her book and sat up straighter. Her eyes widened as she looked between the two of us, noticing our ragged breaths. "What is going on? Did you figure out who Kole is working for?"

I didn't want to tell her that Kole had escaped. I didn't want to cause her more fear, to have to admit that we failed. But she needed to know. She needed to realize how serious this fucking was. She needed to know that she couldn't go off on her own, wandering the library or patrolling the gardens close to the woods, which I knew she liked to do frequently with Abherham. So I told her everything.

She listened.

Once I finished, she visibly swallowed as her hands clasped onto the pendant of her necklace. "So Kole is gone, and no abilities can work on him?" she barely whispered. Her eyes flared with shock, not looking at either of us now. She just kept clutching that damn necklace. The fucking necklace that wouldn't help her now. It wouldn't protect her.

I knelt in front of her, trying to get her to look at me. "Yes," I said slowly. "The possibility that others are working with him are high, so I want you to always be with Peter or me. I am serious when I say I don't want you alone. I don't trust anyone else, so please don't go wandering off on your own, at least until we can figure this out." I expected her to fight me on it like she had did earlier this morning, but she just nodded her head.

"Okay," she murmured and then finally looked up at me. Her beautiful eyes swirled with tears that threatened to spill over her high cheekbones. Her bottom lip was swollen from her endless gnawing. "I'll stay with you—with one of you."

I knew she meant Peter.

# TWENTY-NINE
## SCOTLIND



THE NIGHTS HAD BLURRED TOGETHER SINCE KOLE escaped, and I'd spent every one of them with Peter since I refused to be alone with Sie. We fell into a comfortable routine together. I slept in my bed. He took up the sofa. He didn't mention my nightmares or the fact that I woke screaming my lungs out most nights. I didn't mention his snoring. It took me a while to finally fall asleep in front of him. The memory of Kole pulling up that chair, dragging it across the floor, and watching me. How he'd waited until I finally slept to attack me—I had Peter get rid of the chair, so only the sofa remained.

I'd seen the healer a few more times since then and I grew to like her. I hadn't realized how beautiful she was the night she helped me. I was too consumed by pain to pay attention to any details of her. I wanted to ask her about Lux. What was it like? How long had she lived there until she came to Tennebris by a work visa? It was comforting and painful to be around someone from my home kingdom. I found myself getting lost in her rare eye coloring, which was a coral pink, wondering what colors my parents had.

She told me that my slight limp shouldn't be permanent. But regardless of her promising news, Peter and Sie had been acting as if I were fragile. Like I was a glass vase sitting on the edge of a table during a storm, waiting to be knocked over and shattered.

They both tried to act relaxed, bored even, around me. Sie did a better job of it than Peter. But I saw them. How Peter moved the sofa to face the door. How each of them scanned every room I walked into. I saw them whispering softly to each other when they thought I wasn't paying attention. I'd tried to sneak up on them to overhear their conversations, to listen for news of Kole or whoever might be behind what happened, but with my stupid leg and my new limp, they heard me coming every time. It was annoying to be coddled. My nightmares aside, I was fine. I could handle whatever news they had for me. I wasn't broken, at least not entirely.

But they were scared.

This morning was no different. "Mmm, that smells good," I said to Peter, taking in the scents of my room as I sleepily yawned and stretched my arms out in front of me. "What are we having for breakfast today?"

We hadn't been able to do our usual morning training session, so it had been replaced with breakfast and the promise that once I was healed, he would train me twice as hard.

He flashed me that dazzling, warm smile of his. "Go wash, and you'll find out when you're done." I stuck my tongue out at him. Then, groaning softly, I climbed out of my warm bed, feeling sticky. The sun was shining through the windows, filling the room with light as I grabbed a candle and made my way toward the bathing room to wash. That was another part of our unspoken deal. He never asked why I was drenched in sweat every morning. He could assume as much from my screams.

When I sat back down for breakfast, my eyes went wide as I took in the whole spread and filled my plate with hot oatmeal, eggs, fruit, and an assortment of pastries. Peter laughed at my full plate and said, "This is our last morning together, so I thought we would go all out."

"What do you mean?" I said in between a large bite of a juicy apple, not bothering to cover my mouth. "Did you guys catch Kole?"

He gave me the most puzzling look. "Are you serious, Scottie? You really don't know?" I shook my head as I took another bite of my apple, a bit of the juice dribbling down my chin.

Peter leaned back in his chair, almost laughing as he put his hands behind his head. "You're going to spend the rest of your nights and *mornings* with Sie."

"No, I'm not," I snapped way too quickly. "I mean… I'm not until we are married since we aren't allowed to. He said I was supposed to stay with you."

The look Peter gave me made me choke on the piece of apple that had now lodged itself in my throat.

"Is it starting to make sense now? Did it finally click in that pretty head of yours?" He laughed as I forced myself to swallow the lump. "Happy wedding day, Scottie," he added with the most triumphant smile as he reached to grab a croissant off my plate.

I suddenly lost my appetite. How had I lost track of the date? I had been purposely trying to avoid thinking about my upcoming wedding, and worse—my wedding night, but I thought it wasn't for another week.

"Fuck," the word slipped out of me before I could think better of it.

Peter's laughter filled my bedroom as he smirked. "Yeah, I guess you will be doing a lot of that tonight." I chucked the remainder of my apple at him as I felt my neck and cheeks burn. That only made him laugh harder.

"I'm glad you got a good night's rest last night. You probably won't sleep at all tonight or the next few nights. Rumor has it that Sie can last for *hours*." He winked at me.

I leaned over the breakfast spread and threw my hand up, readying to slap him as he laughed.

"Okay, okay. I'll stop teasing you." I slumped back into my chair as he added, "Come on, finish your breakfast. You really will need your strength today. It's going to be a *long* and *hard* day."

So much for not teasing me. I shot him a glare. "I'm not hungry anymore."

Peter jumped from his chair, wiping his hands on his thighs. "So eager to get to it, Scottie." My eyes went wide as I attempted to hit him again, but he quickly stepped out of the way. I hated my limp so much at that moment. Then he said in a serious tone, "He's a good guy, Scotlind. You're going to be fine."

"Then why don't you marry him?" I quipped as I slumped back into the chair.

"Tempting as that is, he doesn't have the right parts," he winked at me again.

"You mean he doesn't have red hair and boobs?"

"It's not my fault your friend is hot."

I laughed. "You are the male version of Vallie, so I guess it's fitting."

"I'm the male version of your best friend? Is that supposed to be a compliment?" he asked.

"Oh, most definitely, but Vallie is much prettier than you. And nicer too."

"I can't disagree with you there," he started making his way toward the door but stopped. "I meant what I said about Sie. I don't have any brothers, but Sie has always been one to me. Regardless of how he portrays himself, he cares for you. He will kill me for telling you this, but he does care. He won't treat you badly."

"He already treated me badly."

"He's done nice things for you too, Scotlind. Many things. He looks out for you and always thinks about your needs, about what will make you happy."

I huffed a laugh. "Yeah, right. Name one."

He didn't hesitate as he said, "It was Sie's idea to spend the night at LakeWood when we were touring so you could see Vallie and Miles. We were supposed to stay in Addler, but he changed the schedule. He told me to say it was my idea, but it wasn't."

"One good thing doesn't make him a good person," I said, but I couldn't stop thinking about it. Did he really care for me?

"Maybe not, but I've watched Sie do many good things. Did you know he watched your Trial and had me petition to make you a guard before he even knew you? He saw Synder had marked you as a servant and thought you deserved better."

I was silent after that. Peter continued, "He doesn't do good things to be recognized. Many Advenians think he's an asshole because he's good at putting on that front. He had to wear that mask for many years to protect himself from his father. But I do know that he cares for you and that he will keep you safe." He shook out his shaggy locks as he walked toward the door. "Anyway, your servants are here to get you ready. Abherham is just outside. I have to go, but I'll see you tonight."

Our comfortable, easy routine was gone.

I took in the surroundings that had been my room for the past couple of months. Maybe Peter hadn't reminded me that today was my wedding day on purpose. Maybe he knew that if I had been aware, I wouldn't have slept last night.

I tried to savor this moment. Being alone. I would spend tonight with Sie, and that scared me more than Kole did. The servants would move my belongings into his chamber, making it *our* bedroom.

I let out a groan as I sank further into my seat. I couldn't help thinking about him these past weeks. How he'd come running into my room when I pushed the button on my necklace. How he'd looked at me when Kole held the knife to my throat. The sheer terror and anger that radiated off him.

Then, how he'd been covered in Kole's blood afterward. He had a different look in his eyes when he left the dungeons. They had turned fully black as he wore the face of death his gaze promised.

Sie scared me.

Not because of his sheer power and ability to kill someone in seconds, but because I didn't understand my own feelings toward him. He was awful to me, yes, but I couldn't shake the feeling that he really did care for me like Peter had suggested.

My mind kept replaying how he kissed me in his bathing room. It was like his mask had come off, and I saw his face for the first time. He'd looked young and innocent, hopeful and wishful, and I wanted more. I wanted more of that Sie.

I couldn't stop thinking about how every time I had been in the same room as him, my heart thudded so loudly against my ribs that I couldn't hear. How my chest tightened when I heard his deep voice. How my toes curled whenever he stood near me.

I didn't want to start liking him. If I liked him, it would make things worse. I didn't want to go down that path of giving myself hope, just for it to be taken away from me. It was only a matter of time until they discovered I was from Lux.

Unless we never had children—Lakimi was centuries away. The chances of us conceiving were slim. Or maybe Sie would go elsewhere for that kind of pleasure. Maybe he wouldn't even want to have sex with me at all.

I didn't know what to make of sex other than what Vallie had told me—that it was rough and sweaty and definitely not just laying on your back. I'd asked her awkwardly one time if a male would see a female's back when they were intimate.

She'd looked at me funny but answered, *Yes Scottie-cat. They see everything. But to be honest, most males aren't really interested in a female's back. There are a few other parts they like better.*

A minute later, a knock sounded on the door as Roslyn, Annabel, and Ashley entered my room. They fussed over me for the next three hours, but it felt much, much longer. In between getting ready, they tried and failed to get me to eat more of my breakfast. I managed to nibble on some fruit as they curled my light brown hair into long, delicate waves.

Ashley told me that no one was allowed to see me until I walked down the aisle. Which meant I would be cooped up in my room until the ceremony started. That would explain why Peter had left and why Abherham waited outside my door.

Once they were satisfied with my hair and makeup, adding coal to my eyes and rose to my cheeks, they helped me into my gown. It took all three of them to get me into it, and I realized with complete dread that I would need help getting out of it.

Annabel was at my side smiling. "You look gorgeous, princess," she said as she gave my shoulders a squeeze. Her silky, black hair brushed against my face.

Ashley pulled me into a hug as Roslyn rolled her eyes. "The girl is getting married," Roslyn sneered, "not going off to war." Ashley huffed at her as I caught my reflection in the mirror.

I looked like a living, breathing diamond.

My long hair was mostly down, falling in beautiful curls behind my back. The few pieces around my face were swept up into a small silver crown that was too snug on my head. My lashes were thickened and elongated, making the sapphire in my eyes stand out against the diamond earrings that dangled to my neck.

Ashely tried to remove my necklace, saying something about how the gold clashed with the silver in my crown and earrings, but I insisted I wore it. She settled with tucking it between my breasts so it was mostly hidden from sight.

And my gown—it was the most opulent thing I'd ever seen. The material hugged my chest, exposing the top half of my breasts before it flowed and cascaded past my waist to the floor. Diamonds were sewn into every inch of the dress, making it sparkle as it swayed and moved with me. The sweeping neckline hung off my shoulders, exposing my collar bone and more cleavage than they usually dressed me in, but somehow was still elegant. The sleeves were sheer, exposing my skin that ended just before my wrists, displaying my two zeroes. The only thing that looked off was the white scar across my neck. It was a thin line, barely noticeable like the healer had said, but it contrasted against my olive skin.

I nodded thanks to Ashley as she helped me into a pair of flats. She was aware of my leg—my limp was impossible to ignore—but it was written off as me being clumsy and everyone in the castle thought I fell. I didn't know if I should be bothered that everyone believed the lie so easily.

Annabel came up behind me in the mirror after a few moments. "It's time."

Ashley held out her hand, and I took it as I walked between the two of them toward my fate. The halls were eerily quiet as Abherham trailed behind us. Everyone else was already gathered in the throne room where our wedding would be held.

I didn't know if I was more nervous about marrying Sie or the fact that the royals of Lux would be present for the ceremony. It was tradition for the kingdoms to come together for special events. I'd never met anyone from Lux before, besides the healer Sie had, and I couldn't help but wonder if they would recognize me. Would they be able to tell just from looking at me that I was one of them?

We stopped behind two white marble doors—the largest set I'd encountered since I'd arrived. As the doors opened on a phantom wind, my jaw slackened. I gaped and took in the ornate details. It was by far the most elaborate and extravagant room in the castle.

I forgot about the massive, looming crowd all gawking at me. I forgot that today I was supposed to marry the Prince of Tennebris. I forgot that Kole had tried to kill me. I forgot that I was in the Dark Kingdom when I should have grown up in Lux. All I could think about was this room before me. Room—if you could even call it that. It was a castle within itself.

The Tennebrisian Kingdom wasn't a court that liked to show off their wealth at every turn. That much could be told by the fireplaces and torches throughout the grounds and the ancient-looking interior, but this room was different. This room was made for kings and queens.

Everything inside the throne room was light, which contrasted the rest of the dimly lit, dark castle. Looming chandeliers dangled from the tall ceiling, and the stained glass windows that the kingdom seemed to favor, aligned the golden walls, casting hues of blue throughout the creamy room. The floors were clear marble with specks of gold that met and blended seamlessly into the walls, tying the room together.

Everything was golden, everything but me. I was dressed in silver and diamonds, such at odds with the gilded room and what the Dark Kingdom stood for. Gold represented their power, and the only ounce of the material I bore on me was my necklace, hidden beneath my breasts.

A raised dais was positioned on the opposite side of the room. Golden swirls, much like the designs of the Tennebrisian markings, were embedded into the platform. A dais that Sie was now standing on. Goddess above. I blinked. Once. Twice. He looked divine.

The sunlight seemed to point directly at me as his eyes narrowed and focused solely on my face. It was as if he could see right through the gown, the makeup, and the jewels, and looked into my bare soul. I felt exposed and naked as my body clinked with each diamond-filled movement.

I tore my gaze away from his lingering stare, and that was when I noticed everyone else. The room was packed with Advenians from both Tennebris and Lux, all turning to stare at me. I swallowed as a soft melody began to play, and I took that as my cue to begin walking down the long aisle. I was thankful for the shoes Ashley gave me as I tried my best to mask my limp. If whoever hired Kole to kill me was here, I didn't want to give them the satisfaction of seeing my injury. I also didn't want to make it seem like I was an easy target.

King Lunder and Synder were seated in seats on top of the dais with Sie, but it was a male from the first row that caught my eye. He was beautiful in a different way than anyone else here. He appeared older, but not in his looks as he didn't have a single wrinkle etched on his tanned skin, but more in how he presented himself, how his presence demanded attention.

It wasn't the crown atop his head that gave him away, but his eyes. They were white, so clear and light I thought I was looking at glass. Hints of silver lined the inner and outer rim. They were eyes that weren't a normal color. Eyes that were Luxian. His hair was bright silver, and was tucked into a thick, black crown. It looked so heavy I couldn't comprehend how he kept his head held high.

The Lux King.

I swallowed as I passed him, fully aware that his silver eyes lingered on me.

I turned my gaze to Sie. I was inches from the dais now. He was wearing a tailored suit, black as usual, with a feathered cape falling off his shoulders. It was held together by two gold interlocking circles that matched the crown resting atop his black waves.

He outstretched a hand for me as I ascended the raised platform to join him. His fingers were rough against my skin. I thought he would drop the hold once I stood next to him, but he kept my hand in his as the priest began his speech.

The ceremony was a blur. The priest, clad in purple robes etched in gold and black, rambled on about our union in marriage to the point where my thigh was throbbing from standing on it too long. His gaze was kept out to the crowd watching us, scanning them as if that would help them soak up his words better.

The priest finally turned to Sie and I as he said, "Do you, Princess Scotlind Mae Rumor, take Prince Sie Axel Noren to be your husband from this day forward until it shall be your last?"

I shifted slightly on my good leg to face Sie as I whispered, "I do." Sie met my gaze, his expression unreadable.

Then the priest turned to Sie. "Do you, Prince Sie Axel Noren, future ruler of Tennebris, take Princess Scotlind Mae Rumor to be your wife from this day forward until it shall be your last?"

Sie didn't hesitate as he answered, "I do." His voice echoed across the throne room. He sounded sturdy and sure of himself, where my voice had been weak and soft.

The priest grinned as he continued the ceremony. "Then let it be known that today is the day we bring these two together in a binding marriage. Pylemo has spoken to me and instructed that they shall become one. Rule as one. Act as one. Let their blood become one from this day forward until forever. Let their *blood bond* unite our Kingdom of Tennebris, leading us to a peaceful and prosperous rule. Let them rule as true as the bond they are about to make."

I didn't notice King Lunder stepping forward with a white and gold dagger until he was right before us. For a brief moment, Sie's unreadable masked expression faltered. It was so fast I would have missed it if I hadn't been staring at him.

I'd never watched a royal wedding before, and I didn't know what to expect, but whatever was about to happen, Sie seemed surprised by it.

A blood bond. I'd read about it once. The words sounded familiar, but I couldn't wrap my brain around it. What was it, and why were they forcing us to make one now? A pang of grief contorted in my gut as I instantly thought of Vallie, of how she would know what the blood bond was. I pictured her spitting out every minuscule detail regarding it due to her ability.

Sie took the dagger from King Lunder and made a clean cut on the palm of his hand. His gaze never left mine as the tip of the blade dragged across his flesh.

Then he grabbed my hand, cutting a straight line in the same spot to match his. The blade stung as it dragged from pinky to thumb. I jerked slightly at the touch and bit my lower lip to prevent any sound from coming out. I would not appear weak while everyone was watching me. If Sie could cut his own palm without flinching, I could certainly have mine cut without wincing too. A rank zero could be just as strong as a rank five.

My jaw dropped as Sie brought my bloody hand up to his lips. His *lips*. He took a long sip of my blood before bringing his hand to my mouth. Following his lead, I cupped my free hand over his and drank. I expected to gag, to have a curdling feeling hit my stomach as soon as his blood sank into my mouth, but I didn't. It tasted sweet, like wine.

I tried not to focus on the lingering drop of my own blood that settled on Sie's lower lip as his tongue swiped out of his mouth and licked it up.

The priest ushered us to join hands so our blood could flow into one another. I didn't feel anything different as our hands came together, but being this close to Sie, I felt the urge to kiss him. It left me feeling dizzy and energized and breathless all at the same time.

I tried to mask what his closeness was doing to me. I tried to focus on my breathing, bringing it back down to a normal pace. In through my nose, out through my mouth. Could Sie feel this too? Did he want to kiss me?

King Lunder grabbed a delicate cream cloth with gold etches sewn into it replicating the twin moons and wrapped it around our hands, tying us together.

"The blood oath has been done. The blood bond is set," the priest declared.

Panic rose in me at his words. What the heck did we just do?

"You may now kiss your bride," the priest continued.

Sie turned his body to face me completely as he bent down slowly. His lips pressed into mine with such softness, unlike our kiss in the bathroom. This felt different, more gentle, aware of all the eyes on us. Whereas the bathroom kiss had been urgent and aggressive like we couldn't get enough of each other.

His bloody hand tightened around mine as his other reached for my neck. My lips parted for his tongue as it made its way into my mouth. Slowly grazing over my teeth at first, before exploring and meeting my own tongue.

I leaned forward on the tips of my toes to reach him better, to feel his lips harder against mine, to give him better access. For a moment, he matched my needs. I forgot where I was as his lips moved faster before he pulled away.

It wasn't enough. I wanted more. I still felt breathless and dizzy from whatever blood bond thing we were forced to carry out. My body felt like it was electrified and awake, but I knew it was because of him. I wanted him. I *needed* him.

I fell back down hard on my feet, wincing slightly as the pain in my thigh throbbed from the impact. Everyone in the crowd watched. Sie removed his hand from my neck. Our bloody ones were still wrapped together as he turned to face the crowd.

"I now pronounce you bound to one another. Please join me in welcoming for the first time, Prince and Princess Noren." Everyone rose and clapped, breaking the unnerving silence that followed our kiss. We made our way down the aisle with our hands still bound—a trail of blood left in the wake of where we stood. I had no idea what we'd just done, but I got the feeling it wasn't normal for a wedding ceremony, even a royal one.

## THIRTY
# SCOTLIND

Within minutes, the throne room was rearranged to accommodate dining and dancing for the reception that followed.

We were told our hands had to remain bound for an hour for the blood bond to set, so two thrones were placed on the dais for us to sit on. It was uncomfortable holding Sie's hand for so long, and no one had told me the purpose of the bond. I kept replaying the exchange Peter gave Sie as he moved to stand behind us. He didn't say anything as everyone formed a line to congratulate us, but I swore the pair shared a silent conversation.

It wasn't until the silver-haired male from earlier approached the dais that I noticed Sie sitting up straighter. Stiffer. Broader. A younger looking male and female flanked the Lux King's side. The female was petite. She looked even smaller than me, and my height was unheard of for an Advenian. They all had the same hair coloring that matched their eyes, but where the king had only flecks of silver in his eyes, the two younger Advenians' eyes were completely silver. It was like looking at glowing molten metal.

"Prince Noren, let me introduce you to King Arcane Xandrin the Seventh of Lux," someone from below the dais spoke, breaking the tension.

"The pleasure is all mine, King Arcane. This is my wife, Scotlind Noren," Sie said, his voice low and smooth.

It was weird hearing him say Noren instead of Rumor, but I didn't have much time to process it as the King of Lux turned his gaze to me. He looked me over slowly, pausing slightly at Sie's and my bound hands. My fingers flexed unwillingly against Sie's grasp. I could still feel his blood against mine, warm and sticky. I shifted in my seat.

"A true beauty. You are one lucky male," the King purred after a long moment before meeting my eyes again. "And those eyes. How striking. A true rarity amongst your Tennebris Kingdom, I presume. Keep her on a close chain."

I started shaking. Could he tell that my eyes were Luxian? He offered a smile before continuing, "May I introduce to you my eldest son and heir to the throne, Prince Arcane the Eighth and my lovely daughter Princess Dovelyn."

The King gestured to the male and female by his side. Both bowed slightly at the acknowledgement. Their silver eyes penetrated through me, so hot that I thought I was melting.

The King continued, either unaware of my panic or he just didn't care, "Unfortunately, my youngest could not attend the ceremony as he has diplomatic affairs to attend to. But he sends his regards and is looking forward to meeting with you both at your upcoming coronation."

Prince Arcane spoke next. His voice was soft and light compared to his father's. "You look beautiful, Princess Noren. Congratulations to you both."

Princess Dovelyn didn't say anything as she stared between us, and I couldn't muster any words to say back. Something about her assessing gaze was unsettling. It was somewhere between awe and disgust, and I didn't know what to make of it.

I thought I would feel something. I thought I would feel at home looking upon them, knowing I was the same and that I belonged to their kingdom, not Sie's.

But I didn't.

Instead of feeling at home when I looked at the Lux King and their prince and princess, I felt a cold, numbing darkness. I found myself leaning closer to Sie without realizing it. As if sensing my unease, Sie squeezed my hand, but loosened his grip once I winced from the cut that was still bleeding into him.

"We will be looking forward to meeting with the youngest Prince of Lux soon. Thank you for coming to our wedding," Sie said, his voice sounding regal and every bit the king he would soon become.

The King of Lux smiled before sauntering off with his two children in tow. But even from across the room, I felt his eyes on me. The pale white and silver pinning me to my spot on the dais, fixated on our blood bonded hands. There was no light in his eyes, just dull emptiness like staring into the bottom of the ocean, unable to gasp for air. Like he was sucking the oxygen out of me from the moment he stood before us. I was drowning on land.

When they were out of hearing range, Sie leaned forward and whispered into my ear, "Whatever you do, Scotlind, don't ever be in front of that male without your necklace on. In fact, any of them. Him and his children." A chill went down my spine. The feeling the Lux King had given me made me realize his warning held some sort of truth.

I found myself saying, "He is coming to your coronation? They *all* are?"

"Yes, three months from now."

"And he has another son?" I pressed.

"Yes. They are all known to be ruthless. All three of his children are ranked five. Prince Arcane will inherit the crown. He takes after his father the most and has devoted his life to politics."

"Inherit," I mumbled, forgetting for a moment that the Luxian Kingdom did not operate the same as Tennebris. They didn't have a King's Tournament where males competed to rule. They lived by rankings for status amongst their court, but as for their ruler, it had always been one bloodline passed down from the same family. One powerful, scary family.

"Princess Dovelyn is as cunning as she is beautiful. And the youngest prince is rumored to be the worst of them all. There is talk that the Lux King offered him the crown because of how strong his abilities are, even though it is unorthodox to skip over the eldest, but he declined. Since he refused, he took up the military route. He has been the commander of the Luxian army for almost a century, and they are brutal. He makes our King's Guard seem like nothing."

According to my classes at LakeWood, all the Luxian royals had arranged marriages with the strongest ranked Advenians, creating stronger and stronger heirs. They must think of me being Sie's queen —with him being the only rank five in Tennebris—a complete joke. I shuddered thinking about just how powerful they had to be. How there were many rank fives in Lux and only one in Tennebris.

As if Sie could read my thoughts, he added, "He's strong. They all are. Their entire bloodline has been rank fives for many generations, and the youngest prince's powers are rumored to be the strongest amongst our kind throughout both kingdoms. He is someone you do not want to get to know."

I reached for my necklace as I asked, "What are their abilities?"

"I'm not entirely sure," he admitted. "They each have multiple. I know the two you met today both possess air abilities. The youngest prince possesses fire. I'm not certain what else they have, though."

My calf ached as I thought about the damage a fire ability could do. I tried not to touch my leg as I felt the heat of the flames burn my skin all over again, dragging me back to when I was seven.

"The Lux King said that the youngest prince was busy in a diplomatic affair, but I thought all meetings were held together?" I asked.

Sie glanced around the room before whispering softly, "They are. He's not in a meeting. The youngest prince is in battle right now."

"Battle? With who? Tennebris and Lux have been at peace with one another, have they not?"

"Shhh," Sie hushed as he glanced around the throne room. Everyone was too drunk and far too into dancing to pay attention to our conversation, and the dais was positioned furthest from the crowd. "There's a rebellion. It's been going on for the past three hundred years. It's been kept hidden from the general public as best as possible. The Luxian army is larger and stronger than our Guard, so whenever the rebellion attacks, they fight in it. And the youngest Luxian Prince is their leader. He chooses to fight right alongside his men. He has been battling against the rebellion for the past century ever since he took up the role of commander, and since he joined, there isn't much left of it."

"A rebellion," the words were breathless on my lips. "Against what? What are they fighting for?"

"For things to be equal. To get rid of the ranking system. Most of the rebels are made up of the lower ranks. Twos, ones, and zeroes. They are sympathizers to nixes."

"How do you know all this?"

"From King Lunder. It is kept a secret, Scotlind, so you cannot do anything with this information. Only members of the royal court and the High Councils of each kingdom are aware of this. The men in our Guard don't even know as they don't fight in it. Only Lux's soldiers are and they are sworn to secrecy."

"How have they been able to keep it a secret, though? Surely battles are difficult to keep hidden."

"Most are happening in Lux, and they are capable of handling it swiftly. But when the rebels attack their castle, we have set Advenians that we send over on work visas who have compulsion abilities to wipe the memories of anyone that might have witnessed it."

"Why are you telling me this?" I asked, unable to hide the fact that my voice rose an octave. I was not the only one who wanted things to change. It gave me hope and exhilaration knowing that a group of people already wanted what I sought. That they were battling for it right now. Sie and I could work with them. We could fight with them. That was if I could convince Sie. Maybe Peter would help.

"Because," he said, breaking my thought, "I want you to understand how dangerous what you want is. Because any time the rebellion attacks, the prince's army wipes them out entirely, and I mean that literally. The Luxian army is powerful. Everyone in it is strong, way too strong. You should avoid all of them. Especially the prince.

His fire is so powerful that he leaves the battlefields in flames. There are no survivors—no bodies to bury. Just ash."

I swallowed. Fire. The ability that killed my real family. The ability that haunts my nightmares. And the one prince who has killed thousands with it.

# THIRTY-ONE
## SCOTLIND

I looked around the room, mortified. It was bad enough to be in Sie's chambers knowing I had to sleep here, but after the celebration, Synder insisted on escorting us back with three other members of the High Council. My gaze landed on Sie, confused and wide-eyed. He briefly looked me over before turning toward Alexander, my new overnight guard since Kole escaped. Although, he barely ever stayed with me since I spent every night with Peter.

"You are relieved of duty for the night," Sie ordered. Alexander opened his mouth to speak, but Sie added before he could, "I promise you that I can guard Scotlind better than anyone here. Since I will be spending the entire night with her, your services are no longer needed. You will be notified if I have to leave her for any reason during the night."

Alexander nodded, then bowed at the waist. "As you wish, Prince Noren. Congratulations to you both."

I swallowed. Once. Twice. I couldn't get rid of the knot that was lodged in my throat or the butterflies endlessly flapping in my gut.

Once Alexander left, Sie turned to Synder and his men. "Leave us."

Synder looked me up and down, his eyes lingering on my cut now that our hands were no longer bound together. He stepped further into the room. "I can't do that."

Sie growled, noticing where Synder's eyes had gone. "And why is that?"

"I'm afraid," Synder said slowly, enjoying this, "that we must make sure you consummate your marriage."

A muscle in Sie's jaw quivered as he clenched his fists at his sides. "I am not having you or your men watch me have sex with my *wife*."

"I'm afraid the High Council insists on it."

"The High Council insists on it, or you do?" Sie snapped as he took a protective step in front of me, mostly blocking me from Synder's view.

Synder smiled. "Well, we are one and the same. I am the head of the Council."

"For now," Sie challenged.

The other three men behind Synder shifted uncomfortably where they stood. An unsettling silence filled the room. The tension was palpable until finally, one of them spoke, "Perhaps we can just wait outside your chambers, Prince Noren. That way we can still confirm the act is done while giving you and your wife some privacy."

"Get out," Sie spat. "I don't care where you stand or where you go as long as it is not in this room."

Synder took one last look at me before saying, "Make sure it's done. We'll be listening." Then he and his men turned swiftly on their heels. I cringed as the door slammed behind them.

Sie released a ragged breath as he turned around to face me. He stood so close that I had to crane my neck to meet his gaze.

"I'm sorry about that," he mumbled before walking over to the leather sofa across the room. "How about a drink first?"

He filled my glass with a strong smelling amber liquid and then his. I took it with shaky hands. His fingers lingered on mine before I slowly sipped on the contents. He downed his in one gulp before filling it again.

One moment he was sitting across from me on the sofa, the next, I blinked, and he was behind me. He had *teleported* behind me. Something about him using his abilities freaked me out like I almost forgot who I was alone in the room with. I tried to create distance between us, but his hands grabbed my shoulders, pinning me to my seat.

"Trust me," he purred into my ear as his hands made their way down my neck. Then, in one motion, my necklace was off. He pocketed it before sitting back down to finish his second drink.

I swallowed as I tried to hide my shaking. I was alone in the room with Sie, the most powerful person in Tennebris, and Synder and his men blocked my only exit. Why did he take the necklace off me? Did he want to force me to do things with him? Vallie's words of how men liked it rough flashed through my mind.

*Relax. As tempting as that is, I'm not going to do anything to you. We don't have to have sex tonight,* I heard his voice say, but he hadn't stopped drinking. Was that in my head? Did I imagine it? I gave him a puzzling look before I heard his voice again. He lifted a finger to his lips, ordering me to not make a sound. *You didn't imagine it. I'm talking to you in your mind so they can't hear.* I didn't know he could do that. My hands instinctively went to my throat, now bare where my necklace had been, as I sucked in a breath. *There is a lot that I can do that you don't know about. I have more mind control powers than just compulsion.*

"You can hear me? My thoughts?" I whispered.

*Shh. Yes, I can read your thoughts right now, so don't speak out loud. Just talk to me in your head, and I will hear you.*

*Get out of my head,* I screamed in my thoughts but didn't dare say out loud.

He looked at me for a moment longer before saying, *I will, soon. But we need to get Synder and his men to leave. They are listening.*

*Is this total mind control? That you can do this?* I gestured between us— to the fact that we were having a conversation without speaking. I couldn't help but ask. I didn't really know the full extent of his abilities.

He frowned at me as if contemplating whether or not he wanted to answer before saying, *It's part of it. It's called telepathy. It's rare, but it is what's allowing me to communicate with you right now. As far as my total mind control... with compulsion, you know that you are being forced to do something. I can compel your body to obey but not your mind. Even though you are forced to do it, you are aware of it. You are aware that I am making you do something and that you don't want to do it. With total mind control, I can make someone believe that what I am compelling them to do is their idea, that they want to do it. I can alter someone's brain. Change their thoughts.*

*Have you ever used it on someone?* I thought to him.

*Not by choice. My father used to test how far my abilities went, but I've never used it willingly. I use compulsion when I need to, but I haven't used total mind control in years. To change someone's beliefs and actions like that is a violation. It's not right.*

*But you can read my thoughts? All of my thoughts?* I pushed further. I wanted—no, I needed to know what he was capable of, what he could do right now.

*If I push enough, yes.*

*Doesn't that get tiring? Draining? Always hearing what everyone around you is thinking?* I asked in my head.

He laughed softly. *It's not like that.* I must have looked confused because he added, *I only hear thoughts of those in close proximity to me and only if I'm trying to—if I'm actively listening for it, actively using my ability to do so. I don't walk around just hearing what people ate for dinner or how they thought the sex they just had went. Although that can be quite entertaining.*

I gulped. The fact that if he pushed, he could know everything I was thinking was enough to make me nervous, and my stupid body decided at that moment to replay our kiss. Visions of him pressed against me flashed in my head. I chugged the disgusting drink, praying he wasn't reading my thoughts in that way now.

*It's different with you, though,* he said quietly, his voice soft even in my head.

*What do you mean different?*

*It's stronger,* he replied after a long pause. *When you aren't wearing your necklace, it's like my mind is begging to connect with yours. Usually, I have to focus on getting inside someone's head. I have to actively keep a connection going. But with you, it just happens. Even if I don't want it to. Sometimes you just send your thoughts or images to me, and I can't block it. It's like my powers are stronger when you are around. It's like my abilities are drawn to something about you.*

*Then please give me back my necklace. I don't want you in my head,* I begged. My heart stammered in my chest as I tried to keep my mind blank.

He sighed. *I will as soon as Synder and his men leave.*

*How?* I thought to him. *They won't leave until we…* I couldn't finish my thought, and he knew it. Being in my head, he could see how terrified I was to have sex.

He gave me a small smile before saying, **We make them think we are. They want a show so let's give them one.** Then he flipped the small table between us over. It landed with a loud thud on the floor, causing me to jump.

**Moan for me, Scotlind.** My eyes widened as he picked me up in one swoop and threw me on the bed. He stood over me and grabbed the edges, shaking the entire thing with me on it. The bed creaked beneath his touch, making it sound like it was groaning back and forth. It sounded like we were…

**Come on, Scottie. If you want them to leave, you have to be convincing. There hasn't been a female that I've been with who hasn't moaned for me or begged for more.**

I rolled my eyes but couldn't help it when a small laugh left my lips. *In your dreams,* I thought back.

**You moan loudly in my dreams.** My mouth dropped. Was he serious? Did he seriously dream about me like that? **Scotlind, if you want them to leave, we have to convince them. Synder isn't stupid.**

I pressed my lips together. I didn't even know what a moan would sound like or where to begin. Then images of our first kiss flashed before my eyes as Sie played a vision. A vision in which I moaned loudly into his mouth as he grabbed me from when we first kissed in the bathing room. *Like that,* he purred with a wicked smile on his face. *Moan for me like you did then.*

I tried to shake the image from my mind, but whatever he was doing held strong as he forced me to watch as we kissed and grabbed each other. I watched Sie touch me, his hands roaming over me like he couldn't get enough. I watched as I leaned into his touch, practically crumbling from it.

My face grew hot and flushed at once. I knew he wouldn't stop making me watch it until I did as he said. I took a deep breath as I tried my best to mimic what he played for me from his memory.

I let out an audible moan as he scooped me up again, throwing me against the door where the men were listening. "I've been waiting a long time to have you, Scotlind," he groaned breathlessly, and I realized that he was saying this out loud for them to hear. "And I've had a long time to think about how I've wanted to fuck you."

*Moan again.* I did. He slammed his fist into the door as he groaned out loud, "Fuck, you feel so damn good."

A smile crossed his face, lightening his dark features. I couldn't help but wonder if it was real. We were both still in our wedding attire and looked foolish. But my body realized how he wasn't touching me. How he stood close, close enough that I could feel his breath on my ear, but he didn't put a hand on me. I suddenly wished he had.

His lips formed a half-grin, making it known he'd just read my thoughts. My mortification grew, knowing that he was still in my head, that he knew exactly what I wanted. *Get out of my head,* I thought to him as he continued to bang his hand on the door above me. It made it seem like he was thrusting over and over again. He let out a guttural groan.

I tried not to think about the fact that he was turning me on, the fact that I now had a growing sensation between my thighs, and how I wanted him there. How I wanted to know what it would feel like for real. What he would sound like. Taste like.

Was this normal? To be so attracted to someone that you wanted them so badly, even when you weren't touching?

Reading my thoughts, Sie pressed into me, finally offering me what

I sought. I could feel him harden against my abdomen, giving me my answer. I could feel the full length of him throbbing into me. I let out a real moan this time as my eyelids fluttered and my head slammed back against the door.

He leaned forward, and I caught my breath as I thought he was about to kiss me. But he stopped short before my lips and whispered, "They're gone."

Pinning me on the door with his hands plastered on either side of my head, I slowly stepped out of his grasp. "Now get out of my head."

"Done," he smiled as he threw his hands up in the air, acting innocent. "You did a convincing job with those moans. Especially the last one." Then he reached in his pocket and tossed me my necklace. "If I'd known any better, I would have thought you weren't faking it by the end."

I ignored his comment and focused on something else as I quickly clasped the necklace back on. "Have you done that before? Been inside my head?" I whispered as the horror of his ability fully sank in.

I was all too aware that I was now going to be sharing a room with the most powerful male in all of Tennebris. Not just sharing a room, but he was my *husband*. One who could teleport and move quickly enough that my necklace could be off before I even blinked. He could get me to do whatever he wanted. He could read all my thoughts and plant visions inside my head like he'd done with the memory of our first kiss.

"Yes," he admitted. "Back when we first met before we left for the castle. I didn't mean to, but your mind kept connecting to mine because you weren't wearing Alluse."

I stood there stunned as he continued, "It's how I knew you were going to that party. I was staying in LakeWood after you were selected, and just being in the same village as you without your necklace on, connected us. The Alluse in your necklace protects you from it—from me." Neither of us moved for a moment as we stared at each other. It made sense now. How he knew it was my first time drinking and how he showed up so quickly.

"Why?" I asked. "Why does my mind connect with yours?"

"I honestly have no idea. It's been baffling to me too. I can't figure it out."

When I didn't respond, he gestured behind me. "Take the bed."

"You aren't sleeping with me?" I asked, confused.

"Scotlind, I'm not going to force you to do something I know you don't want to do." He sighed. "I was just inside your head. I know how scared you are. We don't have to."

"Right. You have other people to fulfill your needs." Jealousy snapped out of me before I could think better of it.

He gave me the most bewildered look and laughed. "Scotlind, I haven't slept with anyone since our engagement."

"Oh," I said. It hadn't stopped him from kissing others, though. I was disappointed and relieved at the same time. I was happy that we didn't have to have sex. I didn't want to risk anything that might expose myself. I didn't want him finding out I was Luxian. It terrified me, but some part of me wanted to sleep with him too. And I still wanted him to want me. Worried that he could still read my thoughts, my hands instinctively went to my necklace. I surprised myself when I asked, "How many have you been with before our engagement?"

He turned to look at me. "Are you sure you want to know the answer to that?"

I shook my head. That was an answer in itself. The fact that I loathed him and he still turned me on was bad enough. I didn't want to think about what he would do with females he was actually trying to seduce.

"I wish I could read your thoughts right now," he said as his gaze pierced through me. Then he said, "Scotlind, *when* we have sex, I want you to want it. It won't be because some middle-aged males are forcing us to. You're going to be begging for it." I noticed the choice of *when* and not *if*. And *begging*. I swallowed.

"Someone thinks highly of himself," I retorted back. "And I won't beg."

"So you admit you want to have sex with me then?"

When I didn't respond, he smiled. I started to make my way

toward the bed but came to a halt as Sie added, "You need to take off your dress."

"What?" I said, whirling around to face him. "You just said we don't have to?"

He just laughed at me. "If you sleep in your gown, the servants will know we didn't consummate anything. Then Synder and his men will be back tomorrow night, and they won't be outside the door."

"Oh." I looked down at my dress and frowned, remembering how it had taken Annabel, Ashley, and Roslyn to help me in it. There was no way I could undo the forty-plus buttons going down my spine holding the heavy fabric together.

I frowned further, and Sie noticed. "Let me help you." I didn't stop him. I didn't move, didn't speak. I didn't even know if I was breathing as he made his way toward me. He lightly grabbed my shoulders and turned me around so that my back was to him.

I was facing the massive bed with the black silk sheets, trying my best not to think about what it would be like to share it with him as I felt his fingers graze my shoulder. He found the first button, letting it come undone. He continued down my back, slowly, neither of us saying anything. I was irritated that they'd picked a gown that took so long to get off. I swore they did it on purpose. I was going to yell at Ashley and Annabel for this.

I started to feel Sie's touch on my skin as the buttons were halfway unclasped. I hugged the top of my dress to my chest, covering my breasts as he continued to work, slowly undoing it. I flinched as his fingers grazed over my lower back. His hands were cold and rough and sent a chill in their wake. I felt more exposed and bare and vulnerable with him looking directly at my back than I did the night Alec compelled me.

"Done," he said softly. "Now get some sleep. I know you had an exhausting day." He made his way toward the other side of the room. He blew out all of the candles, but even with the curtains drawn shut, I could still make out his silhouette. He didn't bother picking up the side table that was still upside down.

"Where are you sleeping?" I asked shyly, still holding the dress up so it didn't slip.

"I don't trust myself to share a bed with you," he admitted. "Being so close to you, I don't know if I would be able to keep my hands to myself. Especially just after the—" He stopped mid-sentence as he sprawled out across the leather sofa.

I took in the length of him through the dying embers of the fire. He was so tall that his feet hung off the edge of the sofa. It looked uncomfortable, but I didn't say anything. The feathered cape he wore during the ceremony was off and tossed on the floor, his shirt unbuttoned, but otherwise he still wore his usual black attire. "I'm fine on the sofa."

When he realized I was staring and hadn't moved, he added, "Your nightgowns are in the bureau over there." I followed his gaze and grabbed one of the thin, white fabrics, taking it into the bathing room to change.

I returned and slumped down onto the comfort of the bed. The silk blankets felt like a caress against my bare skin. They beckoned me to sleep, but it didn't come. I laid there wide awake, with my hands clasping the necklace like a lifeline. My eyes stayed glued to the ceiling as I listened to the sound of his breathing.

When sleep finally found me, I didn't have a single nightmare.

———

THE NEXT DAY, I awoke to find my three servants hurrying about, cleaning up our room. I glanced around and saw no sign of Sie. I knew without looking that Abherham was just outside the door.

Roslyn glared at me. "Looks like you two had a good night."

I glanced around the room and took in what my maids saw. It looked like Sie and I had destroyed it. I cringed thinking about the rumors that were probably spreading around the castle of us consummating our marriage.

I turned bright red as Ashley added, "Don't be embarrassed, Scottie. It's normal for a husband and wife to have sex. We just didn't know Sie was so wild." Then she winked at me before going back to her tidying. *Wife.* I would have to get used to that.

I threw myself back onto the bed and covered myself with the comforter. "No time for that now," Annabel mused as she threw the blankets off me. "You have to get ready for the grand breakfast celebrating your marriage. It starts in an hour. Quickly, get dressed."

At breakfast, everyone's eyes were on me as I filled the empty seat next to Sie. To my horror, Alec and Reagan sat across from us, Peter to my left.

"You look tired, Scottie. Did Sie keep you up all night?" Alec grinned as he shoved a forkful of eggs into his mouth.

Reagan finally met my eyes and looked ready to murder me as Peter said, "Enough, Alec."

But Alec didn't listen. "Relax, Peter. I'm just making sure our princess held up her end of the bargain and pleased Sie."

I knew he was referring to the night they made me participate in their sick game. I was also aware that I wasn't supposed to remember it. "I don't recall ever making bargains with you regarding my personal life, and I don't plan on discussing anything now," I said as my eyes narrowed over him.

He met my gaze as he lazily leaned back into his seat. "No matter. I'll just ask Sie for the dirty details later."

Sie's hand gripped the edge of his seat as he sneered, "I think there are more important things to discuss."

"On the contrary, Sie, everyone has been talking about your wild night. It's the highlight of the maids' gossip this morning. They kept going on and on about how your room was destroyed and how loudly you had Scottie moaning. They say the shy and timid ones are the freaks in the bedroom, right? Besides, you might have me to thank for your wife being so willing to accommodate your pleasure." Alec winked at me then turned to Sie. My stomach turned, and I lost my appetite.

Sie's hands turned white as he gripped the armrest even harder. "That's enough, Alec."

Alec, at least, had the decency to finally stop his taunting, but it was too late. The entire table had stopped talking and was listening. Synder was the first to break the silence. "Well, I'm glad we found you a wife that is satisfactory, Prince Noren."

I wanted to die. I wanted to curl up and die from embarrassment and then die all over again.

The death stare Sie gave Synder made everyone go silent. Everyone wordlessly resumed eating their breakfast. The only sounds were of silverware clinking against the plates for the rest of the morning.

Synder smiled.

# THIRTY-TWO
## SIE

I took an ice bath after breakfast in an attempt to relax myself. No one would know it was the day after my wedding based on how I'd been avoiding my new wife since last night.

It took every single ounce of self control I had to not crawl into that damn bed with her. The way she'd been moaning against the door made me want to make her moan for real. I thought about every single fucking way I would, knowing exactly how I would start.

I tried to shake her out of my mind as I looked down at the paperwork sitting before me. King Lunder had been letting me run the kingdom over the past month. To be honest, I hadn't seen much of him since the first month of my orientation. He'd only been around at council and war meetings about the growing rebellion. He was way too happy to push off this kind of work onto me, and I could see why.

It was much more tedious than I thought. I devoted the next three hours to the large stack of papers, sorting through and responding to the massive amount of letters the kingdom received. It was only a step above organizing the royal budget.

I felt it before any of the guards came to warn me—the warning sign I had programmed into Scottie's necklace went off. It alarmed, but the tracking system was dismantled, and there was only one way to dismantle the tracking. Either Scottie realized what it was, or someone did it for her and that would mean—

I half sprinted, half teleported to our bedroom as fast as I could, praying she would still be there, pushing away anyone in my path. I scared more than one servant and many guards with the stream of curse words leaving my mouth, but I didn't care. All that mattered was her.

When I arrived, our bedroom had been sacked. The guards who were stationed with her were all on the floor. The only guard still breathing was Abherham, and he was lying in a thick pool of blood. I didn't bother checking to see how extensive his injuries were as I turned toward him and growled, "What happened?"

Red was everywhere, it stained the floor, and I had no way of knowing if Scottie's blood was mixed in with it. A window was bashed in, broken glass scattered across the floor in shards of varying sizes. The furniture had been overturned, broken bits of wood sticking out every which way. And Scottie was nowhere to be found.

Abherham huffed too slowly, his voice was strained and barely audible. "They took her." He tried to lift his arm, but it barely raised an inch over the blood-soaked floor. He held a flimsy paper in his broken hand. I stepped forward, ripping it from his fingers. The note was smeared in blood, but the writing was still legible.

*We have your wife. If you want to see her alive again, do exactly as we say. Tell no one. Burn this note immediately and head to the back garden. Someone will meet you there. It is best for your wife if you cooperate. Come alone with no weapons. You have ten minutes, or you will find her returned to you in pieces.*

Shit. Shit. Shit. I read the note twice, cursing as I did, before throwing it into the fire. I waited until it went up in flames, then stormed to the gardens, ignoring Abherham's weakened plea to wait.

A hooded figure approached as I entered. I couldn't make out any details of his face, but I knew it was the Advenian I was waiting for.

"Drop your weapons," the male rasped as he held out manacles for my hands. "And princeling, one wrong move, and she dies."

I yanked my daggers out of my belt and unsheathed the blade from behind my back. Once I threw my weapons onto the grass and out of reach, the male approached me. I had no choice as I let him clamp the shackles over my wrists. I felt the Alluse working through my system, spilling into my veins and freezing my abilities the moment the cold metal hit my flesh. Then a bag went over my head, and my world went dark.

# THIRTY-THREE
## SCOTLIND

I CHOKED ON THE GAG IN MY MOUTH AS SOUNDLESS SOBS broke from me. I couldn't see anything through my blindfold, nor could I move to feel my surroundings. I was bound. Shackled to the floor, the metal digging into my wrists. No matter how hard I yanked and pulled on the chains, they wouldn't budge. So I just sat on the cold ground. Shivering. Listening. Waiting.

My head throbbed, and my heart pounded hard against my sternum as I strained to hear anything. I wanted any information I could get about who held me captive.

Then I heard it, a soft laugh. That laugh. I could recognize it from anywhere.

Two brown eyes seared into me as my blindfold was ripped from my head. Kole. I tried to scream, but the gag only allowed for a weak, muffled sound to escape.

I looked around to see where he had taken me. It looked like an abandoned warehouse. Two stories were visible with balconies surrounding the upper level.

Then I noticed all the males. Hooded figures were scattered throughout both floors. Every single one of them was armed to the teeth with weapons, but they weren't focused on me. Their arrows were notched and pointed toward the front door like they were waiting for something or someone.

I squinted, trying to get a better look. They all wore black masks beneath their hoods. Silver and gold designs were etched into each one, mimicking plastered facial expressions contorted into a haunting grin. They looked terrifying.

I tried to count the hooded figures, maybe thirty or forty. I scanned the different weapons they held—swords were strapped to their backs, knives and daggers of various lengths were held in their grips—whips, chains, axes, arrows... Then there were objects, no... torture devices that I had never seen before.

I swallowed or tried to with the gag as Kole grabbed my chin and forced me to gaze at him, preventing me from seeing anything else. Maybe it would be a good thing not to know.

Kole laughed, his grip tightening as he ushered me into a seated position. I winced as my jaw throbbed, knowing he would leave a bruise. He held my gaze as I started to shake under his grasp. My thigh aching all over again as I remembered the pain he inflicted. I remembered how he'd tried to kill me that night in my room.

I didn't know how much time had passed since my kidnapping or if anyone even knew I was gone. But I wouldn't be leaving this warehouse alive. I knew it by the pure hatred in Kole's eyes.

Something shimmered in his hands—my necklace. I tried to retreat, but my chains were already pulled taut.

"Curious thing this is, little nix," Kole sneered, waving the golden chain in my face. "I always wondered how your prince got to you so fast that night. I wondered how you didn't obey my compulsion and fought back. Then, I discovered this lovely button on the back. It alarms him, right?"

He paused as if to wait for my answer, but I was still gagged, and all I could do was stare at him. "Well, I guess we will find out if he comes for you. I already took the liberty of pressing it." I shook my head violently. *No. No. No.* Sie can't come here.

The males who were scattered throughout the warehouse had covered their faces with masks and hoods. Kole was the only one who openly showed his face. Probably all too aware that he was a known threat to the kingdom now. Tears ran down my cheeks as I crawled awkwardly away from him. I put as much distance between us until my chains pulled taut which wasn't much at all.

"What do we do now?" one of the hooded males asked Kole. They looked to him like he was their leader.

"Now," Kole said to the group, "we wait." Most of the men nodded. Some looked toward me.

"What if he doesn't come?" someone else asked.

Kole's eyes never left mine as he said with a sickening, wicked smile, "Oh, he will. He'll come for her."

Bile rose deep in my throat, turning sour. I wanted to vomit.

Kole bent over to remove my gag. I gasped for air, gulping in as much as I could. With my hands still bound in front of me, I staggered slightly forward. The males snickered.

When I finally caught my breath enough, I rasped, "Why are you doing this?" I couldn't hide the hurt in my voice or the tears in my eyes.

Kole slapped me hard across the face. The power of his arm forced my head to slam against the floor as I fell. I groaned in agony as I tried to lift my hands to my head, but the chains stopped me short from the angle I was in.

"You'll get what's coming to you, nix. You will wish I'd killed you that night."

I kept quiet and waited with the males, my gaze transfixed on the door. I didn't know if I was half expecting Sie to just walk through them. But the longer I waited, the less confident I became. He wouldn't come. Sie wouldn't risk leaving the castle to come for me. I wasn't worth it. It was better this way. Better if he didn't come because whatever Kole had planned, I knew it would be awful.

The hooded figures started to pace. I watched the sun shift in the sky through an open balcony from above. I thought over and over again about how I could escape. If I could just get out of these chains... The front door was too heavily guarded, but if I could make it to the second floor and run to that window, I could jump. I knew it was wishful thinking. The males were dressed in weapons like they were jewels. I wouldn't make it two feet before someone shot me down with an arrow. Not to mention the thick chains that were digging into my wrists and secured to the floor wouldn't budge.

I heard a commotion coming from the front of the warehouse. Kole rubbed his hands together. "It's time."

He stepped behind me, loosening my chains just enough to pull me to my feet, and pressed a knife against my throat just as Sie emerged through the door. Every single male tightened their hold on whatever weapon they possessed, all were aimed toward Sie as if they could sense the threat he promised. Their anticipation for bloodshed was palpable.

Sie walked into the warehouse, the door shutting heavily behind him, locking us in. He was flanked by another masked male who held twin blades. Sie carried no weapons. I squinted through the blinding, unending sunlight and saw that he was shackled. Chained just like me. They had captured him.

"One more step, and she's dead, prince," Kole sneered, pressing the knife further into my neck right over my scar. The scar he already gave me. I felt a small drop of blood ooze out and roll down my collar bone.

Sie stopped dead in his tracks once he spotted me. "Let her go. I came alone with no weapons. You have what you wanted. Now release her."

Kole nodded to his men, who positioned themselves closer to him. Sie took a step toward me, but Kole held out his other hand. "I wouldn't do that if I were you." Then Kole lazily dragged the knife down my almost healed thigh, reopening the cut as blood poured out of me.

I fought against the urge to scream as agony shot through me, taking over my senses and narrowing in on the pain searing through my thigh. "Now, this looks familiar, doesn't it? Scottie with her thigh bleeding open. You with that crazed look on your face. Only this time, I win."

"What do you want?" Sie growled, clenching his jaw. I could almost hear his teeth grinding against one another.

"I want you to kneel before me, *prince*," Kole taunted.

*Kings bow to no one.* Kole knew what he was doing. He was testing Sie, seeing how far he could take it. To my horror, Sie listened and dropped to his knees before us, his eyes locking on mine. An echoing thud sounded throughout the warehouse as he slammed onto the stone floor.

"Please. Just let her go," Sie begged. "I'll do whatever you want. Just. Let. Her. Go."

Kole took his time answering as if thinking it over before agreeing. "Alright, but I need to make sure I can trust you. You could be lying." He nodded toward his men as six bulky figures stepped into the light. Still on his knees, Sie's gaze held mine. He didn't look toward the threat that was approaching him.

"Sie, don't," I yelled, my voice raw from the gag. "It's a trap. Don't agree to whatever he wants!" Kole dug the knife further into my thigh to silence me. I yelped as tears blurred my vision. My breathing turned ragged.

Sie gave me a gentle, sympathetic look as if urging me to stop resisting—that I might make things worse. I blinked away the tears and tried not to focus on the searing agony shooting up my leg.

"Now," Kole purred, "don't fight my men as they beat you. If you pass, then I'll know I can believe you."

Sie laughed and held up his shackled wrists. The chains rattled from the movement. "I don't think I could fight with these chains, but I accept."

Kole huffed. "I'm not an idiot, *prince*. I know you can take many of my men out even with those Alluse shackles."

"Alright. I won't fight back. You can do whatever you want to me as long as you let Scotlind go."

Kole's smile was answer enough. I watched in horror as the six males took turns punching, kicking, and beating Sie. He did nothing. He just knelt on the ground taking it. Occasionally, they would knock him off balance, and he slowly, painfully, would rise again to that same kneeling position.

Sometimes the men would switch out their fists for weapons, laughing as the metal landed on his flesh. Sometimes I would hear a bone crunch.

"Stop!" I yelled. "Please, stop." I begged over and over, but no one paid attention to me. It felt like time stilled, and I was awake, forced inside a nightmare, stuck on repeat, unable to wake up. No one could hear me over the pounding of fists and clang of metal.

The stone around Sie's knees turned red. He didn't scream. He just took it, only grunting occasionally from the harder blows. His eyes lingering on my crying form. "Please, stop it," I sobbed through my tears.

Kole finally spoke, "Alright that's enough. I don't want him dead yet. We have orders to kill him by morning, but not a minute before, and I still want to have my turn with him."

Sie managed to get to his knees again, blood dripping from every part of him. "We had a deal. Now let her go."

"I'm afraid you might be a male of your word, but I'm not one of mine." Kole laughed as three men grabbed Sie by the arms and held him down. "I'd like Scottie to know how you tortured me all night in the dungeons. Enlighten her to the monster you really are. I think I'll show her. Maybe I can demonstrate and do the exact same thing to her as you did to me. I can repeat every single cut, every burn, every punch."

This was all planned. He just wanted to weaken Sie, so he wasn't as much of a threat. Kole wasn't going to let either of us walk out of here tonight.

Sie realized it just as I did. He attempted to stand, ready to lunge, but Kole pressed the knife against my throat again. Standing up, my chained hands didn't reach past my breasts. I could do nothing as I felt the steel of the blade bob. I tried not to swallow. I tried not to breathe.

"I wouldn't do that if I were you," Kole mused, his voice laced with power. "Back on your knees." Sie sank onto the ground in front of me.

"You two will be begging for mercy by the time I'm done with you," Kole spat as he stared between us. The expression on his face held borderline insanity.

I couldn't look at Sie. I focused my attention on the floor in front of me, on the blood that was now pooling around my reopened wound. I tried not to think about how the blood around Sie was worse, so much worse.

"What should I do to you first?" Kole drawled. He loosened his hold on the blade at my throat as he grabbed my chin with his bloody fingers—my blood on his fingers—and pulled hard, forcing me to look him in the eyes.

The twisted smile he gave me made my stomach turn. Some of the males around us laughed. Some took a step closer to me, eyeing me up. One twirled a blade in his hand as he licked his lips. I tried to wriggle out of Kole's grasp, but I was too weak, too far drained to fight back. I noticed Sie out of the corner of my eye do the same as he pulled against his restraints to get to me. One of the males holding him threw a punch to his temple, forcing him back down.

"If you touch her," Sie growled with such deadliness to his voice, "I will kill you. I will kill all of you."

"I'd like to see you try," Kole grinned. "You see, *prince*, we are much larger than you even realize. We've been gathering for quite some time now, and thanks to you coming tonight, we have exactly what we need."

"Which is what?" I breathed.

"Besides giving nixes like you what they deserve?" Kole spat. "King Lunder will be dealt with soon enough. He will be easy to kill. It won't be difficult to fake his death. But you, Sie, you're talked about everywhere, constantly watched. We knew once you got on the throne, we wouldn't be able to get you off. We knew your rule would be long. You would win the King's Tournament for as long as you breathed. We also knew your ideals don't align with ours."

"Who are you working for?" Sie ground out.

"I can't tell you that or our main purpose. But it's really not going to be a concern to either of you as you won't live to see the morning.

But I will tell you something we have been working on. Or rather, I want to *show* you. We have far more advancements than you do. There are three different kinds of Alluse. The first is Complete Alluse. Just like the necklace you gave her," Kole gestured to me as he swung my necklace in his hands. "Which prevents all abilities. The wearer of this item can't use abilities, nor can any abilities be used on them.

"But our men discovered a way to yield Alluse into more than just objects like a necklace or shackles. We now have tonics and serums of all three kinds of Alluse."

Three kinds of Alluse.

I must have said it out loud because Kole clarified, "There is Sui Alluse, where someone can use their own abilities just fine. It only acts as a shield or a block to prevent others from using their abilities on them. That's the injection I had in my system when you kept me in the dungeons. It's why your compulsion didn't work on me. The last is Vir Alluse. This one is my favorite. If I inject someone with this Alluse, their powers will cease to exist for a time, leaving that person completely defenseless. Making them into a nix, so to speak, while I can still use any abilities I want on them. We have Vir Alluse in your shackles, prince, as well as injections on standby. Why don't you demonstrate for him, Fern," Kole sneered at the masked male standing next to him. His hood was down, exposing chestnut hair, differentiating him from the others.

"With pleasure," a rough voice said as he strode in front of Sie, making a point to crack his knuckles and neck before he started. But then he didn't do anything. His golden markings appeared over his body, but he just gazed down at Sie, neither of them moving.

Sie's screaming filled the room moments later. I might have been screaming too, begging Fern to stop whatever it was he was doing to Sie, but I couldn't hear myself over the noise. Finally, the male released his hold. Sie sagged to the ground, his shoulders dropping. His breathing was ragged, coming in and out too sharply to be normal.

Kole stepped in front of me as another male grabbed Sie by his hair, forcing him to look up. "Fear illusion," Kole smiled, practically breathing into Sie's face. "It's the worst kind of torment because the illusion feels so real that it's hard to tell when you're out of it."

Sie spat on him. It was more blood than saliva, but Kole just laughed. "What you just saw, what Fern showed you in your head... that's what we will do to her."

They both turned to look at me—Kole grinning and Sie fighting against his restraints.

"The Vir Alluse in those shackles," Kole said as he pointed to the handcuffs on Sie's wrists, "will completely eliminate your powers. You will find yourself defenseless as you are forced to watch what we have planned for your wife. Maybe you will even feel her pain for yourself with that disgusting blood bond the two of you share. If you ask me, I'm doing you a favor by getting rid of her."

"If you want me dead, then kill me. You want vengeance for what I did to you in the dungeons? Then do it to me, not her. Scotlind is innocent in this. Please, just let her go," Sie begged.

"Innocent? It's nixes like her who are tainting and ruining our society in the first place. Once we take over the throne, they will be nothing. To be honest, it's pathetic they even forced you to do the blood bond. They only did it because they didn't think you would want her. But I think you would have come even without the bond. The only reason she is involved is because we needed you to care about something. You had no weaknesses, no reason to agree to the shackles long enough for us to kill you. So they forced it. They forced your feelings for her by performing the bond."

Kole yanked on my chains, forcing me to stumble toward him. "I could let her go. She isn't really important in this now that we have you here, but I don't think I will. You both ruined my life. I was a King's Guard, and instead you made me into a traitor. Now I'm forced to hide out here until I finish my task." He laughed again. He was insane. We'd made him insane. "But thanks to you, prince, my task will end tonight with you both dead. Once my master comes to the throne, I'll be forgiven. I'll be a hero and welcomed into the High Council, where we will change the laws and give the ranking system the revisions it deserves. The high ranks will rule while the low ranks serve. That's how it should be. That's how it will be after tonight."

I met Sie's gaze and found him already staring at me. Neither of us were making it out of here alive.

# THIRTY-FOUR
## SCOTLIND

The sun was peeking through the window in the upper balcony, illuminating the warehouse and exposing every inch of this awful place. The constant Tennebrisian sun made it hard to tell how much time had passed. I only knew that it was the next day from Kole talking to the other men.

I wondered if he would stay true to his word and kill us soon. He promised that we wouldn't make it to see the morning, and I suddenly wished and prayed that it was true. I couldn't take it any longer.

Whatever fear illusion Fern showed Sie was coming true. I could barely stand anymore. I couldn't make out the color of my skin through the dried and fresh blood caked on me. Sie wasn't much better. They took turns on us. Torturing us while forcing the other to watch. I didn't know what I hated more—being forced to watch Sie or when Kole turned his attention to me.

The smell of eggs and meat filled my nostrils. My stomach grumbled, begging my body for fuel, but I barely had the energy to lift my head. The food wasn't for us.

All I wanted to do was die. I wanted to die in this cell right now while Sie held me close to his chest. I wanted to die in his arms. I didn't want to die on that table where Kole had strapped me down. I didn't want to die looking into brown eyes while Sie's screams filled the space as he pleaded for Kole to torture him instead of me. Those were the only times Sie would scream. No matter what Kole did to him, he refused to budge. But when Kole went to me…

No. Right here was good. Right here, we'd found peace in this hell.

We'd been sitting like this for maybe an hour, or maybe it was only a few minutes. Time didn't exist anymore, only pure agony and pain. Sie leaned against the dirty cell wall as I sat in between his legs. My back resting on his chest, my head turned toward the nape of his neck.

The cell was positioned in the corner of the main room, enough so that the table wasn't in view. There were rusty bars to our makeshift prison, so we could see Kole, and he could see us. I tried not to look.

I wanted to lift my head to look at Sie, but I didn't have the energy, so I just curled up into him, embracing the only warmth this place had to offer. Sie wrapped his arms around my chest, holding me tight, and hadn't let go since. The hold was awkward with both of our chains getting in the way, but I wanted to be close to him. I felt terrible that they'd captured him because of me, but a selfish part of me was grateful that we would go together. I didn't have to die alone. I felt safer with him here, even though I knew deep down he couldn't do anything to save me or get us out of this situation.

We didn't say anything. We didn't dare speak. So we sat there, curled into one another, and held on, savoring this last moment.

Kole threw his plate away, rubbed his hands against his pants, and stalked toward us. They'd changed, all his men had as their previous attire was stained with our blood. Now they were rested and fed, ready for another day of this nightmare or to finally end it.

The cell bars groaned open as Kole stepped forward. Sie's grip around my chest tightened.

"I think the time has come, Sie, for you to watch your wife die," Kole said with a smile as he grabbed me by my hair and pulled us apart. I screamed as he dragged me across the stone floor, my knees scraping against my already raw flesh.

I saw Sie move out of the corner of my eye. He fought the males around him. He fought without any abilities, his shackles barely hindering him as he tore into Kole's men, ripping them apart, trying to get to me.

Kole yelled, "Fucking inject him. Inject him now!"

A needle flashed in the morning sun. Then a grunt came, and I heard more than saw Sie fall to his knees. The injection rendered him powerless. With the tonic running through his veins and the shackles on his wrists, he could do nothing but watch.

He wasn't going to save me.

"I'll kill you. I'll fucking kill every single one of you if you hurt her!" Sie screamed.

Kole just smiled and continued to drag me toward the center of the warehouse. Toward a tub of water that wasn't there before.

"I wouldn't doubt you. I know what you are capable of firsthand from my night in the dungeon cell. But you see, even if you broke out of those Alluse shackles now, it would be too late. My men injected you with the Vir Alluse serum. You will find in a few minutes that you won't have any power left circulating in your veins for a long, long time."

I struggled against Kole's tight grip on my hair as he lifted me. My eyes briefly met Sie's frantic stare before Kole plunged my head into the cold water.

I kicked and pushed as hard as I could against him, but his grip held firm, keeping my head submerged in the water. He was killing me. Drowning me. I could hear Sie screaming. I could hear him struggling against the men and the chains, but I couldn't make out what he was saying.

Kole's voice came through, muffled by the water, "Bring him closer. I want him to watch this."

I fought against his death grip, but it was useless. I could feel Kole's chest heaving as he laughed at my efforts. "Watch her."

My head started to throb. My lungs burned and ached as I felt my chest caving in on itself. Air. I needed air. I fought the urge to open my mouth. I knew it would only make things worse with the water rushing in, filling the space as I struggled to breathe.

I would have been crying from the pain, but I couldn't muster the strength. My tears would just blend in with the water, going unnoticed. My fighting against Kole grew weaker and weaker as the seconds dragged on. I was going to die. I was already dying. Weakened from the hours of torture, I could barely fight against Kole's strong hold.

This was wrong. I wanted to die in Sie's arms, not Kole's.

He pushed me further into the tub until my legs were the only thing not submerged. My neck was twisted, and my face was pressed against the slick bottom surface. The burning in my lungs overtook any common sense I had left as I opened my mouth and swallowed. The water came rushing in.

Maybe it would end this torture sooner. Maybe I would die sooner if I just gave up.

I expected more pain, but instead, my lungs expanded. I could breathe. The fire in my chest extinguished. I thought I might already be dead, but then Kole pressed my head further against the tub, his grip tightening around the nape of my neck. I opened my eyes. I was still underwater.

I could breathe underwater. *My Luxian ability was water.*

My head stopped throbbing as I greedily breathed in the water like air. I could see, smell, and hear everything around me now. The water was no longer blurring my senses but enhancing them.

I could finally hear what Sie was screaming, "I'll kill you. I'll kill you. I'll kill you." I could feel his anger stir in me. I heard him fighting against the chains that kept him down.

I fought Kole for a few more seconds, this time acting in pain before I let my body slump. Kole, thinking I had drowned, let me fall. He dropped his hold on me as I slid onto the stone floor. I could feel him watching me as he turned my body over with his boot. The upper half of me was soaking wet. Sie fell silent.

If Kole thought I was dead, maybe I could attack him when he wasn't expecting it. So I laid there, listening and waiting.

"Such a pity that she was born a nix. She *was* gorgeous," Kole tsked. "Was it worth it, prince? Was she worth it?" I could feel Sie staring. I could hear his ragged breaths, but he didn't respond. A slap sounded, then another. "Answer me!"

"You will die for this." Sie's voice was deep and promised bloodshed.

"You're pathetic," Kole taunted. "You're a waste of a high rank if you fell for someone like her. She was all it took for your demise? A pretty face and that was it? You could have been great. You could have been the one to make Tennebris as strong as Lux. You could have ruled and reigned for a long time."

"What is this to you? You want me to admit that I cared for her? Well, I did, and you will fucking regret this."

A laugh. "My master took a gamble on her. He knew that you liked her after our Trials. Your mistake was having your second demand that she be made into a guard instead of a servant like they had planned. He knew he could use her in some way to get to you. He was testing you to see how far those feelings went, but you really stumped everyone by playing the role of an asshole so well, making it seem to the world that you hated her. That's why he had you perform the blood bond, so you would have no choice but to come here to save her."

I tried to steady my breathing. Sie willingly came here last night. When he walked through the door in shackles, I thought that they had captured him. I had no idea that he accepted this fate in an attempt to protect me. He let Kole's men beat him up to save me. The most powerful male in Tennebris, who could probably kill every single Advenian in this warehouse if not for the Vir Alluse, made himself weak for me.

"And who is your master?" Sie asked Kole.

*Scottie, are you okay?* Sie. He was speaking to me in my mind. That's why he seemed so calm now. He knew I was alive, that I hadn't died. He was buying us time by distracting Kole.

"Wouldn't you like to know?" Kole responded, but I didn't hear what else he said. I was too focused on Sie inside my head.

*Yes, I'm fine,* I sent back to him, not daring to move a muscle from where I laid on the floor. *How are you talking to me? I thought they injected you with Alluse? I thought the Vir Alluse made it so that you couldn't use your abilities?*

*They did, but for some reason, I can still use my powers with you. It's draining fast, though. I don't have much time. I can feel it working against me. I need you to listen to me very closely, Scotlind.*

*Okay,* I thought, waiting for his plan. If we could surprise Kole, maybe we could get out of this. Hope swelled inside me.

*I want you to lie there. Do not get up for anything, no matter what you hear. Let them think you are dead. Once they kill me, I want you to run. Run like hell and get as far away from here as you can. Go to Peter. He will help you. He will protect you.*

*No!* I almost yelled out loud before reminding myself to not give anything away. *I'm not leaving you.*

*Scotlind, I'm not asking you. I'm telling you. Please. I need you alive. Once you get out of here, go to Peter. Tell him everything that Kole said. He will know what to do.*

"If you aren't going to tell me anything about who you work for and you're planning on killing me anyway, why not get it over with?" Sie said out loud to Kole.

No, no, no. I couldn't let this happen. Sie couldn't die. He couldn't leave me.

"So eager to join your dead wife?" Kole stepped toward Sie, and I reacted. I couldn't let this happen. I didn't know what I could do against him, but I had to try. I couldn't let him hurt Sie while I just laid there.

"Scotlind, no!" Sie screamed at the same time Kole spun around.

"What the hell?" Kole spat, his face dazed in confusion.

I lunged at him, wrapping my legs around his waist, tackling him to the ground. My chains hooked around his neck as I pulled hard. A choking noise rattled from his chest as he struggled to breathe.

Kole's men leapt toward me, but Sie was faster and took out as many as possible. Sie was on me in an instant and helped spring me to my feet. Then we ran like hell.

# THIRTY-FIVE
## SIE

We only made it to the damn door before one of the males grabbed Scotlind. I heard her thin nightgown rip. I whirled and punched the mask off the male who was holding her. I flung Scottie to my chest, pulling her close, even though I knew I couldn't truly protect her, not without my powers. I'd already failed her. What Kole and his men did to her last night... What they tried to do to her this morning...

Scottie would have drowned if—I couldn't let myself go there.

Kole's men had us surrounded in seconds. Our slim chance of escaping was gone. I looked at Scottie and took in her sapphire eyes. They were wide with fear. Agony lined her face, tear tracks left marks on her cheeks as they parted the blood that hadn't washed away from when Kole had held her in the tub. All I wanted to do was wipe the tears away and get her the hell out of here.

I pulled against the chains that clung to my wrists and tried to break out of them, but it was no use. I willed my ability to surface, attempting to call upon the flickering power that I felt in her presence. I just needed enough to teleport her away from here, but it came back empty. It was gone. My reserves were wholly depleted from the Alluse.

I still didn't know how I had managed to use my telepathy with her earlier.

Images of last night flashed in my mind. I couldn't get the sight of her on that table out of my head. I wanted to fucking murder them all for it. If we survived this, her screams would haunt not only my night-mares but my every waking moment.

Kole recovered and stalked toward us. His eyes gleamed red, matching the mark that Scottie just gave him across his neck. I wrapped my chain around her, pulling her into me, and pressed my hand flat against her stomach, pushing her back against my chest.

Water was dripping down her wet hair and onto her thin night-gown. There was barely any material left. The few stands that remained left nothing to the imagination and the males around us glowered at her.

Some smiled at the sight, taking her all in. One of them had his eyes glued to her chest. "Since she survived, can we at least have our fun with her before you finish her off again?"

A low growl escaped my lips as I turned her away from them, trying to put myself between her and the men that surrounded us. Laughter filled the warehouse as one of the males lunged for her.

Kole hesitated, enough that I thought he would say no, but then, "I guess Sie wouldn't mind us using his nix for a little bit." His men didn't wait. They swarmed us and ripped her away from me. I fought like hell as she screamed my name.

This was worse. This was worse than any damn torture Kole did to me. I couldn't stand seeing her scared, pleading for me when I couldn't do a fucking thing to stop it. And what they were going to do to her...

The male named Fern pulled Scottie by her gown, ripping it further, leaving her back completely exposed. Everything stopped. The males halted and gaped as she attempted to turn her back away from them, but it was too late. With the water glistening down her spine, the black markings on her were as clear as day.

"What the hell is this?" the male holding her said. Kole pushed him out of the way and threw Scottie face first against the wall to get a better view of her back.

"She's Luxian," Kole whispered to himself as he processed what he saw.

"Does *he* know?" Fern asked.

Kole ran a hand over his mouth, trying to think everything over. "I don't know."

"What should we do?"

Kole started to pace. "He just said to kill them both once morning came. That it didn't matter how we did it as long as the job was done. But she's not a fucking nix."

He ran his hands down her back. Scottie was shaking so hard as he pressed her further into the wall. "This kind of information… Send word to him now. He needs to know this. And put Vir Alluse chains on her too. We don't know what Luxian powers she possesses. Throw them both into the cell until we hear back from him." His touch on her was possessive. I fought against my chains and the males holding me down as Kole ran his fingers over her exposed skin.

Then someone exchanged her previous chains for Alluse ones. Scottie winced as the metal clamped over her skin, no doubt feeling her powers leave her body. The Vir Alluse felt like someone was taking a part of you away, like it was bleeding you of life.

They threw us both into a cell. One that didn't have bars but concrete walls. The door slammed shut, leaving us in the dark, waiting to find out what Kole's *master* wanted to do with us.

My knees scraped against the stone as I slid over to her. The cell was damp and cold, and I could barely make out her silhouette. "Scottie, are you okay?"

She crawled toward me and sagged in my arms. I let out a sigh of relief, thankful that she was alive. I wrapped my arms around her, pulling her into me.

"What's going to happen now?" she whimpered. Her skin was frozen from the water. Her body was overtaken by shaking.

I couldn't give her an honest answer. "It's going to be okay." She didn't call me out for lying because the truth was I didn't think either of us would make it out of here alive. She knew it too. Instead, she leaned further into me, sinking into my chest—our blood, dirt, and sweat mixing as one.

She let out a small sigh as her head tilted back into my neck, and I savored her warmth.

———

I DIDN'T KNOW how much time had passed as I held Scottie in the dark, waiting for our end. We both jumped up to our feet as a loud thud echoed off our cell.

The clang of metal against metal sounded. I heard bow strings pulling back and then releasing. Then the screams came one after another after another. I glanced over at Scottie, but I couldn't see her face in the darkened cell.

She was standing next to me, ready to fight. Even with the chains on her wrists, the Alluse seeping into her skin, she stood steady. I couldn't help but admire her after the living hell we'd been through in the past twenty-four hours. The fact that she was even standing right now was beyond me.

I grabbed her hand in mine as we waited together, listening to the fighting and the screams. Then silence.

Our cell door creaked open on a phantom wind. A telekinesis user probably. Scottie went to leap out, but I held my hand in front of her, keeping her back. I wasn't about to let her walk out first into danger.

I had a sinking feeling that whatever just happened was worse. I crept quietly out of the cell, scanning the surroundings. The smell of death filled my nostrils as I saw the masked males lying in pools of their own blood. Fern was facedown outside our cell with an axe through his back.

They were dead—all of them.

I scanned one more time, making sure there wasn't a threat before I nodded to Scottie. We silently collected whatever fallen weapons we could hold. I grabbed two swords and a crossbow. Scottie grabbed a dagger. I crouched down and picked up a thick set of keys before placing them in my pocket. I didn't want to stay in this warehouse for a second longer than we had to. We would unchain ourselves later. For now, I needed to get Scottie far away from this place. I grabbed her chained hand in mine and ran toward the door.

———

WE HAD BEEN RUNNING for hours and hadn't come across a single village yet. Whatever warehouse they'd brought us to was deep in the forest.

Feeling confident that we had put enough space between us and that hell, I finally let her rest under a thick tree. The only thing that was letting either of us still run was the adrenaline and I could see hers was started to fade.

I surveyed her body through one eye—my right eye was bruised and swollen shut. She was covered in blood and bruises and too many cuts to count. Her thigh was reopened from Kole's knife and was still slowly dripping blood, but it luckily wasn't as deep as the first time he cut her. I tore off the sleeve of my shirt and wrapped her thigh as best as I could. Then I tended to some of her smaller cuts in silence. Neither of us spoke.

When I was finished, Scottie sank to the ground. I squatted next to her and reached in my pocket for the keys. She stared into my eyes as I tried each one into her shackles until it finally clicked and unlocked.

I did the same to mine before sitting down next to her. She was shivering, despite her panting and sweat glistening off her forehead. I shrugged what remained of my shirt off and wrapped it around her. She opened her mouth to protest, but I stopped her. "You can't stand the cold as well as I can, and you've been beaten for hours and submerged in water. Take it, Scottie."

She nodded weakly, sinking into the warmth of my shirt as she rubbed her raw wrists over her zeroes. The cold wind ripped at my bare chest, but I managed. My only concern was keeping her alive. We were both in terrible shape and wouldn't make it long at this rate. I could feel the Vir Alluse still in my veins from the serum, so teleporting us back was out of the question.

I glanced around the woods, scanning for anything that could help us. Addler was known to have the most greenery, but that was too far away. The area between Kitlarn and Palm was also known for their forests, so that was my best guess as to where we were. We couldn't be more than half a day from the castle, but I couldn't tell if we were even running in the right direction.

I had to keep Scottie moving. I was worried that once she stopped, she wouldn't start again. "Come on, let's go." I ushered her to her feet. I thought she would protest. I knew she was beyond exhausted, but she didn't.

I helped her to her feet and she fell into step next to me as we walked—our bodies couldn't last at the pace we were sprinting before. Neither of us talked, saving our energy and breath.

Scottie's teeth were chattering so hard, I could hear nothing else in the forest. We hadn't had proper food in almost two days. Earlier, we'd stopped by a creek long enough to drink murky water and eat some berries that I knew weren't poisonous, but she needed rest and a fire. And fast.

Scottie's body was starting to shut down. I thought it was damn freezing, and the cold usually never bothered me, but Scottie... her lips were bloodless, her fingers purple. I had to get some warmth into her again.

I finally slowed down as I recognized a small cabin to our left. I remembered it from hunting with Peter and my brother when we were younger. It confirmed my fear that we were heading in the wrong direction. This cabin was north of Kitlarn, but at least I knew where we were now. We weren't lost, but we definitely weren't going to make it back to the castle tonight.

I led her toward the broken door. "Come on. We'll stay here for the night. We need to recover. Once the Alluse leaves my system, I'll teleport us back to the castle."

She nodded, too tired to speak as I shut the door behind us. The wind swept through the cracks in the foundation. It was warmer in the cabin but not by much. The cabin hadn't been stocked or taken care of for quite some time. Once my father learned I would be a rank five, he refused to let us come. The days of doing anything for enjoyment were long over.

Scottie fell to the floor. Her shivering worsened as my shirt fell off her shoulders. Her nightgown was still damp from earlier this morning. Shit. "We have to warm you up."

I carried her toward the small fireplace in the corner of the room. "I'll be right back," I said to her as I went back into the cold to search for firewood and rocks. She didn't look up or respond. I was losing her rapidly.

After hurrying back, I found old blankets in a trunk to the right of the door. I dusted them off before covering her with them. She moaned softly as the blankets engulfed her.

I tried to talk to her as I made a fire. I needed to keep her conscious. "This was an old hunting cabin. Peter and I used to come here as boys, but we haven't been back in years." Her eyelids fluttered. "Scottie, stay with me."

Once the fire started, I positioned her as close to it as I dared. Then I started taking off her wet nightgown.

"What... are... you... doing?" she puffed. Her voice was barely audible. I could see her breath lingering in the air.

"Scottie, whatever is left of your nightgown is soaking wet from your blood and the water from earlier. Your skin is frozen, and you're shivering. I need to warm you up before the cold kills you."

She narrowed her eyes at me but didn't swat my hand away when I reached for her again. I knew she was still uncomfortable with being naked, so I added, "Whatever fabric is left of your nightgown isn't doing anything to hide your body. I already saw everything. The only thing it's doing is making you cold, and the wetness of it will prevent you from warming up. Please, Scotlind."

"Turn... around..." she breathed. "I'll... do it... myself."

Too slowly. Too slowly, she undressed out of her slip. Once she did, I scooped up her clothes and laid them out before the fire to dry. Then I followed suit and pressed my body against her back, throwing the blanket over us both. She gasped, and I thought she would protest but instead settled back into the warmth of my chest.

"What... are... you... doing?" she asked between chattering teeth.

"I'm warming you up with my body heat. You can sleep now, Scotlind. You're safe. Just sleep." I whispered in her ear as I patted her wet, frozen hair. Her hand settled on my arm, and shortly I was listening to the sound of her breathing. I prayed to the Goddess that my words would be true and that she would make it to the morning. I'd never prayed before. I'd never cared or believed in Pylemo. But tonight, I prayed and prayed until my own body gave out and darkness overtook me.

# THIRTY-SIX
## SCOTLIND

I WOKE UP THE NEXT MORNING TO THE *SMELL* OF BURNT
wood. I *heard* the crackling of the fire. I *felt* the heat from the flames. I
screamed, my body not yet registering that I was alive and safe. My
half-conscious self brought me back to my burning childhood home.

"It's okay. You're okay," Sie gently soothed as he reached for me. I
was panting as I focused on the sound of his voice. Vague memories
surfaced—us escaping, running in the woods, a cabin, then warmth. I
glanced around. A dying fire explained the smell. We were in a small
room, lying on a dusty floor, curled up together.

Then I glanced at him. Sie was looking up at me through hooded
eyes, rubbing small soothing circles up and down my arms, careful to
avoid the tender areas that Kole had carved into. I felt his calluses
scrape against my skin. I looked down at myself and screamed again as
I reached for the blanket. We were both completely and utterly naked.

I pushed Sie away from me, but he barely moved as my strength
was spent.

"Good morning to you too, wife," he smiled. He actually smiled at
me, despite everything that had happened the past two nights. He was
so cold and serious on a normal day, but we had just been starved,
tortured, and almost killed, and yet, he smiled at me. It wasn't his

usual smirk or half grin either. I'd never seen him smile at me like that before. It seemed so genuine.

He let out a small grunt as he repositioned himself. "You know, shoving someone is not the nicest way to wake them up. Especially when they just took a beating." Was that a joke? How was he joking about this?

I sat up straighter, clutching the blanket like it was my lifeline. I was suddenly very aware that I had pulled most of the covers off him in the process. His chest and abdomen were now exposed as he sat up with me. The blanket now rested on his lap. He was peppered in dried blood and bruises. Images of Kole's men taking hit after hit on him kept replaying through my mind.

I turned away, unable to look anymore. He could have beaten them up, he could have fought back, but he didn't. He'd let them chain him and put the Alluse around his wrists, making him weak. The cocoon of togetherness we made seemed to vanish now that we weren't in that warehouse and about to die.

"Why did you let them take you? Why didn't you fight them? Why did you do that?" It was the first thing I said.

He let out a low sigh. "We should really go back now. You need to see a healer. I'm strong enough to teleport us now. The Alluse is almost all out of my system."

"No," I stopped him as he was about to get up. What he just said honestly sounded amazing. My entire body throbbed, agony coursing through me with each subtle movement. It felt like acid was pouring down my throat and slowly burning me from the inside out. I needed so many things that the castle would provide—a healer, sleep, food, water—*water*. I didn't let myself think about water right now… of how it almost killed me, of how it saved me, of what I could do with the element.

"Please, just be honest and answer me, Sie." I didn't know if things would change when we got back to the castle. I didn't know if he would don his mask again, and I needed answers. I could work through the unrelenting pain for a little bit longer.

He looked me up and down, slowly taking me in before saying, "If I fought back, I would have really lost. I couldn't let Kole hurt you, not again. If those men did what they wanted... if they did what Fern's vision showed..." He shuddered. "I can't lose you."

"Why? Back at the castle, you treated me like I was nothing. You avoided me in public. So I don't understand. I don't understand you. I didn't think you were going to come." My voice rose as I let out my frustrations. Tears were brimming in my eyes.

I tried to calm my breathing. I knew I couldn't risk yelling. Whoever killed Kole's men was still out there. But I was emotional and pushed past my breaking point and... I was confused.

"I know. I'm sorry for that," he admitted as he sat back down next to me. "I had no choice. I had to be cruel and distant to you. I thought it was the only way."

"You had no choice?" I snapped, then stifled a groan as my head ached from the sudden movement. I said more slowly, "What do you mean you had to? You just had to mess with me, confuse me, kiss me, and get inside my head? Only to then ignore me and watch as your friends completely humiliated me time after time? You just had to let random girls stick their tongues down your throat while I watched?"

He winced at my words. I knew I wasn't being fair or rational. He'd just saved my life, and here I was chastising him, but I couldn't help it. I didn't know why him being with other people seemed to be at the forefront of my issues. Goddess knew I had more pressing matters. We almost died, and yet here I was acting as if I was jealous?

"I had to act like I didn't like you," he said softly. "If they knew how much you really meant to me, they would have done this much sooner or worse. You are my weakness, Scotlind, and now they know that. Alec was testing me that night to see if I cared about you. He was seeing how I would react. He was being a dick, doing all those things to you, because of me. He wanted to get under my skin. Don't you understand that if anyone wants to get to me, the fastest and easiest way to do that is to go through you? I tried my best to keep my distance from you in public, to act like I didn't care about you when people were watching. I tried to do everything I could to not let this happen. To not let last night happen." He pointed between us, gesturing at our wounds and what we had just gone through. "Do you think I wanted to watch Alec humiliate you? Do you think I wanted to sit there and watch him have his way with you?"

"I can see how difficult that was for *you*," I sneered. I didn't know why I wasn't dropping it. Why I *couldn't* drop it.

"Scottie, please," he breathed as he placed his shaking fingers around the sides of my neck, moving closer. My eyes traveled to his throat as it bobbed when he swallowed. "Please. I don't want anything to happen to you. I know what I did wasn't fair or right by you, but I would do it again in a heartbeat if it meant avoiding what happened last night. I would take Alec playing his games over being forced to watch Kole strap you to that table again." He paused before adding, "You need to train."

"I train every day with Peter, or I did before my thigh," I said as I tried to push his hands off my face but failed.

"That's not what I meant. You need to train with your abilities," he said. His face shifted again to his expressionless stare that I couldn't read. His smile faltered. The playful joking moments before were long gone.

"What do you mean?" I said slowly and cautiously as I held up my wrists, exposing the large zeroes that were forever burned into them, branded into me. "I have no abilities."

"You and I both know that isn't true. It will be a lot easier if you stop denying it. I saw everything."

I pulled away from his grasp. His eyes lingered with this hunger for me to tell him the truth. Everything was a blurry daze. I recalled the men ripping my nightgown open, Kole pinning me against the wall and exposing my back. There was no denying it, even if my brain was hardwired by now to do so. But when my back was on display, Sie didn't seem surprised. In fact, he held me against his chest, covering my back as if he already knew about my markings there. "How... how long have you known?" I stuttered as realization dawned on me. "Since when?"

"From the first time we kissed," he said slowly, studying my face. "When you fell, you tore the back of your gown and landed in the water. I saw your back as you ran out of the bathing room."

I crawled backward as his words hit me, not bothering to care that I was still naked, or that I pulled the entire blanket with me. That had happened my first night at the castle. How could I have been so careless? One kiss, and I'd messed up everything I worked so hard to hide my entire life. How many other Advenians saw me as I walked around the halls that night?

"I had a suspicion the moment I met you," he continued. "I knew something was different about you. I just didn't know you were from Lux until that night in the bathing room. You didn't wear Alluse when we met at the banquet and your thoughts were rushing into mine. They were all jumbled and I couldn't piece them together, but I knew you were hiding something. I was intrigued by you. I wanted to know why you trained so hard. I wanted to know what drove you. I wanted to know everything."

"Before we were married." I started as I processed his words. "You knew about me before we were even engaged?"

"Yes."

"Why did you do it then?" I cried, not caring about the tears, not caring that I was now screaming. My pain seemed second to the shock raging in me.

"Do what?" he asked, taken aback by my sudden anger.

"Why did you marry me? If you knew I was Luxian, why did you make me go through with it? Don't you know how dangerous this is for me? For *us* now that we're married? They will kill me when they find out. They can kill you too for just being with me. It's illegal for our kind to mix."

"I won't let that happen. I won't let anyone hurt you," he said slowly.

"It already happened!" I shouted as he winced, but I didn't drop it. "Whoever Kole is working for already knows I'm from Lux. And that's not what I asked. Answer my question, Sie. Why did you marry me? Why did you go through with it?"

He rustled and weaved his fingers through his hair. "Because I'm selfish. Peter told me not to, begged me not to marry you, but I wouldn't listen. I couldn't... I couldn't stand the thought of not being with you. I couldn't stand the thought of you with anyone else. You're intoxicating and different, and I..." He stumbled over his words. "You're the first girl who hasn't thrown herself at me. My entire life, ever since I was little, everyone used me and only wanted to date me or be friends with me because of my title, because they said I would be the future king long before the tournament. You were the first person, the first female, who didn't care about that stuff. You saw me as a person, not a title. It was refreshing and—"

I cut him off, unable to listen anymore. "So you married me, forcing me into this, putting my life at risk just because I didn't throw myself at you? Just because I didn't *want* to marry you?"

"No. That's not what I meant. I just..." he started, then paused. A pained look came over him before he continued, "I love you." He moved closer, inching forward on his knees until they were touching mine. "I truly, deeply love you, Scotlind. I don't know why. I don't know how to explain it, but I couldn't let you go. And for that, I'm sorry."

"I'm going to die because of you," I muttered into his chest as my sobs took over. He pulled me closer to him, and I let him as he ran his fingers through my matted hair.

"No, you won't. I promise," he said, but it seemed like he was trying to convince himself more than me. We both knew that someone out there had the knowledge that I was Luxian. Whoever Kole was working for now knew about me too.

———

IT TOOK MULTIPLE JUMPS, but once we were close to the castle, Sie teleported us right into our room. Peter was already waiting for us, along with a healer. Sie told me that he had used his telepathy to explain everything to Peter once we got in close range of the grounds. I could tell using his abilities was taxing on him, the Alluse injection wasn't entirely out of his system. His face was drained of color, and beads of sweat had formed on his forehead by the time we stumbled into the room.

Sie looked at the healer. "Heal her first." He walked away before the healer could respond. I strained to listen from the sofa as Sie and Peter spoke softly.

The healer worked on me, scanning my body for cuts and bruises, allowing them to heal faster as that strange blue light radiated from her fingertips. I recognized her from the first time Kole attacked me. The only difference between now and then was that there was more of me to heal. She didn't waiver. Even as her hands shook with the effort, she kept healing.

When she started to restitch my thigh, I asked, "What's your name?" I needed a distraction. Not from the pain of the needle, my body was oozing in agony already, but from my thoughts, and I realized I'd never asked her before.

Her beautiful, coral eyes locked onto me. They were the deepest pink I ever saw with small specks of gold so tiny that I wouldn't have noticed it if I wasn't gawking at them. She was breathtaking. Her black, coily curls were tied up in a high bun, showing off every detail of her rich skin. Three large freckles rested on the center of her cheek like a triangle that I couldn't tear my eyes away from. "I'm Molilyn," she said sweetly, "but everyone calls me Moli."

"Thank you, Moli, for helping us."

She paused from her healing, her blue light fading back into her as she looked me over. "It is my pleasure, princess." Beads of sweat rolled down her beautiful face and were slowly drenching her healer's uniform. A golden sun was etched onto the fabric between her breasts, indicating that she was from Lux and here by a visa. Looking into her gaze, I would have known even without the symbol of Light that she was from my home island. Her eyes reminded me of a setting sun, so low in the sky that the colors of gold and pink took over its descent. I hated that Tennebris didn't have sunsets, that I could only see them through pictures in a book.

"Scottie. Please call me Scottie." I smiled as Peter made his way over to me with food—bread, fruit, pastries, and eggs. My mouth watered as I filled my stomach with as much of it as I could.

Sie walked into the bathing room shortly after eating. I assumed to bathe and wash off the blood. Once he re-emerged with wet hair and mostly clean skin, he ordered me to do the same.

Sie barely sat for ten minutes with the healer before walking out of the room. He only had her heal crucial injuries and his superficial wounds. Enough to appear that he wasn't injured underneath his clothes.

"Where is he going?" I asked Peter. I instinctively reached up to clutch my necklace, but my hands came up bare, remembering that Kole took it off of me.

Peter looked over in the direction Sie had left. "Just wash, Scotlind. You will find out soon enough." I didn't have the energy to fight back or ask more questions. I realized that I trusted them, both of them, so I did as he said.

The walk to the bathing room wasn't as bad as I thought it would be. I was surprised at the extent to which Moli had healed me. I barely limped as I opened the door.

But then I saw it. I vomited three times before glancing at the tub. I couldn't do it. I couldn't get in it. I kept thinking about Kole pushing my head against the tile, holding me there. I could feel his chest vibrate against my back as he laughed while I struggled. My body felt chilled from the coldness of the water. I heard Sie's muffled shouts. A burning rose in my chest as I started hyperventilating.

No. I couldn't get in. Even though I knew now that it wouldn't kill me. *Water couldn't kill me.* There was something about the tub itself I couldn't face yet. I asked Moli to wet some washcloths for me and bathed the best I could after she left.

I'd almost gotten all the blood and grime off of me by the time Sie cracked the door open and stepped inside. I tried to cover myself with the fabric I was holding, but Sie didn't seem to notice.

He glanced from me to the empty tub. I was sitting furthest from it on the other side of the room, doing a terrible job of a cloth bath. He didn't say anything about why I hadn't gotten in it, or why I could barely look at it. His eyes drifted back to mine as he said, "We have to leave."

"Leave to go where?" I asked as I quickly grabbed fresh clothes to change into.

He smiled lightly, but it didn't quite reach his eyes. "I believe I owe you a honeymoon."

# THIRTY-SEVEN
## SCOTLIND

Sie must have teleported us thirty times before we reached our destination. I swayed on my feet when he finally set me down on the ground, my vision still blurry from the dizzying world that flew by from the speed we were traveling. I made it all of two jumps before my stomach threatened to spill the remainder of the food Peter gave me, and I had to clamp my eyes shut the rest of the time. I was still too scared to open them as my knees wobbled and I tried to steady myself. A wave of nausea ran through me as my stomach was in a constant flutter.

"That feeling is normal," Sie said. "It used to take Peter an hour before he felt okay after a teleport. Now he refuses to come with me when I jump."

I nodded my head, unable to muster a conversation, too worried I would vomit. Taking a few steady breaths, I finally willed my eyes to open. I gasped as I looked around.

I'd never seen anything so beautiful. A massive lake stretched before me with white glaciers settled in the back. A fog was floating above the surface, but underneath it, the water was unmoving. A few birds chirped from within the shield, an echoing song, letting me know I was alive. I survived. I hadn't truly let myself believe it yet.

My toes curled into the rocky ground. Small pebbles and stones ran from the woods at our backs to the edge of the water, a long wooden dock stretching between them. I inhaled deeply, letting the woody scent linger in my lungs. It was so refreshing after being locked in that cell—after only smelling blood and sweat.

Other than an occasional chirping, we were alone.

"What are we really doing here?" I asked Sie as he started to set up a camp with a makeshift fire and tent. One tent. I didn't know what a honeymoon was, but I had the feeling he'd made it up.

"It's not safe right now for you in the castle," he said as he continued his tasks. "Whoever killed those men knows about you, knows *what* you are. We have to figure out who they are before they come out with the information they've learned."

"So you think camping by a lake is magically going to give us the answers we need and let us know who Kole was working for?"

He laughed gently. "No. Peter is going undercover to figure it out. In the meantime, I want you where I know it's safe. We weren't seen at the castle yet. The Council believes that we are on a honeymoon. Whoever Kole is working for either thinks we're dead or still lost in the woods. It gives us an advantage. It gives us time. They won't do anything with the information until it works in their favor. If they can't find you, they can't do anything. That is, if they aren't already a member of the High Council. And if they are, it's best for us to keep our distance while we're still healing and weak." He stopped what he was doing with the tent and looked up at me. The sun glinted in his dark eyes, making the inner edges appear lighter. "I also thought it would be a good idea for you to *really* train. Do you know what your abilities are?"

I shook my head.

"I thought so," he said. "It's time you figured it out. Whoever is behind this isn't going to stop. They could attack you again, and I want you to be as strong as you can be. I want you to be ready so this doesn't happen again."

"I don't even know where to begin," I admitted.

"I know. That's why I'm here to help you in whatever way I can.

We'll figure it out together. But you do have abilities, Scotlind. You wouldn't have survived in the water if you didn't. And your back is enough proof of that. A true nix wouldn't have markings."

"Well, they might not be fighting abilities," I paused. "I could breathe under the water when I opened my mouth. It felt the same as breathing in air. What if that's all I have?"

He gave me a wicked grin. "Don't you want to find out?"

And I did, I realized. I wanted to know that answer my entire life, and now Sie was giving me the opportunity.

———

THE NEXT TWO days were torture. It was a whole new level of embarrassment. Sie had me trying every element of Lux to see what abilities I *might* possess. I failed at every single one. The only thing we knew for sure was that I could breathe underwater. Which I hated, absolutely hated doing as Sie made me go into the freezing lake and instructed me to stay under the surface until I couldn't anymore. His reasoning was to test how long my reserves would last. He explained that every Advenian had an ending point to their abilities, that they could only use their powers for so long before they needed to rest and replenish.

I gave up after two horribly long hours of straight-up shivering underwater. But at least it wasn't a confined tub. The open lake didn't feel constricting. As long as I didn't see the bottom, the memories of that night with Kole didn't surface. So I swam to the middle of the glistening water and submerged myself.

Once I dried off, Sie made me try to summon water out of thin air. He had me trying to create a force shield around us to see if I was an air user. I tried to shift the wind, grow a flower, move the dirt. Nothing happened. The only thing we knew was that I wasn't an Alluse user since Sie could use his abilities around me.

The worst exercise was on the first night. He made me stand in front of the empty fire pit for *four* hours, trying to get me to summon flames. I didn't tell him that even if I had fire abilities, I would never use them.

"This is stupid," I said. "I've been staring at these dumb logs for hours, and nothing is happening other than me freezing my butt off. Can't you just start it?"

"Keep trying," he smiled.

On the second day, after hours of pointless training that amounted to nothing, we finally sat down by the fire to rest, one that he'd started the old fashioned way. The sky was so clear, there weren't any clouds above the shield. It made me wonder how Miles and his team were doing with their research. What else was out there? Could we really go back to our home planet one day?

Sie was quietly sitting with his head tilted up. He must have noticed me staring at him because he asked, "What are you thinking about?"

I couldn't bring myself to ask the question that had been on my mind since we were captured, so instead, I said, "You told me that Peter is undercover trying to figure out who is behind all of this?"

"Yes."

"How? How is he doing it without putting himself in danger or getting caught?" I asked, feeling guilty that it was the first time I'd thought about my blonde-haired friend. He was putting himself at risk for me, and I was just camping and utterly failing at my abilities.

Sie frowned before saying, "Do you not know Peter's abilities?"

I shook my head, again mad at myself for not knowing much about Peter. Peter, who was my friend, probably my only friend at the castle. Peter always tried to distract me from court life, but we rarely talked about him, and we definitely never talked about his abilities. He'd never brought it up, and I never bothered to ask.

Sie continued, "Well, let's just say Peter's abilities make it very easy for him to be where he isn't supposed to be and do what he needs to do."

I tried to wrap my brain around it to figure out what that meant. The only ability I could think of was using invisibility, but that was a trait only Luxian air users had. I frowned, clearly puzzled. "Can't you just tell me what they are?"

"It's not my story to tell. You'll have to ask Peter yourself."

"And when will that be?" I asked, trying to figure out how long he was planning on keeping me at the lake. I liked it here, especially after what had happened. It was nice to be away from the castle, but I couldn't shake the feeling that we were running. I hated it even more, knowing my friend was out there putting himself at risk while I was doing nothing.

"We will be here until Peter figures out who is behind this or until you figure out what your abilities are."

I frowned. "That could take forever."

Sie laughed. "From what I've seen from you, yes. On your part, it could take forever but don't underestimate Peter's abilities."

"Don't you think King Lunder and the High Council will find it suspicious that we're gone for so long?"

Sie looked at me sideways. "Don't worry about that."

I got a bad feeling about what they thought we were doing. "Why? What did you tell them?"

"Are you sure you want to know?" When I nodded he said hesitantly, "They think we are occupied because of the blood bond."

The blood bond.

I'd wanted to ask him about the bond ever since we were forced to make it, but every time I mustered the courage to ask, nothing left my mouth. Kole said that it forced Sie's feelings for me, that Sie only came for me because of the bond, and part of me was scared to find out the truth.

I took a deep breath before asking, "What is the blood bond?"

Sie ran his fingers through his hair, leaving it tousled and messy in the front.

"Please, just be honest with me," I added when he didn't answer.

He blew out a breath. "Okay. Do you remember when we had to cut our palms at our wedding, and we drank each other's blood? Then they wrapped our hands together and bound them?" I nodded. How could I forget? I looked down at my palm. It was now scabbed over from where Sie had dragged the blade. How was that only a few days ago?

Sie continued, "What they did, it's called a blood bond. It connects two people on a different, deeper level. It doesn't always take, though. You have to be compatible with whom you are forming the bond with. It's rare for someone to find their bond mate. But if it takes, your souls will be connected and intertwined for life."

"Is it not a common thing to do?" I asked because I hadn't heard of it before. It wasn't something they taught us at LakeWood.

"No," he answered tightly. "It used to be common back when our kind lived on Allium, but it's rarely done anymore. I was really surprised they had us do it. It wasn't supposed to be part of the ceremony, but I couldn't say anything to stop it without making it obvious."

"You said it connects people on a different level? What do you mean by that? I don't feel any differently toward you, I mean."

"I know. It's because we didn't finish the bond," he looked down at his hands before adding, "The bond worked. At least I think it did. Two souls have to be aligned for the bond to take. In the past, couples broke up over it if it didn't take. For males, we feel it first. I can feel it, feel you, I think. Whenever I'm around you, and your necklace is off, it's like my powers are amplified. I've never felt that way with anyone before. It's like you make me stronger." I swallowed, listening to him speak. "But in order for the bond to last, you have to accept it."

"Me? How do I accept it?" I asked.

He didn't answer for a long time. Then, "We have to have sex."

Oh—OH.

"They thought we did," Sie continued. "I think that's why Synder and his men stood outside our room that night. They wanted to make sure the blood bond worked. That's why Kole thought I went to you in the warehouse—because of the bond. Because if we were blood bonded, we would feel each other's pain. Legend claims that a bonded pair feels each other's heightened emotions, until one of them is dead. I wouldn't have had a choice but to come for you. He was banking on me saving you because of that. I don't know why yet. I've been trying to figure it out, to figure out what they are planning. Why the blood bond was important. Was it really only to lure me out to the warehouse, or is there more to it?" He threw a rock in the fire. "But we don't have to. We can let the bond fade."

"It will fade?"

"Yes. If we don't..." he started and cleared his throat. "I don't know how long we have until it fades, but we have to complete the bond with each other's blood in our systems."

"What will the bond do if we have it? If we don't let it fade, I mean. You said your mind abilities are stronger with me, would that go both ways?"

He turned to face me, and my cheeks heated, thinking about what we would have to do to complete the bond. I looked at the fire, hoping he wouldn't notice.

"I don't know much about the blood bond, but if my abilities are stronger with you, I would think that it could make your Luxian abilities stronger too. Which is why you need to learn and understand them so you can control them. If we complete the bond and you don't know what you possess, your powers might manifest without you even meaning to use them."

My mind whirled. If that happened, if the bond made my powers stronger, but unpredictable, I could give away to anyone around me that I was from Lux. Was that why he was trying to get me to figure out my powers? Did he not want to sleep with me until I did? Did he even want the bond?

I swallowed as he continued, "But the bond would also link us together. It connects two people, and once it's formed, it's permanent. Rumor claims that the sense of each other's safety and feeling one's heightened emotions occur even thousands of miles away. I'm not entirely sure how true that is, but there are written documents of bonded couples being able to communicate with each other in their minds within close proximity. Just like my telepathy allows us to. Some say bonded pairs don't have to have mind abilities to do it. But in truth, no one knows entirely what the bond does. It's been a practice that hasn't been used in centuries."

"Do you want the bond? Do you want to accept it?" I asked.

He shook his head no almost immediately. I tried not to look offended. "I don't want to force you to do anything you don't want to do, Scottie. The bond would make it easier for me to protect you, but we don't need it. We can let it fade. Besides, the High Council wanted us to be bonded, maybe it's part of their plan, and we will have the advantage of them thinking we are when we aren't."

"I still don't get why they would think that we would be preoccupied with the blood bond, though. Do they think we want to get away from everyone just to talk to each other in our own heads? Why is that a good reason for us to be gone?"

Sie spit out the water he was sipping on and coughed hoarsely as he tried to recover. Once he composed himself, he glanced over at me and cleared his throat before saying, "If the blood bond was activated and if it took, the two people generally wouldn't be able to keep their hands off each other for *a while*. It's just as much a physical reaction as it is mental."

I felt the heat rush to my neck and cheeks. Not knowing what else to do, I grabbed for the water and took a long sip to distract myself.

"So you told everyone in the castle that you are taking me away to basically have sex with me over and over again?" And then another thought hit me. "And everyone believed that?"

Sie shifted uncomfortably in his seat. "Well, after they thought we destroyed our bedroom the first night, it didn't take much convincing when I told them that if they wanted their castle still standing, it would be best for us to go away for a little bit."

My mouth dropped open before anger took over me. "You weren't going to tell me about this, were you? You were going to let the entire castle think we're on some sort of sick fucking spree while you kept me in the dark?" I gritted my teeth, trying my best to keep my hands at my side and not smack him across the face.

"Fucking spree?" he laughed but stopped once he realized how seriously furious I was. "I wasn't planning on telling you because I didn't want you to feel pressured. I didn't want you to think that you had to sleep with me. It's not a big deal, Scotlind." Then he got up from his seat and walked over to the edge of the lake.

Our wedding was only a couple of days ago, but it felt like a lifetime ago. So much had happened since then. I didn't know how long our blood would stay in each other's systems, but if Sie felt his telepathy stronger with me... I swallowed as I realized that we still had some time to complete the bond if we wanted to, and now I was alone with him in the middle of nowhere.

"Who do you think Kole is working for?" I asked Sie, not wanting to discuss the blood bond any further.

Sie walked back over to the fire to sit down next to me. "It has to be someone of power to be able to get Kole released from the dungeons earlier and to give him an arsenal of men and weapons. I think it's someone from the High Council. The problem is figuring out how many."

"Do you think it's Synder Phillips?" I asked.

"Possibly. That's what Peter thinks, and what he is trying to find out now," he sighed. "But we need proof. I also think it's bigger than just Tennebris."

"What do you mean?"

"The night Kole first attacked you, I beat him up badly. Then afterward, when you were with Peter, I went back to the dungeons." He looked into the fire. The expression on his face seemed remorseful. "I did things to him that I'm not proud of. I was furious with what he'd done to you and desperately tried to figure out who he was working for. I tortured him all night, and it wasn't pretty."

I shuddered. Kole mentioned Sie coming to his dungeon cell, but I didn't know the details. If it was anything like what Kole had done to us, I knew it was awful. It made sense why Kole was so set on vengeance. He never liked me to begin with, but if Sie did all that—

"Kole shouldn't have been able to stand for months after what I did to him. I know some time had passed since that night, but..." He stopped. Swallowed. "Hell, I don't even know if he should have still been alive, but yet..."

I finished for him, "He was fine." Kole didn't have a scratch on him when I was still limping from the one cut he gave me that same night.

"Exactly," Sie continued. "The only people who possess that kind of healing are from Lux. And they have to be extremely powerful healers. Most of the Luxian healers that Tennebris has access to can just speed up the process of healing like Moli. But powerful ones who reside in Lux have such strong abilities that they can completely heal your wounds. On top of that, Kole also had Alluse. Complete Alluse like the necklace I gave you is hard to come by, but Vir and Sui Alluse..." Sie shuddered. "I think whoever in the castle is facilitating this has the support from the Advenians of Lux, if not the Lux King himself."

I swallowed the lump in my throat as he went on. "There is someone at the castle who knows about you now. Who knows you are from Lux, and yet, they let us go. They let us live that night. We just walked out of the warehouse. You saw the mess. Kole's men were brutalized. We shouldn't have survived, Scotlind. The question is why and when they plan to use that knowledge. It's only a matter of time before someone else discovers what you are, and it's going to be hard to keep that a secret." He paused. "It's going to be hard to protect you."

Suddenly his insistence on training made sense.

"Do you think Kole is alive?" I asked. We'd left the warehouse in such a rush, but I didn't remember seeing his body among the dead.

"I do. I scanned the warehouse. He wasn't there. I need you to tell me everything, Scottie. Tell me everything about how you got here and what you know. Why are you Luxian and living in Tennebris?"

I looked at Sie, and for the first time since I came here eleven years ago, I spoke about my past. The normal urge to swallow everything back was gone and I told him everything—from the little bit I remembered of Lux, the night those strange males came into my room, to waking up on the black-sanded beach. I told him about the lies they told me about my parents dying in a fire. I told him about how I kept this a secret and never told anyone about it except the one counselor who threatened me. I told him about my time at LakeWood, why I chose the guard, and how everyone called me a nix. I told him about my past with Kole and how he'd always despised me, how he'd compelled me to do awful things. I told him everything up until how I ended up here with him.

Sie didn't interrupt me once. He let me get everything out, listening intently. When I finished, I let out a ragged breath I didn't realize I'd been holding. It felt like a weight was lifted off my shoulders, finally letting all my secrets out and no longer keeping them buried.

I didn't notice the tears slipping down my cheeks until Sie gently wiped them away. "You never told anyone that?" he asked hesitantly. "Not even Miles or Vallie?"

I shook my head. "No one. You're the only person I ever told that to. After the counselor threatened me with treason when I first came here, I never dared to speak of it. And anytime I thought about telling Vallie, I could never get the words out."

"I'm sorry. I'm sorry you went through all this, and I'm sorry for my part in your suffering," he whispered, still holding my face in his strong hands. I felt the tip of his thumb brush against my lower lip, our breaths intertwining as one.

I felt free for the first time without having to be alone. Free to share my true self with someone. Free to have someone know everything about me and not run. To have someone I could trust with my secrets and not have to shoulder my burdens alone. So I smiled at Sie as I leaned into him. I swore I heard his breath hitch as he stopped breathing. He went wholly still as I pressed my lips against his.

# THIRTY-EIGHT
## SIE

Holy shit. Scottie was fucking kissing me. I wasn't expecting her to. I wasn't expecting her to even talk to me again or forgive me after hearing her story and how much she'd suffered. How alone and afraid she had been her entire life. And how my selfish need to be with her only made things a whole hell of a lot worse.

Her lips were so full and soft against mine as she hesitantly moved them, pressing further into me. I leaned in and tasted the salt from her tears that had escaped down her cheeks while she was talking. I told myself to calm down, to let her lead this. I didn't want to initiate anything that she would regret later. I didn't want her to form the bond, only to realize that she didn't want it. I wouldn't be able to live with myself if she was tethered to me and hated it. I wanted her to want the bond—to want me.

But fuck.

The way she moved, the sound she made as she moaned into my mouth. I couldn't help it. I cupped my hands around her neck and pulled her further into me, deepening the kiss. I couldn't get enough of her. I had to feel her breath and her very soul against mine. I'd never felt so alive. So drawn to one person.

I knew the blood bond was working against me, making it hard to resist her. At least that was what I blamed it on as my desire for her grew. I wanted more than just a kiss. The past two nights with her were testing my patience. I had to take many, many cold swims in the lake to calm myself.

Everything she did pushed me over the edge, even her bending over to tend to the soil while she was practicing ground abilities sent my insides roaring, wanting me to take her then and there. But now... Now she was kissing me and moaning my fucking name. Her hand pressed against my chest. The other hovered over my lower abdomen, then lower.

I knew she would have to be the one to pull away.

———

THE NEXT MORNING, I woke up to Scottie curled up on my side of the tent. The tent was just large enough that it could fit two bedrolls. But she'd moved around in her sleep, and I didn't stop her as she made her way closer and closer to me.

I told myself that it was the warmth she was clinging to as the air had dropped twenty degrees overnight, sending chills throughout our makeshift camp.

"It's time to get up, Scotlind," I said gently. I was thankful that she hadn't woken up screaming with more nightmares like she did that first night in the cabin. After hearing her story last night, I started to understand some of what haunted her. Peter warned me about her nightmares when I forced him to give me updates on her. He would say that most nights, she woke up screaming and drenched in sweat.

I watched every detail of her as her eyelids slowly fluttered open. Her sapphire irises were blinding, and all I could do was focus on the color as it swirled like the lake just outside. Scottie stretched her arms over her head, letting out a little yawn. She had done this since we arrived at the lake, and I'd come to look forward to it, wanting to watch her small morning routine as she adjusted to the sun.

I wished for a different life for her. One where she could wake up this way every morning. One where her past didn't chase her while she slept. She was so damn beautiful and serene when she was at peace, and I hated myself for playing a role in her terror.

She noticed that she had gravitated toward me again and gave me a small smile before mumbling sorry and shifted back to her bedroll.

"Come on," I said as I opened the flaps of the tent. "We're going for a swim this morning."

"What?" she snapped as she followed me out. "I'm not getting in that water again. It's freezing!"

"We can start a fire and warm up afterward, but we are doing this."

"And why is it so important that we freeze our butts off in the middle of the lake? That doesn't sound like fun to me. I don't care if I never find out how long I can hold my breath. And I can practice attempting to control the water from the dock, thank you very much."

"I want to look at your markings to see if they can give us any indications to what abilities you have. Generally, Tennebris' golden markings are just swirls and spirals that cover our bodies. They have no meaning, but according to my studies, some of Lux's markings actually indicate their ability."

She thought about it for a moment as she shifted on her feet. She looked so damn cute as she bit her bottom lip and stared at the lake with dread. "Fine. You can look at my back, but I'm not staying in that water a minute longer than I have to."

I didn't know what all the symbols of Lux meant, but Peter was going to try to find old texts from Allium to see if there was any information on her markings. If I could trace and memorize her back, we could later compare them to what was in the books. Maybe it would give us more insight into what she might possess.

Stripping down until I was in only my trousers, I smirked as I noticed Scottie staring at me, but I pretended not to notice. Let her look. I jumped into the water without thinking twice about it and tried my best not to make a damn sound as the water instantly numbed my skin. Shit. It really was freezing. The constant sun did nothing to demolish the frigidness.

Scottie was still standing at the edge of the lake with her clothes on. "Scotlind, it's cold in here. I don't want to freeze my balls off while you just stand there and gawk at my body. Get in here."

Her cheeks turned pink as she gnawed on her lower lip some more. "Absolutely not. I am not getting undressed and going into the lake with you." Her hands went up to her now empty throat. I couldn't find her necklace when we had escaped that morning, and I could tell that not feeling protected bothered her. I had ordered Peter to see if he could find a necklace with Sui Alluse, so she could still practice her abilities while being protected at the same time. I didn't want to tell her about it, though, and give her false hope. I'd already sent Peter out to do way more than was physically possible for one person.

"Come on, Scottie. What do you think is going to happen? I just want to look at your markings." I would have thought that after last night she would have warmed up to the idea of being more uninhibited around me. We'd kissed for a damn long time. I had willed myself to not go further unless she initiated it. But then I couldn't take it anymore. I needed more. As soon as I had picked her up and carried her into the tent, she became shy and awkwardly pretended to fall asleep which left me with fucking blue balls and an uncomfortable as shit night of sleep.

Neither of us said anything about the kiss she'd given me. I didn't want to pressure her to complete the bond, so I did my best to hold back. I knew if I started it, I wouldn't be able to stop. But damn, she was really testing me.

"I hate you," she grumbled. "And I don't care what happens to your balls." She was feisty this morning. I couldn't help but grin as she added, "Turn around."

I saw her naked three days ago in the cabin. Hell, I hadn't just seen. I had held her naked and felt every inch of her skin on me, but I decided against bringing that up as I turned around and gave her privacy. It was probably best for my sake to not look at her anyway. There would be no way I could hide how I felt around her with only my trousers on.

I waited until I heard the splash before turning toward her. And holy fuck, I was thankful for the cold water as I took in the sight of her. She was made for the water. The blue of it reflected and enhanced her features. The water rolling down her arms glistened, making her olive skin shine through her freckles. And her eyes—they were breathtaking.

She screamed. "Sie, are you crazy? This is freezing!" She shivered, her teeth chattering a mile a minute as she wrapped her hands over her arms and started wading closer to me.

"I forgot Luxians have weaker skin and the cold bothers you more," I teased.

She laughed and rolled her eyes at me. "Just hurry up, please," she begged through chattering teeth.

"Turn around," I ordered. We weren't deep in the lake, so the water lapped around my hips, but Scottie was much smaller than me. The water rested just below her chest, blocking most of her markings from view. I pushed her long hair in front of her shoulders as I scanned her back, trying to focus on the markings and not the softness of her skin. My fingers trailed up some of the black inky designs before I unclasped her top undergarment.

"What are you doing?" she snapped, whipping her head to look at me while clutching her breasts.

"It's blocking my view," I replied matter-of-factly. "I want to look at all your markings. You will get it back in a minute." And then I entered her mind, sending images of what I saw to her, allowing her to look at her back markings just as I saw them. Her mind was wide open for me, so I did my best not to go to her thoughts, keeping myself void, and only focusing on the task at hand. But it was really fucking tempting to push further, to figure out why she stopped kissing me so suddenly last night, why she pretended to fall asleep, to know exactly how standing here made *her* feel.

"The water is too deep. The bottom half of your markings are cut off," I said as I looked down at where the water hit her back. I wrapped my hands around her waist, lifting her up so her entire back was now exposed. She let out a small yelp as the chilly air hit her but stopped protesting as we both focused on the images of her back. I could hear her breath quicken as my hands tightened around her hips.

"Am I interrupting?" a familiar voice laughed from the distance. I set Scottie down immediately as she grabbed her bra out of my hand, ducking into the water to hide herself from Peter.

"We'll be right there," I yelled over to him and then looked at Scottie.

She was giving me the death stare. "You didn't think to warn me that he was coming?" she bristled.

"I thought he wouldn't be here until later." I shrugged, then started walking out of the lake before she could protest.

Once we were all dressed, we sat in front of the fire. Scottie dragged one of the blankets out to wrap around herself. She was still shivering but sat slightly further from the flames than Peter and I did.

"It seems like I got the wrong end of this deal," Peter finally said, breaking the awkward silence. "I'm out here dealing with a bunch of disgusting old males from the High Council and rusty ancient books, while Sie gets to swim naked with Scottie." He grinned at her. I wanted to smack him for that comment. There would be no way of getting her back into the water now.

Scottie turned bright red as she pulled the blanket up higher on her neck. I was surprised when she spoke before I did. "Shut up, Peter. We were doing research."

"Right. Research. Researching what? The opposite sex? Sie, I didn't know you needed help in that department." Peter was cut off by the slap Scottie threw across his face. I couldn't help but laugh. Peter grinned at her as he rubbed his cheek. "Ow. I haven't seen you in almost a week, and that's how you greet me? No hug? No heartfelt hello? Just a slap across my pretty face?"

"Did you find it?" I asked, bringing the attention back to why he was actually here. Peter reached into his pack and pulled out an ancient leather-bound book.

"Here." He smiled as he chucked the book at me, causing dusk to fly off the edges. "This was the only one they had in Addler. There were none in Palm. I checked their library first."

"What is it?" Scottie asked as she watched me open the book and flip through the pages.

"It's a book on Lux. It has information regarding their powers and markings. We thought it might be helpful in figuring out your abilities," Peter said.

"A book about Lux? But how did you get it?" Scottie asked Peter, her eyes flaring wide.

Peter shrugged. "It was in the restricted section in the library in Addler."

"What are your abilities?" she asked suddenly.

It was weird seeing them interact together. I knew they had grown really close and had become friends, but I was never around to watch it firsthand. I tried to distract myself in the pages of the book and not pay attention to them.

"Well, well, well, Scottie. Why so curious all of a sudden?"

She narrowed her eyes at him as she stuck out her tongue. Such playful banter they had. Their relationship seemed easygoing and care-free. I couldn't help but be jealous of Peter.

"Hmm. I would rather not tell you."

"What?" Scottie practically yelled as she grabbed his upper arm and shook him. "That is not fair. You have to tell me!"

Peter smiled, exposing both of his dimples. "I'll make you a deal, Scottie. Figure out what your powers are first. Then I will show you mine."

"Show me?"

"Yeah," he grinned. "It will be more fun to show you than just tell you."

I interrupted the two of them. "Here, look," I said as I pointed to the page I had opened. "This says that Luxian markings typically have meanings behind their symbols. It has some examples, but pages are missing once it gets to the rare abilities, almost as if someone wanted to keep those powers hidden." I held up the book for them to see. Flames symbolized fire. Waves were water. Wings were air. Ground users were the only elemental ability that seemed to be depicted over multiple designs. Mountains, trees, and flowers were all used inter-changeably.

"So you think Scottie has a rare ability? One that they don't want to keep in the books?" Peter asked as Scottie paled.

"Possibly. Scottie, your markings are unique. It has pieces of every-thing in it. You have symbols for fire, water, air, ground, healing, and other ones I can't recognize, all over your back." I flashed the images of Scottie's wet back from the lake into Peter's mind, so he could see what we were talking about. He nodded as he took it in.

Her upper back had two beautiful feathered wings entwined in flowers that spread across her shoulder blades. One wing was dripping in water while the other had feathers burning to ash. Straight down the center of the wings was a large trunk covered in thick bark, sepa-rating the two sides. Then scattered throughout, I noticed the healer's cross and the blade for Alluse. More water designs were painted up her sides mixed with other symbols that I didn't recognize.

"Do you think she possesses all the Luxian abilities then?" Peter asked as he took in all the symbols scattered across her back.

"No. I don't think so. We have been trying to get her to summon any of Lux's elements, but she can't. It has to mean something else. Plus, she has the symbol of Alluse here," I said as I showed both of them telepathically her lower right portion of her back. "And we know she doesn't have Alluse. If she did, no one would be able to use their abilities on her." I tried to wrap my brain around it. "We need these missing pages, or we need to break into Lux's official records."

"Lux has official records of their powers?" Scottie asked, still pale as she processed everything.

I nodded my head. "Just like we do. Both of our kingdoms record everything. We have records of the first Tennebris Advenians dated years and years ago. They go all the way back to when we were on Allium. The problem is, they are restricted. Even Peter would struggle to get past the ability wards in place. And getting into Lux's would be impossible."

"Not impossible," Peter said. "You know I can do it."

"No," I shot back. "I'm not risking you for that. Let's keep looking. Maybe we can find the missing pages first, and in the meantime

Scottie will keep practicing. We will try to do this without Lux's records. I'm not sending you to Lux."

They both nodded at me, at the authority in my tone. I knew Peter wouldn't question it, even if he wasn't happy about it. I couldn't send him to Lux. I wouldn't risk him, not yet anyway. "Were you able to get the other item I requested?" I asked him. I didn't want to flat out say the Sui Alluse necklace in front of Scottie in case he didn't have it.

"Yes," Peter smiled as he reached into his pack and pulled out a long golden necklace. The chain was similar to the one before, but the pendant was a rectangular crystal, a beautiful shade of sapphire that matched her eyes. He held it out to Scottie as she swallowed. Her eyes went wide as she took the necklace with shaky hands. "It's Sui Alluse so you can keep practicing your abilities while being protected from anyone using their powers on you. It will act as a shield."

"Thank you," she whispered.

"Any news regarding the other thing you were working on?" I asked Peter as Scottie clasped the necklace around her neck.

"Yes," he said through gritted teeth. "But you aren't going to like it."

# THIRTY-NINE

# SCOTLIND

I looked between Peter and Sie from across the fire, wrapping my blanket tighter around me, bracing myself for the news Peter had discovered. Peter's gaze was unwavering on Sie as he said, "Your father is back. Apparently, Synder begged him to rejoin the High Council, and he accepted the position as commander of the Guard."

Sie's jaw clenched as his teeth ground together. He hated his father. I'd gathered that much from the night I spent at his house, and I could see why.

"You know your father's opinions of the ranking system," Peter continued in the most polite way he could without bashing me. "And you know his feelings about Scottie. I think we would be stupid to write this off as a coincidence. I think you both might need to come back to the castle, and soon."

"Okay. Follow him and track his whereabouts," Sie replied, not meeting either of our gazes. He instead stared at the lake's white glaciers in the distance. "Did you make any headway on the High Council itself?"

"Nothing concrete yet. Other than Synder reaching out to your father, no changes have been made. Braven and Synder have met twice this week, unofficially." I must have looked confused because Peter clarified, "Braven is Alec's father." Then he turned back to Sie. "I have been tracking their movements but still have not been able to infiltrate their meetings. Their next one is tonight, though, and I plan to be present."

"Good," Sie said, standing up. As if that was some indication for Peter to leave, he rose as well. "Scottie and I will stay an extra day. See if she can practice any more, and I'll read through the book. I don't want to risk bringing it into the castle. We'll return tomorrow night."

Peter nodded and went to leave. I quickly glanced at Sie before I shrugged off my blanket and ran after my friend. "Peter, wait." He was at the edge of the camp, about to enter the woods, when he halted and turned toward me. "No, goodbye?"

He smiled. "You're only going to be away from me for one more day and you can't help but miss me? I'm seriously flattered."

"Stop messing around. I'm serious. What are you doing to find this information out? Is it… dangerous?" I asked him, unable to meet his gaze.

"Only if I get caught. I'll be fine, Scottie. I'm good at what I do."

"Right, and you won't even tell me what that is yet. I don't understand why you have to keep your ability a secret from me." I crossed my arms over my chest, and he laughed lightly.

"I told you that I would make you a deal. I'll show you mine when you show me yours."

I frowned at him. "That's not fair. I don't even know what my ability is."

"Then all the more reason for you to work hard to figure it out. But I think swimming naked isn't going to get you any closer to finding it," he said with his glistening smile. I was about to shove him and refute that we weren't skinny dipping when he added, "For now, stay with Sie, and you'll be safe."

"I hate this. Feeling weak. Feeling like I need someone to watch over me while you go off and do what I should be doing. Instead, I'm just hiding away at some lake to avoid whoever is trying to use or kill me."

He looked at me for a moment before saying, "You aren't weak,

Scotlind. You've just never been given the opportunity to grow with your abilities. That's why you are here. You aren't doing nothing. Sie is trying to get you to discover what you can do. With the castle heavily guarded, you won't be able to practice much there. If you can access your powers, it will help protect yourself if you ever need to again. It will also help you hide that you are Luxian if you can learn to control yourself. Think about it. You don't know what you are capable of. What if you were to accidentally use your Luxian ability in front of everyone at the castle? Before, Sie gave you a Complete Alluse necklace, unknowingly preventing you from ever accessing your powers. Now, you have a necklace of Sui Alluse, meaning that your control could slip. We wouldn't be able to protect you if that happened. I know this seems silly, but it's important, Scotlind. You're important."

"I guess." I let out a sigh. Sie said as much to me about controlling my powers.

"You guess? That's it? What about, 'you're right, Peter. You are always right.'" He teased me as I gently swatted at his arm. I smiled at him as he gave me a quick hug goodbye. "I'll see you tomorrow night. Work your butt off today and tomorrow, so you can show me your ability."

"Thank you for this," I said softly as I held onto the gold and blue necklace. He nodded once before he turned toward the woods. I was left puzzled about how he would get back to the castle since Sie brought us here through teleportation.

Once Peter was gone, I slowly made my way back to the camp. Sie was reading through the pages of the book. If he'd heard Peter's and my conversation, he didn't show it.

"I want to try a different approach for your training today," he said, not looking up.

"What would that be?"

"These past couple of days, you have been working to *create*, which is generally a higher ranking Luxian trait. Fire users can bring a flame to light out of thin air, and water users can call upon waves that previously didn't exist. But maybe that's not the same for you. I want to try all the markings on your back, each one again, but this time use a different approach with them. I want you to use the water from the lake that is already there and see if you can do anything with it. Maybe you can't *create*, but you can *manipulate* what's around you. It usually means you have a lower ranking, but it's worth a shot."

What he said made sense. These past couple of days, I'd been trying to produce the elements from nothing. Maybe I could control them, but only with what I had in front of me. "And what if I can't even manipulate?"

"Well, we aren't going to find out by just staring at each other. Just try it."

"So, what do you want me to do?" I asked awkwardly, looking at the vastness of the lake before us.

"See if you can move the water at all. In any way, any amount, even if it's just a drop."

I walked over to the wooden dock that was off to the side of the lake. There was no way I was getting back into the freezing water when I was just finally starting to dry off. Sie followed, and I noticed him staring at me. I tried to ignore him as I focused on the water in front of me. I closed my eyes and imagined it moving, but nothing happened.

Another hour passed, and still nothing. All I'd managed to do was stare at the deep water while it stared back at me, completely unmoving.

Two hours in and something jumped out of the water, causing a splash as it returned to its home under the velvet caress of the blue. I jumped with excitement thinking that I'd finally done it, that I finally made the water move, only to realize it was just a fish. Sie laughed at me.

I turned my gaze to him. "Can you not mock me?" He threw both of his hands up in the air before leaving me alone. I could still see him smirking as he slumped into a seat by our tent. I waited to resume trying until I saw him open the Luxian book.

I stared at the water for another forty minutes before it rippled. I thought it was the wind at first, but the air was stagnant and the small wave was moving faster and faster. I did it. I could move the water.

My heart thundered against my chest because, for the first time, I let myself believe that I was not a nix. I knew I could breathe underwater from what Kole had done to me, but this was the first time I could actively do something with my abilities. It was an absolute rush. I felt like I had power. Like I was strong. I was no longer the weak little girl afraid of flames. If I could master water, I could douse any fires that came my way. Except, the amount of water I'd moved wasn't even big enough to harm an insect. I also had no idea how I did it.

I'd known my whole life that I wasn't a nix. I just never let myself truly believe it because I had never been able to use an ability. I always felt weak and useless when it came to powers, which was why I wanted to train my body well in combat to make up for it.

I felt the mental exhaustion take over as sweat started dripping down my neck, and a headache was pounding at my temples. I couldn't believe I'd been freezing just hours before because the exertion of trying to use abilities had me panting.

I looked over my shoulder to steal a glance at Sie, who was still consumed in his book. I didn't want to call him over yet. I wanted to keep practicing. I wanted to get better before I let him know. I wanted to be able to control the water on my own without it being a fluke accident, so I turned back to face the vast blue of the lake and tried again. And again and again and again. I tried until the small wave turned into the size of my palm, until I could make a wave big enough to spray the bottom of my pants as the water crashed upon the dock.

Manipulate not create. Sie said it meant I had a lower ranking, but I could still do something. I was so focused on moving the water that I didn't realize Sie had come up behind me until his breath slithered over my exposed neck. The water I was hovering over my head came crashing down, drenching us both.

He gave me a lazy, half-soaked grin. "Good."

"Does this mean that I'm a water user?" I asked him.

"I'm not sure," he admitted with a frown. I could tell he hadn't gotten very far in deciphering my markings from the book. "You definitely possess water abilities, but it's different from what others claim to have. I don't think it's the same. And your markings still don't make sense, unless you have two powers." He paused, then shook out his wet locks, sending water spraying over my face. "Once you can control water enough to be able to bring a wave to douse a fire, I want you to turn to that. To practice fire. See if you can move fire in the same way. Then once you master fire, we can move onto ground abilities. Tomorrow we will head to the force shield on our way back to the castle to see if you possess any abilities of air as well."

"Will I still be able to train when we are back at the castle?"

"Not much. I want you to practice the big stuff while we have privacy here. In my room—*our* room," he corrected, "we can practice smaller, less noticeable things like Alluse and healing."

"How will we do that?" I asked.

He shrugged. "I'll have you try to block my mind powers without your necklace on for Alluse. I don't think you possess the ability, but maybe it's similar to my mind reading where you have to actively use it."

That scared me. I wasn't ready for him to enter my mind. "And to see if I have healing abilities?"

"You can heal me."

"Heal you from what?"

"A small cut won't kill me, Scotlind."

"I'm not cutting you." I spat out quickly, horrified that his mind went to that.

He arched a brow. "Then I'll do it to myself. Get back to work."

I nodded my head as he walked back over to the fire. I wasn't going to let either of those things happen, but there was no use in arguing with him over it now. I'd find another way to test if I possessed healing and Alluse powers.

Even though my body ached and throbbed all over and my eyelids grew heavy, the adrenaline pumping through my veins was nothing I'd felt before. I felt wired even though I was drained. I wanted to cling to this feeling—of feeling strong—of controlling elements with my mind. If I could master my abilities, I could fight back. No one would be able to capture me again. I silently made a promise to myself that I would never be locked up in a cell ever again.

I didn't realize how much time had past until the chill of the night crept back in. I stood on the dock all day practicing. I was thankful whenever I did spray myself with water, even if it was by accident. It helped to wash away the sweat and grime that I knew was all over me. I'd still never properly bathed since the night with Kole, and I didn't know when I would have the courage to get in a tub again.

A massive wave moved along the lake's surface, breaking my concentration. Shaking and throbbing, I did my best to focus my thoughts and send it toward the shore but I couldn't control the momentum. The water had a mind of its own. I turned from the dock to see where it had landed and realized our entire camp was soaked with water.

Oops.

Luckily, the wave just missed our tent and was still relatively dry, but the same couldn't be said for Sie. The fire was now doused from the water, and Sie was completely drenched. His dark wavy hair fell into his eyes as he peered up at me. I would never forget the smile he had on his face—he seemed alive and carefree for once.

"Nicely done. I could have done without being soaked, but good work. Now you need to eat. You look exhausted. Then we can move onto fire." His grin was flashing wickedly and brilliantly and everything I wanted it to be as I walked over to him and took up a soggy seat by the water-filled fire pit.

———

I SPENT the rest of the night roasting in front of the hot flames of the fire Sie had relit. He stayed awake with me the entire night. I knew he had to be just as tired as I was, but he didn't show it.

I told Sie about the night I was captured, how my parents died in the flames, or at least, I thought they did. I left out the burn mark on my right calf, and the fact that the flames still haunted me. I didn't want to possess fire. I didn't want the ability that killed my family and changed my life. I thought knowing I had water abilities would help overcome my fear of it, but I was wrong. As I stared at the red amber flames licking the night, I heard my mother's scream. I heard my own screams as the males dragged me over the tiled floor, as they held me down, as the skin on my leg melted off. I saw their dark masks, lavender eyes, and smoke seeping in.

So I stared at the flames, watching the wood crackle. The summer sun hung low in the sky, reaching slightly lower and lower each day, warning us that winter was approaching and that the constant six months of darkness was coming.

The water from earlier had dried up. Sie used the remaining sunlight and the orange glow from the pit to continue researching through the Luxian book. I didn't mind his presence now. I didn't feel so foolish being around him because I knew at least I had something —some ability. I hadn't realize how badly I'd wanted that my entire life until I felt the power of commanding the water with my mind, or attempting to. Now, I didn't know how I'd lived without it.

I slumped down in the seat next to Sie. Only a single small spark flew from the fire throughout the night, and I couldn't convince myself that it was my doing. I knew I didn't do anything to the flames. I hadn't tried as I stared and stared at the thing that haunted me. The fire became a living creature in my nightmares. It moved and breathed and acted on its own accord.

Sie finally convinced me to go into the tent to sleep. "You need to rest, Scotlind. Your mind needs rest and recovery just as much as your physical body does, and you're shaking from exhaustion. Your reserves aren't used to being under constant stress."

"I know," I admitted, looking down at myself. I'd seen better days. I hadn't had a proper hot meal since our wedding, and my body was still bruised and cut. "I just really wanted to keep practicing but not with fire anymore."

He looked at me through the glow, and I thought he was going to ask me why I didn't want to keep practicing with fire, but instead, he just nodded. "Okay. I know you want to keep going, and we will figure it out, I promise you. But you aren't doing yourself any favors running yourself thin. We won't leave until tomorrow night, so you can practice all day tomorrow if you wish. We can move onto air and ground. I'll find other excuses for us to leave the castle once we return for a bit. You will have more opportunities to practice. We just have to be careful about it, but I need you to sleep now."

"Okay." We were both quiet for a few moments. I still hadn't moved to go inside the tent. "Sie, can I ask you something?"

"Anything."

"When we get back, and you become king, will you change things?"

"What do you mean?"

"You told me on the monorail when I first came to the castle that the High Council was going to make me a servant before my Trials just because I was a rank zero. That's not fair. There are many rank zeroes in Tennebris. They deserve more than that. They deserve to be treated the same as other ranks. They deserve for things to be fair, to be equal. You will have the power to change things. So will you?"

He sighed loudly, and I knew right away that he wasn't going to say what I wanted to hear. "No, Scottie. My only concern is you. It will always be you. My focus is to keep you safe, keep you alive. Right now, that's all I care about."

"How can you say that when you are going to rule these people? How can you say that you only care about me, one person, when thousands of our kind need your help? You can make a difference."

"You aren't a nix anymore, Scotlind. You aren't one of them," he said with such a bite that I cringed. The words *nix* and *one of them* rang through my mind. He'd never said it to me before. He'd never called me a nix.

"Does that really matter? I am still seen as a rank zero to our kind, and even if I wasn't, it shouldn't matter. I was treated like one. I know how they feel, what they go through. They're abused, Sie. I know what they suffer. I know what Alec does to them, and that's only one Advenian. I cannot stand by anymore and let it happen. I want to fight, to go up against the Council. I want to fight this—"

He cut me off. "They want to kill you. This isn't the time. Maybe afterward, when you are safe, we can talk about how they are treated and try to come up with a better solution, better conditions for them. We can make it so servants are respected."

I was fuming. *Servants.* He said servants like they still only deserved that role. I looked away from him, barely able to stomach it. I was thankful I hadn't admitted to him that I wanted to join the rebellion. That I'd been thinking about it more and more every day. Even if that meant I had to go up against the youngest Prince of Lux—the Fire Prince.

"But for now," Sie continued, "I just want to focus on keeping you safe and finding out who is behind this."

I nodded before stepping inside the tent and crawled over to my bedroll. Despite being furious with Sie, exhaustion won, and sleep found me immediately. If I had a nightmare, I didn't remember it.

———

I woke up to the sound of footsteps. Multiple footsteps. My eyes bolted open to find Sie in the same shocked position as me. I was about to ask him what was going on when he leaned forward and pressed his hand over my mouth. His other hand went to his own as he held a finger over his lips, ushering me to keep quiet as his golden markings spiraled out across his arms.

I knew he was using his ability to access the minds of whoever had come to our tent, so I kept quiet and waited. When his markings faded, he couldn't hide the terror on his normally blank face.

"Stay here," he breathed, but someone pulled open the flaps to our tent just as he was about to exit.

I blinked, once, twice, before my mind believed what my eyes were seeing. Sie's father, along with ten other guards from the castle, were standing outside our camp.

His father drew a mischievous grin. "Son, I think it's time you and your nix get out of your tent." Nix. *Nix.* He couldn't even refer to me by my name or acknowledge me as Sie's wife. I'd been called that my entire life, but something about the way he said it, his tone, seemed different. Like I was nothing more than Sie's property.

A muscle quivered in Sie's jaw as his hands balled into fists. Releasing, flexing, releasing, flexing. I kept staring at his hands, waiting for what Sie would do. He finally nodded and said, "We'll be right out. Give us a minute."

His father looked at me and smiled. "Make it fast."

As soon as the tent flapped shut, Sie swung over to me and had my necklace off before I could even blink. ***Don't tell them anything, Scotlind. Not a damn thing.***

My eyes felt like they were going to bulge out of their sockets as I stared into his black ones. I swallowed and nodded as he reclasped the necklace back around my neck and tucked it into my shirt. Then, he took his calloused hand in mine and ushered us out of the tent.

"Interesting," Sie's father mused with a horrid smirk on his face as he looked between the two of us. His gaze flicked over my disheveled hair, then our hands. "It's funny. I returned to the castle to find out that my son, the future king, had decided to take a little trip with his whore. You must have had a rough night because she doesn't look well."

His father ignored Sie's death glare and the puff of breath he released. Instead, he held up the restricted texts of Lux. "It's interesting how you found the time to do leisurely reading amongst all the fucking. That is what you told the Council was it not? That you wanted alone time with her?" Now his gaze rested on me.

"First off, she is my wife. Not a *whore*. You can refer to her by her title as she will be your future queen. I don't care if you and I are blood-related. If you offend her again, it will be your last." Sie paused. I saw his chest rise and fall. He squeezed my hand before he continued, "And secondly, I will be the king. I thought it would be best to do my research regarding the Lux Kingdom. A good ruler would be wise to know their potential enemies and what they are capable of. I do believe that was one of your lessons. Wouldn't you say so, *Father*? Or should I say commander now? I guess congratulations are in order. You seemed rather busy while I was away."

The commander laughed. "I hope you enjoyed her while you could.

You're needed by King Lunder and the High Council. I'm afraid I'm going to have to cut your little trip short. My apologies."

"Fine. We'll meet you back at the castle tonight," Sie said, unflinching, unyielding any hint if he was nervous about what was to come. I didn't know if the commander's comment meant something more.

"I'm afraid we are leaving *now*."

"You and I both know I am capable of teleporting. I'll take Scotlind back to the castle myself," Sie remarked.

His father held out a piece of paper and passed it to Sie. Sie dropped my hand as he reached for it. I tried to see what it read but couldn't with the blinding sun in my eyes. "As you can see, it's a direct order from the king himself. We will be escorting you both back by our own transport immediately. Your teleportation is not necessary. I think it would be best for your *wife* if you did as you were told. And I would strongly advise that you don't ruin everything we've worked for just for one girl because it won't matter in the end. According to that," he gestured to the paper, "we have permission to use force if you do not comply."

Sie's jaw tightening and clenching was the only indication of worry on his face. He didn't say anything back to his father or the other guards. He didn't bother packing up our camp as he stalked off after them, forcing me to follow as he didn't let go of my hand. Whatever that letter said, it wasn't good.

They directed us into a black car that zoomed off immediately for the monorail. No one said anything. No one spoke. Once we got to the monorail, I was all too aware of the three guards hovering close to me and the other seven by Sie.

Then everything happened at once. They separated us, pushing us into different compartments. My stomach tightened as the commander followed me into mine, the door sliding shut behind us.

"What a magnificent little thing you are. I have to commend you for your efforts. You almost, almost, got away with it," the commander sneered. Shackles clamped down on my arms and my legs. I immediately felt the Alluse running through my veins, working fast to halt my newly-found powers. I was about to fight back when a sharp pinch flared on my thigh as one of the guards injected me with something. I saw a flash of the clear liquid before it disappeared beneath my skin. I looked into the commander's dark eyes before the world around me went black.

---

ANOTHER DAMP, cold cell greeted me when I woke up from whatever sedative they had injected me with. My hands reached for my throat, but my necklace was gone. I was stripped of my clothes, and in its place was a thin, scratchy, brown slip. At least I thought it was brown through the dim flicker of a torch a few feet away.

A shiver went through me as my bare thighs touched the cold stone floor. My back was propped against a concrete wall while the other three walls were contained of thick iron bars, clustered together so tight that only my arm could pass through them. My legs just barely stretched out in front of me. I brought my knees to my chest, holding on to myself for warmth and comfort that didn't come.

Closing my eyes, I tried to steady my breathing as I desperately convinced myself that the walls weren't caving in on me, that I was breathing. I was still alive, that had to be a good sign, right? How could I end up chained again and in another cell? What did that letter say to change everything? The past couple of days, Sie talked about how he would protect me, how nothing would happen to me, and now here I was in another prison, but this time I was alone.

I didn't see Sie again for the rest of the day. I didn't know if I would ever see him again.

# FORTY
## SIE

I knew instantly we were caught. My father knew about Scottie and wasn't planning on keeping it a secret any longer. There was no other explanation as to why he was here. But I didn't think it would go down like this. I thought, at least, we would make it back into the castle. Then I planned on grabbing her, finding Peter, and teleporting us away.

But they pushed her into a compartment before slamming me into another one. Seven guards held me back as I started to fight them to make my way toward her. I was seconds away from using my compulsion even though I hated it. It felt sick and wrong to control people, but I didn't care. I would use it to get to her. I would do anything to keep her safe.

But then I felt it. My powers fading into nothing until I was empty. Alluse shackles were clamped around my wrists and chained to the wall.

My father wasn't in the compartment with me, and a horrible feeling washed over me once I realized who that meant he was with. Shit. Shit. Shit. I couldn't do this again. I couldn't watch her get hurt again.

I kicked the door to my compartment, trying to startle the seven guards that were watching me before I charged at them. I made it three feet before the chains went taut, keeping me in place. I pulled at them again and again, trying to rip them off the Goddess-damn wall.

I heard Scottie scream. One small shriek from her and then silence.

"If you hurt her," I sneered between gritted teeth at all seven of the males with me, "I will fucking murder you. Every single one of you."

The guards my father had brought tensed, watching me closely throughout the entire trip. I didn't stop pulling at the chains, even when all their weapons were angled at me. The monorail ride was short. It didn't take long to get back to the castle from where I had teleported her days earlier. When it finally came to a halt, I jolted up. "Care to unchain me?"

"Not yet, prince," one of them snapped back. I stared him down first, taking in his features. I'd remember every single one of them. I heard the door to the compartment click open across the hall, and then I heard shuffling. Scottie was being dragged across the floor. Dragged for fuck's sake.

The guards assigned to me were smart enough to wait ten minutes after they pulled her away before unchaining me from the wall. The shackles remained on my wrists, the Alluse still working, as one of the larger guards yanked on the chains, forcing me to follow.

Again, probably smart of them considering how deathly pissed off I was right now. I glanced into the compartment that Scottie was in and swore under my breath as I noticed a small pool of blood on one of the cushions. I tried to steady myself. I needed to remain calm to focus on what would come ahead. Plead Scottie's innocence, free her, then revenge. Revenge on every single one of them. And not just the males who came with my father, but whoever planned her kidnapping with Kole. And Kole. I would track him down and find him. Later.

I let the guards pull me through the grounds toward the small meeting room used by the High Council for more intimate proceed-ings. Good. This would be easier if it wasn't a public affair. The fewer people that knew about Scottie, the better. I noticed the servants and housekeepers gawking as I passed.

The prince, who had been missing from the castle for a few days, was now being escorted back in shackles. I could imagine the rumors spreading around the halls and had no doubt the entire court would know within minutes. I didn't care what they thought about me as long as they didn't see Scottie. I was sure my father's men were discreet about wherever they'd put her, waiting for the right moment.

Once directed inside the small meeting room, I was thrown in the center of the floor. No one bothered to offer a chair or to unchain me. My father—no, commander—seated himself behind a table situated across from me. Synder Phillips and Braven Bask flanked either side of him. King Lunder was nowhere to be found.

I was surprised to see Peter. He wasn't sitting with them but standing to the left side of the room where the guards were gathered. He tugged on his ear, the gesture so casual it seemed like he just had an itch. It was our signal for me to enter his mind, but I couldn't with these damn shackles. I tried to give him a sideways glance to read anything from his expression, but I was jerked by one of the guards and forced to look at my father. The Luxian book was positioned front and center on the desk.

Synder gave me the wickedest grin as he eyed my shackles. I knew the sick bastard was enjoying this. "Like what you see?" I scoffed at him.

His grin only widened. "On the contrary, prince, it brought me grave despair to have to call upon this meeting today. I don't wish to see you chained. Although the same can't be said about your wife."

I glanced around the room again, looking to see how many guards were here and who they were. Were they loyal to me or to Synder? "Care to enlighten me as to why I'm chained and my wife was taken from me?"

Synder tapped his thin finger on the book's brown faded leather. "No denying it. Your father found this at the lake with you. This is an illegal text and brings up the question of why you would have it."

"I already told him," I gestured toward my father, "why I was reading it. I see no reason for the shackles based on some light reading," I said in a bored tone. I needed them to take these off of me. I needed to get inside Peter's head to figure out what the hell happened.

"Interesting that it went missing from Addler the day before. If you weren't worried about the consequences, why steal it?" Synder remarked.

My father waved his hand in the air and gestured toward the guards. "Release him," he said to them. "Our quarrel is not with Sie but with the female he calls his wife. We only had to chain you to keep you from getting to her. Now that she is properly locked up"—he smiled at me. He actually had the audacity to smile at me—"you won't need those chains. You won't be getting to her."

Synder frowned and I had the suspicion that his goals weren't aligned with the commander's. My father probably had no idea what was going on and just wanted to make sure our bloodline didn't lose its power, wanted to make sure I didn't lose my power. Wanted Scotlind as far away from my bed as possible, Goddess forbid I taint my blood with a lower rank. Except she wasn't really a zero. I turned my gaze toward Synder, trying to glean what he knew, what he sought from this, what the hell he wanted. My father—easy—he wanted me to have a different wife and make sure my spot as king was secured.

My teeth ground together as the guards stepped up and started to remove my shackles that I was surprised they didn't chip. "What does Scotlind have to do with this?"

"We have reason to believe that she is not who she says she is. We have reason to believe that she is a spy, a traitor to the throne," Braven said, speaking for the first time.

"Be careful of what you are suggesting, Braven. She is my wife," I growled at him, at all of them.

My father lazily waved a hand in the air. "Oh, stop playing these mind games." As he spoke, the door opened behind me, and Kole walked in. I tensed. He just walked right fucking in, casually, strolling toward the table with his hands in his pockets. It took everything in me not to lunge myself at him.

"What is he doing here?" I gritted out as a guard starting working my chains. "He kidnapped Scotlind and tried to murder us."

"Oh, please. Don't tell me that you are suggesting that one guard, a rank four, has overthrown our prince, our only rank five." Synder almost laughed.

My father chimed in, "That is what can happen when you mix your blood with a nix. They make you weak. Or is she even a nix?"

Finally, with the shackles off, I wielded my mind into Peter's. **What the hell happened?**

Peter didn't dare look at me as he thought back, *They know she is Luxian. I don't know when Kole came back. I was just summoned here a couple minutes before you.*

"Kole here is actually a hero to the crown. I expect you to reward him well," Synder continued. "He has informed us all about the night at the castle. How he saw Scotlind's Luxian markings while he was being a loyal guard and protecting her, and how she tried to murder him in cold blood when he confronted her. Then, she framed him when she couldn't get the deed done. She even went as far as cutting her own leg for the theatrics of it."

I saw Peter tense out of the corner of my eye. Kole was fucking twisting the story for his own benefit. I knew exactly how this looked to them.

"I am telling you that is not true. Your future king is telling you that this male is lying. Are you going to believe one guard over—"

Synder cut me off. "Sie, you would do best to hold your tongue. It has already been confirmed. We searched your wife's body before we locked her in her cell and saw her Luxian markings for ourselves. There are rumors that can also frame you for treason as well. How do we know that you weren't involved? You were married to her after all, and we found you together, alone at a lake. She is a gorgeous female, don't pretend that you didn't explore every inch of her body. Don't pretend that you didn't notice her back when you fucked her."

My father chimed in then, "You will annul your marriage to the wretched girl, claiming that she fooled you, that you had no idea she was from Lux. You will be the one to draw the blade at her execution to prove your innocence in the matter."

Fuck Pylemo. Fuck all of the twelve lesser Goddesses too, because they were not on my side. They wanted me to murder my wife—to kill Scotlind.

Peter stepped up to stand in front of me. "With all due respect, if this girl is really from Lux and Sie kills her, we are opening ourselves up to a war with the Lux Kingdom. It is illegal to kill another race, it's in the Treaty itself. Lux could claim Sie's life in exchange for the murder. I don't believe we should start a war over one worthless girl. If you would allow it, I would like to suggest something else."

"You're friends with the girl. Why should we listen to you?" Braven barked.

"I was acquainted with her out of duty for my prince. And you and your High Council were the ones who hand-selected her for Sie to marry. I'm sorry if I'm being presumptuous, but aren't you to blame as well?" Peter said casually. He shrugged before stuffing his hands in his pocket.

"Be careful what are you are implying, boy," the commander sneered.

Peter ignored it before continuing, "Annul their wedding, make it public if you want, have Sie plead innocent or make up your own story. It doesn't matter."

*What are you getting at?* I asked Peter, but he shrugged off my thought before continuing out loud. "But don't kill her. Contact Lux, set up a meeting with them. Use this to Tennebris' advantage. Send her home where she belongs, but make it known we are watching them. That we suspect she was a spy. Let us have something over Lux."

Peter stared at the three males as he thought to me in my head. *Convince them. Send her to Lux. She won't survive here. Not with these males in charge. They will make you kill her, Sie. I think Synder is banking on you not being able to do it.*

**He thinks if I have to kill Scottie myself, I wouldn't be able to because he thinks we have the blood bond.** I replied into Peter's mind, realizing for myself what was happening.

He thought back to me, *I don't think Synder wants you on the throne. When they took you two to the warehouse, they were probably just testing your blood bond. If they make her execution public, and you can't kill her, it would prove that you're guilty too. It would be enough to send you to the prison. That is if the Light Kingdom doesn't find out that you killed a Luxian and demand your life in exchange. They don't have enough evidence to deem you guilty now. But if you save her, claim you love her even though it's publicly known she is Luxian, that is treason. That leaves the throne empty. And if they make you kill her, it will start a war. Either way, you end up dead or locked up.*

**I can't send Scottie to the Lux King. You know how he is. That is just as bad as death for her, or worse. You know how he will treat her, how he will use her.**

*It's the only thing I can think of to keep Scottie alive right now,* Peter interrupted our secret conversation in our heads. *She will die if we keep her on our soil. They will force you to kill her, Sie. If Kole is with them, they definitely are using Sui Alluse. You can't compel them. You can't win. Send her to Lux. Keep her safe for now. We will come up with a way later to make sure she is okay. I have a plan.*

I looked up to meet the eyes of my father, and although it killed me, I said, "I'll annul the marriage." My father smiled as I forced myself to say what I had to next. "Send her to Lux."

# EPILOGUE

The Fire Prince

Blood and dirt trailed behind me as I made my way toward my chambers. My labored footsteps echoing throughout the empty halls. I felt more fatigued than usual, my thighs burned and my calves shook slightly with each step. The battle dragged out longer than expected, taking me days to find their leader.

Images of the gore engraved in my forevision. They would linger until I could wash the remnants of battle from my body—remnants of rank zero sympathizers. The lower ranks retaliated more and more every day, fighting for equal rights. How many of their blood coated my skin, embedded in my scars, consumed me entirely until all I felt was death? The only thing that kept my feet moving was knowing that a hot bath was waiting for me. It was all I really missed about the castle, being able to wash off the dirt and grime and sleep for days in my own bed sounded like a gift from the Goddess herself.

"You're back." The King's voice echoed down the open hall. "I have a task for you."

I slowly, stiffly turned to face him. His silver eyes were hard. No hint of concern for the son he sent out to fight while he remained seated on his throne. I was expendable, just another being to serve him. He had Arcane, his eldest son, to carry on his bloodline, and me to carry out his orders.

"Can I wash off the gore from the last task first?" I asked through gritted teeth. The scent of death clung to me like a shadow. I could still sense the fear in the blood that splashed onto my uniform and matted my hair, turning it from white to red.

The King clicked his tongue as his glowing eyes surveyed me. "Speaking of which, can I presume that everything was dealt with accordingly?"

"The rebels are all dead."

"Good. Now you just have to deal with the families. I don't want any low rank sympathizers alive. Our ranking system is crucial and anyone that is left breathing is at risk for spreading—"

I cut him off, which given by his glare, I would pay for later, but I really didn't give a damn at the moment. I didn't have it in me to listen to him lecture about the importance of compliance and amenability. "This is your task that couldn't wait until after I bathed? I have done this enough times to know what is expected of me."

"No. That's not your task this time. Send your men to kill the wives and children. I have something else planned for you." His calculated smile unnerved me—I knew whatever this task was, it meant something to him.

"Prepare a cage. We are going to Tennebris to get ourselves a prisoner."

———

THANK you so much for reading *Lake of Sapphire*. Scotlind's story continues in *Ocean of Silver*, Book Two in the Allium Series.

OCEAN OF SILVER

---

WANT to stay up to date with all my releases? Follow my newsletter!

NEWSLETTER

# ALSO BY MALLORY BENJAMIN

THE ALLIUM SERIES

Lake of Sapphire

Ocean of Silver

Illusion of Hazel

River of Lavender

ALLLIUM COLLECTION

Advenian Omnibus

IMMORTAL HUNTERS

Hunted by the Dead King

# ACKNOWLEDGMENTS

First and foremost, to anyone who picked up this book and read it, THANK YOU! I hope it brings you as much joy reading it as it did for me writing it. Creating these characters brought magic to my life. They are my fictional best friends and I hope you love them as much as I do.

To my Nana. I love you dearly. Thank you for helping me bring this book to life and the countless hours you spent editing my words. I am so blessed to have you as my grandmother. As a little girl, I remember you editing some of my school papers, and now, you've edited all my books. You are the first person to get a copy, and the only person to read them as many times as I have. Everything you have done means the world to me. Every time I pick up this book, I will think of you.

To my love, my soulmate, Anthony. Thank you for everything—for being a dreamer with me. I love that we never stop encouraging each other, and we support each other fully, no matter how crazy our ideas are. Nothing is impossible and everything worthwhile is worth the risk. I absolutely love you with all of my heart. My soul belongs to you always.

To my family. Thank you for putting up with my rambling for hours on end about all of my story ideas. Thank you for the endless support and encouragement. To my Dad, you can read my book now. To my little brother. Thank you for listening to all my ideas regarding cover art for my story and helping me design the water element of my cover.

To my mom. I love you. I love you always. I'll love you forever. It means the world to me to have you believe in me and in my story.

Your continued support has been uplifting. Ever since I was little, I wanted to write. You were always patient with me and listened to every idea that came to my mind. You and Dad are my role models, a reminder to manifest my dreams and live the life I want. I will always cherish how you helped me celebrate all the little moments that came along with writing this story. Thank you for everything.

To my sisters. Kelly, thank you for being the first person to ever read anything I wrote. I gave you my book when it was only eight chapters long and didn't have a plot yet. You were the reason that Sie got a point of view. Kasey, I will always cherish our writing sessions. Our nights together, eating Taco Bell and doing writing sprints are some of my favorite memories, even if we talked more about our book boyfriends than actually writing.

To Lisa Worthy. Thank you for being my biggest supporter throughout this entire series. Your optimism for my characters means the world to me. It was incredibly motivating to hear your excitement as you were reading. If it wasn't for you, my story would have ended abruptly, so the epilogue is dedicated to you! I appreciate everything you have done for me and my book. I can't thank you enough.

To Kat. Having you as a writing bestie, critique partner, beta reader, and just an overall friend has been a gift. I appreciate all of our video chats discussing each other's books. You have been my book cheerleader, picking me up when I had doubts. I cannot express enough how thankful I am for you.

To Lana, I am so happy that our significant others became friends so that we got the chance to meet. I love talking with you about all of our favorite books. It means so much to me that you read my story. You have been my go-to person for asking opinions about all the little, gritty details that went into making this book come alive.

To Glasswing Editing. Morgan, thank you for editing my book and being patient with me through all of my changes. I am so honored by your encouragement and kindness throughout this entire process, and I appreciate all the work you have put into my story.

Thank you to all of the beta readers that took the time to read my story. Every word you read, every feedback you gave, meant the world to me. Whether it was listening to my ideas, reading a few chapters, or finishing the entire book, I can't thank you enough. Special thanks to Lisa Worthy, Nancy Kohutka, Lana Gooch, Lynn Christ, Lauren Ettaro, Kimberly Valois, Nick Hartman, Kat Turner, Dayana Soto, Lindsay Hartman, Kelly Pepper, Kasey Benjamin, and Mary Benjamin.

My list of thanks could go on and on. I feel so blessed for everyone in my life. Thank you with all my heart!

# ABOUT THE AUTHOR

Mallory graduated from Penn State with her bachelor's in nursing and spent eight years working as a nurse before becoming a full-time author and mama. You can usually find her drafting stories, chasing her toddler around the house, and surviving on energy drinks. When she isn't completely consumed by imaginary worlds and fictional characters, she's spending time with her family, capturing everyday moments through a camera lens, or treating herself to buffalo wings.